A Place to Hide

Becca Lynn Mathis

A Place to Hide

Copyright © 2022 by Becca Lynn Mathis

This is a work of fiction. Names, characters, places, and incidents either are the product of the author's imagination or are used fictitiously. Any resemblance to actual persons, living or dead, events, or locales is entirely coincidental.

All rights reserved. No part of this book may be reproduced in any form by an electronic or mechanical means, including information storage and retrieval systems, without permission in writing from the publisher, except by a reviewer who may quote brief passages in a review.

First paperback edition July 2022

ISBN 978-1-7331626-6-1 (ebook)

ISBN 978-1-7331626-7-8 (paperback)

ISBN 978-1-7331626-8-5 (hardcover)

Edited by *Vicky Brewster (www.vickybrewstereditor.com)*

INTERIOR FORMATTING & DESIGN - *T.E. Black Designs—www.teblackdesigns.com*

Cover by *Joolz & Jarling – Julie Nicholls & Uwe Jarling*

www.beccalynnmathis.com

The world is kind of a dumpster fire, so I'm going to let this be long.
Because we all could use a little positivity.

Let's start with the obvious, shall we?
This is for my readers most of all.
You guys continue to love these crazy stories of mine, and that means the world to me, so this one—like all of the others, really—is for you! Thank you so very much for all of the love and support!

But I would be remiss to not also dedicate this to the people who helped make it possible.
To Trishinator, my sister from another mister, I love you so very much and am so so glad for all of your patience with my questions at all hours of the night, and for all of the hours you've spent beta reading both the outline and the (mostly) final draft.
To my absolutely stellar critique partner, Ben, for reading this beast before it even made sense, and for helping me to make it make sense.
To Stina, for beta reading my ridiculous outline and then following through to beta read the (mostly) final draft like a full-blown critique partner. Watching your comments come in as you worked your way through the completed story absolutely gave me life.

To Andie and Myri, for all of the amazing support and encouragement as you beta read on such a tight timeline for me! And, of course, to Vicky for all your hard work and patience in helping me to get this story to really shine! Your expertise has been instrumental in bringing this story to life!

To my absolutely wonderful family, for all of their sacrifices as the muse stole my sanity and replaced the momma bear of the house with a cranky zombie that couldn't keep a consistent sleep schedule.

SPECIFICALLY, to my utterly magnificent husband, Kevin. You are, without a doubt, the best brainstorming partner I have ever known. The amount of patience you have for me while we talk through my stuck bits means the whole wide world to me, and I could not have asked for a better forever person through the writing process. Your love and support keep me going, and I am so damn grateful for everything that is you, and everything you do.

Of course, this is ALSO dedicated to my patrons, most especially Amy Lynn, whose support has been instrumental in getting this book out into the world!

And, one last thing:
to Elisa, for being so much of an amazing friend I made you Naiya's as well, and to Shaun, for lending me your likeness when I was looking to add a real-life person I knew to the passing mention of people in Naiya's life.

PROLOGUE

Valerie

Ungh, brightness. Ew. I moved my arm away from my face and squinted against the daylight invading my living room. The sunbeams drove spikes into my head with needle-like precision. Last night had been a hell of a party. How many hours of sleep had I managed to get in? I sat up with a yawn, my vision hazy and unfocused as I swung my legs heavily off the couch and reached to check the time on my cell laying face down on the coffee table.

Two in the afternoon.

And I'd gotten in as dawn started to light the sky. So … what? Like seven-ish? I counted it out on my fingers. Seven hours. I shrugged. Good enough.

I wiped at my face with both hands, pushing sleep-mussed rainbow strands of hair back and out of my face. I needed to get something into my system to kick out this dull throbbing in my head.

I opened the music app on my phone for inspiration. Eptic? Nah, dubstep is better for sex or dancing than for waking up. Nirvana? Mmm, no. Not enough weed in my system for that yet. Diamante …? Hmm … yeah, actually. That'd be perfect. Punchy rock music with female vocals. I added some

Halestorm and New Year's Day into the mix, and—a few taps later—the heavily distorted guitars of Diamante's "Bulletproof" sang from my home sound system and pounded into my hangover headache as I padded into my kitchen.

The bottle of Cuervo next to the coffeemaker caught my eye. Hair of the dog, that's what I needed. Elias wouldn't approve, but he wasn't here, was he? Besides, there was only a little left in the bottle. It seemed a shame to leave it all by its lonesome.

I twisted off the lid and took a shot straight from the bottle as I started the coffeemaker. As the coffee percolated into the carafe, I rolled myself a fat blunt. Thank God the Colorado lawmakers had the good sense to make this shit legal. I lit it as I leaned back against my kitchen counter, closing my eyes in anticipation of the hit as I took the first long inhale. I pulled another long drag and held it until I became aware of the fact that the coffee had stopped dribbling into the pot.

About damn time. If I didn't drink so many cups of coffee to keep going during the day, I'd get one of those stupid single-cup coffeemakers. At least those didn't take half an eternity.

I poured most of a cup of caffeinated goodness for myself, topping off the mug with more tequila. That left the Cuervo bottle just this side of empty, so I finished it off and tossed it into the recycle bin before heading back to the couch, coffee in hand. I took another long drag of my blunt before setting my mug down on the squat table, letting the guitars and drums of the music wash over me as the high started to hit my system. I flopped onto the couch and dialed the volume higher, aching to feel the thump of the bass in my chest. I threw my arm over my face again as I lay back into the cushions, pulling another long drag from my blunt.

I had it finished and half the spiked coffee down when my head finally started to clear. But I couldn't be sure if the thump I'd just heard was a part of Halestorm's "Do Not Disturb" or if it'd come from my front door. I sat up and listened more carefully, not yet turning down the music.

Thump thump thump.

Well, that was between lines in the next verse. Had to be my door.

"Yeah, yeah, keep your pants on." I gulped down another mouthful of tequila-laced coffee and got up from the couch. I didn't get a lot of visitors, so my curiosity was piqued.

I opened the door as the next knock started and found myself face-to-face with First Lieutenant Elias Clark. He was probably the hottest lupine the Buck had on that base, which was saying something, as most of the lupines on base were hot as fuck. I hadn't seen him in a while, but he was still the same—strong jaw, cheekbones that could cut glass, sun-kissed pale skin, dark hair, and smoldering dark eyes, all on a deceptively slim frame that practically towered over me. His olive shirt was tucked into his camo pants which were, in turn, tucked against the top of his boots. He had a manila folder tucked against his side, under his left elbow, and it looked like he hadn't gotten a good night's sleep since the last time he'd stayed over.

He took in my appearance with a slow scan from my bare toes up, drinking in the sight of me like a starving man. I was only in an oversized shirt and neon green panties, and his gaze on my body sent warmth straight to the spot between my legs. That he hadn't touched me yet spoke volumes about his control. And, since I liked to tease him, I leaned alluringly against my doorframe, running my fingers lightly up the top of my thigh before propping my hand on my hip.

"New ink." His dark eyes met mine and flicked down to my latest tattoo: a patch of intricate black lace on my right thigh with delicate chains supporting a richly detailed heart-shaped gemstone in a kaleidoscope of colors. "It suits you."

I arched my back, watching his eyes follow the motion of my hips, and licked my lips. "Glad you think so. It's been a while, Lieutenant Clark. I thought you'd forgotten about me."

He closed the distance between us then, his control slipping as he attempted to crowd me back inside. His chest pressed against me—and I was only a little slip of a thing at just barely over five feet tall—but I didn't let him move me, not just yet.

"You and I both know that's a lie." It was a little hard to hear him over the music, but his voice was dark as he reached a hand for my face, his fingers brushing against my cheek before burying themselves against my scalp.

His eyes were on my mouth, which I tantalizingly parted for just a breath as his heart pounded against me. He bent his head, clearly intending to kiss me, but I gave ground with a smirk, backing into my entryway. His answering smile as he followed me was somehow both radiant and dark. My panties were going to be soaked before he even touched me.

He shut the door behind him with a soft click as I stepped over to my phone on the coffee table, turning down the music with a few taps on the screen. The distance broke the moment between us, but that was almost certainly only temporary. At least, it was if I had anything to say about it.

He cleared his throat, apparently feeling the same break. "How's life?"

He meant, 'How's life on the bench?' At least he

had the decency not to rub it in my face. Didn't make General Buckheim any less of a dick, though.

"Oh, y'know. Same old, same old." I picked up my coffee and downed the last of it as he moved toward me with the awkwardness of someone who wasn't sure where we stood.

He reached a hand out and brushed more of my rainbow hair from my face, cupping my cheek lightly before brushing his hand down to my shoulder. Warmth followed the trail his hand traced, a faint tingle in its wake.

Shit.

It'd be a positively intimate gesture if it didn't immediately sober me up. But that was reliable healer Elias, ruining my highs ever since the Buck swept me off into this identity. At least he had the good grace to take the hangover with the high.

I sighed and headed for the kitchen, empty coffee mug in hand. "Business call, huh?" My voice was clipped.

He growled low in his throat. "Val …"

I turned and arched an eyebrow at him as I put my mug in the sink. I couldn't be sure, but he may have been slimmer than he'd been before. "Y'know, I think those pants would fit me."

He matched my arched brow. "Are you trying to get into my pants?"

Now, there's an idea. Not that it hadn't already crossed my mind.

I sauntered back over to him. "I wouldn't be so sideways about it." I grabbed the waistband of his pants and tugged him close, running the ball of my tongue piercing along my lips. "But now that you mention it," I murmured, unbuckling his belt and pulling it free in one smooth motion.

Look. If he was gonna ruin my high with business,

the least he could do was give me a few O's for the trouble.

His lips twisted upward as he plopped the file on my coffee table and stripped his shirt off. He may have been built slim, but he was solid muscle. He wrapped an arm around my waist, grasping me firmly against him as his mouth crashed against mine.

Well, good. We were on the same page. And fuck, did he ever taste good. I practically melted against him as the space between my legs turned molten. And then his thumb brushed across my hardened nipple, and I could think of nothing beyond how badly I wanted him inside of me.

Pulling away as he rucked my shirt up my body, he practically tore it off me and ran his big warm hands along my bare skin. Despite being a lifetime member of the itty bitty titty club, his hands felt amazing as they cupped each of my little girls, though they didn't even fill one of his palms each. I leaned into his touch, sighing with pleasure at the warmth of him as I felt him come to full attention in his pants. I ran my tongue along his lip and pulled away to work on the fly of his pants, but he caught my hands before I made any real progress.

He fished a contacts case from his pocket and offered it to me. "For you."

I frowned at him. "I don't need contacts; I can see just fine."

"They're colored contacts." He smiled and jerked his chin toward the file. "I need you to make contact with this girl."

Was the Buck putting me back in play? Really? And how the fuck could Elias still keep a damn level head when he clearly wanted my body as bad as I wanted his?

"Get as much intel as you can about where she

comes from and what she's capable of," he continued. "Then get her in the path of the *purgatum*."

I tapped the contact case against the palm of my other hand and pouted at him. "All work and no play?" I tried to ignore the niggling question that dangled at the thought of taking someone to the one who'd fixed me, more or less.

With a husky chuckle, he plucked the contact case from my hand and dropped it on top of the manila folder before gripping my hips. He pulled me to him, licking a line up my neck and nipping gently at my ear as he thumbed my hardened nipple again. "Plenty of play, but there's still work to do, too."

I pushed him to sit on the couch. At least he was closer to my height there. His hands cupped my ass, pulling me closer to him so he could lick another line up between my breasts, sending more heat thrumming through me.

"Fine," I said, trying to play it cool despite his hands and mouth on me. "So, you want me to play spy? What's her deal?"

He nipped gently at the tender skin below my breast as he slipped my panties to the floor. He sat back and admired me for a moment before bending to pull off his boots. "We haven't seen wereleopards before, and that's a variable we can't have as an unknown out there." He spoke more to the ground than to me, but the words still sent a chill down my spine and cooled my jets.

My fingers found the scars on my stomach, and I traced the ragged edges of the four parallel pink lines, staring at him until he looked back at me.

"There's wereleopards?" There was decidedly more anxiety in the question than I wanted.

He stood quickly then, grabbing my jaw firmly and tilting my head back as he towered over me. He placed gentle kisses against my neck as he spread a hand across my scars, lining a finger up on each of the shiny pink marks and holding his warm palm firmly against me until my heart finally stopped trying to keep time like the happy hardcore beats of the rave last night.

"She needs to be the last," he said quietly against my hair. "We don't need more of her kind."

The hand that had been over my scars crept lower as his other hand held me firmly against him, instantly reigniting the warmth that had gone out. Fuck, if I didn't love his hands on me.

And then his fingers found the pearl among my folds, and I panted against his neck as he ran circles around my clit. Steady, unrelenting circles that I ground into and against. I bit his neck as my orgasm crashed into me, turning my knees to jelly.

"There's my good girl," he whispered as I shuddered against his hand. I'm a damn sucker for praise during sex.

Well, two can play at that game. I was far from done with him.

I reached up to pull his face down to mine as I released his truly impressive dick from his pants. I ran my hand over it a few times, pumping his length until drops of precum slicked my palm.

I looked up at him with a wicked smile and pushed him back onto the couch. I followed him down, straddling his lap and guiding him into my still sensitive core.

His eyes rolled back in pleasure. "God, I've been away from you too long."

I bounced on his dick a couple of times, reveling in the way that he filled me almost to bursting. "Mmhmm. It's only been about a month."

I bent my mouth to his as I ground my hips against his lap. Running my hands up his chest, I clawed at the back of his head, seeking purchase in the close-cropped hair there. He twitched inside me as I moved against him, and I finally closed my fingers around the dark hair at the top of his head, my nails scraping against his scalp as I yanked his head back and away from me.

He smiled at the rough play, making a pleased little noise deep in his throat.

"Maybe you shouldn't have let the old Buck bench me." I licked his Adam's apple, tracing a line up his throat. "I miss fucking you in the exam room."

He hummed agreeably as he wrapped an arm around my waist, lifting me from his lap and plopping me on my back beneath him on the couch. He buried himself in me again in a single stroke.

"I miss fucking you in the back of the humvee," he replied, gripping my left ankle and lifting it over his shoulder for better access. He held my leg up with a firm grip on my thigh as the thumb of his other hand found my clit. "But now, I want you to come for me. Again."

It was his specialty. He knew *exactly* how to touch me to make me fall apart for him. And as his thumb fell into sync with his hips pumping against me, I came loudly, my hips bucking against his hand with decidedly wet noises.

"Yes," he cooed. "Good girl."

He kept his hand on me, kept pumping into me as I ground against him until the aftershocks subsided, at which point he pulled out, despite the needy little whine I gave him.

"Oh, there's more," he said, throwing me easily over his shoulder. "But I want a little more space."

Sure. More space. Wetness dripped down my thigh. I watched his firm ass from where I was draped over his shoulder as he padded into my bedroom.

"No hospital corners for you, huh?" He swatted

my butt once, and the spot he slapped wasn't the only thing that warmed.

I snorted and propped my chin in my hand, my elbow braced against his shoulder blade. "Since when do I do anything at all neat and orderly?"

With another little chuckle, he dropped me onto the mess of pillows and blankets on my bed. "Fair."

He lowered himself on top of me again, kissing me until I gently pushed him away. I was two orgasms in; I could at least try to get my head a *little* clear. He wanted me to pretend to make friends with some girl—some wereleopard. She wasn't mooncrazed, was she? A cold finger of ice flicked at my spine.

He rolled onto his side and propped himself on his elbow. He watched me think as he traced a hand over the bright rose vine and dark chain tattoo that twisted around my left arm from shoulder to hand. "What thoughts lurk behind those eyes?"

I hooked a leg over his hip, mirroring him with my head in my right hand. "Why me?"

He rolled a shoulder. "Because I'll be missed."

"Isn't the old Buck the one who wants this info? Wants her to stop being a leopard?"

"Mmm, I'm sure he wants the info," Elias replied. "But I'm not sure he'd want her to stop being a leopard."

I studied his face. He was masking something there, I was sure of it. "He doesn't know about her yet, does he?"

It would make sense. Buckheim would probably want her for himself. Test her skills and endurance, and then see if she's pack material. Did leopards even pack bond?

He pressed his lips into a line before leaning forward to kiss my temple. "Please don't make me lie to you, Val. I need you to do this for me." He pressed his forehead against mine. "And I need you to just trust me. With any luck, it'll get you off the bench for good."

"Hmm." I pushed him over and straddled him, letting his rock-hard length lay along his body instead of pressing into me. "What if I like the bench?" I rolled my hips along his shaft, slicking him with my considerable wetness.

With a laugh that twitched along his length under me, he propped his arm behind his head, resting the other hand on my tattooed thigh. "You only like the bench because you can sit around here getting high all the time."

I wriggled and readjusted until he was inside me again, rolling my eyes back at the delicious sensation of fullness. "And fuck hot ass werewolves whenever I want." I slid up and down his length a couple of times.

His left eyebrow shot up as he grabbed my hips with both of his big warm hands, thrusting hard into me. "Werewolves, plural, huh?"

"Well …" I fell forward, brushing my lips against his without quite kissing him. "Maybe just the one, for now," I whispered against his mouth.

He tightened his grip on my hips and gave me another hard thrust. "I see."

I couldn't help but love the way he didn't try to be terribly gentle with me. And as he pumped into me, he left little scratches on my butt and teeth marks in my collarbone that would have bruised if he hadn't immediately healed them. But he left the teeth marks. He always left the teeth marks. And I fucking loved it. I loved knowing I was his. I loved knowing how much he liked having me.

And I *really* loved the sounds he made when my next orgasm drove him over the edge.

As his dick slowed its twitching, I rolled from the bed and stepped into my obnoxiously large bathroom. It had Jack and Jill sinks and a huge claw-foot bathtub along with a shower stall with two oversized rainshower heads. It was entirely too much for just me, but I hadn't had the chance yet to pull Elias into the shower with me.

I called to him from the bathroom. "So, how do you want me to do this?" I pulled a washcloth from the basket on the counter and ran water onto it, which I wiped over my face before rinsing it and wringing it out again. "Do I need to dye my hair and cover my ink?" Hopefully not, I liked my rainbow hair.

He made a deep pleased sound that rumbled from his chest before replying. "You don't have to go that far. What we know of her so far is in the file on your coffee table. She just got dropped into Saint Dymphna's Institute for Behavioral Health in Dallas. I'll get you admitted there for rehab."

I narrowed my eyes as I cleaned myself up with the damp cloth. "Win-win for you, huh?"

"Look," he said, "you get clean, Buck pulls you off the bench, whether you get the intel or not. It's not like former werewolves are easy to come by."

I tossed a towel to Elias as I leaned against the doorframe, pressing my right shoulder against the cool wood. "Easier now that Lynn's around."

He cleaned himself off. "Val … come on, you just gotta learn what you can and earn her trust enough that she'll go with you when I send my guys. They'll be in suits. You'll know them by their orange pocket squares." He tapped his left pec.

I bit my lip. "It's just … I'm not a *spy*, Elias. She's gonna see through me."

"Maybe if you're stupid about it."

I threw my damp washcloth at him. "I'm serious! If she's anything like you lupines, she's gonna see through any lie I tell her, colored contacts or no."

In almost a single motion, he stood and threw an

arm around my waist. He pulled me to him as he gripped my chin with a little growl that sent heat coursing through me again. He kissed me then, biting my lip where I had just a moment ago.

"So, don't lie," he said, releasing me and taking a step back.

And then he doubled over, his body contorting into impossible angles and proportions as he shifted to his wolf form.

My heart rate spiked, my spine hit sub-zero, and my jaw went slack at the creature he became. His wolf was black-streaked grey on top with creamy white on his legs, belly, and the underside of his tail. But all I could think about was the thing that turned me into a manic, slavering creature of violence. My vision unfocused as I crossed my arms tightly over my belly, hunching into myself and taking a single step backward before clenching my eyes shut and forcing air as deep as I could into my lungs. I forced myself to hold my ground, reminding myself that if I ran, he would chase, and that would be worse.

Except he wouldn't.

He wasn't mooncrazed. He had control. He'd had control for longer than I'd even been alive.

I heard the cracking of joints and bones rearranging themselves as he shifted back. And then the warmth of him pressed against me, wrapped around me. It melted the fear I was working so hard to drive away with logic. There was my Elias. He wouldn't let that happen to me again.

"See?" His voice was a gentle whisper of breath against my ear. "Shifted creatures are terrifying. Better she get rid of the leopard anyway." He kissed my temple. "And you *do* have a drug problem. You abuse the shit out of your Ambien and Xanax, and you know it. One of these days, you're gonna end up dead. And that's unacceptable. Rehab will be good for you."

I hummed a noncommittal noise and opened my eyes. He wasn't *wrong*, I just liked it better when I was using an off-label strength of my meds.

"Please, Val. Just get her to the *purgatum* and call me when she's human."

He lifted me from the floor with his casual strength and dumped me onto the bed, following me down onto the sheets. He was already hardening against me again. But I wasn't sure I was ready to let him have me. Not after that stunt of his. I hooked a leg over him and forcefully switched our positions. Well. He probably let me.

"What a rude trick to pull, scaring me like that. You'll have to make it up to me before you go running back to the Buck." Mischief dripped through my tone as I wrapped my tattooed hand around his dick. I lowered my mouth to that magnificent shaft and circled the tip with my tongue, flicking the ball of my piercing against the sensitive little spot just under the head.

"Ffffuuuuck, Val." His voice was breathless. "It's not like I was gonna get you all hot and bothered just to leave you playing DJ to the little man in the boat."

I nearly choked on my laughter as I sat up. "Holy shit, where the *hell* did you learn that one?"

He laughed with me, throwing his arm behind his head again. "Jones said it to Lawson the other day. I wasn't sure what he meant until she kneed him in the groin for it."

I continued laughing. "That's fucking hilarious."

"No," he said, shaking his head as he rolled over back on top of me again. "What's *really* hilarious is how many more times I'm going to make you come before I take you to the airport and put you on a plane to Dallas."

Fifteen was the number. Seven more that day, three in the middle of the night, four in the morning, and once more in the car in the garage at the airport.

Fuck, I was gonna miss the feel of his hands on me.

But there was work to do, and the sooner I got it done, the sooner I'd be back in his arms.

ONE

Naiya

I EYED the nametag of Dr. Kaleb Anderson, my assigned therapist at Saint Dymphna's Institute of Behavioral Health, as he perused my chart yet again. That's Kaleb with a K because, apparently, his mother didn't want to be too mainstream with his name. Memorizing the spelling of it—again—was better than watching the phlebotomist's vial fill with more of my blood. He wore his reading glasses today, though they usually sat on his desk during our conversations.

"How many of those are you going to need while I'm here, anyway?" I asked as she pulled the needle from the crook of my arm.

Her voice was clipped as she pressed a cotton ball to the spot where the needle had just been. "One every day, Ms. Kateri. It's in your chart." She nodded to the folder resting under her tray of supplies on the cart.

I'd swear the staff here were a bunch of vampires. Probably starving from the pittance of blood in a single vial. But there were at least twenty other residents, so maybe twenty-ish vials every day was enough to sustain them? Pfft. Not likely. If vampires were real, I'd guess they'd need a hell of a lot more than just a couple vials of blood a day to keep going.

After securing the cotton ball to my arm with a band-aid, the phlebotomist wheeled her cart out of the room, closing the door behind her with a soft click. I put my arm back into the sleeve of my cardigan.

I couldn't stand those books, though—the vampire romance novels. Who the hell sees a violent, vicious predator and thinks, 'ah yes, that's what I need to get into bed with?' You'd have to be dealing with some serious unhealed trauma for that.

Dr. Anderson's nasal drone interrupted my thoughts. "You've been here a few days now and haven't spoken to anyone but the staff. Why do you insist upon solitude here, Naiya?" His hands were folded on top of the yellow legal pad in his lap as he watched me, holding an uncapped pen between his fingers. His hooded eyes had little crow's feet in the corners, though they were probably only visible thanks to those reading glasses of his.

"It can't be all that uncommon to not want to make friends in rehab." I shrugged a shoulder and looked over at the bookshelf lining the wall next to the door. Every book on the shelf was related to substance abuse, trauma, or regulating emotions. Shocking.

"It's not," he agreed, nodding. "But there's a difference between not making friends and choosing to only speak with staff. You even sit alone in the cafeteria."

I resisted rolling my eyes at him. "Almost everyone sits alone in the cafeteria." And I barely even speak with the staff unless I'm spoken to. The less I said here, the less they'd have to hold me on, and the sooner I could leave.

Dr. Anderson's pen scratched across the legal pad,

but he looked over the top of his reading glasses at me. "Naiya." His tone was chiding.

I huffed out a breath. "There's no point in making small talk with anyone. I'm not going to be here long. I don't have a drug problem."

He scribbled something else down. "Perhaps not. But the alternative is more troubling, don't you think?" He placed his hand down deliberately on the pad of paper before looking back up at me. "Because that would mean you have clearly lost touch with reality and could be a potential danger to yourself or others, should your perception of the world be threatened."

I sighed and looked away, placing my chin in my hand as my eyes focused on the clouds outside the window. "Or so my mother says."

"Your father, too," he added. "Why don't you tell me more about this leopard story you now claim is a contrivance?"

I rolled my eyes at his 'I'm so smart' vocabulary but didn't look back at him. "It is, obviously. No one can just turn into a leopard."

The pen scritched on the paper again. "Why abandon it so quickly? Is it because of what happened with your father?"

No, what happened with my father wouldn't have happened if my stupid mother hadn't screamed when she found me as a leopard in my bed. I wouldn't even *be* here if they hadn't assumed I'd drugged them instead of trying to figure out how the hell me turning into a leopard was even possible. I had to tell them something to try and get out of being sent to this stupid place.

I shook my head. "I only ever wanted attention." Which really wasn't true, but it was an easier explanation than trying to get yet another person to believe I wasn't lying.

"Hmm." More scribbles.

"Look," I continued, taking my head out of my hand and turning back toward him, "the way-too-tanned-to-be-white adopted child of a successful white businessman and his too-perfect wife?" I shrugged. "My parents only ever wanted me around when I was quiet and prim and proper. They did not like me when I was wild." Which was true enough.

"So, when they accused you of drugging them, you came up with a wild story." He nodded and returned to scribbling notes.

"The wildest I could think of," I confirmed, leaning forward as I crossed my legs in the armchair. "Something so wild they would have to talk to me instead of just dumping me here or shoving me off onto Abigail." Who also hadn't believed me the first time I tried to tell her.

He looked over his glasses at me again. "Your nanny?"

"She's the 'house manager' now, but yes." I put air quotes around Abigail's current title. It was the third my parents had given her as I'd grown up. First housekeeper, then nanny, now house manager.

He looked at his notes a moment, his face a careful mask, but his eyes told me I had his curiosity. "And where will you go when you leave here?"

I made a face, curling my lip before answering. "Anywhere but back there. I'm old enough to get a place of my own." Better to live alone than with parents who are so convinced you're lying, they're willing to dump you in a mental institute.

He nodded. "Uh-huh, and how will you afford that?" He sounded like he was talking to a five-year-old.

I sucked on my teeth and tried hard to keep the edge out of my voice. I dropped my legs back out of the chair and sat up straighter. "I'm not a child anymore, Dr. Anderson. I'm twenty years old. Father won't want his stakeholders to know his adopted daughter was committed to rehab. He won't cut off my funding if he wants to keep his job."

He pointed at me with the back end of his pen. "That's blackmail, Naiya."

His judgmental tone could take a long walk off a short cliff.

I folded my arms across my chest and didn't bother keeping the edge out of my voice. "No. That's them upholding their commitment as parents. Don't adopt a kid if you aren't going to support them."

He looked away as he scribbled more notes. I kept my arms crossed and sat very still, watching him until his pen came to a stop. He flipped through some of his notes from our previous sessions. "Tell me more about the nightmares, then."

I slumped back in the chair. Yeah, right. Like I really wanna talk about all the times the bloodthirsty predator stalked and caught me in my dreams. No, really. Let's chat about that one time it caught up to me and then forced me to watch from its eyes as it literally disemboweled my parents—who didn't take such abuse silently, mind you.

I shook my head, stopping the motion when I realized Dr. Anderson was watching me.

No. Freaking. Thank. You.

"Naiya," he chided, gesturing to the clock when I glanced his way.

I sighed. "The night terrors, you mean."

He shook his head. "We've been over this. You remember them—"

"So they're not night terrors. Yeah, I get it." I leaned forward, my elbows on my knees. "But you said that if someone or something wakes the person having the night terror, then that changes things.

Makes it so they're more likely to remember the nightmare, right?"

"Yes. But Naiya, nothing is waking you up."

I huffed out another breath. Yeah, right. Nothing but changing into a damn pointy-toothed, sharp-clawed predator, that is.

He glanced at the timer on the coffee table next to him. It was turned so that I couldn't see how long was left from my angle, but I suspected we still had about ten to fifteen minutes to go today. "Tell me about the nightmares. Are they what cause you to use?"

Ugh. Leave it to the therapist at a rehab center to always assume everything leads back to drugs. "I don't use … and I'd rather not talk about what happens when I try to sleep."

Dr. Anderson took off his glasses and pinched the bridge of his nose. "If you're going to insist that the reason you were admitted here is a fantasy, I'll have to treat you for what I can. You'll have to learn for yourself the value of truth over lies." He replaced the reading glasses and gestured to my file. "Now, your drug tests have come back negative, but you have also had a couple of nightmares since you were admitted. How long ago, before you came here, did those start?"

I jerked my chin toward the file in his lap. "It says there in my chart, I'm sure."

His eyes met mine. "I'm asking you."

I pulled my feet into the chair then, my knees pointing toward the door of his office. "It's been months now, for sure. So …" I shrugged. "Maybe a year ago, I guess?"

His pen scratched across the paper again. "And what did your parents do when you started having these nightmares?"

"They got rid of all the sodas and hired a nutritionist who doubled as a chef." I ran a hand through my hair and sighed. "Helen tried virtually every diet she could think of—gluten-free, sugar-free, keto … hell, they even tried to make me vegan."

More scribbles. "Did it help?"

I snorted. "Not at all. If anything, it made them worse. Except when we went Paleo. At least the food for that diet was tasty."

"Did it help the nightmares?"

I sucked on my lip and thought for a moment. "No."

He bobbed his head as he made more notes. "So, how did you cope with the diets and food restrictions?"

"I got my friend Elisa to take me places, so I could get snacks I actually liked."

He nodded like that was an expected response. "And what did your parents do when they found out?"

The corner of my mouth pulled up. "They didn't find out. I kept my snacks in a box on the top shelf of my closet. If they searched my room, they've probably found it all by now."

He didn't look up from his notes. "What about the dreams themselves? Any recurring themes?"

Yeah. The vicious leopard. Sometimes it was me. Sometimes it stalked me … dammit. That would only keep me here longer. I pressed my lips into a line and traced a pattern in the upholstery as I tried to pick just the right words to say.

He looked up at me then. "Naiya, I can't make you talk to me, but I can't let you leave until our time is up, so you might as well—"

"I'm always being hunted." I stopped tracing the upholstery and met his eyes. "Something is after me in the dark—breathing, snarling, claws scraping on things that set my teeth on edge to think about." The words tumbled over each other like rushing river stones. I couldn't tell him anything about me being a leopard, or he'd surely extend my stay, but I could tell him everything else. Maybe that would be enough to fill the requisite minutes. And if he could help me with that, well then, at least this wouldn't have been a complete waste of everyone's time. "It's big and evil, and it wants to consume me. It's faster than me—always ends up ahead of me, even if I run. And I wake up screaming every time it catches me."

Or I wake up snarling, covered in fur, fighting against the blankets and sheets of my bed with four black, claw-tipped paws. As it turns out, I have faint spots in the blackness of my fur, something I only noticed when I got stuck as a leopard for most of the night once. But even in the dark, I could see them—spots of impossible black against the all-consuming darkness of the rest of my fur.

I suppressed a shudder, glad that Dr. Anderson was too engrossed in his scribbling to see. He nodded along with whatever notes he was making, as if pieces were falling into place for him.

He probably had the wrong idea.

The wind-up timer began its sharp ring, and he stopped taking notes to end its incessant noise-making.

"Saved by the bell," I breathed.

He took off his glasses again, laying them on the coffee table next to the timer. "So it would seem."

The door opened, and a bulky orderly who was past his prime stepped in. His nametag read 'Jimmy.'

"We'll talk again on Monday," Dr. Anderson said as I stood to follow Jimmy the orderly. "Make a friend, Naiya. Non-staff."

I rolled my eyes and waved dismissively before shoving my hands into the pockets of my cardigan. "Fine."

TWO

Jimmy led me through a couple of hallways back to my room, a path I'd already grown familiar with in the three days since I'd been admitted.

My room was the last one on the right in the east wing. My neighbor was a girl who cried herself to sleep on my first night. The light wasn't on in her room, so she was probably off in the rec room or playing a round of air hockey upstairs with one of the guys from across the hall.

I flipped on the lights as I entered, but hit the switch to turn them off again as soon as Jimmy left. No light was more comfortable than the buzzing harshness of the fluorescent tubes overhead. Plus, there was plenty of ambient light coming in through the window, thanks to how well-lit they kept the courtyard—likely so they'd see if someone decided to try to make a break for it.

I peeled off my cardigan and tossed it over the back of the chair by my dresser before flopping facedown onto the bed. Belatedly remembering the band-aid on my arm, I rolled over with a quiet grumble and ripped the sucker off. A glance at the spot it vacated confirmed what I already knew.

There wasn't even so much as a dot where the needle had pierced my skin. The band-aid had been completely unnecessary. I dropped my arm to the bed with a heavy thud.

I stared blankly at the ceiling for a bit, hating that my parents had so blindly dumped me here. They wouldn't even let me talk to Abigail first; she'd always been able to help them understand me better. They just rushed me here without any real discussion or explanation. And my father had been in one of those moods where he wasn't going to let me get a word in anyway until I did whatever he said. Not that I could blame him, really. Not after what happened when he found me.

Eventually, I picked up the worn copy of *Pride and Prejudice* from the dresser and went back to the sordid affairs of the Bennetts and Mr. Darcy. But I could hardly focus.

The rest of the day went about the same as yesterday. I eventually finished Austen's classic and chose another book from the well-loved options on the shelf in the rec room—an old copy of *Romeo and Juliet*. Since I'd somehow managed to miss having that foisted upon me in high school, it seemed only right to give it a chance. I went to the cafeteria for my allotted dinner time, ate what little of the offerings that seemed palatable, and returned to my room to read until curfew. There was no mandatory lights-out, just a time that everyone had to be in their rooms and quiet, but it was a decent enough chunk of time to get a good sleep in.

Soon after curfew, right around the point when Juliet took the potion to appear dead, the night nurse came in, flicking the light on. His name was Ethan, and I squinted up at him in the sudden brightness as he rolled his cart in. He was probably only a couple of inches taller than me, though I was admittedly taller than pretty much all of the ladies at Saint Dymphna's. His wavy black hair was pulled into a low ponytail, and he had a dark goatee to match. He looked like he was probably only a couple of years older than me. He wasn't particularly muscular, nor particularly skinny, just kinda average.

He looked around the room, his eyes passing over me like I wasn't there, and made a face as he reached for his radio. He pressed a button on the side, and a crackly voice said, "Go ahead."

"Kateri in the rec room?" he asked.

Didn't this guy get how curfew worked? Well, at least he knew how to pronounce my last name. So many folks here tried 'kate-er-ee' before being corrected to 'kuh-teehr-ee.' But the question implied that he had not, in fact, seen me, even though I was sitting right there.

Beautiful.

I loved that I'd figured out how to pull this trick on people. There was no reason it should ever work, but it did.

"Nope," replied the voice on the other end of the radio. The front office, if I had to guess.

I stayed still, smoothing my expression into a passive mask, despite the smile trying to tug at the corners of my mouth. This was not the first time the staff here had failed to notice me.

Ethan rubbed the back of his neck. "Cafeteria?"

"Dinner time is over for her ward."

Dinner time is over for everyone, Ethan. The corner of my mouth pulled upward in a slow, smooth motion, controlled so as not to draw attention. How do you miss a girl sitting on the bed right in front of you?

He huffed out a breath. "Well, is it her counseling time?"

Y'know. Because Dr. Anderson is known for staying late and seeing clients after hours in a freaking substance abuse center. And I'm the Czar of Russia.

There was an audible sigh from the other end of the radio. I could practically hear the eye-roll in the guy's voice. "Trust me, man, she's in there."

Ethan pressed his lips into a line and looked blankly around my room. It wasn't like it was even that big of a room—barely more than a closet, really—and the only place to hide would be under my bed, which he bent to check even as I thought about it.

He straightened and cleared his throat, looking a little more nervous than he had before. "Naiya?"

I thumped the book onto the bed next to me and gave him a blithe look. "Yes?"

"Shit!" Ethan jumped like I was the boogeyman come to tear his soul from his body, and I couldn't help the smile that spread across my face. He took a slow deep breath and put his hands out in a steadying gesture as he collected himself.

I tried to force myself not to laugh, but that only made a quiet burst of giggles bubble up from my chest. I shook my head and allowed myself a couple of silent ones as Ethan rubbed at the back of his neck.

Once he'd reclaimed his chill, he eyed me like he hoped that would glue me to the spot as he grabbed my file from the cart and flipped a few pages. "Medicine ti—" He looked at the medicine in the cup on his cart and back at the paper in his hand, his brow furrowed. "Hmm, that can't be right." He flipped a page or two and then back to the page he was on. He shook his head. "One moment." He plopped the file back onto the cart next to the medicine cup and stepped out of my room in the direction of the front office, his keys clacking against the keycard and ID clipped to the waistband of his scrubs as he walked.

I didn't know how long he'd be gone, but that was my chart he was apparently having trouble with. So, I stood from the bed and took a look at it myself. The first couple of pages were filled with jargon I couldn't readily follow, but then I got to a summary page with my basic statistics. Female, twenty years old, five-foot-ten, 135 pounds, non-smoker, drug tests negative, blood type AB positive, and my allergy to silver was highlighted in yellow in the upper right corner of the page.

Waitaminute. AB positive? That wasn't right. I gave blood once a year at my father's charity gala, had since I was sixteen. I was O negative, a universal donor.

Keys jangled in the hallway. Ethan was coming back.

I put the chart down and hurried back to my spot on the bed. It wasn't like I wasn't allowed to know any of the information in my own chart, right? But it still didn't feel like something I wanted to get caught perusing. It'd probably lead to more questions from Dr. Anderson.

"Alright, Ms. Kateri," Ethan said as he stepped into my room again. "Just the one pill tonight to help you sleep. We'll double-check things in the morning." He tapped two pills from the little cup into a spare one he pulled from a drawer in the cart.

He checked my vitals, as he had the night before, and as had been the routine every night and every morning, before handing me the little cup with only a single pill in it and a bottle of water. I swallowed the medicine down as he turned to leave, and picked up my book.

Why the language of Shakespeare was easier for me than the rambling sentences of Austen, I'll never know. But I finished the lovers' death by suicide just as the sleeping pill kicked in.

THREE

IN THE MORNING, the nurse with short curly brown hair—her name was Leslie—took my vitals and had me pee into a cup. She checked my reflexes with her little rubber hammer and did a lot of the same tests they'd done when I was admitted, including yet another blood draw. I was pretty sure that had something to do with whatever Ethan had found in my chart last night. If I had to guess, someone in admissions wrote something down wrong, and they had to recheck everything else to be sure they had it right.

After the poking and prodding and questioning, I went to the cafeteria for breakfast, only to learn Nurse Leslie had kept me so long that the only options left to me were wheat bagels and cold eggs. Or some unholy abomination that passed for eggs. It was rubbery and disgusting, whatever it was. So I grabbed a bagel and ran it through the toaster. All of the little single-serve cream cheese packets were gone, but there was still some butter, which was better than nothing.

After breakfast was group therapy. Or at least, it would have been if I was actually using. Dr. Anderson had at least believed me enough that he didn't make me go to group with all the others. So, I had some time to kill in the rec room, which was a dumb name for it. It was basically just a large living room with a couch, some armchairs, and some card tables set up for board games and puzzles. But at least it meant returning *Romeo and Juliet* to the particleboard bookshelf and picking a new adventure from its sagging shelves.

Or so I thought. It was slim pickings at Saint Dymphna's Institute of Behavioral Health, unless I wanted a self-help book that echoed the sentiments of Dr. Anderson's collection. But there were a number of historical classics like Mary Shelly's *Frankenstein* and J.D. Salinger's *Catcher in the Rye*. I picked up and put down half a dozen of those well-worn classics, but none really grabbed me. I wished for my copy of *The Last Unicorn*, but I hadn't thought to grab it on my way out the door. Thanks to my parents' gross misunderstanding of the nature of my problem, I hadn't had the chance to think of anything to bring with me.

The news anchor on the TV grabbed my attention. Some strange weather anomaly had caused a freak lightning storm in Times Square, and nearly all of Manhattan had been plunged into middle-of-the-night darkness for two hours in the middle of the day. No power, no lights.

I absently stepped over to the worn leather couch and sank down onto the faded cushions.

According to the news anchor—a woman with so much hairspray on her shoulder-length bob that it didn't even move as she shook her head—this same thing had developed in Miami last week, and again in Los Angeles just a few days ago. The correspondent on the scene in Times Square mentioned reports of another anomaly in New Orleans about a month ago, but eyewitness accounts from the scene had been conflicting.

They switched to a meteorologist who talked

about how the late spring weather patterns across the US were all a little warmer than usual. Apparently, that meant things would be drier, allowing the ions in the atmosphere to become negatively charged and then arc to the ground as lightning. It sounded like he was making up his explanation on the fly, but the anchor nodded along, her expression thoughtful, as if she believed every word.

A door banged open in the hallway, and voices drifted my way. Group was out, which meant it was time to go sit outside and reflect. Or, at least, it was for them. I had to go, too, of course, but for me, it meant time to climb a tree and pretend I was elsewhere for a while.

The orderly in the rec room escorted me out to join everyone else in the courtyard, which was enclosed on all four sides by the three-story building. It had huge oak trees scattered around, providing lots of shade for the numerous benches. A multi-tiered fountain provided nice white noise to keep conversations from echoing off the walls, and a long swing set was situated over on the south side. The swings were almost always the first to fill, but that wasn't where my sights were set, so I didn't care.

The tallest tree in the yard just so happened to also be the furthest from the door we came through, though there were entrances on all four sides. That particular oak had branches that stretched well past the roof. It was far enough away from the building that it wasn't a likely escape, so the orderlies didn't pay it much attention—or, at least, they hadn't in my time here so far. Not that I intended to stage a breakout, but I could have made it work if I wanted to. Running would only show my parents they were probably right about the drugs, regardless of what the tests said. No, better that I stayed put and waited out my time here.

So, I wandered over to that tallest oak and started climbing. I didn't stop until I had cleared the roof—until there was nothing but sky between me and the skyline of downtown Dallas. The air seemed clearer up here, the breeze a warm promise of the sweltering heat that was to come this summer. Up here, I almost couldn't hear the other residents. Up here, if I closed my eyes, I could almost forget that I wasn't in my favorite tree back home. I clambered around from branch to branch in an attempt to find a good place to prop myself. I used to nap sometimes in my tree back home, and—if I could just find the right spot—maybe I could nap here, though it would be more entertaining to watch the others.

The oak split into two trunks about halfway up its height, but none of the branches this high up were big enough or close enough together to support a nap. So, people-watching it was. Corey looked better today than he had two days ago, as did Elaine. Rhonda still looked like she had one foot in the grave, while Nickolas seemed downright chipper. I didn't know the rest of their names. None of them really mattered to me. They weren't my friends, and they weren't going to be. Why make friends with druggies? Even if they were trying to get clean, I didn't want to be associated with them. I was not one of them.

And then, cliché as it sounds, *she* stepped outside. A tiny little thing with rainbow hair so bright it was almost painful to look at. She wore cutoff shorts with a hot pink tank top and tennis shoes, though her laces had been confiscated. She had a tattoo in vibrant green, red, and dark grey that wound around and down her left arm, and another on her right thigh that poked out from beneath her frayed denim shorts. She looked lost, wildly whipping her head around like she was shaking her hair out of her face as she eyed everyone in the courtyard. I watched her try to get her bearings, watched her try to find whatever it was she was looking for.

"Dammit, where is she?" she finally muttered, probably intending it to be more to herself, but I could just make it out over the rustling of the leaves.

I picked my way down a handful of branches until I had a decent jump to the ground. The orderlies would give me hell if they saw me, but I'd probably been still for long enough up there that they'd forgotten about me … again.

Rainbow Hair had wandered closer to my tree, probably hoping to get some distance from everyone else so she could find whoever she was looking for. This close, I could see the details of her inked sleeve. It was a rose vine and a dark chain that wound all around her arm, ending in a big red bloom that covered the back of her left hand.

I dropped out of the tree behind her with a soft thud. "Lose someone?"

She jumped as I landed, her tattooed hand brushing her stomach as she inhaled sharply. Her face crinkled for a moment as she looked at me, and then she shook her head. "Nope." She eyed the tree and then looked at me with wide-set brown eyes that seemed a bit bloodshot. "They don't freak about you being up there?"

I smiled at her. "If I sit still long enough, most of them forget I'm there. They even left me out here my first day. But then they put me in lockdown for three days once they found me."

"The bastards."

"Right?" I nodded. "They don't do a headcount or anything. It's not like this is a high-security operation here. But still, 'you can't deviate from your treatment plan.'" I mimicked Dr. Anderson's nasally voice and shook a finger like my mom used to do when she scolded me when I was little.

She snorted a laugh. "So, you just sit still, and they forget?"

I shrugged. "People are twitchy, always in motion. A hand in their hair, a bouncing knee. But movement draws the eye. Our brains are wired to notice it. Kinda like how you didn't notice a whole freaking person up in a tree until I landed behind you. A person doesn't look anything like tree branches. But when I sit still, I can nearly cease to exist."

She made a face at that last bit. "You cease to exist?"

"I might as well." I shrugged. "I'm very good at it. And it's freeing, watching people who have forgotten I'm there." My tone turned mischievous. "And I can't deny it's fun to watch them jump when they realize I never left."

"I bet." She extended her hand toward me. "Valerie Jenkins."

I chewed my cheek. Rainbow Hair—or rather, Valerie—was probably here for the same reason everyone else was. But I suspected it was about to get very lonely at Saint Dymphna's, now that I'd exhausted all the reading options I actually cared about.

Make a friend, Dr. Anderson had said.

Well, fine. At least, if I picked her, I wouldn't have to explain why I hadn't said a word to her until now. Here's to hoping she wasn't too terribly crazy.

So, I took her hand and shook it once. "Naiya Kateri." Releasing her hand, I jutted my chin at her. "What's your story?"

She tucked a section of hair behind her ear. "The same as everyone else, really. I just like being high too much."

Probably true if she got herself admitted here. "So, court-ordered rehab?"

She rolled a shoulder. "Something like that. What

about you?" It was a brushoff. Her tone told me she didn't want to talk about the real reason she ended up here.

I pressed my lips into a line. "Mmm. Admitted for drugs I didn't take. So now, they're keeping me here because I've lost touch with reality and have chronic persistent nightmares." I rolled my eyes. "Or so they say."

"Chronic nightmares?"

"I wake up screaming, and no one knows why. So, I've got that going for me." I clicked my tongue as I winked and shot finger guns at Valerie.

"Aren't those night terrors, then?"

I shook my head. "Apparently not, since I remember every visceral detail afterward."

Her brown eyes turned lustrous as her tone went sultry, and she winked at me. "Y'know, there are better reasons to scream in bed than nightmares."

I blinked. What the hell? Was she flirting with me?

"So, you're still high, then?" I tried to make my tone playful, but I was admittedly thrown. I mean, she was pretty, sure, but who hits on someone they just met in rehab? "What'd you last take?"

She put her hands together like she was praying and looked to the sky before closing her eyes. "The holy trinity: Mary Jane, Molly, and mimosas—heavy on the prosecco." She dropped her hands and looked back at me. "But the buzz wore off during intake."

"The vampires." Maybe there was more vitriol in the statement than I'd meant, but I was tired of the damn needles.

Her eyes went wide. "What?"

"The staff," I said with a huff. "They're vampires. They take a vial of my blood every freaking day. Didn't they take yours?" Maybe I *should* have been talking to some of the other residents while I was here.

Her eyebrows knitted together, and she shook her head once, setting the rainbow hair in motion. "No. That's not what recovery centers do. They just have you pee in a cup or clip a bit of hair from the back of your head on intake."

"What?" What the hell were they taking my blood for, then?

"You said they're taking your blood on the daily? Maybe they're trying to make sure your medicine isn't fucking with your organs or something."

I made a noncommittal noise. I wasn't so sure.

"I'm glad you were just making a joke about the staff," she added. "For a sec there, I thought you might be one of those crazy conspiracy theorists."

"Mmm, nope." I shook my head. "Despite my presence in a mental health facility, I have not actually joined the ranks of the foil hat-wearers."

"Do me a favor?"

I arched an eyebrow at her.

"Don't."

FOUR

THERE WAS something about Valerie that made it easy for me to just be around her, and she and I spent the hour before they brought everyone back inside lurking around the courtyard like a pair of stray cats. Valerie had, of course, been given the grand tour upon her arrival at Saint Dymphna's, and it wasn't like I was going to be able to wander off to give her a tour myself anyway. But I pointed out the residents whose names I knew, and we made up wild stories about how they got here: Rhonda turned tricks on the corner for rails, Corey's band threw him in here so he wouldn't OD on heroin, Nickolas drank to numb the pain of all the girls who wouldn't sleep with him, and Elaine just got hooked on Adderall after cramming for her midterms. None of it was true, of course—at least, not as far as I knew—but it passed the time.

Valerie apparently had her first therapy appointment scheduled for immediately after outdoor reflection time, so I grabbed a tuna sandwich from the cafeteria and wandered back to the rec room to eat it and kill some time. Killing time was all there was to do, really. There were a couple of air hockey tables in the upstairs rec room, but they usually got claimed pretty readily. Besides, you had to have someone to play against, and—up until now—I hadn't had anyone I'd so much as talked to, let alone someone I'd want to play a game with.

The book selection in the rec room hadn't improved in the time I'd been gone, so I plopped down on the leather couch and took a bite of my sandwich as a different news anchor droned on about the stock market. The guy was so old he could have been my grandfather, with skin so wrinkled and liver-spotted that it was easily visible through whatever stage makeup they'd applied. Or … God, maybe that *was* the stage makeup and he looked even worse beneath it! Either way, I couldn't follow his droning on and on about numbers, so I quickly finished eating and peeled myself off the couch to go take a shower and otherwise kill time before dinner.

I take inordinately long showers and even longer baths when given the opportunity. And since there weren't any bathtubs—likely because they'd be a drowning hazard—I tried my hardest to find the end of the hot water. I thought since I liked to get the bathroom good and steamy before I even ducked under the water, I'd for sure get to the end of their water heater's capacity. But after forty-five minutes of hot water, an orderly came in to check on me and told me to wrap it up.

It may not have been the swankiest recovery center around, but Saint Dymphna's had it where it counted. Hot water for that long was nothing to scoff at.

At dinnertime, I was already seated with my slab of dried-out meatloaf and reconstituted mashed potatoes when Valerie made her way through the line. She brought her tray over to where I was seated, which was at one of the tiny high-top tables that lined the outer edge of the cafeteria. The big round tables were all about half full of faces I wasn't interested in getting to know.

She looked over her shoulder at the other tables and then back at the empty chair at my table. "This seat taken?"

I shook my head. "Not yet."

She smiled at me with perfectly white teeth and sat down.

I eyed her dinner selections. "Ooh, careful of the jello there. It's, uh, not the flavor you think it is."

She looked at it and then up at me. "What is it?"

"I dunno. But it's wrong. A charlatan parading around as whatever green or red flavor it's supposed to be." They had both as options pretty much every day, but they both tasted the same flavor of wrong, so I didn't get the point of offering the illusion of choice.

She scrunched up her face, her expression of disgust somehow so cute I wished for about half a breath that we were close enough friends that I could boop her nose. I pushed that thought out of my head the same way she pushed the jiggly fraud of a dessert away from her tray.

"Good to know," she said, poking her fork into the overly firm meatloaf. "And is the meatloaf just as suspect?"

I smirked at her. "Nah, it's just dry and bland."

She nodded as she shoved a forkful into her mouth. "At least the eye candy is nice." She waved her fork at me.

I blinked and stilled. "What?"

Look, I can appreciate girls just as well as I can appreciate guys. Hell, I gave my v-card to the girlfriend I'd had during my senior year of high school. But Rachel had transferred mid-year when her parents moved to DC, and there hadn't really been any other women in my life since. There had been a few guys, but nothing lasting. Valerie was out of my league, even if she *did* have a drug problem. At barely five feet tall, she was skinny and wild, all party girl by the look of it, and her pouty pink lips looked dangerously soft. I may have had some sort of vaguely international look—with my dark olive skin, my pin-straight long black hair so thick it broke hair ties on the regular, and my bright green eyes that were almost too big in my face—but I was too skinny, too lanky.

She nodded over my shoulder. "Oh *please*, you can't possibly tell me Mister Beefy over there isn't hot as fuck."

I turned in my chair to look at the door on that side of the room, somewhat relieved and yet also somewhat disappointed that she wasn't talking about me.

She meant Tyler, the orderly who looked like he could bench press at least five of me.

He stood with his arms crossed, looking as intimidating as he could. It probably meant he was just a huge teddy bear, but his job was to keep us all here in the cafeteria while they changed everyone's sheets and checked the rooms for contraband.

"Uh," I said. "He's not really my type." Which he wasn't. I liked my men just a bit … well, *smaller*.

"Not your type?" Her brown eyes refocused on me. "Are you blind? That man could break me in two, and I would thank him for it."

"Wow." What the hell do you do with information like that?

"Okay, Miss Judgey." She shook her fork at me with her tattooed hand. "What *is* your type?"

I chewed my lip and thought for a moment. I mean, she fit, I suppose, though I'd want to get to know her before getting involved with her. But Rachel had been a curvy girl with thick thighs, and the guys I'd dated all kinda ran the gamut: nerdy Geoff who spent more time with his war games than with me, lanky jock James who cared entirely too much about his image, drummer Eli who just would not get his shit together, stoner Blake who had zero ambition in life … I'd even dated this one theater kid named Shaun who was shorter than me, though we just didn't vibe as well as I'd wanted us to.

"Well?"

"I'm not really sure I have a type," I finally said. "I keep pretty busy. I dated a lot in high school, but these days my only socializing is at my father's mixers. Only, it turns out all the eligible bachelors in my circle are entitled assholes. So, I guess, not that."

"Oof," she said. "We'll have to work on it, then."

"Work on what?"

"You not knowing your type." She bounced her leg under the table.

Had it been doing that the whole time? I usually noticed that kind of thing.

"It's not like it's hard to figure out, y'know," she continued.

"Well, okay." I finished the last of my mashed potatoes. "So big, dumb, and likely to break your furniture is your type?"

"Mmm, I'm not really picky. But I *do* have standards."

"Which are …?" I rolled my hand in a gesture for her to keep going.

She put her fork down and looked at me. "Well, let's see. Dark hair, big eyes, looks vaguely Indian or Persian or something like that—"

"Valerie!" I balled up my napkin and threw it at her.

"Look, you asked, sexy thing." She shrugged. "I'm just dealing in truths here."

I blinked as I watched her stand and take her leftovers to the trash. If it weren't for the fact that she was clearly an addict, it might be nice to be closer with her. And either way, she did have a nice ass.

I shook my head.

Don't hook up in rehab, dumbass.

She turned and looked back at me. "There's still some time before curfew. Wanna see if the air hockey table is open?"

I smiled as I shoved the last of my meatloaf in my mouth. Tyler had moved away from the door, which meant we were free until ten o'clock curfew.

"Sure," I said, standing to clear my own leftovers. I saved the dinner roll to eat as we walked.

We had to wait for a game to finish, but then we did indeed get our turn at air hockey. And I won every match. Her eyes gave her away. Well, that and she shifted her weight when she was trying to trick me into juking left while the puck went right. She got a couple points on me before I figured out all her tells, but after three matches in a row of me shutting her out of any points, she was done. She had been pinching the bridge of her nose more and more between shots in the last game and had even started wincing when the puck hit the sides of the table. She went to bed a full hour before curfew.

I wandered back to my room as well and slept better that night than I had my whole time there. Not a nightmare in sight.

FIVE

It turned out Valerie was just as fidgety as everyone I'd ever met. No surprise, really. But she touched her stomach a lot and was kinda jumpy. When the typically chipper Nickolas slammed the door to his room after what was probably his therapy session, she nearly jumped out of her skin, but her hand went right to her stomach. And when she realized she was being super aggressive at the hockey table, she pressed her palm to her belly as she apologized. I finally decided to ask her about it after Chase—who we decided had a problem with getting blackout drunk trying to go shot-for-shot with the seasoned alcoholics in sports bars—gave one of her explosive sneezes in the rec room.

I watched Valerie's wide eyes and dropped my voice so the others wouldn't hear. "Are you pregnant?"

She blinked at me, her face going slack with confusion, as she pulled her hand away from her body like a child who just got burned by the stove. "What?"

"You rub your stomach a lot, particularly when something surprises you," I said, relatively certain she'd heard my initial question. "Are you pregnant? Or just always hungry?"

She ran a hand through her rainbow hair. "No, I …" She looked around the room and leaned closer, dropping her voice to a barely audible whisper. "I have a scar there." She eyed the orderly and turned a bit on the couch as she pulled up the bottom of her shirt.

A scar, she'd said. She didn't just have a little surgery scar like her simple wording would suggest. Marring the smooth pale skin of her soft stomach were four mostly parallel lines of pink scars. The edges were ragged, and the scars themselves a bit raised.

Something had tried to kill her.

"Holy shit," I whispered. "What happened?"

She took a deep breath and sucked on her bottom lip as she pushed her shirt back down. I thought for a moment that she wasn't going to tell me.

"It's okay—"

"I was attacked coming out of a club one night, and … well … I've been a little jumpy since then." Her head drooped.

"I would be, too," I said, placing my hand on her shoulder.

Some of the tension left her at my touch. It was kinda nice.

The rest of the day went exactly as scheduled. I puttered around the rec room while Valerie was in group, and when that let out, we sat at the base of the tallest oak in relative silence, dozing in the warm breeze. They called us in for dinner as the courtyard grew shadowy in the half-light of dusk. We got another shot at the air hockey table that night, but we only got halfway through a game before she called it. Her eyes were unfocused as she said good night.

I didn't see her much the next day. She had back-to-back therapy and group. And, since it was rainy and we couldn't go outside, group went for longer than usual. I, for one, wouldn't have minded going outside. I liked the rain.

Sadly, I wasn't the one who got to make that call.

I brought her a coffee after group let out, but she only drank half of it before deciding to head back to her room. Tyler, her favorite orderly, brought her a bag of hard candies. Supposedly they would help her keep her mouth busy so she wouldn't want to smoke so bad.

The thought danced through my head of other things she could do to keep her mouth busy, but it was more a passing 'that's what she said' joke than an actual desire to kiss her or anything.

She had another therapist appointment that day, which made three for her since my last one. She must not have been kidding about the drugs she'd been on. I knew they put her on a cocktail of meds to level her out, but I guess it hadn't occurred to me how far down the rabbit hole she'd been before coming here.

Besides, Dr. Anderson had obviously had just about enough from me. Or he couldn't actually help me. I suspected it was the latter, since he and I both knew I wasn't using any type of drug.

It didn't stop them from taking vial after vial of my blood every day, though. What the hell were they even monitoring? It wasn't like I was diabetic or anything.

The part of me that bristled a little at the thought of being brushed aside while a new and more interesting client crossed Dr. Anderson's desk was easily dwarfed by the growing frustration that I couldn't get any answers for the one question I actually had.

The door to Dr. Anderson's office opened, and Valerie came through, along with Ethan, the orderly who'd noticed something about my file.

Valerie was in rough shape after her appointment. Her eyes were red-rimmed, and she didn't even look up as she brushed past me to her room. She didn't slam the door or turn on music. She simply shut the door with a quiet click, which was followed by the more solid clack of the lock.

And I was alone again.

Before she came around, it hadn't bothered me in the slightest to be alone in this stupid place. But the finality of the lock hurt. Her sniffles and obviously quieted crying didn't help. I wanted to hug her. To be there for her. But I was nobody to her—just another junkie who had somehow conned her way out of group.

I didn't sleep much that night. I even ghosted through the next morning, blithely offering my arm for the morning nurse and her needle. It was too easy to revert back to how I handled this place before Valerie came along. It had only been three and a half days that she'd been around, anyway. I passed her room after breakfast, but she wasn't there, and her sheets were a mess.

After group ended and all the residents went outside, I climbed my tree again, staying as far away from everyone as I could. But I watched her as she sat and stared blankly at the fountain. She seemed so damn lost. She needed some encouragement to get her through this stay, or they were going to take her to wherever they kept the padded rooms.

So, I devised a plan. Jenny, the orderly keeping an eye on us today, always had a couple of markers sticking out of her back pocket. It couldn't be hard to grab one as I came inside. I just hoped Valerie's room wasn't locked.

The plan went off without a hitch. Jenny didn't even check her pocket after I snagged the marker, and Valerie's room was wide open. But I hadn't accounted for what to write, and as I stood there, staring at the mirror above her dresser, I drew a blank.

"What're you doing?" Valerie asked just as I raised

an arm to start writing something I'd seen in a video online.

Shit.

I dropped my arm and recapped the marker. "Uh … I was gonna leave you a note." God, did I really sound that freaking lame?

"Oh."

"It was probably gonna be cheesy as hell, anyway."

She nodded.

I chewed my cheek for a moment, watching her. She seemed hollow, sunken, and I guessed she hadn't slept very much in the past couple of days. She absently rubbed a finger over her stomach, probably tracing the line of one of her scars through her shirt.

And I knew what to put on her mirror. I uncapped the marker and started writing.

She read it out loud as I wrote it. "Not. Even. A. Monster. Could. Take. You. Down. You. Bad. Bitch." She half giggled, but it was quickly swallowed by a sob.

I hurriedly capped the marker, leaving it on her dresser as I rushed to hug her. I just held her as she cried out whatever she needed to. I couldn't fathom what she was going through, but I could be there for her. At least for as long as my stay. I had stopped counting the days. Well … I wasn't about to check the math while she cried.

When she was done, we sat on her bed—it was the only place in her room where we could sit together—and she laid her head on my thigh as I sat cross-legged on top of the woven blanket. We sat in amiable silence, and I ran my hand through her rainbow hair, smoothing it and tucking it behind her ear.

At dinner, we ate without conversation. I liked that I could just be quiet with her, that she didn't need to fill the silence. But when dinner was done, it was like the spell was broken. Something about the expression on her face and the tension in her shoulders told me she wanted time alone. Really alone. She went back to her room, and I went to take another long-ass shower before bed.

She wasn't at breakfast the next morning, but there was a note on my mirror, written in big bubbly letters: *I'm really glad to have met you —Val* .

We were a lot like ships in the night the next couple of days. It turned out Dr. Anderson wasn't done with me, but his sessions were a lot less invasive. He didn't bother trying to get me to talk about my nightmares; instead, he asked more about my family and friends. It felt like he was killing time. I tried to ask about the vials of blood, but he told me that the orders for that came from the doctor who checked me out at intake, and that I'd need an appointment with them to learn more. And since I wasn't sick and wasn't having issues with my meds, I got put on the waiting list.

When Valerie and I did manage to meet up, I asked her about calling her Val, since she'd signed the mirror that way. She smiled at me and told me it was fine. But she alternated between pretty spacey and super antsy in the coming days, which had me worried. When she was spacey, we ended up sitting on the bed in her room in much the same position as that first time, her head on my lap. Sometimes, she dozed off. Sometimes, I leaned back against the wall and did the same. But when she was antsy, we roamed the halls of Saint Dymphna's—at least, the ones we were allowed—until we could get our turn at the air hockey table.

And when we were outside, I taught her how to climb trees. Specifically, my tree. I showed her how to tell when a branch was strong enough to support her weight, and how to shift her weight smoothly so she didn't always feel like she was going to fall. She wasn't great, but she got the hang of it pretty readily.

It only took two days before an orderly had something to say about it. Bryce was new, but he had an attitude and thought he was the big man on campus just because the admins had given him a keycard and ID badge.

"Hey! Get down from there!" He was across the courtyard, with the fountain between him and us, but he was loud enough that I heard him.

Everyone else did, too, and they all looked to see who he was yelling at. I looked to Val, who sneered at him.

"Shove it up your ass," she shouted, grabbing the next branch. "My insurance will cover it if I get hurt!"

The corner of my mouth turned up as I watched her climb higher.

He stormed toward us. "That's not how it works around here, Miss Jenkins!"

"Then try to stop me!" But there was a shake in her voice. I don't think she knew what she was going to do if Bryce caught her.

Well, in for a penny, in for a pound, right? I darted for the tree at the other corner of the courtyard. "You'll have to stop both of us if you're that set on it!"

Bryce was past the fountain by then, but he stopped as I scrambled up this new tree. He looked between Val and I as he reached for his radio. Whatever he said to the front office, I didn't hear clearly other than the simple word 'backup.' My attention was split between climbing my own tree and Val. As I got up past the roof of Saint Dymphna's, a warm breeze blew across my face, and I closed my eyes, taking it in and letting it slow my racing heart. I was too high up for the branches to support someone as big as Bryce.

A sharp yelp drew my attention to the other tree.

Val had misplaced her weight and dropped a couple of branches before she caught herself. She probably scraped her palms, but that bad ass bitch just kept climbing. And since she was smaller than me, she got much higher than I could.

They had to borrow the custodial staff's scissor lift to get us down. It took them over an hour.

The nurse checked us out afterward. Val's palms were indeed scraped up, and Bryce made sure the front office confined both of us indoors—her for three days and me for the remainder of my stay.

The next morning, Dr. Anderson scolded me like a child. He probably did the same for her as well, but it didn't matter. It had been absolutely worth it to see them all lose their shit like that.

SIX

THE NEXT DAY, I was finally getting discharged, and Val definitely seemed more on edge. I'm not sure if it was because she had done the math and wasn't looking forward to my departure, or if it was simply that she was working through the tail end of whatever she'd been hooked on, but I worried for her and how she would handle this place without me. She still had a little less than a week to go on her treatment plan. I wanted to ask her about it, find out what was really making her so antsy, but her own appointment with Dr. Anderson immediately followed mine, so she wasn't around as I signed off on all the requisite paperwork.

The morning nurses were still taking my blood, and the admitting doctor still hadn't found room in his schedule for a consult with me—which was frustrating, to say the least. I wasn't sure if I would be able to see him after I left, which meant I would be left with this bullshit unsolved mystery about my stay.

As I handed the last of my paperwork to the lady at the big round desk that separated the lobby from the doctor's waiting room, the automatic sliding doors at the front of Saint Dymphna's opened, letting in a warm breeze along with two people in suits—a man and a woman. Something about the way they smelled set my teeth on edge, but I couldn't place it. So I stilled and watched them as they approached the desk with matched movements.

The woman was maybe in her early thirties. Her hair was blonde, set in a tight bun at the nape of her neck. Her suit was well-tailored, but it was in that particular shade of non-descript black that told me she was private security. Expensive private security, judging by the cut of the suit, but private security all the same.

So was her partner, a vaguely middle-aged man with short dark hair, whose suit matched hers like they were cut from the same bolt of fabric. They even had the exact same silver pocket square. His face was clean-shaven and held a seriousness that made me wonder if he even knew what a joke was. I doubted he'd ever laughed in his lifetime. Or if he had, he'd long forgotten how. But his eyes were a curious shade of pale brown that I could have sworn was almost gold.

The woman in the suit met my eyes. "Ms. Kateri?"

I blinked. It shouldn't have surprised me to hear her address me directly—she even said my name properly—but I had grown used to going unnoticed. I was the only one standing in the waiting room, and there was no one else in the lobby either, beyond the admin at the desk. Of course she'd noticed me.

"Ms. Kateri," the man said, gesturing with an arm toward the door. "If you'll come with us, please, we'll get you where you need to be." His deep baritone voice held a polite deference mixed with a no-nonsense air that confirmed my suspicion that these two were private security.

My parents had probably hired them to pick me

up discreetly. Can't have their druggie daughter riding home in her recognizable car.

"Wooow," I said, drawing out the word and arching an eyebrow at the guy. "My parents couldn't even be bothered to pick me up themselves, huh? Are they even in the country these days?"

I don't know how I missed seeing the woman move, but she was suddenly beside me, placing a hand at my lower back as I snatched my bag of possessions from the counter where the desk admin had placed it.

"We'll answer your questions in private, Ms. Kateri," she said, eyeing the room behind me. Her palm was warm even through my shirt.

My heart rate spiked. Private security is only allowed to touch me when my life is in danger. I swiveled my head around the room but didn't see anything amiss.

That was when Val burst through the door to the waiting room, slipping on the tile floor as she rounded the corner. "Don't go with them, Naiya! They're not who you think they are!"

Tyler, her favorite orderly, was hot on her heels. He wrapped an arm around her waist and smoothly lifted her from the ground, pulling her back into the hallway like it was a matter of course.

But her panicked expression told me all I needed to know.

I looked outside the automatic doors, narrowing my eyes at the vehicle there. It was a plain black SUV with blacked-out windows. The kind that screams FBI or CIA or possibly something else entirely.

I turned back to the woman in the suit. "Which of my parents—?"

"I'm sorry, Ms. Kateri," the man said as he jabbed a needle into the spot where my neck met my shoulder. "It appears your questions will have to wait."

My vision fogged. How had he gotten over to me so fast? My knees turned to jelly. Who the hell were these two? My mouth went dry, and my body fell limply into someone's waiting arms as the world went dark.

SEVEN

I opened my eyes to a low-lit metal room. I was lying on a firm bunk with a soft pillow under my head. My feet were bare, but I was otherwise wearing what I had been when I was discharged from Saint Dymphna's—a black tank top and my acid-wash skinny jeans. Next to the bed was a metal table with a crystal clear glass, half-filled with water. I swung my legs from the bunk and picked it up.

It was plastic, not glass.

"What the …?" My mouth felt like it was filled with sand.

"Naiya?" Val's voice sounded like it came from the room next to mine.

"Valerie?" I brushed some of my hair back from my face and took a sip of the water. It was barely cooler than room temperature, but it at least cleared the dry itch from my throat.

"It's still okay to call me Val," she said, but her voice seemed a bit … strained, maybe? "Are you okay?"

I stretched my neck. My head felt like a balloon, and my heart started to pound as I looked around the room. Across from me was a metal toilet with a black privacy curtain half pulled around it. Next to that was a sink with a white hand towel and washcloth laid over the bar on the wall. The wall facing the foot of the bunk held a metal door that fit nearly flush with the surrounding wall. Bars covered a large triangular opening that was set in the upper right of the door, above where the handle would be. On this side, there was simply a round piece of metal, but there was a black card reader just to the right of the door. To the right of that, and a bit higher up, was an empty shelf large enough to hold maybe a microwave or a folded blanket. And in the top right corner of that wall was a digital clock that also displayed both the day and date —11:23 a.m. on Thursday, May 28th. It emitted no light, but instead resembled an old-style black-and-grey LCD screen in reverse.

"I'm alright, I think," I said. "Are you?"

"Seems like it," she replied.

I had started the lengthy check-out process at Saint Dymphna's at around eight in the morning. I must not have lost much time to unconsciousness. Where the hell *was* I, anyway? Why did this place look like a slightly swankier version of a prison cell?

And where the *hell* were my shoes?

I pushed my hand through my hair. "Where the hell are we?"

A man's voice came from across the hall. "Some kind of research facility, best I can tell." His accent had an almost musical lilt, hitting the long vowels a little hard while cutting the consonants short. I couldn't place it.

I narrowed my eyes and stepped over to the window. Beyond my door was more cold steel coupled with harsh lighting and too-clean white tile. I squinted against the almost painfully sharp brightness and backed a step into my room, which was, thankfully, distinctly darker than the hallway.

It was also distinctly darker than the room across the hall from me, where a man in maybe his mid-twenties stood at his window, his light brown hair a short mess atop his head. He wore what looked like a plain white t-shirt, but I couldn't see what else he had on thanks to the limited view the window afforded me. His too-dark eyes gazed into my own, and I couldn't be sure even what color they were. Maybe dark blue? Maybe brown? Either way, they sparkled with intelligence in a way I couldn't quite put my finger on.

I looked away, searching the walls of my room for a dimmer switch to explain the darker state of my room. "How did you know those guys weren't sent by my parents, Val?"

No dimmer switch. No thermostat. Nothing that gave me any control over the way this room was kept beyond the bedsheets, toilet, and sink. And thanks to the lack of door handle, no escape. Peachy. I gulped down the rest of the water from my cup.

"I saw the SUV they got out of," she called. "It looked sketchier than I figured your family for."

I nodded. "Thanks for trying to warn me, at least."

There was a heavy flop onto something soft in the room next to mine.

"Fat lot of good it fucking did," she grumbled.

"It counts that you tried," I said.

"Well, wherever we are," she said, "you can bet your ass you're not getting your phone call. This place reeks of off-the-books activities."

My heart had at least stopped slamming against my sternum, but at that, it picked up speed. Ice danced along my spine as I leaned back toward the door and squinted down the hall. There were skylights in the hallway, which was where the almost blinding brightness came from.

I bet there's a beautiful breeze out there, too.

And suddenly, the air felt stuffy and old, and my

racing heart ached for my tree back home. I swallowed around a lump of fear and closed my eyes as I took a steadying breath. There was no way to know whether this place was actually dangerous just yet. I didn't have enough information. My instincts screamed at me that it was decidedly unsafe for me to be there, but maybe being locked in my cell-like room was for my own safety. Maybe the same was true for all of us.

I forced myself to visually trace the lines of the hallway, my vision adjusting to the brightness as I did. I couldn't see far enough down the hallway to the right to see how it truncated, but to my left, the hallway ended three doors down, another keycard door set into the perpendicular wall closing off the hallway.

"It's sealed," said the guy across from me.

He apparently hadn't stopped watching me, and curiosity danced across his expression.

I nodded. "Of course it is." I met his eyes again, focusing past the light of the hallway to try to figure out the mystery of their color. They were a deep blue so dark they were actually almost purple-black, the kind of thing you'd only see with colored contacts. No one's natural eyes were that color. Still, it suited him.

"So, who are you?" I asked him.

He tilted his head toward me in a little half-bow, the corner of his mouth turning up ever so slightly. "Andrezmes Kjelliho. You?"

The bow was cute, but I swear it was like he was speaking a foreign language.

"That's a name," Val said. "Run that by me again?"

He straightened and said it slower this time. "And-*raze*-mess k-yell-*ee*-ho."

Well, at least I was relatively certain I could recreate *those* sounds.

"Naiya Kateri." I hooked a thumb toward the room to my left. "That's Valerie."

"You might as well call me Val, too," she said.

He smiled then, his teeth bright. "A pleasure, ladies. I thought I might end up alone here for the rest of my days." He quickly ran a hand through his messy hair, which made it worse but in a somehow charming way. "That's what I get for meddling in the boundaries."

"Boundaries?" I arched an eyebrow at him.

He nodded once. "This is not my home."

"Welcome to the club," Val said. Something gave a low creak as she said it. Maybe she stood from her bed?

He smirked. "Perhaps. But I suspect this is more your home than it is mine, if your speech is anything to go by."

"What?" I made a face at him. "They literally just kidnapped us and dumped us here!"

"Sure." He shrugged. "But this *world* is yours."

I stilled. "What do you mean by that?"

"Ooh," he said, interest and intensity glittering in his dark eyes. "Did you know? Your irises contracted just now. Your pupils are tiny little pinpricks of black in a field of bright green."

The hell? I stared at him for a moment, but he held my gaze without continuing.

"What. Did. You. *Mean?*" I tried to keep the animosity from my tone, but I was disoriented, confused, and frankly tired of being so damn out of the loop.

"I'm not from here." His hand came into view again. It was covered in geometric tattoos. "Is this an accent you have heard anywhere before?" He gestured at his face.

Val snorted out a rueful laugh. "So, where're you

from, then?" She sounded like she was right at her door—right next to me, but for the wall.

"Arcaniss."

I cocked my head to the side. "What?"

He pointed at the ceiling and swirled his finger in a circle. "You know those anomalies that have been manifesting?"

"I know there are some strange lightning events going on around New York and Miami," I said. "Is that what you mean?"

He nodded.

"It's not lightning," Val said. It wasn't a question.

"No," Andrezmes confirmed. "They're rifts, tears in reality, portals to my world, gateways to where I came from. These people seem to think I'm responsible for at least some of them. But I'm not powerful enough for that." He deflated a little. "Not yet, at least."

Maybe this was another mental institution. Had Dr. Anderson somehow arranged for this?

"No way," Val said.

But if Dr. Anderson had decided I was delusional and this was a mental institution, why was Val here? She was just a recovering addict.

"There is a way," he said. "Only I'm not sure *how*, exactly. But I can prove I'm telling the truth."

Nice of him to offer before either of us called him a liar … or a nutjob.

His tattooed hand came into view again, this time palm up. In his hand was a large translucent purple crystal, about the size of a closed fist. Half a breath later, the crystal unfolded itself. Val squeaked her surprise as it split eight slender little legs off a gracefully faceted body and began to crawl from his hand. At the edge of Andrezmes' fingertips, it reached for the window and bridged the gap with tiny little taps of crystal on metal. Sliding between the bars of the opening, it tinked down the front of his door, moving not entirely unlike a sizable tarantula. And the way it clung to the vertical surface of the door absolutely defied physics.

I couldn't help but smile at the little thing. "Oh! How cute!"

"Are you fucking insane?" Val's voice bit through the air. "It's not *cute*! Keep that thing away from me!"

As if in challenge, the crystalline spider darted diagonally across the hall and made its way up her door. She let out a little scream, and the thump against the back wall of her room told me she had backed all the way up to get away from it.

He had to be at least a little unhinged, even if he did sound like he believed what he'd said about the weird weather patterns.

I met Andrezmes' dark eyes. "Don't torture her! She's obviously afraid of spiders! Likely moreso for crystal ones that aren't native to any country on any map I've ever seen!"

He sighed and looked over at the spider. "You might like him more if you ever get hurt." He whistled quietly and jerked his head toward me. The spider jumped from Val's window, tumbling in the air to land on its feet in the hallway, and skittered up the wall toward my window.

Maybe if I humored him, went along with what he was saying like it was truth, I could understand what was going on here.

"Why's that?" I placed my right hand next to the door, palm up, as the little creature reached the bars. It slowly, gingerly stepped onto my hand with legs that ended in sharp points like thumbtacks. It wasn't uncomfortable, but I certainly believed this little creature capable of defending itself.

"He helps knit closed minor injuries," Andrezmes explained. "He can't heal broken bones, but … we'll get there, won't we, Chad?" He said the last bit like someone talking to their favorite pet.

The spider answered with a quiet shrill screech. Except he didn't even have any internal organs. How did he inhale air to make a noise like that?

I mean, that'd be pretty cool if the healing thing was true. And that guy *definitely* sounded like he believed it was.

I brought the creature closer to my face, trying to make sense of how he worked as I brushed a fingertip along the cool facets of his back. They were sharp, like he was made of cut glass. He leaned into my touch with a little chitter that sounded decidedly happy.

"His name is Chad?" Val sounded full of disbelief.

I was more in disbelief that this thing was even capable of independent locomotion. No brain, no lungs, nothing at all that indicated this thing was anything more than a highly detailed crystal paperweight.

"Chadmahrazhalorne, actually," Andrezmes said. The name flowed smoothly from his mouth and leaned hard into his musical accent. "But it's easier to call him Chad."

I tore my gaze from the creature and looked across the hall. "Does that mean we can call you Andy?"

He rolled a shoulder. "Most of my friends do."

I nodded once and looked back at the crystal spider, who cocked his head at me and twitched his little translucent mandibles. It was really bizarre, but also very cute. He reminded me of all the misunderstood spider pictures on social media.

I glanced up at Andrezmes—at Andy. "How does he work?" I lifted my hand holding Chad.

He gave me a wry little smile. "I'm not exactly sure. I thought it was because of the magic back home, but that's obviously not the case. I'm glad he still works here, though."

Chad lifted his little head and I got the distinct impression he was pridefully puffing his chest out at me.

"I'm surprised that thing isn't living in a contained little box of its own," Val said.

"I don't know who these people are," Andy said, gesturing toward the door at the end of the hall, "but they certainly tried that. Except if Chad cannot connect with me, he reverts to an inert crystal until he can detect my psychic presence again."

He paused then, watching me.

I brought the finger of my left hand up to point at one of the legs of the little crystal spider. Chad reached that foot toward my fingertip and tapped it. I pointed at a leg on the other side of him and he did the same with the leg I'd indicated. A smile pulled at Andy's mouth, but it turned sour.

"When they couldn't get a response from him in his inert form, they tried chipping away at him when he was active," he said, his voice somber. "It … hurts. I refused to cooperate with them until they put a stop to it."

Chad ignored my last pointed finger and instead danced to the fingertips of my hand with a little chitter, anchoring himself and reaching for my window using his front legs. I extended my hand toward the bars, and he skittered up my doorframe this time, crossing the ceiling to get back across the hall to Andy, where he nuzzled against his neck with a low hum.

"Now," Andy said, "I'll do what I am capable of to cooperate with their search for knowledge of my world and the rifts, so long as they leave him alone."

I watched him recollect himself. Chad must mean an awful lot to him.

"Wait," Val said. "If you're from a whole different world, how do you even speak English?"

I looked up at him. She had a point. He may have had a strange accent that I'd never heard, but he spoke English *very* well for someone who claimed to be from elsewhere.

"I wish I knew," he said. "The people here asked me the same thing. My current theory is that something in the power opening the rifts is translating everything I know into the common tongue of the land."

"That's convenient," she said with a huff.

I couldn't help but agree, even if he did sound genuine.

He nodded. "I agree. I think I'd be in an even worse mess than this place otherwise. Everyone here seems so anxious and suspicious of strangers."

Understatement of the year.

"How long have you been here?" I asked him.

"Here in this facility? Or here in this land?"

"Here in this facility," I said.

He glanced up at the top corner of his cell, presumably where the digital clock was in his own room. He nodded in time with the seconds blinking on my own clock. As 12:57 became 12:58, he answered me. "Twenty-one days, four hours, and fifty-two minutes."

Holy shit. My heart started to pound again.

I ran a hand through my hair. "Are they going to try to hurt us, too?"

Andy shrugged and shook his head. "I don't know. But I don't think they want to kill us."

"We'd already be dead if that was the case," Val said.

I took a breath, trying to force my heart to slow down. She had a point.

"Okay," I said. "And how long have you been in this land?"

"Thirteen days beyond that count," he replied.

A little over a month, and most of that here.

There was a soft beep at the end of the hallway, breaking my train of thought. The sound of a metal cart rolled toward us, dishware clattering as it rolled over the tiles. The scent of roasted beef and vegetables wafted down the hall as the cart came into view, followed by two personnel—a pair of wiry men in black scrubs. The one pushing the cart was much paler than the other, with curly tufts of red-brown hair on his head. The other guy was deeply tanned, and his head was smoothly shaved. Neither seemed much older than thirty, and they didn't so much as look up as they approached.

This close, they smelled vaguely wild, but I couldn't quite put my finger on what gave me that impression. My pulse pounded in my ears. The one with the shaved head held something up next to my door, and after another soft beep, my door swung outward to admit the curly-headed man, who held a metal-covered platter as he immediately crowded into the doorframe.

"Where are we?" I asked him. "Who are you people?"

"They don't speak," Andy said.

I flicked my eyes toward him and then back to the guy with the platter. Curly didn't look at me.

"Don't?" I asked. "As in, they can't? Or they won't?"

"Not sure," Andy said. "They just don't."

Well, that was going to change.

"Hey!" I stepped toward the curly-haired guy, raising my arms to shove him.

"Don't!" Andy's voice rang out as I pushed the guy into the doorframe with a solid thud.

The platter clattered to the ground—spilling meat, potatoes, and green beans—as something sharp jabbed hard into my shoulder. My knees went first this time, and I hit the tile hard next to a pair of dinner rolls as blackness invaded my vision.

EIGHT

I was still on the ground when I came to, though the spilled food had been cleaned up. My head rang as I sat up, and my shoulder throbbed.

"Goddammit," I groaned as I tried to get a look at my shoulder. There wasn't a bruise, as far as I could tell, but there was still the ghost of an ache. I massaged it as I craned my neck up to look at the clock.

I had only been out about fifteen minutes, and I was alone in my cell again.

"If you try to force an interaction with them," Andy said, "you get one."

I pushed myself to my feet and moved toward the mirror mounted above the little sink. "In the form of a sedative, apparently."

"Are you alright, Naiya?" Val's voice sounded like she was at the door to her room.

I looked at my shoulder in the mirror. No bruise, and the ache was gone in both my head and my shoulder.

"Yeah." I stepped over to the shelf next to the door. A fresh platter of meat and vegetables sat there, complete with a pair of dinner rolls. "At least I still got lunch … assuming it's not laced with anything."

I couldn't help but wonder if Curly and Baldy had

just picked up the rolls from the floor, though the meat and vegetables looked like they had been arranged by whatever chef this place had. It all certainly looked better than the cafeteria food of Saint Dymphna's.

"Unlikely," Andy said. "That's not the way they do things here. At least, that's how it's been for me, anyway. If they want you unconscious, they simply sedate you."

I screwed up my face as I pulled the tray from the shelf. "Apparently at range, like a damn wild animal." Which isn't terribly far from the truth of things, really.

"Well, are you?" He was studying me again with those too-dark eyes.

"Am I what?"

"A wild animal?" It wasn't concern on his face; it was genuine curiosity.

How odd.

"Umm, no," I said, turning back toward the bunk.

It wasn't a complete lie. I was only *sometimes* a wild animal. And only when I had a bad enough nightmare. And I didn't really have any control over that bit anyway.

"I bet you are if you get enough drinks in you," Val said.

I shook my head as I sat cross-legged on top of the blanket, placing the tray in my lap. "Mmm, sorry to disappoint. I went shot-for-shot with a guy on a dare once. He got black-out wasted, while I barely felt even a little buzz."

She snorted. "And you weren't at Saint Dymphna's for addiction?"

"I was," I countered. "But I was also clean and sober because I don't *do* anything."

"What's Saint Dymphna's?" Andy asked.

"A rehab facility," Val replied, utensils clinking from her room.

"Rehab?" He sounded genuinely confused.

I put my tray beside me on the bed and stood to look at him. Who doesn't know what rehab is? I couldn't explain his crystal spider, but that didn't mean I was ready to buy into him being from some other world—especially after such a convenient explanation for why he spoke English so well.

"Do you live under a rock?" Snark oozed through Val's tone.

He shook his head, and the light brown mess of hair brushed his brows as he did so. "No. I have a house."

Did he also not know how sarcasm works?

"Rehab is where people go to stop being addicted to drugs and alcohol," I explained, watching him through narrowed eyes, my head cocked to the side.

Val sighed. "It's generally a place full of fuckups, so no one goes there unless they have to."

He caught me watching him and nodded at me. "So, what are you addicted to?"

I blinked and straightened, frowning. "I'm not addicted to anything. My parents are just a hell of a lot stupider than I ever thought they were."

"How so?" Val sounded like she was talking around a bite of food.

I went back to my bed and pulled the tray into my lap, spearing the roast and sawing at it with the flimsy plastic knife. "They thought I was so addicted to drugs that I'd slipped them mushrooms or something when they saw something they couldn't easily explain." I shoved a bite of meat into my mouth. It was juicy and surprisingly tasty, even if it was a bit colder than I'd have liked.

"What was that?" Andy asked. He was moving around in his room, though I couldn't see him from my spot on the bed.

I shook my head. I wasn't going to tell them about

the leopard. I wasn't going to tell anyone about the leopard anymore. Not after what happened to my father. Not until I knew what the hell was happening to me with it.

"Naiya?" Val's tone was probing.

I sighed. "They just couldn't easily explain what they found in my room."

"You snuck a boy in? You rebel!"

I snorted a wry laugh at her assumption. "What am I, sixteen? No, I didn't sneak a boy in!" I poked a potato wedge with my fork and took a bite. "Anyway, if I was going to do something like that, I'd probably take him to the lake house instead."

It was quiet for a moment, and then Andy asked, "So, what'd they see?"

I finished another potato wedge while I thought of what to say. I rolled a shoulder and shook my head again. "You wouldn't believe me even if I told you," I said. "No one does."

"Well," Val said, "it must've been one hell of a surprise for them to automatically jump to drugs and rehab for you."

"I guess I can understand," I replied, cutting up the rest of the meat. "What were they supposed to think? My parents are straight-laced and professional. My dad is a super successful business type—a marketing executive for a tech company. And my mom is his perfect little wife, running the graphic design company that supports his work. They barely had time for me growing up. They love me, I know that, and I love them dearly. But my nanny, Abigail, was more of a mother to me than anyone."

It was quiet as I finished the vegetables on my tray.

"But I get it," I said. "I mean, adopted kids have a history of being problematic, right? So, why shouldn't my parents immediately jump to drugs?"

"Wait," Val said. "You're adopted?"

Except she said it like she'd already figured it out.

I shrugged. "I figured out early on that I was adopted. I don't look anything like my parents."

"Are they white?" she asked, once again sounding like she already knew the answer.

The corner of my mouth pulled up in a wry half-smile. "Yup."

"And let me guess," she said. "Your adoption is closed, so you don't know anything about your biological parents."

I blinked. I mean, I knew my situation was pretty stereotypical, but I didn't know it was *that* well-known.

"Naiya?" Val sounded like she was next to her door again.

"I'm alright," I said quickly. "I just didn't realize it was such a common story. There's not much in my records. My parents literally found me as a child, got licensed to be my foster parents, and then formally adopted me as soon as the state would let them. My parents said I was about three. They don't know who my birth parents are, and neither does the State of Texas. The Davenports had me keep my own last name, since I seemed to know it, in case I decided to try to find my birth parents myself later on."

"Will you?" Andy asked.

"Maybe?" I took another bite of the roast and sighed. "I don't know. I mean, what kind of parent just abandons their kid? I'm sure there're all kinds of explanations, but still. And the Davenports are good parents, even if they are a little distant."

"Just not good enough that you ever changed your name to theirs," Val pointed out.

"I just couldn't ever get their name to fit me," I said. "It always felt weird. And I found out a few years ago that my mom can't have kids of her own, which explains why my dad always said I was meant to be with them. They let me pick my birthday, since they didn't know … but then I learned choosing your own birthdate wasn't normal when I was talking with the other kindergarteners about our upcoming birthday parties."

"What day did you pick?" Andy asked.

"October 31st," I said. "Halloween seemed as good a day as any."

Val snorted. "Or did you just like the candy options?"

I clicked my tongue with a nod, not that she could see it from the door of her room. "That too."

"So," she said, "if the state doesn't have your birth parent information, do you even have a birth certificate?"

"Of course I do! It'd be hard to get my driver's license if I didn't."

"But it doesn't have your name on it?" She sounded confused.

"It has my name on it," I explained, "but it lists the Davenports as my parents, even though they're technically not."

"Well," she said, "what does it say for your race, then?"

"Mixed race, not Hispanic." With a huff, I stabbed the last bit of roast with my fork and speared the last potato wedge to go with it. "I should try doing one of those DNA tests to find out my heritage."

Maybe then I'd finally have an answer. Everyone I'd ever tried to be close to wanted to pin down my ethnicity, so I shouldn't have been surprised that Val did, too. She probably just didn't want to end up saying some super racist joke or something.

"Or here's a thought," Val said as I shoved the last bite of my meal into my mouth. "Maybe don't? Those guys aren't entirely on the up-and-up with what they do with that info."

Andy sounded like he was back at his door again. "What info? What's DNA?"

He genuinely didn't know? Really?

"Deoxyribonucleic acid," I explained patiently. "It's your genetic makeup, kinda like a biological blueprint specific to each individual, but made up of stuff they've inherited from their parents. These days, people collect their spit or something and send it to a lab to find out their genetic background. The people they send it to build a database from all the samples they have and try to connect you with every individual they can, based on your genetic markers."

"That sounds great," he said, the smile plain in his voice.

"Sure," Val said. "But they definitely aren't telling anyone everything about what they do with your DNA once they've sequenced it and put it into their system. I mean, sure, you're related to all these others in their database, but what good does that do you? More importantly, what good does having that information do *them*?"

"They use it to help find others who could be related, don't they?" I stood and put the tray, with its remnants of my lunch, back on the shelf.

"Of course they do *that*," she said. "But I'm just saying there's no way that's all they do when they are literally building a database of the entire world's genetic information." She was quiet for a moment. "Anyway, fostering and adoption? That's a pretty expensive process for a child they just found. Even if it was 'meant to be.'"

I rolled a shoulder. "It's not like they don't have the money. We've never really struggled to afford things."

"Must be nice," Val said.

I leaned against the wall next to my door, pressing my cheek as hard as I could against the cool metal, trying to see her door. "What about you?"

She was quiet another moment before answering. I could only really make out the change in the light when she moved closer to the door—I couldn't see her face.

"My parents were garbage," she said finally. "My mom was a floozy drunk who slept with anyone who would give her the time of day. My dad was the same, except he was a sloppy drunk. They split when I was six, and I spent weekends with my dad after spending the week at my mom's. They both ignored the crap out of me, which was fine by me since they were annoying as hell anyway. Most of my meals came from a can or the freezer, so I got out of there as soon as I could."

Oh my God. Poor Val.

"I'm so sorry, Val," I said. "You deserved better."

"Most kids do," she agreed. "I think that's why my parents signed my emancipation papers so readily."

"Emancipation?" I couldn't keep the shock from my voice. Most kids I knew went through a phase where they considered the notion of having the state declare them a legal adult early, even if it was only a brief and fleeting consideration during a heated argument. But I'd never heard of anyone actually going through with it. "How old were you?"

"Fifteen," she said. "It was the earliest Colorado would let me do it."

"You're from Colorado? What the heck brought you to Texas?"

"Life," she said simply. "This may come as a shock to you, Naiya, but I haven't always made the best decisions."

Ouch. I hadn't even considered any of that as a possibility. She was still a kid when she went out on her own. Hell, she hadn't even graduated from high school yet. And here I was with my dad trying to get me to take over for him at his company when he retired.

"I'm so sorry," I said.

"Don't be," she replied. "I don't need pity. I got this. Y'know, except whatever the hell this place is about." The water ran in the sink in her room for a minute, and then her cup clacked onto the table.

"You both had absent parents," Andy pointed out, "but you feel wildly different about them. Why is that?"

"My parents always encouraged me to pursue what I was interested in," I said. "Between gymnastics in elementary school, dance in middle school, and my extracurriculars in high school, they were always really supportive, even if they weren't *there*."

"You were student council president and valedictorian, weren't you?" Val said.

I rolled my eyes. "Salutatorian, actually. By a hundredth of a point. And, thanks to color guard and winter guard, I didn't really have time for leadership on the student council."

"What's winter guard?" she asked.

"You know the kids spinning wooden rifles and swords in the gym after football season was over?"

"Yeah," she said. "Those guys were always really intense."

I huffed out a laugh. "Well, that was winter guard. That was me."

"What about summers?"

"Summer band camp," I replied. "Color guard tryouts and prep for the upcoming season took a lot of my time. And when I wasn't there, I spent a lot of time sitting up in a tree back home, reading. Or playing hide-and-seek with my cousins, though they'd always lose interest in the game before they found me."

"Why didn't your parents ever freak out about the tree-climbing?" Val asked.

"They probably would have if I ever got hurt," I said. "But they believed in me having the freedom to learn stuff on my own. And I fell out of a lot of trees when I was younger. I just never really got hurt."

"Do you think your parents are worried about you? Since you didn't come home from Saint Dymphna's?"

My throat closed up at that, tears stinging my eyes. Sure, I was angry at their stupidity for putting me in the rehab facility in the first place, but I hadn't really meant what I'd said to Dr. Anderson about getting a place of my own. It might not have been long enough since my discharge for them to notice I was gone, and if they were on a business trip, that'd be even more true. But it also didn't look like I was going anywhere anytime soon, and *that* was not a comfortable thought.

"God, I hope so," I whispered.

NINE

A few hours later, Curly and Baldy came back with dinner. It smelled like fajitas, if I had to hazard a guess. Curly stayed out in the hallway this time, while Baldy took my empty tray from lunch and brought in my dinner tray. He eyed me with startlingly gold eyes as he did so. I hadn't noticed their color last time, but his expression now was one of challenge.

Except I wasn't about to get sedated again.

I simply sat very still on my bed and watched him place my dinner on the shelf next to the door. His eyes—which stayed on me the entire time he delivered my dinner—darted to my cup before he left, but he nodded as he stepped out of the room, leaving it where it sat on my bedside table.

I looked at my cup—it was still full from before. And he hadn't glossed over me like everyone did when I was still. I chewed the inside of my cheek as I thought. Would Baldy have refilled the cup if it was empty? Even if it meant coming within arm's reach of me? Maybe he just wanted to make sure I hadn't destroyed it.

But the smell of dinner made my mouth water.

"Mmm," Val said, her mouth clearly half-full of food. "At least the food's good."

I grabbed my tray and sat back on the bed to eat.

She wasn't wrong. The steak fajitas were really good. So was the guacamole, for that matter, and the refried beans tasted like they were made with bacon grease, which gave them a really delicious flavor. The tortillas were thick and handmade, and even the rice—which was always the blandest part of a meal like this—was super tasty.

"Just wait till it's baked stacked pasta and toppings night," Andy said.

Val coughed out the water she'd apparently been drinking. "The fuck?"

I looked at the window of my door, but couldn't see anything from my vantage point on the bed. "Do you mean lasagne?"

"Is that what they call the thing that looks like a pasta cake?"

Val laughed. "I'm never not calling it that!"

I smiled at the surprisingly accurate description. "It's lasagne. Big, wide noodles with white cheese, red sauce, and meat?"

"Yep," Andy confirmed.

"Lasagne," I said, standing to place my empty tray on the shelf. I looked across the hall. Andy was sitting on his bed with Chad on his shoulder.

"Lasagne," he repeated, looking up at me.

I nodded. It sounded better in his accent.

"And these were fajitas," Val said. "Y'know. In case you didn't know."

He looked over to her door. "Thanks."

So wherever he was from apparently had noodles and pasta, but not rehab, and they weren't scientifically advanced enough to know what DNA is. Or maybe they just called it something that didn't translate. All of which hinged on the concept that what he said about rifts was even true. But I didn't get the sense that he was lying about it, even if it did seem a bit inconsistent with reality as I knew it.

And for all the camaraderie we'd gained just by being three relative strangers trapped in the same situation, the awkwardness really set in when one of us had to use the bathroom. At least there was a curtain, and there was no water in the toilet to make any splashing sounds, but turning on the faucet prior to pulling the curtain around seemed like a better choice for at least a little audio privacy on top of the visual privacy. Though, I suspected Andy didn't have the right angle to see that far into my room unless he pressed himself flat against the wall perpendicular to his door. But if Val's room was a mirror image of mine, he probably could see hers.

My room stayed dim the rest of the day and—in point of fact—got even darker right at ten at night. Val and Andy's rooms did the same, and the hallway light went out, too.

It wasn't much different from curfew at Saint Dymphna's.

The leopard stalked me from the outskirts of my tense—but not terrifying—dreams that night, haunting me from the shadows as I played hide and seek with my cousins at my parents house during the football game on Thanksgiving. Any time I turned to look directly at it, it simply faded into the shadows, reappearing somewhere on the opposite side of me from where it had been. I still didn't like it, but at least it wasn't bad enough to make me wake in its skin. I got the feeling that I didn't want to have that happen here if I could help it.

The clatter of the cart rolling down the hall woke me. The lights in my room had brightened some, but they were still distinctly darker than in the hallway. Eggs and sausage and pancakes and syrup wafted in the air, along with the glorious scent of coffee. Baldy and Curly accompanied the cart again, and I couldn't help but wonder if there was any other staff here beyond them and the unseen chef. I somehow doubted either of them were the culinary type.

As they had yesterday, they dropped off my meal first, taking the empty tray from the night before with them. To my surprise, they even included a mug of coffee and a cup of orange juice.

"How generous," I said.

"What's that?" Andy asked.

"Beverages that aren't just tap water," I replied as Curly shut the door to my room.

I had most of my eggs down—because cold eggs are disgusting—by the time the pair had finished delivering meals to Val and Andy.

"Huh," Val said.

I gulped down a mouthful of coffee. "What?"

"There's pills here with my food, along with a little note that lists them as the ones Saint Dymphna's put me on."

"So, on top of the good food, they're keeping up with your maintenance medications. Real philanthropists, they are," I said wryly.

"Mmm, no," Andy said around a bite of his food. "I don't—wait. That was sarcasm, wasn't it?"

I clicked my tongue at him. "Little bit, yeah." I'd have shot finger guns at him, too, if I thought he'd have seen them.

"He can be taught," Val declared with a giggle.

"I've been told I'm actually remarkably intelligent," Andy said. "At least, that's true back home."

We didn't talk for the rest of breakfast, but as I was finishing the last of my sausage, the hallway door beeped open, and the lights in my room brightened a little. I set my tray down next to me and stepped over to the window in the door. The hallway was still brighter than my room, but less so now. Two people, a man and a woman, approached on smooth, matched footsteps that were nearly silent. Her hair was blonde, pulled into a low ponytail, and his was close-cropped and black, but he had a couple of days' worth of scruff on his chin. Both wore tank tops and tearaway track pants. Her tank top was black, his white, though both their pants were grey with two white stripes down the outside of the leg. And she held a pair of black slip-on shoes in her left hand.

I looked across the hall to Andy, who had also come to his window. His brow was furrowed in what looked to be concerned curiosity. I was pretty sure my own expression matched his.

The two were closer to my door now, and—with a start—I recognized them. It was the pair who had picked me up from Saint Dymphna's. I should have known it from the mirthless look on the guy's face.

Maybe these two would actually speak to me. "Who the hell are you people?"

The dark-haired guy looked at me and pressed his lips into a line, making his expression even more grim. He didn't answer me, but he beeped open my door and swung it wide, allowing me to step into the hallway if I wanted. The pale brown of his eyes looked decidedly more golden here. Maybe he and Baldy were brothers?

"Please come with us, Ms. Kateri," the woman said, her tone the same no-nonsense deference as it had been at the rehab center. She proffered the shoes.

Well, at least one of them talked to me.

I looked past them to Andy and narrowed my eyes. The concerned curiosity hadn't left his face, but there was a thoughtfulness to it now as well—as if he were analyzing and rearranging information he already knew. He gave me a single slow nod.

I didn't know what that meant, so I took the shoes from her and sat on the bed to slip them on.

I met her eyes as I stood. "Where are you taking me?"

The guy outside the door sighed.

"To someone who has answers." She gestured down the hall.

Pushing past the shiver of nerves that traced my spine, I blew out a breath through my nose and stepped out of my room. Looking to my left, over my shoulder, I confirmed what I had suspected—Val's room was a mirror image of my own, though hers was bright, like Andy's. Curious that mine had been kept dim. Not that I was complaining; the dimness was more comfortable. Val stood near the door, watching me. Her dark roots were starting to show, adding another shade to the kaleidoscope of color that was her hair. Her brown eyes were serious, but held a hint of curiosity as well. Taking a note from Andy's book, I nodded once to her as she pulled her bottom lip between her teeth. She returned the nod.

The woman led the way, and the mirthless guy with the almost-golden eyes fell into step behind me.

Blondie and … Grump. Giving them names was an easier thing to focus on than the creeping dread of the unknown.

Blondie beeped the door open at the end of the hall, and Grump made sure it closed firmly behind us. I tried not to let that add fuel to the nerves chilling my spine.

TEN

Blondie led me through a series of bright hallways, with long corridors branching off to either side. Wherever we were, this place was sprawling. I tried to keep track—two hallways down and a left, then the first right, then another left after the first door—but by the time I got to the fourth turn, I'd forgotten the first steps. The air smelled filtered, maybe a little metallic, but it was hard to get a read on what sort of facility this was. The windows in the doors were all mirrored, though I suspected it was two-way glass because why would there be a mirror instead of an actual window? Still, interesting that there was any glass at all in these doors, since the ones in the hall Val and Andy and I were being kept in had only bars.

Grump's eyes on the back of my head made my neck stiff. Or maybe it was just the anticipation of the unknown. I cracked my neck as we walked.

I raked a hand through my hair. "What the hell even is this place?"

It wasn't a rhetorical question, but Blondie and Grump definitely acted like it was.

"Let me guess," I continued. "If I don't keep going with you, I get another jab in the shoulder followed by a cold nap on the floor."

Grump snorted at that. "You learn quick."

I nodded once. "But you two aren't the answer people. You're the retrievers."

After the next turn, Blondie beeped us through a door where the hallway darkened slightly. Maybe it was because the walls here were a darker grey than where we'd come from. But something else floated on the air here—like a housekeeper or cleaning crew had been through recently. Maybe not today, but definitely this week.

We kept going past all the doors in that hall, and when Blondie beeped us through another security door, it was like I had stepped into the pre-exam room of a doctor's office. It was a pretty spacious room, really, with a digital scale to my left and the kind of chair they use for blood draws to my right. Next to the chair was a counter with drawers underneath, except for the space that was meant to be used as a desk, where a middle-aged woman with dark umber skin and slick black hair pulled into a neat bun sat on a black rolling stool. She wore a lab coat over a loose blue shirt and black knee-length pencil skirt, and she stood when we entered.

"Ah, Ms. Kateri," she said, smiling as she folded her hands in front of her. "Perfect. Step on the scale, please."

Blondie and Grump stationed themselves against the wall with their backs to the door we'd just passed through.

I blinked at the nurse. "What?"

"The scale, dear," she said, gesturing to it as her brows knitted together.

"I can see where it is," I said, not moving. "But what are you doing?"

She cocked her head and studied me for a moment. "Checking your vitals, of course."

"Why?"

"Because we need to know your baseline."

I narrowed my eyes at her and noticed the door behind her, set into the far wall. She was between me and it, and Blondie and Grump were between me and the other door.

She gestured to the scale again, but her eyes flicked to Grump over my right shoulder.

"And if I don't want to?"

"Please, Ms. Kateri," she said. "I mean you no harm. This is simply a matter of routine."

Behind me, Grump shifted his weight, the quiet rustle of his clothes breaking the tense silence.

"Fine." I sighed and stepped onto the scale.

Grump cracked his neck and relaxed his weight back into his stance against the wall.

I'd dropped a couple pounds since the start of my stay at Saint Dymphna's, which was no surprise, really. Stress—and barely palatable meal options—will do that to you. But the nurse simply wrote it down without comment and continued along. She measured my height and took my temperature before having me sit in the chair for a blood pressure check.

And for another damn blood draw.

Only she didn't bother with the cotton ball and band-aid combo when she was done. Instead, she simply had me press my index finger to the spot.

"I'm good at my job, Ms. Kateri," she said to my likely quizzical expression. "You won't need more than a dot of pressure, and you won't bruise."

That was more explanation than anyone on staff had given me about anything this whole time.

"What is this place?"

"I'm not authorized to answer your questions," she replied. "Beyond what is necessary for my job, that is."

She didn't bother having me pee in a cup—not that there appeared to be any bathroom connected to this room—but she did clip a small section of hair from the back of my head, like Val had mentioned they do for drug tests.

"You won't find anything there," I said. "I don't use."

She didn't even look at me as she put the strands of hair in a specimen bag and sealed it.

I pressed my lips into a line.

She also didn't have me sign any paperwork or privacy policy like every doctor's office I've ever been to, which was … troubling.

Instead, when she was done, she looked past me to Blondie and Grump and nodded as she tucked her pen back into her lab coat pocket. She pulled a hair tie from the pocket on the other side of her coat and offered it to me.

"Thanks," I said slowly, taking it from her. I raked my fingers through my hair, pulling it into a high ponytail as I tried to piece together what information I had.

No questions answered. Basic vitals. Cell-like room that was almost like a private hospital room, but without the hospital bed and hookups. A step up from a jail cell, for sure, but not as good as a basic hotel room.

And I didn't know anyone's name beyond the identifiers I'd given them.

The nurse turned to the door behind her and opened it. The lights were dimmer on the other side, but it looked like it was perhaps another hallway.

"This way, please," she said, gesturing beyond the door.

I looked back at Blondie and Grump, who stepped toward me as well. I didn't have much of a choice here if I didn't want another surprise nap.

So, frowning, I went.

ELEVEN

I WAS RIGHT; it was a hallway beyond the door. A short one, though, relatively speaking. Perhaps the length of a football field? Another door was at the far end, and two more doors were evenly spaced along its walls.

The nurse led us all toward the second one on the right, beeping it open.

Inside, the walls were bare steel, like the walls of my room, with high ceilings and exposed beams and air ducts, like you'd find in a warehouse. There was a mirror that was likely a two-way set high in the wall opposite the door, and the floor was smooth pale concrete, the texture more like a sidewalk than a glossy garage floor. The room itself was roughly the size of a tennis court, and three pitching machines—like the kind tennis or baseball players practice with—were set up at the far end of the room, one in each corner and one in the center. Aside from the ball machines, the room itself was bare.

"The first activity we have for you today," came an older man's voice over a loudspeaker, "is a simple test of your reflexes."

I furrowed my brow and looked over my shoulder at the nurse. "You could have just tapped my knees and elbows like the pediatrician used to do."

Grump snorted at me, the smirk on his face the first sign of any emotion beyond annoyance I'd seen in him. Blondie shot him a look.

"Those aren't the sort of reflexes he means," the nurse said.

With a little *fwoomp*, the center machine shot out a tennis ball. I hopped to the side as the ball hit the wall behind me.

"It's more a game of dodgeball, Ms. Kateri," said the loudspeaker.

"What?" I narrowed my eyes at the window, knowing full well I wouldn't be able to see beyond it. "Why?"

"It is not every day that we get someone with such extraordinary abilities as yours," the disembodied voice answered.

There was a click behind me—the sound of the door closing.

And I was alone in the room.

Fwoomp.

Another tennis ball.

With a little grumble, I dodged to my right this time.

The nozzle on the machine followed me.

Fwoomp.

I took a step to my left.

Again, the machine followed me.

Fwoomp. Fwoomp.

I jumped to my left again and then juked back right.

"Good," praised the loudspeaker.

The machine kept me targeted as it launched tennis ball after tennis ball at me. It slowly picked up speed, sometimes launching two or three balls in quick succession. But it was easy to keep track of where the next ball was coming from, so it wasn't like this game was even hard.

And then the machine in the left corner started launching balls at me too, tracking me just as the first had. The first few volleys from it hit me with a stinging *thok*, though I still managed to keep the first machine's shots from hitting.

"The game is *dodge*ball, Ms Kateri." The voice from the loudspeaker was chiding.

I huffed out a breath and nodded as the second machine picked up speed, not taking my eyes from the nozzles shooting tennis balls at me. I got hit a few more times as that second machine occasionally launched two or even three balls in quick succession. Tennis balls were collecting on the floor, creating a mild trip hazard, but I fell back into a rhythm, dodging the balls from both machines with a focused smile on my face. The activity was … actually really nice. Certainly fun. Even the worries about what the hell I was doing here faded into background noise as I played this rather novel version of dodgeball.

With three more little *fwoomp*s, the third machine in the right corner of the room joined the fray, shooting fuzzy neon balls at the same rate as the other two. Two of its initial volley hit me, as did one of the next two shots.

"Ms. Kateri," said Mr. Loudspeaker, the implied warning of another unwelcome nap clear in his tone.

Because, really, what else was he gonna do?

"Shut up, and let me concentrate!" I suppressed an eyeroll, sure that it would mean more hits if I looked away from the machines for more than a blink.

Fwoomp. Fwoomp.

I dodged the next shots, finding the rhythm again. There wasn't a pattern, per se, to the machines' shots, but there was a little click of the next ball being prepped that I could hear if I concentrated. Pinpointing which one it came from helped me figure out what I needed to do to dodge it.

It was challenging, to be sure, but now we had a game!

A ball hit the wall next to my head, where I'd been only a half a second before. Another hit near the corner of the room and bounced off the perpendicular wall before bouncing toward the center of the room. The next shot zoomed past my knee, and I somersaulted backward.

I hadn't somersaulted since I was a kid.

And it felt good.

"Excellent," praised the loudspeaker.

Fwoomp. Fwoomp.

No time to reminisce. I danced and dodged around the next shots, but the ground on this side of the room was nearly carpeted now with tennis balls. My foot landed on one and rolled out from under me as I tried to shift my weight off it. I started to fall, but turned it into another somersault to dodge the next three balls headed toward where my head would have been. I got to my feet again, but there were already a number of shots headed toward me.

The machines were not interested in whether I was ready for their volley.

I hopped backward and then ran at the side wall, taking a couple of steps up it like I'd seen once in a martial arts movie, and launched myself off it, landing on the ground with only a hair of a breath to catch my weight before needing to sidestep the next tennis ball or four headed my way.

Holy shit. I just did that.

No time. Focus!

That's when a panel slid open in the middle of the wall opposite the door, directly below the center of the two-way mirror. From it emerged the nozzle of a fourth ball launcher, which was already shooting at me at a rate much faster than the others.

Thok. Thok. Thok.

Three stinging shots hit my thigh, my shoulder, and my elbow, causing the sudden shocking pins-and-needles feeling of a direct hit to the funny bone. As I shook it off, five more balls hit me from the other machines.

"Dammit!"

"Ms. Kateri …"

"I *know*!"

I shook loose strands of hair back from my face, taking a deep breath to try to find the rhythm again. I had been doing just fine before that fourth machine joined the fray, but now, I struggled to get out of the way. I was losing track of the balls as they flew in my direction, but when the next ball would have hit, I caught it instead and threw it off to the side in frustration. I still dodged some of them, but I was angrier about it now.

How many of these damn machines was Mr. Loudspeaker gonna turn on me? How many balls did I need to dodge before this test of my reflexes was done?

I huffed out a breath and chucked the next ball I couldn't dodge back at the machine it had flown from. It collided with the next ball *fwoomp*ing from the nozzle, sending them bouncing off in opposite directions.

Now there was an idea.

If they weren't going to turn the machines off, maybe I could disable them entirely.

Fwoomp. Fwoomp. Fwoomp.

Dodge. Somersault. Catch.

Fwoomp.

Dodge. Throw.

I don't think it hit anything but the wall. It was hard to track where my shot was going while dodging the tennis balls coming at me.

"Beautiful!" There was almost a chuckle in the voice from the loudspeaker.

I started catching any ball I could, dodging away or somersaulting over what I couldn't, and threw them back at the machines. But I wasn't hitting anything. Or, at least, I didn't think I was. I had to focus better.

Fwoomp.

Catch. Throw.

Fwoomp.

Dodge.

Fwoomp.

Catch. Throw.

Fwoomp. Fwoomp.

Dodge. Catch. Throw.

KLUNK.

One machine—the one in the center—ceased shooting tennis balls.

Finally!

"Don't lose focus," I muttered to myself. "There's still three more."

Fwoomp.

Catch. Throw.

Fwoomp. Fwoomp. Fwoomp.

Dodge. Catch. Dodge.

Fwoomp.

Somersault. Throw.

KLUNK.

The one on the right did the same.

Yes!

Fwoomp. Fwoomp.

Catch. Catch. Throw.

Fwoomp.

Dodge. Throw.

KLUNK.

As did the one on the left.

Fwoomp. Fwoomp. Fwoomp.

Dodge. Catch. Dodge. Throw.

Fwoomp. Fwoomp.

Dodge.

THOK.

The last shot hit me square in the forehead, and I blinked, knocked from my rhythm. I shook my head to try to clear it. I swear the machines had kicked into an even more frenzied speed.

Fwoomp. Fwoomp. Fwoomp.

THOK. THOK. THOK.

Three more shots hit my temple, knocking my head to the side so my left ear touched my shoulder.

Fwoomp. Fwoomp.

THOK. THOK.

Fwoomp.

THOK.

Two hits to my hip and a third to my knee, and I fell onto my ass amidst a sea of tennis balls.

Shit.

Fwoomp. Fwoomp. Fwoomp. Fwoomp. Fwoomp. Fwoomp.

I pressed myself to the ground, willing myself to be skinnier than the tennis balls were tall as six balls of neon fuzz zoomed past me, bouncing from the back wall with six little *thok*s.

"Absolutely superb, Ms. Kateri," the loudspeaker lauded, and I stilled.

I waited a few slow breaths, but no more balls flew from the nozzle of the machine in the wall. So, I sat up slowly, rubbing my forehead as the fourth machine receded into darkness with the sound of a quiet motor and metal sliding against metal. The wall panel slid back into place as a soft beep sounded and the door behind me opened.

I shuffled tennis balls out from under me and got to my feet as the nurse came in.

The three machines on the far side of the room all had their nozzles bent at odd angles.

I'd thrown the tennis balls back that hard.

Holy ... just *damn*.

"Well done, Ms. Kateri," the nurse said, her expression pleased. "Now, if you'll follow me." She gestured back the way she'd come.

I arched an eyebrow at her. "Back to my room?"

"Not just yet," she said. "This way, if you would."

I pulled the hair tie from my hair, raking my hands through and fluffing my thick strands off my neck before re-securing the lot of it in a low messy bun. I stepped past her out into the hallway, and she turned to the door at the end, the one opposite the door we'd initially entered through. Blondie and Grump took up positions behind me as the nurse beeped open the next door, which led into a blindingly bright hallway.

TWELVE

I was beginning to lose my sense of direction. Too many turns and too many doors and too many hallways that all looked largely indistinguishable from each other, aside from their lighting conditions. Worse, none of these doors had any markings on them, so how did any of these folks have any clue where they were even taking me?

But the nurse clearly knew this place like the back of her hand. She didn't hesitate at any of the intersections, and her strides were purposeful and long.

The hallway in front of me had rooms to both the left and right before taking an odd forty-five-degree turn off to the right. We followed the bend, passing a single door on the left and two on the right before the nurse beeped open the third one.

It looked like a home gym. Or one for athletes, maybe? There was a treadmill to the right, with all sorts of wires and tubes draped over the side railing, and to my left was one of those digital resistance machines, the kind with heavy metal arms that extended from either side of the bottom of a vertical readout to straddle the head of a workout bench. Foam-wrapped handles attached to cables rested at the ends of the arms down at the floor, and I suspected the whole machine simulated a bench press of whatever weight was input with cables run on a series of pulleys of varying resistances.

As I contemplated it, I realized the readout was turned around, facing another large mirror, which I again suspected was two-way. Against the mirror was a table built into the wall, with a set of drawers next to it, forming a sort of desk. But there wasn't a chair.

I furrowed my brow. "You want me to work out?"

The nurse smiled at me as Blondie and Grump took up positions on either side of the door.

"The benchpress, Ms. Kateri," said Mr. Loudspeaker.

The nurse gestured.

I gave the mirror a hard look. It was big enough that I could see nearly all of myself in it. And I looked like shit. My tank top was stretched out from multiple days of wear, and my hair was dull and full of flyaways.

I closed my eyes and set my jaw. "And if I don't cooperate?"

"Please, Ms. Kateri," the nurse said.

I rounded on her. "That doesn't answer my question."

"There are consequences for noncompliance." Mr. Loudspeaker's voice was flat.

I rolled my eyes. "Yeah, if I don't do this, you'll sedate me, right? Another cold nap on the tile?"

"Sedating you to get these measurements is counterproductive," came the answer from the loudspeaker. "We could hardly expect you to run on a treadmill while unconscious."

"It's a simple exercise," the nurse said. "We simply seek to establish a baseline of your capabilities."

"Dodgeball establishes my baseline?" I didn't bother to hide the skepticism in my tone.

The nurse flicked her eyes toward the mirror.

"It does," said Mr. Loudspeaker. "And the sooner you cooperate, the sooner you can get back to your new friends."

"What I want is out of here," I replied.

"All in good time," said Mr. Loudspeaker.

The nurse gestured again to the bench.

I couldn't help but be curious myself about what I could lift. I'd managed to not need phys ed in high school—thanks to color guard and winter guard—and I certainly wasn't the gym rat type.

So, I stepped over and laid down on the bench. The nurse pulled the handles over to me, and I took them, settling my hands on the bench above my head. I craned my neck up, trying to see if I could catch the reflection of the starting weight as the machine beeped in acknowledgment of the nurse's input. But I couldn't see anything, and even if I had been able to see the mirror, she was between it and the display.

With another beep, tension mounted against the handles of the bench press.

"Ten reps, please," said Mr. Loudspeaker.

It wasn't even hard.

"It'll take all day if you start me at a child's weight limit," I said. "I may be skinny, but I'm not a weakling."

A few more beeps.

"Ten more reps, please."

It still wasn't hard. Harder than the first, perhaps, but I didn't even have to work at it. It wasn't much harder than lifting maybe a couple of soup cans.

"I guess for science sake, you can't just skip these low weights, huh?"

A few more beeps.

"Again."

I pushed my hands up ten more times and sighed. I didn't bother with any more commentary on the weight. I just waited as the nurse dialed in the next weight and did the next ten reps when prompted. The next weight actually felt like I was lifting something. It wasn't hard, really, but the muscles in my upper arms were definitely doing work. When it was done, I waited for the nurse to put in a different weight and for Mr. Loudspeaker to prompt me. This time, the weight was significant, and I couldn't push the handles up with the same ease. By the time I got to the fifth rep, I had to slow down. By seven, my chest was burning with the exertion. I almost didn't get my arms up for number ten, and when I did, they were trembling.

"Good," said Mr. Loudspeaker. "More."

"What?" I lifted my head from the bench, craning to look at the window with wide eyes.

A few more beeps on the machine.

"That's not your limit, Ms. Kateri," Mr. Loudspeaker replied. "Keep going. Again."

I screwed my face up, but pushed the handles out and away from my chest again. I could tell there was more weight than before, but I was able to handle it. I couldn't go as fast as I had been, but I got through five at a steady pace. Once again though, by seven, I was struggling, and nine and ten left my muscles feeling like they were on fire.

"You're holding your breath," the nurse said as I finished shaky number ten. "Breathe through the rep. It helps if you exhale as you push up and inhale on the release."

Three more beeps.

"Again."

This round had to go much slower than the last, and I simply could not keep the last two steady, though the nurse's breathing tip certainly seemed to help.

"Deeper breaths," she said, dialing in the next set.

"Again," said Mr. Loudspeaker.

Even slower than before, but the deeper breaths helped me to keep it steady. At least, until the last three, that was. I was sure the spongy handles were going to pull themselves from my hand with the resistance on them.

As the machine beeped again for the next set, I adjusted my grip, stretching out my fingers and wrapping each around the handles, one by one.

"Again."

And I did. Slowly, steadily, I pushed the handles up and away six times before it felt like my arms were turning to jelly. Still, I pushed, getting the next one out with a slowness that left fire spreading along the muscles in my chest and shoulders. The next one trembled so hard the sweat dripped from my elbow. I managed one more, but forgot to breathe and released a gust of air as my arms fell away from the weight. I scrambled to keep my grip on the handles, but it left me in a painfully awkward position with my arms spread so wide that my hands were nearly behind me.

"Recover," Mr. Loudspeaker ordered. "Finish the set."

With a groan, I pulled my hands forward, trying to get number ten done.

Just one more.

Inch by aching inch, I pulled my hands forward yet again. They shook as they came back into my field of view. I gritted my teeth, vocalizing an extended grunt behind them as I pushed them up and away from me.

And I did it.

I have no idea how much weight the nurse had on there, but I did it.

I dropped my head to the bench with a satisfied huff as I released the last rep.

"Excellent."

Three more beeps.

"Again."

"Are you kidding me?" I shot up then, turning to look at the window.

The nurse stepped back, placing herself even more between the display and the mirror, but not before I could see that it was a three-digit number on the screen.

And it started with a four.

I was bench pressing over four hundred pounds? Were they trying to hide that number from me?

"That you got through so many before shaking indicates you are capable of more," replied Mr. Loudspeaker. "Now, continue. Again."

At least four hundred pounds, and I was capable of more.

Holy. Shit.

"You can't be serious," I said.

"I am, in fact, quite serious, Ms. Kateri," said Mr. Loudspeaker. "Please continue."

I stared at the mirror. I couldn't see into the room, so I gave my reflection a once-over. I was drenched in sweat, and my hair was falling out of the bun. Big surprise, since I'd been laying on it to do this damned exercise.

But I couldn't help but wonder how much more I could do. I didn't know what a normal person could lift. I had no idea how much would be considered impressive. But four hundred pounds sure sounded like it was up there.

"Ms. Kateri," the nurse said, breaking my train of thought.

With a huff, I pressed my lips into a line and nodded, shaking a little of the remaining ache from my shoulders. I recovered one of the handles as I laid back down, and—reaching for the other one—

realized that the weight had not been released from them. I was going to have to start from that same overextended position I'd gotten myself into on the last set.

I held it steady for a moment, taking a few deep breaths to refocus. And then I brought my arms forward, pushing them up and away from my chest once again as they came into view. I blew my breath out between clenched teeth as I slowly made my way through four reps. Muscles on fire and arms shaking with the exertion, I pushed out a fifth. And then a sixth. And a seventh. Like before, sweat dripped from my elbow as my arms trembled. But I got number eight.

And shuddering number nine.

And then, agonizing number ten.

I kept hold of the handles as I released.

"Good," praised Mr. Loudspeaker. "Now one more."

A few more beeps.

"Go."

With a deep breath in, I adjusted my grip yet again and pushed.

The handles didn't move.

I squeezed my eyes shut, flexed my fingers, readjusted my grip, took a deep breath in and pushed again. I grunted with the exertion, blowing a slow stream of air out between clenched teeth. And the handles budged. The muscles in my chest lit up with the exertion, but I couldn't let the motion stop, or I was sure I'd get stuck.

Or lose my grip entirely.

So I pushed harder. Or I focused harder. I didn't think I was actually capable of any more force than I was exerting. As it was, it felt like my muscles were trying to dislocate my shoulders.

One.

Even just holding pressure on the handles as I prepped to do the next one hurt.

I took another couple of deep breaths, once again readjusting my grip on the foam of the handles as I did. And pushed. Again, the handles didn't budge at first, until they did. Again, I focused on keeping the motion going. But I shook so bad as I approached the top of the press that my grip started to loosen, and something popped in my left shoulder.

Pain spiderwebbed out from the joint as all the strength left that arm. The handle rolled from my left hand, snapping toward the point where it met with the machine with the kind of force I would've expected to break it. I slammed my left hand to the grip of my right, closing my fingers around my other hand to keep it from doing the same, though I might as well have been doing it one-handed for all the help my left hand offered.

As I eased the other handle back, I realized that I hadn't heard the first handle hit. Looking over, I saw the nurse place it on its hook on the side of the machine.

She must have caught it. Which meant she must have been ready for it?

I looked over her shoulder as I returned the right handle to its hook, trying to read in reverse the number on the display as I repeatedly opened and closed a fist in my left hand.

The nurse moved quicker than I'd ever seen anyone move, obscuring my view of the number again. But I caught that it still started with a four.

And she was definitely deliberately hiding that number from me.

"That's enough," said Mr. Loudspeaker. "Next."

I met the eyes of the nurse. "How much was that?"

She tapped a button on the display, and I saw it go

black in the mirror. She gestured to the treadmill. "Over here, please."

"How. Much. *Was*. That?"

"She won't answer your questions, Ms. Kateri," chided Mr. Loudspeaker. "Now, please, step on the treadmill so we can get you hooked up to the sensors."

THIRTEEN

"I'll do no such thing until I get answers," I replied, taking a step toward the mirror. "Who are you people, and what do you want with me?"

Grump pushed off the wall, reaching into a pocket of his pants as he took a step toward me.

"Ah ah," said Mr. Loudspeaker, stopping Grump's progress. "It's perfectly reasonable for Ms. Kateri to have questions."

Grump narrowed his eyes at me in the mirror and stepped back to his spot next to Blondie, though he didn't resume the relaxed stance against the wall that he'd adopted while I was doing the bench presses.

"There will be plenty of time for answers later, Ms. Kateri," said Mr. Loudspeaker, and I could swear I could feel his attention returning to me through the mirror.

Or maybe it was just the fatigue.

I rolled my left shoulder, releasing the mounting tension there. Another soft pop, and the spiderwebbing ache that had suffused those muscles since the last press released and subsided.

With a start, I realized none of my other muscles ached.

"Many of the answers you seek will come to you

as we continue on," Mr. Loudspeaker continued. "Please be assured, we have no intention of causing you harm."

Maybe I had a bunch of adrenaline running through my system? That would certainly explain things. But I knew what the rush of adrenaline felt like—the tense readiness in my muscles, the rush of my own pulse in my ears—and this didn't feel like that.

Wait a second.

"Continue on?" My vision refocused on the mirror. "You can't just keep me here! Once my parents figure out I'm not at the recovery center anymore, they'll have every police force in the DFW Metroplex out looking for me."

"A bridge I'm sure we'll cross when the time comes."

I swear I could hear the smile in his voice. Though, it was more likely a sneer.

"Please, Ms. Kateri," the nurse said, gesturing for me to move closer to the treadmill.

"Why should I?"

"Because you want to know what you are capable of, just as we do," Mr. Loudspeaker replied. "Likely moreso."

"Not like you're showing me any of these numbers anyway," I grumbled.

"With or without the hard data," he said, "you have already outperformed what you previously thought were your limitations, have you not?"

Dammit.

He was right.

With a huff, I stepped over to the treadmill.

The nurse opened an alcohol pad, wiped a spot on the right side of my chest, near my collarbone, and placed a sensor there. She placed two more on my face, one at each temple, and clamped a device onto my left pointer finger. The latter was likely a pulse oximeter, if I had to guess.

The nurse gestured again to the treadmill, and I stepped onto it.

"This goes over your head," she said, handing me something that looked like an oxygen mask with wires and a big tube coming off the front of it. "It should cover both your nose and mouth."

I visually traced the wires back to the thick column at the head of the machine—the one with all of its readouts facing away from me. And the treadmill was set at an angle, so I couldn't even see the readouts in the reflection of the two-way mirror.

"Ms. Kateri?" The nurse's voice broke my train of thought.

I hadn't moved. I nodded and looked at the mask. It had a head strap to hold it on while running.

But it felt like a trap.

"Ms. Kateri," said Mr. Loudspeaker, warning again in his tone.

"What the hell do you need all this for, anyway?"

"As has been explained to you," Mr. Loudspeaker said, clearly annoyed now, "we are establishing your baseline. Something it is clear you yourself do not know. Now, stop stalling and get moving."

He was right. I was stalling. And I did want to know my own capabilities. Even if I wasn't going to be able to see the numbers or the readouts, I'd already learned I was much stronger than I thought. Maybe I'm much faster, too?

I pulled the mask over my face, and the nurse helped me adjust it.

"You'll want it to be a bit snug," she explained, "so that you're breathing through the mask without feeling air pull in from around the edges."

I nodded once in acknowledgment as she moved around to the front of the machine. She pressed a few buttons, and the belt on the treadmill started moving. I walked to keep pace with it.

"We'll start with determining your peak speed," said the nurse. "The machine will adapt to match your steps, but since you're not a runner, you won't reach that if you just try to run right away. Instead, try to smoothly increase your speed from a walk, to a jog, to a lope, to a run."

I nodded, grateful for the explanation, and transitioned into a brisk walk. Trying to do as she suggested, I counted twenty steps of the brisk walk in my head before going into a jog. Another twenty-five steps, and I lengthened my stride, turning it into an almost lazy lope. I counted a full fifty steps at the lope, falling into a rhythm, before escalating to a run.

But she wanted to know how fast I could go, and so did I.

So, I counted out another fifty steps of the run before pushing myself to go faster. Another hundred steps in, and I pushed myself harder. And harder. And still harder. I let my eyes fall into the soft focus that I used during rifle spins and tosses in winter guard.

Something beeped from the column of readouts.

"Even out your breathing, Ms. Kateri," said the nurse, "or you'll pass out."

I focused on counting the steps as I breathed in, trying to match them on the exhale. And then I focused on taking deeper breaths, increasing the steps on both the inhale and the exhale.

And then I pushed myself even faster.

My shoes were becoming uncomfortable—they weren't built for running.

"My feet," I said. But my voice was muffled through the mask, and the machine and my breathing were making so much noise, I wasn't sure she'd be able to make out what I'd said.

"Your feet are fine," she said.

"Keep going," said Mr. Loudspeaker.

I tried to refocus, pushing my thoughts away from the way my toes were squished into the front of my shoes.

Something twisted in my gut, the feeling all too familiar.

It was like when the leopard caught me in my nightmares.

Oh no.

I started to feel off-balance, and the next step came a hair slower than the one before it.

My gut twisted again.

No. Not here.

I clenched my eyes shut. It had never happened while I was awake. It couldn't happen while I was awake. I couldn't let it happen while I was awake.

My heart pounded in my ears, the air becoming harder to breathe.

And I certainly couldn't let it take me in front of these people.

"Don't slow down now, Ms. Kateri," Mr. Loudspeaker chided.

I opened my eyes, searching for a detail to focus on, to ground me. There had to be something.

There was a hair, like fur from a dog or perhaps a cat, on the nurse's shoulder. I watched it. Focused on it. Willed the thing that stalked me to go away as I gasped for deeper and deeper breaths. I counted the next hundred steps and pushed myself faster again.

"Good," praised Mr. Loudspeaker.

The nurse nodded.

A hundred more steps, and I pushed harder. Not now, dark creature. You stay back, and let me get through this.

A hundred and fifty more steps, and I pushed harder yet again.

I couldn't even fathom how fast I must have been going. But I could feel from the burning in my thigh muscles and in my lungs that I hadn't ever run this hard before.

And then my gut twisted again, and with a cry, I stumbled.

NOT. HERE.

My breathing erratic, I scrambled to keep my feet. But I'd already lost my pace.

"That's enough," said Mr. Loudspeaker.

Not here. Not now. Not like this. Please, God, not in front of *them*.

I slowed to a walk, swallowing around a lump of fear in my throat.

"Alright, Ms. Kateri," the nurse said.

Not here. Not now. Not like this.

"Now, we're just going to see how long you can go," the nurse continued.

Not here. Not now. Not like this.

I took a deep, shuddering breath, trying to calm the pull at my gut.

"Now, Ms. Kateri," ordered Mr. Loudspeaker.

I had stopped. I blinked, my awareness of the room returning to me.

"Um," I said. "Running at top speed like that?"

She gave me a gentle smile. "No. Just a normal run, if you will, please."

I sniffled in a breath, not wiping at my face because the mask was there, and nodded. Like before, I transitioned slowly into the run, counting steps at each stage. When I hit what I'd consider a normal running speed, I switched to counting steps of the inhales and exhales. After a bit, I was able to comfortably increase just a bit more without feeling like I was straining.

And I finally found a rhythm to it.

Not here. Not now. Not like this.

A word for every step. A prayer for every breath.

I wasn't exactly the praying type, but here was where I found myself.

Not here. Not now. Not like this.

It became an endless refrain.

Somewhere along the way, I realized there were no windows in this room. No daylight, no clock. I had no way of knowing how much time had passed.

Not here. Not now. Not like this.

But I didn't feel tired, so I just kept going.

Some amount of time later—I had no way to know how long—I started to slow.

"Keep going," said Mr. Loudspeaker.

"For how long?" I can't even imagine how that sounded.

"Until you can't," replied the nurse.

My eyes went wide, and I stumbled a step.

Not here. Not now. Not like this.

"Until I can't?"

"How will you know your capability if you stop simply because you're bored?" Mr. Loudspeaker sounded like he was talking to a child. "You must keep going until you can't." A pause. "And do try to keep your speed steady, Ms. Kateri."

I narrowed my eyes at the mirror, imagining daggers shooting from them to clip the smug smile from Mr. Loudspeaker's face.

Not here. Not now. Not like this.

I refocused my breathing, pushing myself back into the speed I'd been at, repeating my newly adopted mantra on every breath, regaining that same soft focus to my vision that I used to use in winter guard.

I have no idea how long I ran for. No idea how fast I'd gotten. No idea of the equivalent distance.

Not here. Not now. Not like this.

Not here. Not now. Not like—

I stumbled and had to slow as I tried to regain my rhythm. Awareness of myself returned to me. Darkness loomed around the edges of my vision. My thighs were trembling with every step. How long had they been doing that?

I stumbled again a few steps later, but managed not to fall, and slowed even further.

My head felt heavy. So did the rest of my limbs, for that matter. And it was hard to focus on the details of people and things in the room.

How long had I been running for?

I stumbled again, sliding backward on the machine as I fought my limbs to try to stay upright. My tongue felt like a wad of cotton-wrapped lead in my mouth.

"Enough," said Mr. Loudspeaker as my knee gave out again.

The belt on the treadmill slowed to a stop, and the nurse hurried over to me. She pulled the pulse oximeter from my finger and the sensors from my head and chest. Guiding me forward a step or two, she pulled the mask from my face, and I breathed in the fresh scents of the room, which beat the darkness back a smidge.

The nurse had a similar wild sort of scent underpinning her otherwise light perfume. It was like she and Blondie and Grump all used the same soap. Did they all live on site here? That would certainly explain it.

She pulled a granola bar from her pocket and pressed it into my hand. Blinking, I unwrapped it as my mouth filled with so much saliva I had to swallow to keep from drooling on my own hand. Inside the package was something more like one of those strawberry breakfast bars than a proper granola bar.

But it tasted good, and quelled the growl threatening from my stomach.

I felt a little more alert as I swallowed the last bite of it.

"We'll give you the day tomorrow to rest," said Mr. Loudspeaker. "But first? Shower. And food."

FOURTEEN

THE NURSE LED THE WAY, out of the room, past Blondie and Grump. They looked tired. Or perhaps bored? But they fell into formation behind us as we headed back down the hall the way we had come.

The showers were close, but I was too tired to keep track of the turns. My limbs felt heavy, but the trembling in my thighs stopped well before we'd gotten back to the hall where I played dodgeball, though I couldn't truly be sure that was this hallway.

As we continued, the ache in my legs subsided as well. But my head was foggy and my steps turned sluggish as she beeped another door open. This room was more like the communal bathroom of Saint Dymphna's, with showers lining one wall and sinks with a long mirror above them lining the other. There was a set of drawers under the counter next to the first row of sinks, and the wall directly across from the door had a large full-length mirror. As we entered, to my right, there was a row of shelves filled with towels. Across from them were more shelves, but these were filled with plain white shirts, black leggings, and grey sweatpants.

"Please leave your underwear on the counter," the nurse said as Grump took up a position next to the door out in the hallway. "We'll bring you fresh ones in your size."

Blondie took up a position mirroring Grump's, but inside the door.

I was too tired to care. Too hungry to care.

I grabbed a towel and a washcloth and shuffled into one of the shower stalls, kicking off my shoes outside of it, and pulled the curtain closed. Shampoo, conditioner, and soap were already on the ledge built into the corner. I tossed my towel over the shower curtain rod and turned on the water.

Pulling the hair tie from the disheveled mess that used to be a low bun, I looped it around my wrist and tried to finger comb through my hair. I gulped down mouthfuls of water while I waited for it to get hot, ignoring the discomfort of cool water on my bare skin. Once the water did get warm, I simply didn't have the energy for one of my signature eternity-long showers. But the hot water did revitalize me a bit, and I felt much less like a limp noodle once it was all done.

As I toweled off, one of the drawers outside the shower opened and closed.

"There's a brush and a comb on the counter here for you, Ms. Kateri," the nurse called. "And a dry hair tie."

"No chance for any leave-in conditioner, huh?" I wanted it to be sarcastic, but it came out mushier than I wanted.

Another drawer opened, probably the bigger one on the bottom by the sound of it. And then it closed.

"It's on the counter," she said.

Huh. That's cushy.

I wrapped the towel around myself and shuffled barefoot back over to the shelf of clothes. They were stacked by size, with each shelf labeled, almost like you'd see in a department store. I studied my options. There weren't even sports bras on the shelves, and I really didn't relish the thought of going braless in a flimsy white tee with skin as dark as mine. The odds that you could see every little detail of the goods were just too high.

So I grabbed a shirt that was too small, but would hopefully stretch well enough to work as a bottom layer, and a second shirt that was probably two sizes too large. I pulled a pair of leggings in my size from the stack and ducked into one of the dry shower stalls to dress.

"We'll bring you new shoes as well," the nurse said. "So just leave those there."

Good thing I actually liked being barefoot.

Once I was dressed, I stepped over to the counter to brush my hair. The leave-in conditioner wasn't quite as thick and creamy as I'd like, but it smelled nice and definitely helped get the comb through all the tangles. I brushed through my hair, but just looped the hair tie around my wrist. If I pulled it back now, it would be hours before it was dry.

"Um, okay," I said with a final check at myself in the mirror. I looked decidedly less like shit now, but I pulled at the shirt to try to get it to lay right. I didn't really like the look, but it was what I had, and definitely better than trying to pair it with sweatpants.

"This way, please," the nurse said, gesturing back toward the door.

I knotted the bottom left corner of the shirt as we stepped back into the hallway. Grump rejoined us as well, and we followed the nurse through the maze of hallways. Since I'd lost track of the turns before, I didn't bother trying to keep track now and just followed along.

My stomach growled like an angry feral cat.

A few more doors, a few more turns, and the smell of grilled fish wafted in the air, along with the scent of roasted vegetables. Again, my mouth watered so hard

I had to gulp down a bunch of saliva just so I didn't drool.

Blondie and Grump swallowed audibly as well. I think the nurse did too, but it was harder to tell from behind her.

The nurse beeped the next door open, and the scents of roasted vegetables and grilled meat washed over me in a rolling wave that made my stomach redouble its already vocal complaints at its emptiness. Swallowing yet another mouthful of saliva, I followed her into a small cafeteria, my footsteps virtually silent on the cool black and white checkered linoleum. Glossy white ceramic tiles lined the bottom half of the walls, with stainless steel panels above. Two of those giant white folding tables with rows of seats attached on either side were arranged in the space, parallel to the wall of the door we entered through. We had come in the back wall of the room, and in the front, there was a passthrough made of glossy red tiles with a few covered plates on its counter next to a metal door that apparently went into the kitchens. There were a couple of staff in there cleaning up, too busy with what they were doing to pay any attention to us. There was a third door set into the wall to the left, near the passthrough, and a fourth in the middle of that wall. The whole room was like the lovechild of a fifties diner and a high school cafeteria.

In the center of the table closest to the door, on the side with its back toward the kitchen, was a single place setting, a metal dome covering it like you'd see in fancy restaurants in movies.

"Sit," the nurse said, gesturing to the place setting.

I was too tired and hungry to argue.

She uncovered the plate as I sat down, and handed the cover to Blondie, who placed it on the other table, where she and Grump then took up seats behind and to either side of me, facing my back.

It was as I'd smelled: grilled fish and roasted vegetables. Potatoes, carrots, and string beans, to be precise. But the portion sizes were absolutely huge. There was enough food on my plate to feed me and Andy and Val and then some. And I was too hungry to question it. I shoveled the first bites into my mouth, not caring much how it tasted, even if it was some of the best fish I'd had since the last time I joined my parents on a vacation to the Bahamas.

As I ate, the nurse gathered a glass of water from somewhere in the room and set it down next to me. Not glass, plastic, as I found when I lifted it to take a sip. I should have known it would be like the cup in my room.

How long had I been running, anyway? How fast had I managed to get up to?

I gulped down more water before shoving a forkful of potato and carrot into my mouth.

And what was the rest of the number I was able to lift? How much more than four hundred pounds was that?

I swallowed the next mouthful and a hefty chunk of fish.

"Why the hell are you people hiding what I'm capable of from me?"

The nurse simply eyed my plate and crossed her arms.

"Let me guess," I said. "You're not authorized to answer my questions."

She freaking *winked* at me as I shoved the next bite of fish into my mouth.

I narrowed my eyes at her, suppressing the yawn that tried to escape me.

How long had it been since they'd taken me from my room for all this? The lethargy in my limbs was enough that I was actually looking forward to the not-so-uncomfortably-firm bunk back in my room. Hell, even a surprise sedative-induced nap on the cold hard floor didn't sound like such an awful option.

I shoved the plate away as my yawn broke free. I had made a sizable dent in what was initially there, but it certainly didn't look it. How wasteful of them to pile so much on. Who the hell eats that much food in one sitting?

The nurse's passive expression turned quizzical. "You're full?"

"Well, I'm definitely not still hungry," I replied.

She cocked her head at me, studying me. "You don't need … to eat more?"

I raised a tired eyebrow. "I will tomorrow, or in the morning, or whatever time the next meal is. But yeah, I'm done for now."

She furrowed her brow, apparently processing what I'd said. After a moment, she nodded once to herself and stood to beep the cafeteria door back open.

"You can leave that there," she said. "This way."

"That way better be back to my bed." Or was it a cell?

The nurse met my eyes, the intense challenge in her gaze a sharp contrast to her relaxed posture. "Or you'll what, Ms. Kateri?"

Maybe mouthing off to her wasn't the best idea. I blinked, trying to force my mind to move, to put an idea, *any* idea, into words. But exhaustion had taken root. I needed sleep more than anything, and that was all I could manage to think about.

"Just so," she said with a curt nod as she turned on her heel. "This way then."

Grump nudged my back with his elbow.

I threw my hands up and gave him a look over my shoulder. "I'm going!"

Blondie and Grump took up their familiar formation behind me as the nurse led the way through the halls. I was still barefoot, my steps shuffle-slapping on the tiles as we made our way through the labyrinth. The nurse peeled off around halfway through the journey, pinching the bridge of her nose as she beeped open a side door, and Blondie moved up front to lead the rest of the way back to the entirely too bright hallway that I came from.

Except the hallway was dark. I slowed my steps. And it smelled like fresh laundry and antiseptic.

It was nighttime? How long had I been gone? Moreover, how long had Val and Andy been asleep?

I focused on being quiet as we approached my door, noticing then that neither Blondie nor Grump were making much noise at all, but for the soft movement of their clothes. I was impressed at their near-silence. People usually make more noise than that, even when they're trying to be quiet. Still, their steps were not as in sync as they had been when they'd first taken me from my room.

Probably because they were tired, too. However long I'd been gone, it was at least enough to get to nightfall, and no one particularly enjoys being on their feet all day. I imagined it was even more annoying that they had to just stand there and be quiet the whole time.

Which, come to think of it, is probably why Grump looked like he did.

It was better that it was after curfew anyway. I didn't have the energy for the inevitable questions Val would have.

Blondie beeped the door open to my room.

Would Andy even have any questions about my absence? Had he already gone through many of these same tests?

Grump nudged my back again, and I blinked as I shook my head to clear it.

"Could I at least get a book to read or something

to *do* while I'm stuck here tomorrow?" My voice was barely above a whisper.

"Do not concern yourself with boredom." Ice shot down my spine at Mr. Loudspeaker's quiet voice emanating from somewhere within my room.

He was here?!

Decidedly more alert than I had been a moment before, I darted forward into my room, hoping to confront the disembodied voice from earlier today. But I couldn't see him, even though I could see everything in my nearly lightless room as clear as day.

Someone had come in and cleaned my room while I was gone. My bed was made, and the towel and washcloth on the ring next to the sink were freshly folded.

"On the contrary," Mr. Loudspeaker continued, his quiet voice now coming from above me. "I think you'll find yourself quite busy, really, during your stay with us."

I huffed out a breath. There was a speaker built into the ceiling. Great.

"Who's 'us?'" I asked as Blondie shut the door with a quiet click.

"All in good time, Ms. Kateri," said Mr. Loudspeaker. "For now, get some rest."

Not that I had much of a choice. Now that I recognized there was no one in my room but me, the ice on my spine dissipated, replaced by heavy lethargy.

It had been a hell of a day.

I flopped on the bed, only to remember at the last second that I still didn't know how long I'd been gone. I looked up at the clock display on my wall.

It was 4:57 a.m. on Saturday, May 30th.

I tried to push my brain to count the hours, but really only made it so far as to understand that the whole day had gone by as sleep took over.

FIFTEEN

I woke with a start to the rhythmic metal clank of the breakfast cart, and the scent of coffee, ham, syrup, potatoes, and eggs wafted down the hall.

I checked the clock. It was just past nine a.m.

I'd arrived back at nearly five in the morning, which meant I'd only had about four hours of sleep. Not nearly enough after everything I'd done yesterday. I rubbed my face with a groan.

"Naiya?" Val's voice held surprise.

"Mmmhmm." I nodded, only remembering a moment later that she couldn't see me. "I'm alright."

Curly beeped open the door, and Baldy placed my food on the shelf before I'd even managed to get off the bed. He also placed a bundle next to the tray. It looked like a folded towel, perhaps?

No point in asking him, of course. They wouldn't speak.

"They came and cleaned your room while you were gone," Andy said.

"We were scared you weren't coming back," Val added.

With a huff, I shuffled over to my shelf and caught Andy's eye as Baldy closed his door.

"I'm alright," I repeated.

Andy's dark gaze was intense. "You look like a

grown-up *drekavak*." His accent, beautiful as it was, made it hard for me to get a feel for his tone.

"I dunno what that is." I grabbed the coffee from the shelf and didn't even bother with adding sugar before gulping some down.

Curly and Baldy continued their breakfast delivery.

"It's undead," he said. "Like a zombie, but plague-ridden and more consciously evil. It lives around places of powerful darkness and necromancy back home."

I raised my mug. "Thanks for the compliment."

Val snorted.

"I just mean that to say you look pretty ragged," he said. "What'd they do?"

"*They* didn't do much," I replied, picking up the tray and sitting on my bed with it. "Except maybe shoot about a million tennis balls at me and dodge all of my questions."

Today's breakfast was a thick-cut slice of ham with a sunny-side-up egg on top. It was served with quartered potatoes and toast. A pile of those silver dollar pancakes sat on their own saucer-sized plate, with a little cup of syrup next to it.

"Well, you were gone a long ass while," Val said. "What the hell were you doing all those hours?"

"It started with dodging tennis balls from every direction," I said around a bite of potato. "Then I was lifting weights on this high-tech digital bench press they had—it worked like a resistance machine though, instead of a bar with plates. After that, they put me on a treadmill."

There was a soft scrape of metal on metal as Curly, or maybe Baldy, put Val's breakfast on her shelf. And then the empty cart clunked along back up the hallway, presumably with its two attendants as well.

"How'd you do?" Val asked.

"I dunno." I poured the cup of syrup over the mini pancakes. "How much do people normally lift?"

"Unassisted by magic and otherwise fit?" Andy said. "A *biskyt*, a *biskyt* and a half. Maybe two if they've been doing it a lot."

"A biscuit?" Val laughed. "Like the things you eat with butter and jelly?"

"No," Andy said, running a hand through his hair. "Not a biscuit like you eat. A *biskyt*. It's … like a big block of sand."

I finished the bite of sausage I was on. "What's an example of something that weighs just one *biskyt*?"

Andy was quiet for a moment. "Well, a person usually weighs around a *biskyt* and a half." He came into view and jerked his chin toward me. "You probably weigh between a *biskyt* and a *biskyt* and a half, Naiya. And Valerie's probably right around just one *biskyt*, since she's smaller than you."

"So, like a hundred pounds," Val said.

I dropped my fork. "Holy shit."

"What?" Andy had turned to go back to his bed, but stopped and looked over his shoulder.

"I lifted more than four times that yesterday. Repeatedly."

His expression went slack. "Four times a *biskyt* and a half?"

I shook my head. "No, four *biskyts*."

"Holy shit," Val agreed. "That's some PCP-level shit. And then they put you on a treadmill?"

I nodded, and then remembered Andy was the only one who could see me sitting on my bed. "Yep. But I don't know how long or how fast. I couldn't see the readouts."

"So, they showed you how much you could lift, but wouldn't let you see how fast you could go?"

Judging by the poke-and-scrape, Val was cutting into her ham first. "Fuckin' rude."

I shook my head as I swallowed another bite of potato. "No, it wasn't that. I didn't actually see the whole number that I was lifting. I just know it was three digits, it started with a four, and there were multiple sets of increasing weight in that four-hundred-plus-pound range."

Val whistled.

"Where I come from," Andy said softly, "people can only do that with magic."

I started cutting into my ham. "Magic isn't real here, Andy."

"I dunno, Naiya," Val said. "David Blaine can do some really creepy shit that I definitely can't explain."

I shook my head. "He's just a performer."

"Sounds like they're putting you both through some of the same things they did me," Andy said. "Only I didn't dodge any balls."

"Wait," I said. "Both?"

"Yeah," Val said. "About an hour after they took you, they took me to do the same stuff, minus the tennis balls."

"But she came back a few hours later," Andy said. "They probably figured out pretty quickly that you're just the average girl."

"Hey," Val said, her tone sharp. "I'm way better than just your average girl!"

I smiled. "Can't argue with that. But I think he just means you aren't the weight-lifting, marathon-running champ of the group."

Val snorted. "Well, let's see. You left at around … nine thirty, nine forty-five yesterday."

"Okay," I said. "Good. I hadn't looked at the clock."

"And then what?" she prompted. "Straight to tennis balls?"

"No," I said, stacking the tines of my fork with ham and the last syrup-soaked pancake. "First a physical, then dodgeball, then lifting, then treadmill."

"If you only spent about an hour each on dodgeball and lifting," Andy said, "then you were probably on the treadmill for at least twelve hours."

I nearly choked on my food.

Twelve hours.

"Holy shit," I whispered.

"How do you know what a treadmill even is?" Val's voice was incredulous but held laughter.

"There are a lot of commercials for exercise equipment on daytime television," Andy replied. "And the place I came from before here had that noisy thing on anytime someone was awake."

"Okay, but Naiya," Val said around a bite of food. "You took breaks, right? Like run for a bit and then something else?"

"No breaks," I said, wiping my mouth with the napkin. "Just running."

"Holy shit," Val echoed. "That sounds boring as hell." But she sounded impressed.

I took my now-empty tray and placed it on the shelf, picking up the bundle wrapped in the towel.

"Maybe," Andy said. He was back at his door, studying me through his window. "But sure as the ley lines, I couldn't run that long on my own. I didn't. My version of those tests took about the same amount of time as Val's."

"What're ley lines?" Val asked as I turned back to my bed.

Andy answered her as I sat down and unfolded the towel. Or at least, I heard his voice as he spoke. But I didn't hear the words.

On top of the pile—along with a tan bra and black panties in my size, bundled neatly together with a properly fitting white shirt—was a used copy of my favorite book, *The Last Unicorn* by Peter S. Beagle. I picked it up as my heart started to hammer against my sternum.

It wasn't just any used copy … It was *my* copy.

The one with a faded cover and worn corners.

I flipped through it as my spine turned to ice.

The one with the jelly fingerprint in the middle of page 24.

My jaw fell open.

The one with the creased and slightly torn page 103, from falling out of the tree as I fell asleep in the branches last summer.

How the hell did they get this?

It even had the coffee stain on the top corner of page 237 from when I stayed up all night to finish it and needed the coffee because I was so close to done.

I squeezed my eyes shut and clutched it to my chest, trying to take deep breaths to slow my heart.

My copy of my favorite book.

It even still smelled like my bedroom.

"Holy fucking shit," I whispered.

And it hit me. This was *my* copy of my favorite book. The one that came from *my* bedroom.

These people had been in my house.

Recently.

And none of them were going to answer any questions about it.

Rage filled my chest, and I thumped the book down on the bed. A blue rubber ball, about the size of a tennis ball, rolled out from the middle of the bra and panties bundle. I picked it up and squeezed. And squeezed. And *squeezed*. It deformed and then crumbled in my hand. I threw the pieces against the wall next to the sink and mirror. Little blue chunks of rubber scattered across my floor.

"Naiya?" Andy's expression was concerned as he came into view.

"What happened?" Val asked as I heard the metal scrape of her tray being placed back on the shelf.

"They were in my house," I murmured.

Andy's eyebrows shot up. "What?"

"THEY WERE IN MY FUCKING HOUSE!"

"Waitaminute," Val said. "How do you know?"

I stormed over to the window of my door, fully intending to push my arm out into the hallway to show her my book, except it wouldn't fit through the bars. I smacked my hand on the wall next to the door as I gritted my teeth with a frustrated sound in my throat and looked down to hide the fury on my face.

"It's a book," Andy said.

I took a deep breath, forcing air in when rage made me want to scream. "It's not just any book. It's *my* book."

"You wrote a book?"

I made another frustrated sound in my throat and tried hard not to snap at my friend. She hadn't done anything wrong. I forced my tone to cool evenness. "Now is not the time to be obtuse, Val."

Andy narrowed his eyes my way. "*The Last Unicorn*."

"Oh," Val said. "I remember that movie! It had really sad music."

I set my jaw and closed my eyes. "It did. It stayed pretty true to the feel of the story and the plot itself, but—like nearly all film adaptations—the book is so much better."

"How do you know that's *your* copy?" Val asked.

"This book has been with me for a long time," I said, looking down at it with a sigh. "I've read it probably a million times, and this particular copy shows it. Down to the accidentally folded pages and smudged fingerprints." My vision blurred with my helplessness, and I wiped the wetness from my cheek. "And it still smells like my bedroom, which means it hasn't been sitting in this damn place for long."

"You live close?" Andy asked.

I shrugged and shook my head as I turned to lean back against the wall next to the door. "No way to know. But I've got to get out of here."

Andy nodded. "How?"

I dropped my head into my hands as I slid down the wall to sit on the floor. "I don't know."

There was quiet for a moment. Andy placed his breakfast tray back on its shelf.

"You've only had like four hours of sleep, Naiya," Val said. "Maybe try to get some more rest? We can try to figure things out after, okay?"

"And Val and I can try to come up with some ideas while you sleep," Andy added.

"He'll hear," I said, more hot tears blazing a trail down my cheek. "He talked to me here last night. They can hear you. They can hear me. Nothing we say or do is secret."

"Try not to let it eat at you, Naiya," Andy said quietly. "I've gotten out of worse. And if I can get out of this, if the opportunity presents itself, I swear to you I'll take you with me."

My voice was barely a whisper, torn apart by tears and muffled by my crossed arms over my knees. "You won't want me around so much when you find out what I am."

Their silence told me all that I needed to know about the likely truth of my declaration.

SIXTEEN

The featureless halls were dark as I passed door after door, searching for exits, windows, or even a skylight to the outside world. With breathy snuffs, something dark and menacing stalked me from angular shadows that were too sharp for the light source.

I was dreaming again. I had to be.

The leftover weariness from the day before must've taken the invitation that the rage and tears had provided.

The voice in the ceiling garbled at me, the words unclear, as I turned down one hallway and another. I couldn't even tell if it was Mr. Loudspeaker or someone else. It sounded like some guttural language that I simply hadn't ever learned.

I was going in circles, wasn't I? But none of the doors had handles, nothing to turn, nothing to grasp.

And then one did.

And then they all did.

Except turning the handles was useless—every single door was locked.

The shadows felt alive, grasping for me as I pushed myself ever onward. The ceiling garbled again in wordless noise as I turned down another hallway.

It was a dead end. No doors, no windows, no skylight.

I was trapped.

The darkness coalesced into the leopard, teeth white and eyes glowing green as it placed one deliberate paw in front of the other toward me.

My mouth went dry, and my heart pounded loud enough in my ears to drown out the now incessant muttering from the ceiling.

The leopard growled—a low deep rhythmic thrumming that resonated in my chest. My thudding heart tried to match the beat.

With a wrenching crumbling sort of sound, a door outlined itself against the end of the hall, a handle sprouting from the expected spot with a punctuated crunch. I threw my weight against the newly formed door, wrenching at the handle that wouldn't budge. The low thrumming growl drew closer, and I squeezed my eyes shut in fear, hunching my shoulders over my grip.

A heavy weight hit my back, and my cheek hit the cool door. I took a breath to scream as my stomach twisted and lurched.

The leopard had caught me. It always caught me.

My eyes snapped open in fearful surprise. I was back in my room, awake in the dimness, though light from the hallway shone through the door onto me.

I was covered in fur. And I could see my spots in the light.

My head whipped side to side as my heart rate ratcheted up. No one in here with me. Good. No one could get hurt. Especially not my parents.

And no sooner had my heart started to slow back down before there was a small tinkling at my door.

Oh no. My heart slammed once against my sternum.

With a fearful noise in my chest that came out like

a snarl, I crawled under my bed, pushing myself as far underneath as possible as I curled into the tightest, smallest ball that I could manage, my tail curled around my nose.

My heart rate had gone back to normal. I didn't like it.

The tinkling grew louder as the little purple crystalline spider I'd met just a day ago came into view.

No, wait. It was two days ago, wasn't it?

"No wonder they want to study you," Andy said, his voice coming from across the hall. My left ear swiveled toward the door. Just my left ear. There had been wonder in his tone?

No... not wonder.

Fear.

It had to be fear. No one wants to be this close to a vicious killing machine.

"I can see you," he said, "through Chad."

Another little snarl escaped me, though it was a whimper in my head. My heart pounded in my ears for just a handful of beats before it calmed. But I didn't want him to see me like this.

Not like this.

A paw reached out from my tight ball under the bed—my paw. It batted at the spider, trying to swat it away.

Chad backed out of my reach.

Good. If he stayed out of my reach, I couldn't hurt him—couldn't hurt Andy. I didn't know if leopard claws could scratch or damage whatever Chad was made of, but I didn't want to find out.

I pushed myself further into the corner, turning to press my nose into the point where the two walls met.

"Is she alright?" Val asked.

No, Val, I'm not. Or I am, but I'm not. It's just good there's a wall between us.

"Well," Andy said. "Yes and no. She's a leopard right now. Naiya, can you speak in that form?"

Val made an exasperated little snort. I swear I could hear her roll her eyes.

I made another of those whine-snarls. Y'know, like a goddamn predator does.

Did these people know what I was? Did they know what had happened to my father? Is that why we're all in separate rooms?

Andy blew out a little breath as Chad skittered away. "Looks like no."

Think, Naiya. Think!

I had no way to get back to two legs, no real knowledge of how I got into this furry form in the first place, aside from knowing that the leopard had cornered me in my dream. Again. So, I did the only thing I knew I could do: I stared into the darkness of the corner until sleep took me again—hoping that, when it did, I'd wake as a person.

The lights coming up in my cell woke me sometime later, though I was still curled under my bed. Except now I was naked. And cold.

The door beeped open, and I squinted at the light as I scrabbled at the corner of my blanket, pulling it under the bed as someone came in and clicked the door closed behind them.

"Ms. Kateri?"

It was the nurse from the other day. Yesterday? Shit. I did *not* need to be losing track of time like this.

There was a scrape of metal on metal—the now-familiar sound of a tray being placed on the shelf. A couple of things tapped afterward, like there was more than just the tray up there, and then, she bent down to look under the bed.

I pulled the blanket closer around me, though the space was tight and it caught on the underside of the frame.

She smiled gently at me. "Could you come out here, please?"

I narrowed my eyes at her.

"I just need to get a blood sample," she said. "And I brought you fresh clothes."

I blinked and looked over to the spot where I'd been next to the door when the ... when I changed. There were scraps of white and black cloth where I'd been sitting.

"Why do you need another blood sample?" I asked her.

With a slow patient sigh, she took a step back and stood up. "You know I won't answer your questions, Ms. Kateri."

"Then why should I come out and give you more of my blood?"

Something smelled like lunch meat and pickles. Ew. I curled my lip and took shallow breaths through barely parted lips, trying to avoid getting that sickening taste in my throat.

"Because I can just sedate you and get it myself if I need to," she said, taking a step toward the shelf. "But it's better if you come out here and cooperate."

I was stiff from the nap I'd already taken, and I ached to stretch after being in such a cramped spot.

"Fine," I huffed, crawling out from under the bed and squinting again at the brighter light in my room.

She turned to me as I did, taking another step back to give me room to stand. "I'll only be a minute."

As I straightened and stretched, holding the blanket around me with one hand, she retrieved the bundle of clothes she'd brought from the bed.

"Fresh clothes," she said, offering them to me.

With narrowed eyes, I took them from her and ducked into the corner with the toilet, pulling the black curtain closed as I did. I sniffed at my armpit.

The lunch meat smell wasn't me. There must be a sandwich under the covered tray she brought in. Here's to hoping it tasted better than it smelled.

"That was quite a feat," the nurse said, her tone both conversational and professional, "changing so smoothly like that." I might have even believed she was impressed. "What specifically triggered it?"

Checking that I couldn't see her through the curtain, I dropped the blanket and hurried to put on the underwear. "Why should I answer any of your questions if you won't answer any of mine?"

"Because a stalemate gets us nowhere, Ms. Kateri," she replied. "And because we can find out all we need to know in time. We know it happened while you slept. Why don't you tell me what happened in your dream?"

I pulled the shirt over my head. "Not a chance."

"You'll find things go much smoother here when you cooperate."

"I don't talk to anyone about my dreams." I pulled on the pants.

"You talked to Dr. Anderson," she said. "Something about something stalking you in the dark?"

I yanked open the curtain and glared at her as my heart kicked into a frenzied pace. Ice traced down my spine, but I steeled myself against it and widened my stance, some part of me vaguely aware that my body language proclaimed 'challenge.'

The corner of her mouth pulled upward as she met my eyes. "I wonder, is that thing in the dark a leopard, like you? Or somewhat else entirely?" Her expression turned smug, and I wanted to smack it from her face. "Do not try to lie to us, Ms. Kateri. You will fail."

I had never wanted to attack someone for their words as badly as I wanted to attack her. Everything in my body screamed at me that she was a threat, and therefore so was everyone else here.

And my gut tried to twist again.

No.

I balled my hand into a tight fist.

Not again.

I took a deep breath in through my nose.

Not here.

I squeezed my fist tighter, my nails digging into my palm.

Not now.

I blew the breath out through my barely parted lips, forcing the departing air to be slow and silent. The other hand balled into a tight fist as well.

Not like this.

I took another deep breath in through my nose and tried to keep the vitriol from my tone. "If you have my records from Saint Dymphna's," the words were thinly veiled rage, "then why do you need yet another blood sample? Did the vampires there not get enough?"

"I can assure you there are no vampires at Saint Dymphna's, Ms. Kateri." She held her hand out for my arm. "Now, if you'll give me your arm, and let me take a sample without having to sedate you, I'll give you something else to help pass the time."

I narrowed my eyes at her once again, the boiling rage dropping to a simmer as it was replaced with curiosity. What could she possibly have brought?

She held my gaze and waited. I swear I could hear her heartbeat, slow and steady and utterly unafraid.

And she knew what I was. So what did that make her?

The rage dissipated entirely at that thought.

Eyes still narrowed, I thrust my arm out toward her. I studied her face as she took yet another vial of my blood. She certainly looked normal enough … but was it possible she was something else, like me?

"Finger," she said, extending her hand, palm up, like someone expecting money to drop into it.

I blinked and raised a hand, finger extended. Like she'd done during the physical, she took my finger and placed it on the spot where the needle met the skin.

"Pressure there," she said and pulled the needle from my arm. She nodded once she'd capped the end. "Good." She tucked the capped needle into her coat pocket and pulled a blue rubber ball, identical to the one I'd crushed earlier, from her other pocket. She offered it to me. "Try not to destroy this one."

I gingerly took it from her and watched her as she turned to gather the three needles she'd placed next to the tray on the shelf. She tucked them into one of the pockets on her lab coat and beeped my door open as I considered my options.

She wasn't going to answer my questions, and I had no way to coerce or cajole her into doing so. If I attacked her now, I might get her down, but those needles undoubtedly held sedatives, and I would be no closer to getting out of here if I was knocked out. And I certainly didn't have anything to offer her in trade, though my parents' money could likely help if I could just reach them.

I thought about rushing the door, but I'd seen the maze of hallways. I had no idea how to escape this place. At least, not yet.

But she was already out the door. She turned to watch me from the hallway, not moving until the door clicked closed again. The lights above me dimmed again, contrasting against the sharp brightness of the hallway.

I waited until the door at the end of the hall

closed before I moved to the shelf and grabbed the tray.

"Unless Dr. Anderson kept super detailed records of your conversations," Val said as I sat on the bed, "there's no way she should know what you talked about in your sessions. It'd be a violation of privacy standards. The records should only show diagnoses."

What was under the lid of the tray wasn't exactly what I had expected, but it was close. Two big sub sandwiches, piled with lunchmeat and lettuce and tomatoes, and three pickle spears. It was entirely too much food for me, really.

"Are you telling me you're surprised?" I couldn't help the wry tone. "Aren't you the one who said this place screams off-the-books activities?"

"I said it reeks of it," she said, a smile in her tone.

"These people know more than they tell you," Andy said.

I nodded as I took a bite of the first sandwich. It was tasty, but unremarkable.

"Andy," I said after swallowing the bite. "You have leopards, where you're from?"

"Yes," he replied.

I crossed my legs under me on the bed. "Are they friendly?"

"No more or less friendly than any wild animal would be."

I nodded. "Do they talk?"

There was amusement in his voice. "No, they only growl or roar, really."

I swallowed the next bite of my sandwich. "Then what makes you think I'd be able to speak when I'm like that?"

He came into view by his door. "Where I'm from, people can, sometimes."

I set my tray next to me to retrieve my cup and fill it with water as I considered that.

"People turning into animals is common where you come from?" Val asked.

"Well," Andy said, "it's not exactly common, but it's not rare either."

I took a few gulps of water. "Well, people don't do that here."

SEVENTEEN

Val's voice was quiet. "Is it true, what she said?"

I pressed my lips into a line and tried not to sigh. There was only one place this conversation could go. "Is what true?"

"That something stalks you in your nightmares?"

"It's not really something I want to talk about, Val."

"No, I get that," she said, her voice quiet and gentle. "But it's just … well, we're kinda stuck here, Naiya."

I let some quiet pass as I finished my sandwich. I didn't want to talk about it. I'd never had any luck talking with anyone about it. Why should talking to Val be any different?

But I wanted it to be. We'd connected at Saint Dymphna's, and she was my friend.

I put the tray on the shelf next to the door. "They started when I—that is to say, they started about a year ago."

"Every night?" Val asked.

I shook my head and came to the door. "No, not every night. But a lot of them. I never tracked them. My parents … they heard 'recurring nightmare' and glossed over what would happen. They just thought me waking as a …"

"A leopard," Andy said.

I nodded, looking up and meeting his eyes across the hall. "They thought it was just the last part of the dream. They never understood. And when I tried to tell it different ways, they just … didn't believe me. They told me to get my head out of the clouds. Even Abigail wanted to know what book I got it from."

"Can you control it at all?" Val asked.

I shook my head. "No. Well … I can sometimes keep it from happening when I'm awake, if I focus on it. But it … it doesn't work all the time."

"So, you couldn't show them the truth," Andy said. "That must've been so frustrating."

I nodded.

"How'd you end up at Saint Dymphna's, then?" Val asked.

She already knew, right? She had to. It's not like it was that hard to piece together.

I chewed my lip. I could still see the fear in my parents' faces. I didn't want to relive it.

"Naiya?" Andy's voice was quiet.

I looked at him again, an ache settling in my chest. Val was my friend. Andy … well, Andy could be. And I didn't know how long we'd be here.

"My parents found a …" I swallowed around a lump in my throat, not sure if I could even say it. I swallowed again. "A leopard. In the bed where their daughter was supposed to be. Well, my mother did, anyway. But she screamed and then my father came running in and he tried to shoo the leopard—me— out of the house, and that's when—" My throat closed at my father's face, and I couldn't get the next part out.

Val's voice was gentle. "That's when what?"

I slumped against the wall perpendicular to the door and squeezed my eyes shut.

"Someone got hurt," Andy said softly, "didn't they?"

I nodded. "My father …" I shook my head, dropping my chin to my chest as guilt flooded through my body. "There was a lot of blood. I changed back to human then, right in front of them, and scrambled to cover myself. But suddenly, all the nightmares and stories made sense to them. I was strung out on some hallucinogenic party drug. So much so that I drugged them too, so they could understand what I felt, and then attacked them when they got angry about it. They committed me for drug use instead of facing the truth."

With a shuddering breath, I slid down the wall to sit on the floor and dropped my face into my hands.

"Woooow," Val said, drawing out the word. "So, how did that first convo with Dr. Anderson go?"

I sighed. "About as well as you'd expect." I mimicked Dr. Anderson's voice. *"And do sober people think they're leopards, Naiya?"*

"No," Andy said. "But apparently sober people don't think they got stuck on the wrong side of an interplanar rift, either."

"Pfft," Val snorted. "Yeah, they'd have a field day with you."

"A field day?" Andy sounded confused.

"Ugh, jeez." I swear I heard her throw up her hands.

"They'd have a lot to say," I said patiently, glad to be moving on. "They'd be excited for the anomaly. They'd give you all the meds they could and stick you in a padded room."

"They didn't do that to you?" Andy asked.

I shook my head again. "No. But to the staff of a mental hospital, I'm clearly better grounded in reality than you are."

Something thudded against the wall at my back.

Probably Val leaning against the wall between our rooms.

"Is your father okay?" Andy asked.

I squeezed my eyes shut and pushed the image of his and my mother's terrified faces from my mind's eye. "He was okay enough to drive me to Saint Dymphna's, but my mother kept saying he should go to the hospital."

"How long were you at Saint Dymphna's before I arrived?" Val's voice was quiet.

I swallowed again, pushing the guilt from my mind. "A few days, I think? Less than a week."

"And you hadn't heard from your parents?" Andy asked.

"No cell phones allowed," Val said.

I nodded. "So they had no way to reach me."

"If he could drive," Val said, "he's probably okay."

I nodded again, more listlessly this time. "I hope so."

Silence settled like a weighted blanket. No ticking, no sounds of staff moving beyond the hall we were in, no birds or wind from outside the skylight. Just the quiet hum of the too-bright lights in the hall.

"Why do they—?"

"What'd she bring you?" Val asked, her words tumbling over the top of Andy's.

I blinked. "A ball. Like a tennis ball, but not fuzzy, and a little more firm."

I leaned over and grabbed it off the foot of my bed before standing at the door. I tried to put my hand through the window but, like with my book, the openings between the bars were too small.

But only just.

I put my left hand through one opening over on the left and then pushed the ball through the next opening to the right into my hand outside the door. It only barely squeezed through.

"Can you see this from your door, Val?" I asked.

"Oh! It's a racquetball," she said.

Andy straightened off his wall and pushed an arm through his window. "May I?"

I tossed it to him, but I'm not a leftie, so it was clumsy. Andy bobbled it, but couldn't get a good grip, and it bounced to the floor and down the hall, out of reach.

"Dammit," Val said.

"Chad can get it," Andy said, bringing the little purple crystal up to the window again.

Like before, the translucent creature unfolded itself and tinked out the window, following where the ball had gone.

As he chased after it, I looked at Andy. "What were you asking just then? When Val asked about what the nurse had brought."

"I wanted to ask why they keep your room darker than ours," he said.

"It's darker?" Val asked as Chad finally caught up to the ball. Or, at least, I assumed he had since the tinkle-skitter of his steps stopped. He'd gone into a corner of the hallway I couldn't readily see.

"It is," Andy answered. "Like they'd do for an *ingoeth*."

I cocked my head to the side. "A what?"

"It's … it's like an elf, but with very dark skin and silver-white hair," he said. "They have entire cities underground where I come from. Entire generations of *ingoethi* live and die without ever seeing even a wink of sunlight. So, their eyes have adapted to the dark. They don't see as well in the daylight."

"Well, I'm not one of those," I said. "If that's what you're asking."

Chad came back into view, walking backward on six legs while the front two dragged the ball along.

Andy smiled. "No, I figured you didn't have those here. But maybe something equivalent?"

I shook my head. "Sounds like something out of a fantasy novel." But then, *he* kind of sounded like something out of a fantasy novel. I looked around my room, squinting at the ceiling to see the lights, which were big round bulbs behind diffused glass. "I'm not sure why they keep my room darker, but … it is more comfortable than the sharp light of the hallway."

Andy nodded.

"How would they know that?" Val asked.

I shrugged. "Not sure."

As Chad got closer, I realized his fangs were sunk into the rubber of the ball, securing his grip. He brought the ball to Andy's door, scooting up the metal backwards to the window. He lost his footing once in his vertical ascent, but he quickly recovered, only to find that he didn't have the strength to pull the ball through the bars.

"I got it," Andy said, reaching his hand out in front of his companion.

Chad dropped the ball into Andy's waiting palm and then skittered up his arm to perch at his shoulder.

Andy squeezed the ball. "How did you destroy the other one?"

I rolled a shoulder. "I—waitaminute, what do you mean?"

"She said, 'try not to destroy this one,'" Andy replied.

"Oh … I squished it. Crumbled it?" I toed a piece of blue rubber on the floor near where I stood. "There's still pieces of it here on the floor."

Andy's face filled with curiosity, and he squeezed the ball again.

"Don't break this one!"

"I won't," he said quickly. "I … can't. It's very firm."

I looked away. So I had a freakishly high grip strength then. Great. Another thing I got to have in common with a goddamn vicious predator.

"Toss it here?" Val asked.

Andy nodded and checked his range of motion before tossing it in her direction. His throw was clumsy too though, and it lightly bounced off her door and down the hall in the other direction.

He made a noise that I was fairly certain was an expletive. "Chad." He nodded his head toward the ball, and Chad skittered off to retrieve it.

"Oh no," Val said, her voice already rising in pitch. "I don't need him to bring me the ball. It's fine, you keep it."

"Val," Andy said.

"Valerie," she corrected him. "And no. Say whatever you want, but I don't need to make friends with a giant spider."

"Val," I said. "Who knows how long we're gonna be here. I don't know how long it'll take my parents to get a grip on reality and figure out their daughter's not in rehab anymore. I don't—"

What if they never figured it out? What if they figured I just ran off and didn't even bother looking for me?

"What's your point, Naiya?" Val's voice snapped me out of my thought spiral, and I shook my head as I forced air deep into my lungs, past the sudden lump in my throat.

"My point is, maybe don't eliminate yourself from possible sources of amusement in a place like this. Maybe they're gonna test the hell out of me, but … you're just … I mean, they didn't even do anything beyond a basic physical, for you, did they?"

Chad made it back to Val, again traveling

backward, and scooted up her door. I couldn't see what was happening, but she squeaked as he progressed, likely when he came into view.

"I don't wanna make friends with a giant spider, Naiya!" Her voice was shaking.

"So don't," I replied. "But just try to realize he's not interested in hurting you? He just wants to give you the ball, like his master told him to." I nodded toward Andy.

"I'm not his master," Andy said quickly.

"Not helping," I told him.

He pulled his hand back through his door, raising both hands in a placating gesture. "He's a physical manifestation of my psyche. He's … part of me."

"That, we can work with," I said, shooting a finger gun at him and clicking my tongue. "See, Val? He's not even an actual spider."

"Nnnngh …"

"I know, Val, but he's not going to hurt you." I looked to Andy for confirmation.

He met my eyes and nodded once. "He's never hurt a thing, but in self-defense."

Val made another nervous noise.

"There you go," Andy said encouragingly. "He doesn't even have to touch you. He can just drop it into your hand."

She let out a little squeak, and the ball hit the floor and started bouncing away again.

"It's alright," I told her.

"You had it," Andy said. "Try again?"

Chad skittered off to retrieve the ball.

"Mmm. I don't think I need to." I could practically hear her rubbing at the scars on her stomach.

"C'mon, Val," I said. "He can't be half as scary as the monster that tried to kill you."

"You don't know what tried to kill me," she

muttered. But she gave an exasperated sigh. "Fine. Bring it here, Chad."

He was already doing so, but he chittered out a little noise as he scooted back toward her.

"A little lower," Andy said.

Val squeaked again, but the ball didn't hit the ground. "I got it!"

I leaned back against the wall with a sigh. "I'm really proud of you, you badass bitch."

"Why's he gotta look like a spider, anyway?" Val asked.

Andy rolled a shoulder. "It's just the form he chose. Magic is sometimes unpredictable where I'm from. Mastering the powers of the mind is moreso, and that only compounds if you aren't necessarily fully attuned to the inner workings of your own mind."

"*Temet nosce*," Val said.

Frowning, I shook my head. "What?"

"It's Latin," she explained. "It means 'know yourself.' The Bu—my boss used to say it a lot."

"He probably got it from that movie with the guy who dodged bullets." I nodded. "Any chance your boss is likely to worry about your absence and come looking for you?"

"*Former* boss," she amended.

But it sounded like it might have been more complicated than that.

"So, no," I said and pulled my lip between my teeth.

"Yeah, no," she agreed. "Will he play fetch?"

"That's basically what he's been doing," Andy said. "But he's not a dog."

"Better than just sitting here waiting for the next meal," I said as the ball bounced along down the hall, its soft impacts chased by tinkling skitters.

Andy nodded. "It is a way to pass the time."

Better than waiting to find out whether my parents would ever figure out I wasn't where they thought I was.

Chad brought the ball over to me, and I copied Andy, dangling my arm out of the window so the creature could drop the ball into my open hand.

"Waitaminute," I said.

"What?" Val asked.

"My parents should have been the ones to pick me up. That should have been *their* security." My voice turned frantically hopeful. "They should already know that I'm not where I'm supposed to be! They probably already have the police on the case."

"Unless the staff here managed to find some way to contact them and feed them some line about why you didn't get out," Val pointed out.

I deflated.

"It's what I would do if I were them," Andy said. "If I knew you had family that would worry, and I didn't want them to come looking, I'd find some story to tell them."

"That … makes a lot of sense." I toed another piece of blue rubber before looking up at the dark eyes and mussed hair across the hall. "Any chance anyone from back home knows how to find you? Or might be looking for you?"

The corner of his mouth pulled into a wry smile as he shook his head. "I don't even know if anyone back home knows how to get *here*. Let alone how to find me." He looked down at his hands. "And I doubt anyone's even looking. I'm known to wander off."

With a sigh, I nodded. "So, no."

He looked back up at me. "So, no."

I leaned one way and then the other, trying to see how far I could see down the hall opposite the way the nurse had gone. But it wasn't any better than it had been the last time I looked.

"There's seven more cells on either side of the hall down that way," Andy said, watching me.

Cells. That really was what they were, wasn't it?

I tossed the ball and slumped against the wall once more.

My distant parents really were my only way out of here. Assuming they could manage it. Assuming they wouldn't jump to conclusions and label me something even worse than a drug addict. Assuming they could see through the lies of the staff for a facility that definitely operated under the noses and off the radars of regulatory bodies.

And you know what they say about assumptions.

EIGHTEEN

We played fetch with Chad for another thirty minutes, but conversation had largely died, and I was soon left to my own dark thoughts. I suspected the same was true of Andy and Val.

When the game fizzled, conversation didn't exactly pick up. So, I started reading my book, unwilling to let the fact that they stole it *from my house* deter me from my favorite story. It was easy to get lost again in the tale I knew so well I probably didn't even need the book to retell it.

Somewhere around the scene where the unicorn and Schmendrick met Captain Cully and Molly Grue, the door at the end of the hall beeped open, followed by the clatter of the dinner cart—baked chicken by the smell of it, with … broccoli perhaps? And something sweet and fruity, but it was fainter and hard to identify. Curly and Baldy were its escorts yet again.

Tonight, as that morning, Curly opened the door, and Baldy removed my lunch tray before placing dinner on the shelf. When he exited, he beeped open Andy's door so Curly could deliver the food. It looked like he did the same for Val's door, too.

Interesting.

I wondered if the change was due to them knowing what I was now. It had to be, right? I pulled the tray from the shelf and sat on my bed with it. But what did that mean? Was Curly afraid of me? I mean, he should have been. Everyone should. I didn't know when I was going to turn into this vicious predator again. And I certainly couldn't know what I'd do if people were around when I did.

I was right again: it was chicken and broccoli under the lid of the tray. The sweetness was a berry cobbler with a scoop of ice cream melting atop it. And it was all absolutely delicious. The chicken was juicy, the seasoned broccoli soft without being mushy, and the cobbler's tartness tempered with the creamy vanilla ice cream was as good as any I'd ever had.

It made me angry.

I didn't want to like the food here. I didn't want to like anything about this place. I was a prisoner here. The reality of that was settling into my gut like a heavy stone.

"Is there a single meal this place makes that isn't good?" Val asked, her voice dripping with annoyance that mirrored mine.

"If there is," Andy said, "I haven't had it. Though, admittedly, I'm unfamiliar with most of your foods, so I assumed it was just the novelty of it."

I bobbed my head, though I was pretty sure no one could see it. "I tend to like trying new foods, too."

"Yeah," Val said. "Well, while the food may be good, we're still fucking prisoners."

"Impossible to forget," Andy said.

I poked at the broccoli, wanting to just not eat it—or anything else on my plate for that matter—but it was too good. "Any idea how to *not* be prisoners anymore?"

Andy gave a dark chuckle. "Just go along with what they want until they're done with you."

"If you do that with mobsters," Val said, "they'll just kill you anyway when they're done with you."

"I think that's only in the movies, Val."

"Criminals don't like witnesses," she countered.

I clicked my tongue and shot a finger gun toward my door, but dropped my hand to the bed as I recalled no one could see it. "*Touché.*"

We all ate in companionable silence.

"It's better now that there's company," Andy said quietly.

Val snorted. "I bet. Place like this? Probably boring as shit without someone to talk to."

"Prisoners in solitary confinement for too long start to go crazy," I said, reciting the fact from some forgotten corner of my mind. "Humans are social creatures. We're not meant to be alone. I'm glad you're here, too. Both of you."

"Sure," Val said around a bite of food. "And, Andy, at least you had Chad."

"Mmm, he's certainly better than being completely alone," Andy agreed, his tone reluctant. "But it's also very much like talking to myself."

I bobbed my head again. "Well, if he's part of you, that makes sense."

"Maybe keep an eye out for windows?" Val offered.

"They're likely to take you for more tests of your abilities," Andy said. "They had a couple more for me after the treadmill and the handle pulling. Maybe getting a lay of the land when they do would be helpful."

"You've been here for longer," I said, looking toward his window, though he wasn't in my line of sight from my vantage point. "Do you have any of this place memorized?"

"Only a couple of hallways past this one," he answered. "But none of them had any windows. And I suspect they are likely to test you differently than they did me, since I can't turn into a leopard."

"This place is a maze," I said, swallowing the last bit of cobbler. "I can't even count the number of hallways I went down yesterday. But what I do know is that the place where I dodged tennis balls is in a completely different section than the place they had me lifting weights and running. The showers weren't terribly far, but the cafeteria they took me to was."

"This place sprawls like a goblin nest," Andy said.

I shoved the last bite of chicken into my mouth and stood to put the now-empty tray back on the shelf. "Have you seen any additional staff beyond who's been here in the past couple of days?"

Andy was quiet for a moment. "There was a man in a white coat that ... checked my vitals. And the pair who picked me up from the place your police took me when I came through the open rift were different from the staff I've seen these past few days as well."

I counted on my fingers. Three plus Blondie, Grump, Curly, and Baldy. Plus the nurse made eight.

"Add in Mr. Loudspeaker," I said, "and that makes nine people on staff that we've directly interacted with. And there were two more working in the kitchen when I was there."

"Don't forget the two that came to get Val before," Andy said.

"And there was a different nurse than the one who's been here for you, Naiya, that took my vitals," Val said.

"Which brings the total to fourteen," I said. "But the cafeteria I saw would have held a lot more than that, and I suspect Mr. Loudspeaker doesn't deign to eat with the plebs."

"So any escape plan is gonna have to be stealthy as hell, or we'll have the whole compound on our asses," Val said.

"I think that's likely anyway," Andy said.

I nodded. "They probably have eyes all over this place, right?" With a huff, I leaned against the wall as Andy finished his food and put his tray on the shelf.

There was the scrape of metal on metal from Val's room at my back.

"Of course they do," she said. "Even regular office buildings with no security doing business completely on the up-and-up have cameras everywhere. I'd expect at least twice as many here, and for all of them to be super hi-res."

I sucked on my teeth. "Great."

Andy leaned his arm on his door, looking under it through the window at me. "Why did your people develop sarcasm?"

I narrowed my eyes in confusion. "Don't you use it where you're from?"

"Well, yes," he said. "But it's usually much more overtly obvious."

"Or maybe you're just not clued into the culture here," Val said.

He bobbed his head.

"There are still people who don't really get it," I said. "My friend Elisa only understands sarcasm when it's super obvious. She'd be like 'no, Naiya, not great' to my comment before."

"No wonder you're so patient with him," Val said.

I shrugged. "Not his fault he got stuck in the worst first-world country." I looked up at Andy. "You should've picked Sweden. They'd have been more kind."

"I didn't exactly get my choice," he said, and then his cheeks colored and he quickly added, "though my current companions are far preferable to the people at the place I first went to. Your police are about as jumpy as the inquisitors back home. All told, it hasn't been that bad."

"Yeah," Val said, "well, I'm willing to bet your

inquisitors have the same issue our police do: hard to tell which ones are likely to tell you to shut up and do what they say from which ones will actually listen to you if there's a problem."

Andy blinked at her. "That's ... less than ideal. But yes. Depending on which faith they follow, or whose staff of office they answer to, it can be hard to tell. Though it's certainly easier to tell some from others."

I nodded. I'd had nothing but pleasant interactions with police officers, but I'd seen the news stories. I knew not all of them would be tremendously helpful—especially if they didn't know who my father was.

Which probably meant we couldn't go to them if we got out of here. The odds they'd send any or all of us back to another mental health hospital for raving about being held captive by folks like this ... well, it was the kind of thing you'd see in movies. Not the kind of thing that actually happened in real life.

I looked at the date next to the clock. May 30th. Saturday. I'd only been here for two and a half days.

I leaned against the wall next to the door. "Hey Andy?"

"Yes?"

"You said something in the rift you came through basically translated everything you knew to English, right?"

"Best I can tell," he said.

"So how come it didn't translate the word for that evil undead thing you said I looked like the other day or the word for those underground elves?"

"Likely because you simply don't have them here," he replied and then gave me smile with a rueful tint, "which is somewhat comforting. The words I used were the ones from my homeland. My common tongue is ... decidedly different from yours."

"How so?" I asked, pushing off the wall to face him.

And then he spoke something that was not a language I was even remotely familiar with, the tones musical and words lyrical. It sounded like something straight out of a fantasy movie. Chad danced up onto his shoulder.

"What's it mean?" Val asked.

He chuckled. "'Do you understand this, the language of my homeland?'"

His laugh made me smile. "It's pretty."

"Thank you," he replied.

"Looks like Chad likes it too," Val said.

"I should hope so," Andy said, rubbing a finger along the facets of the crystalline creature. His eyes lingered on my face, the ghost of a smile still playing at the corners of his mouth until my cheeks heated and I had to look away.

I slid down the wall to sit on the floor and hooked a strand of hair behind my ear. God, what was this, elementary school? I liked his eyes on me. I liked his attention. So freaking what?

Silence closed in around us. It was companionable, but there was an undeniable undercurrent of 'trapped' that made it less comfortable than I would have liked.

"How long do we wait for your parents to wise up to our situation here?" Val asked a moment later.

I shook my head. "I don't know. If they're out of the country and only planned to send a security detail or Abigail to pick me up? It could be a week or more before they get home to make arrangements."

"That's … less than ideal," Andy said.

"I know."

"That's assuming they can even see through any story this place may or may not have arranged to get fed to them," Val said.

I dropped my head into my hands. "I *know*."

In the silence that followed, I relocated to the bunk and went back to my book. By the time the lights went out that night, I had only thirty-one pages to go—which was frustrating. But when I found I was still able to make out the words even in the dark, I simply finished it before laying down to sleep.

I had more tense dreams that night: my father telling me to figure my own way out of this mess, Abigail telling me it was all in my head, my mother driving endlessly down a four-lane highway late at night. I could see them all so clearly, like I was a cameraman standing right there with them.

But at least the leopard didn't catch me.

NINETEEN

As it had the day before, the breakfast cart clattering down the hallway woke me, the aroma of coffee accompanying the scent of eggs and sausage and toast. Baldy was once again the one to deliver my food, though Curly delivered Val's as well as Andy's.

Under the lid of the tray, there were avocado slices accompanying the toast, and the sausage was mixed into the scrambled eggs, along with tomatoes, onions, and cheese. I drank the coffee first and had the rest finished in short order, which was right about the time the door at the end of the hallway beeped open. A moment later, the nurse beeped my door open, handing me another pair of shoes. Blondie and Grump stationed themselves out in the hallway again, though Grump held the door open for the nurse.

"We have another exciting day planned for you, Ms. Kateri," she said, her voice much cheerier than I liked. She eyed my tray, which only had crumbs left on it, and nodded.

I looked over her shoulder at Andy, who'd come to his window, nibbling on a piece of toast. He gave me a reassuring smile and, as he'd done the day they took me to dodge tennis balls, nodded once.

I made my return nod part of my response to the

nurse. "Fine. Let's see what you want from me today." I took her proffered shoes and slid them on.

She was quiet as we exited my cell and padded down the hallway. Blondie and Grump fell into step behind us, though the only sound we made as we walked was the rustle of our clothes.

Two hallways down and a left, then the first right, and another right after going through the door at the end of the hall. I was pretty sure this was close to the same way they took me last time. But all the hallways looked the same.

"I'm sure glad I have you folks to guide me around here," I said, sarcasm dripping through every word. "I bet you lose interns all the time." I turned to walk backwards and look at Grump. "How many people have starved to death in this maze?"

He met my eyes with the same indifferent half-scowl he always wore. And then his eyes flicked over my shoulder and back to mine.

I raised an eyebrow.

My back hit the wall at the end of the hallway, and a corner of his mouth turned up. His glance over my shoulder had been a warning that I was walking into a wall.

The nurse turned. "This way, Ms. Kateri."

I blinked and narrowed my eyes at him before turning to follow the nurse down the hallway to the right. We were in a part of the building with higher ceilings and wider hallways now. It got a little colder, and the air was a bit more stale.

I tried to repeat the directions for the path we'd taken. Two hallways down and a left. Take the first right. Need a keycard for the end of the hall, and then a right. Then it was a right into the high-ceiling section? Or was it only a right because I was walking backwards at the time? That must be it. Start over. Two hallways down and a left. First right.

Keycard, and then right. Then a left into high ceilings.

But I lost even that when the nurse beeped open the next door.

It was a huge warehouse space with white cinder block walls. But it was what they had set up here that made my jaw drop. It was a massive obstacle course, largely built out of black walls, grey metal pipes, and brown ropes, the likes of which I'd only seen on TV. Only it was huge. Way bigger than anything on the ninja warrior shows. And instead of water at the bottom of the obstacles, there were either thick black gym mats or a pit of black foam cubes, like you'd see at a trampoline park, and there was a pile of tires without rims somewhere near the center of it. But the obstacle course itself—with all its ropes and pipes and bars and cables—was the showstopper. And maybe the sheer size of the warehouse. They could probably park five or six commercial airplanes side-by-side in this space and still have plenty of room.

"Today should be much more fun for you," the nurse said cheerfully, gesturing at the obstacle course.

I became aware that I was curling and flexing my fingers at my sides, and stopped myself as I looked at her with wide eyes. "You can't possibly expect me to get through all of that?" But a trickle of excited anticipation spread through me.

"Much like the time you spent on the treadmill," Mr. Loudspeaker's voice echoed throughout the space, "and the weights you lifted, you clearly labor under the assumption that you are incapable of such a task. We disagree."

I squinted up at the giant gym lights buzzing from the ceiling and tried to at least see the speakers his voice came from, but with the light in my eyes and all the obstacles in the space, I couldn't make any out. So I visually traced the walls, trying not to focus on the obstacles as I leaned one way and the other, looking for the observation window that he must be behind. When I didn't see any, I spun in a slow circle. Blondie and Grump had taken up position on either side of the door. And there, in the wall to the left of the door, in the high corner, was a large mirror reflecting the obstacles. Below it was a white door with no handle on this side, just a little black keycard reader. I took a step to my left and traced the ground floor, looking for other exits, but with everything in the way, I couldn't really tell what was at the far corner.

"You've gotta be outta your mind," I muttered under my breath.

"Not at all," replied the nurse.

She actually heard me?

I turned my attention to the course itself. We'd come in next to a cargo net set on an angle up and away from the door. But there was nothing at the top, just a drop into a pit of foam blocks. At the end of that was a platform up to a set of six oblong balls suspended from cables at either end.

"The idea is to get through it as quickly as possible," the nurse said. "We'd like to see how fast you can manage this."

I pressed my lips into a line and took a deep breath in through my nose, actively stopping my fingers from flexing and curling yet again.

"You'll begin at the sound of the horn," Mr. Loudspeaker said.

"You're not even going to walk me through all of the obstacles? How the hell am I supposed to know how to get through these?"

And then an air horn sounded, like the kind people take to football games, ringing in my ears, loud enough to make me squint.

"You'll figure it out," said the nurse.

I closed my eyes as my fingers curled into tight fists and took a slow, deep breath.

Fine. Let's do this.

The rope net was no problem at all, and movement through the foam blocks was annoying, but only because it was slower than I'd like. The black platform at the other end was taller than I expected—though the foam pit I was in was a bit deeper than it looked, so that tracked. The ledge was over my head, and I had to jump for it, but I pulled myself up onto it without too much trouble.

I was expecting the first of the oblong balls to bounce a little, suspended on the cable as it was, but I wasn't prepared for it to spin as well, and I fell between the first and the second balls into the foam pit below.

"Back to the platform, Ms. Kateri," said Mr. Loudspeaker.

I looked up at the oblong balls and studied the obstacle beyond: four round cages made of thick grey metal pipes suspended from a framework at a height that was well over my head. I was pretty sure the only way to reach the first of them was to make a jump for it from the last ball.

Which meant I was going to need to be stable on it.

With another sigh, I heaved myself back up onto the platform before the oblong balls. I was pretty sure the trick would be to keep moving to get to the cages.

I fell two more times before I managed to get all the way to the last ball. But my leap for the first cage was clumsy, and my left shoulder wrenched as my weight dropped into the only hand able to get a firm grip.

It didn't help that the cages rotated on their connection point to the support structure like a front-loading washing machine. Only it was mounted at a strange angle, so it was harder to predict where my weight was going as I tried to get a second hand up.

But I managed to get a hand on it. I had to swing myself over to the next one, which I did, despite the burning ache in my shoulder. I managed to get my other hand on that one as well and pulled myself up to swing for the third, and then the fourth.

There was no landing at the end of this obstacle, either—unless the large angled pads counted. There were six of them placed in two rows of three, offset from each other and increasing in height the further from the cages you got. And they were set impossibly far apart with only a thick black foam mat underneath.

Hanging from the last basket, I furrowed my brow as my right shoulder started to ache from the strain, though it wasn't as bad as the left. Not yet, at least.

I was going to have to leap from one pad to the other, wasn't I? The first one was already a handful of feet off the ground, and the last was probably close to eight feet up.

A hell of a fall.

But they had implied I was capable of it. Or, at least, Mr. Loudspeaker thought I was. I took a deep breath as I swung my legs and launched myself toward the first of the pads. I had to scramble for purchase, but I managed it. I looked across to the next pad, which truly did look like it was entirely too far for me to jump to.

Still, I had to try. Even if I wasn't going to see any hard numbers out of this, getting to the end would be an impressive feat in and of itself.

So, I backed up to the edge of the pad and took a single step toward the edge. It was all of the running start I could get, but I managed to get my foot placed close enough to the edge that I could launch off it to get to the next pad, which I landed on belly-first, knocking the air out of me. I recovered for a moment and scrambled up onto the pad as I thought about how to do the next one.

Maybe it was like the balls on the cables: I had to keep moving to truly succeed. I again took a single step of a run to launch myself at the next pad. I landed belly first on that one, too. And the next, and the one after that. I don't know how I was supposed to be doing this, but there was no way this was it. But I kept going. I almost didn't make the leap to the last one and contemplated the distance down to the mat from this pad. That mat wasn't going to do much for an eight-foot fall—it'd still hurt like hell.

Except I didn't fall. I shook my head and pulled myself up. Next to this pad was the start of a heavy square balance beam that was set at an angle and made a wide curve around to the left. It was higher off the ground than even this last pad was. Beneath it, maybe nine feet down, was another pit of foam blocks, and at the far end of it was a wide ladder of big round pipes set up more like steps. I had to pull myself onto the beam to get up there, but I managed it.

And that was when I spotted it. On the long wall of the warehouse, near the adjoining wall, was a set of wide double doors. No keycard sensor, no chain. And the odds were good that it was an exterior wall, because how else would they get all of this equipment in here? I doubted they were likely to transport it through the maze of hallways.

"You'll find them locked, Ms. Kateri," said Mr. Loudspeaker. "And guarded as well, should you be strong enough to break the lock."

Of course they'd thought of that. I *was* a flight risk, after all. I raked a strand of hair back from my face with a frustrated sigh through clenched teeth.

Walking the beam itself wasn't terribly hard since

it was a little wider than my foot, which probably made it about six inches wide? It didn't really matter, I guess. I got to the end and took a step onto the pipe stairs, which lacked any sort of grip tape—forget workplace safety, I guess—and made my way down.

The next obstacle was a series of four walls set into frames. They were each about seven feet tall, and it looked like they were meant to slide up, but I didn't see any sort of pulley system to support that. Then I spotted the handles at the base of the walls. I was supposed to lift them and go under? I'd seen something like that in a video online.

Well, they couldn't be much heavier than four hundred or so pounds, right? I already knew I could lift that much, but I also knew that I had zero frame of reference for how much they should weigh. So I tried the first, which lifted with no trouble, revealing train springs set into the bottom corners so that it wouldn't smash into the ground when I released the wall.

Well, good. At least I didn't have to be gentle about it.

The second wall was heavier than the first, and thicker; the third wall was heavier and thicker still; but the fourth one stopped me altogether. I could only get about an inch of space between it and the ground before my grip failed me.

But I had to get past these, right? I looked up to the two-way mirror and chewed the inside of my cheek. The only way I was getting past this was to go around.

"Ah ah," Mr. Loudspeaker chided as I approached the side. "You must go through, not around."

My fists balled tight at my sides. "I can't even lift the damn thing!"

"Figure it out, Ms. Kateri."

TWENTY

I swear, it was a good thing that guy was where he was. I'm not usually the confrontational type, but I was tired of his bullshit.

But I also couldn't *do* anything about it. Not right now. I was only about a third of the way through the course, and I wanted to try the other obstacles. He wasn't worth my wasted energy and anger, a realization which actually helped me to calm down some.

I turned my attention back to the fourth wall. I bent to grip the bottom and lift, but despite making sure my grip was as secure as I could possibly manage, I still only got the wall about an inch off the ground before it tore from my hands. I shook the sting and ache out of my hands as I looked back at the wall.

Can't go under like I'm supposed to. Can't go around. Then it looks like I'm going over. And if Mr. Loudspeaker didn't like it, he could sedate me.

If he could catch me.

I wondered if he could even complete this course.

I shook my head. No time for the contemplation of that. I jumped for the top ledge of the wall and pulled myself up. It was dirty and dusty from however long it'd been here without being cleaned. In the dust was the wild scent like the nurse, like Grump and Blondie, like Curly and Baldy.

Which meant they'd likely gone through this course, hadn't they? So, it followed that Mr. Loudspeaker likely had too, if he was anything like them.

No time for that. I filed the thought away in my brain and hopped from the wall only to find myself facing another series of walls. These were shorter, set closer together but offset from one another, and the top corners were taken off. There was a black arrow painted on the ground. It ran along the bottom edge of the one closest to me and then curled around the corner.

Oh! I had to weave through them. That was easy.

It was close, tight enough that Grump would've had to shimmy sideways to get through, which would slow him down.

Well, let's see how fast I could do this then. I weaved through the rest of the walls, following the arrows, and came around the end to a pile of tires as tall as the walls I'd just weaved through. I picked my way up and over to another set of four walls, these spaced further apart with a waist-high bar in between them. Another black arrow traced over the top of one while the next ran straight on the ground under the bar.

Over-under, then? I shrugged and tried it. Again, I suspected someone beefier like Grump would have had a harder time, and while my height definitely meant I had to crouch lower than the nurse or Blondie would have had to, it still wasn't terribly hard.

Past the last bar was a heavy climbing rope that was the only way to get up to the monkey bars next to it. So I climbed. I had always been good at that; I was the speed climber in phys ed in middle school. Turned out I still had it—I was up the rope in a flash.

But the start of the monkey bars was farther away than I had initially estimated. And these weren't the typical monkey bars from an elementary school playground. These sloped up and down a couple of times before their end at a pair of inclined ramps set one after the other. I was going to have to get a little higher on the rope to be able to make it. With a grunt, I launched myself from the rope, caught the first of the bars, and made my way across. I had to swing on the last one, so I could drop onto the first of the ramps, but I landed easily and started toward the edge.

"Remember, we're timing you," said Mr. Loudspeaker. "You and I both know you're capable of more speed than this."

I pressed my lips into a line. I hadn't forgotten, but I was still trying to make sure I understood the assignment. I sped up as I landed on the second ramp, which took me to another black platform with a thick, heavy cargo net suspended between it and another black platform on the far side. The net went around a bend halfway through, and there was another pit of black foam blocks underneath, though I felt like you'd have to be trying to fall on this. I picked my way across the net on my hands and knees. It wasn't entirely unlike picking my way around a tree, the way the net gave way under my feet. But as I got to the platform at the end of the ropes, I looked to the next obstacle: a set of three bars set up like a trapeze, only they were solid u-shaped bars, with the bottom flattened out. They were fixed to the top of their frame with a couple of links of heavy chain. The problem, however, was that they were set impossibly far apart.

Except, like the uneven pads early in the course, the implication was that I was capable, wasn't it? And

I *had* made those jumps, even if I'd had to scramble to keep from falling off the pads.

So, I took a step back and then forward again, jumping and reaching for the first bar. It didn't do anything strange, and I sighed with relief. I swung back and forth a few times to get myself as close as I could to the next bar, and tried to time my jump for it at the apex of the swing.

And I made it!

The relieved sigh as I gripped the second of the bars came with a little bubble of excited laughter. Holy shit, I had this!

I swung again and jumped for the third bar, which released from a catch as my weight settled onto it. My grip came loose as it swung toward the three rows of cubes set on thick pipes beyond. I, however, dropped into the pit of foam blocks.

Dammit!

The bar that had dropped me reset, pulling back into place with thin cables on a winch, like those retractable dog leashes. Instead of watching it, I analyzed what needed to happen, ignoring Mr. Loudspeaker's voice as he gave more instructions. I had to jump from the second bar and make sure I was gripped tight for the drop. Then I'd have to time it, so I dropped onto the cubes instead of landing in the foam blocks.

Difficult, but certainly not impossible.

I turned to go back to the black platform at the beginning of the bars. There were canvas straps anchored to the side, like a ladder, which I was able to use to get back up to the top. Better than jumping for it, that was for sure.

Back atop the platform, I jumped for the first bar and swung back and forth a few times before launching myself at the second bar. There, I hung for a second, gathering myself. Then, with a sharp blown-out breath, I made the jump for the third bar. I squeezed my eyes shut as my weight settled onto it and the catch released, but remembered at the last second that I was going to have to time this bit and opened my eyes again to try to get the landing right.

When my feet hit the first of the cubes on the pipes, it started to rotate, and I had to readjust my weight to stay on top. Doing so put me onto the second set of cubes, so I just kept moving. There was a timer going, after all.

On the far end of the cubes was another ramp, this one leading down and into a low black tunnel that curved around to the left. I had to crouch and crawl like a baby to get through it, which meant anyone bigger than me would have to practically drag themselves on their elbows.

As I emerged at the other end, I faced another set of walls, all about seven feet tall. The first had a big square opening, like a window, in the middle of it, and a black arrow indicated that my path was to go *through* the window. Each of the subsequent six walls also had windows, though they were all at different placements on the wall—some toward the left, some toward the right, with a couple in the middle. The walls were spaced far enough apart that I had to get entirely through one window, taking a step onto the concrete of the warehouse floor before I could go through the next. Still, it wasn't hard, just a bunch of crunching and redirecting.

Beyond that was a long stretch of black turf and a ball launcher, only this one had a hopper with footballs in it. A big grey button on the side of the machine had the word "PUSH" in block letters around it, and when I did as it said, a football launched toward the two baskets at the end of the turf. Except the ball fell decidedly short, and I furrowed my brow. At the end of the turf was a huge curved wall that reached toward the ceiling of the warehouse. It was like a half-pipe for skateboarders turned on its side.

"Tick, tock," said Mr. Loudspeaker.

Yeah, yeah. I blew out a breath. Hmm. Well, it looked like I had to get the football into one of the baskets, but the baskets weren't even sitting on the turf, and the ball launcher was bolted to the warehouse floor. And I wasn't even sure how I was supposed to get up that half-pipe. Maybe at a run?

Run.

It was like a light bulb in my brain. Launch the football, run for it to gather momentum, catch the ball, drop it in the basket on my way toward the half-pipe, and maybe, just *maybe*, I'd have the momentum I needed to get to the top of that thing. Again, the implication was that I was capable, wasn't it?

And I'd never know if I didn't try.

So, I hit the button and started running. I bobbled the catch on the football, but managed not to drop it as I continued running toward the half-pipe. I had to slow down a little to drop the ball into the basket, but sped up again and ran up the half-pipe wall with barely any effort at all. I grabbed the top ledge, which was wide and rounded like a firm pool noodle had been attached around the edge to keep people from bonking their heads on the upper corner. But it made for a fantastic grip point, and I pulled myself up. If I jumped from up here, I could've easily brushed the crossbars of the support structure for the ceiling. There were some platforms down from here that put me back at the starting cargo net ramp, indicating that this was a course to be repeated on a loop.

I settled my hands on my hips as I caught my breath for a moment and looked down on the obstacle course from this higher vantage point. If speed was the key, I could probably just go over the top of a lot of the obstacles. With a nod, I turned and looked over at the two-way mirror. I wished I could see through it, see the face of Mr. Loudspeaker.

Who cleared his throat over the intercom as I studied the mirror.

I arched an eyebrow and flipped him the bird before turning back toward the way down. They were tall jumps with wide landings, so I was relatively sure I didn't need to hang from the top of one to drop onto the next. Instead, I just jumped down, landing lightly at the bottom.

TWENTY-ONE

I JUMPED as the air horn sounded at almost exactly the same time my feet hit the ground.

"Faster this time," Mr. Loudspeaker ordered.

And, as much as I wanted to tell him off, to just sit on the floor and refuse, I actually *did* want to see how fast I could do it. Only I hadn't seen a clock anywhere.

I looked at the nurse, because at least I could see her face. "How am I supposed to know what time to beat?"

"We're keeping records," she answered.

"Which is your bullshit way of telling me you're not going to tell me anything useful about my own capabilities," I retorted, my hands curling into fists again.

And then that damn air horn went off again, just as the ringing in my ears from its last sounding had cleared.

The nurse gestured toward the first cargo net with an open hand.

God*damm*it. I shook my head as I started for the net.

Up and over the net, through the foam blocks, and I lightly bounced across the egg-shaped balls on cables. It felt good to still have the rhythm of that one in me. I made my way across the cages but still scrabbled at the angled pads, though not as badly as I had the first time through. The balance beam was as easy as it had been, as were the big pipe steps. Again I lifted the first three walls, and again I went over the fourth before weaving through the offset walls. Tire mountain was no trouble, and the over-under walls and pipes barely slowed me down. I recovered some time on the rope climb, and continued on across the uneven monkey bars. The ramps were as easy as the mountain of tires, as was the high cargo net traverse. I eyed the third of the trapeze-like bars as I leaped for the first one, and I was ready for it when I got there, holding tight as it released and letting go at the apex of the swing. I easily hopped across the blocks on pipes and loped down the ramp to almost dive into the low tunnel. Emerging from it, I quickly got through the windows—center, left, right, left, center, left, right—before launching the football. I didn't bobble it this time and barely slowed even a step as I dropped it into the basket on the way to the half-pipe wall. I bounced down the platforms on the other side and winced as the air horn sounded again when my feet hit the ground.

"Again," said Mr. Loudspeaker. "Faster."

I chewed the inside of my lip and surveyed the obstacle course. I wasn't sure I could do it faster. Except to go over like I'd seen should be possible from the top of the half-pipe.

That damn air horn sounded again, but I used the jolt of it to launch myself at the cargo net. I skipped a few of the oblong balls this time through, jumping instead onto every other one while still landing on the last with the ability to jump for the cages. Those damn angled pads—the leap pads, as I'd dubbed them—still left me scrabbling for purchase, but at least I didn't fall. I crossed the balance beam, went down the pipe stairs, and simply went over the walls I was supposed to lift.

Actually, what I did was pull myself to the top of the first and hop to the second, third, and fourth, before jumping down to go through the weaving walls. After going up and over tire mountain, I did a similar thing with the over-under walls and bars as I had with the lifting walls, hopping from the top of the wall onto the bar and then up onto the wall beyond it and the bar beyond that. The rope climb was never going to be a slow point for me, but instead of jumping from it to hang underneath the monkey bars, I instead landed on top of them and took big, wide steps, placing a foot on each of the bars as I went across.

It wasn't a far cry from moving among tree branches, just without the central trunk to anchor myself against.

I dropped onto the last of the monkey bars to reduce the jump height from them to the ramps, and went across the cargo net at much the same speed as I had the monkey bars. The trapeze swings, by comparison, felt slow, but I made up the time as I swung onto the blocks on pipes, where I was able to skip some of the blocks like I had the oblong balls on cables. I didn't bother to dive for the tunnel, but ran on top of it. The walls with the windows had little roof-like overhangs, so it seemed unwise to try to go over them. I hadn't felt like the windows were slowing me down anyway, so I just went through them.

Then I was on the home stretch. I hit the button for the football, caught it, deposited it in its rightful basket, and kept going.

As my feet hit the ground on the other side of the platforms after the half-pipe wall, the air horn sounded again, and I turned to look at the mirror window.

"Again," said Mr. Loudspeaker. "Fas—"

"Why should I keep doing this for you?" I demanded.

I expected the air horn as an answer, but the silence was more telling. I looked over my shoulder at the nurse, whose arms were now folded across her chest.

"How do you think we got our hands on that particular copy of that particular book, Ms. Kateri?" Something dangerous slid into Mr. Loudspeaker's tone.

My spine turned to ice again. "You were in my house, in my room."

"As has been explained to you," Mr. Loudspeaker said, a smile clear in his voice—which only deepened the dangerous feel of his tone, "there are consequences for non-compliance. Now, get moving."

The air horn sounded again. I winced, but did not move.

"Consequences," I said. "Like what?"

"What is it the young folk like to say these days?" There was no mistaking the implicit threat threading through his words, and the smile had disappeared from his tone. "Oh yes. 'Fuck around and find out.' Now cease wasting your energy on aught but the course. Tick. *Tock.*"

I debated my options as my hands balled into fists again. Punching that asshole in the face was right out, since it was clear I'd likely never see it. If I refused to continue on, they would probably just sedate me and take me back to my room, and who knew if I'd ever get the chance to go through this again.

I couldn't deny that the course itself was fun. But I also wasn't interested in giving these assholes a whole lot more information about what I could or couldn't do. Not that I had any clue myself. It was becoming apparent to me that—leopard aside—I was not at all just your average twenty-year-old girl.

"Ms. Kateri." Mr. Loudspeaker's tone was a warning.

I needed as much information about myself as I could get if Val and Andy and I were going to get out of this place. I had to know how much I could take.

So, I launched myself at the course again. I still skipped some of the oblong balls on cables, but I didn't scrabble as much this time at the leap pads. I lifted those first three walls, as was intended, but still couldn't get the fourth to budge more than an inch or so. So, I went up and over that one. I did the over-under walls and bars as intended, and did the same for the monkey bars, and the tunnel when I got to it.

The air horn sounded again at the end, and Mr. Loudspeaker didn't hesitate.

"That could have been your fastest yet, had you not wasted so much time at the start. Again."

My fastest yet? Despite going over on some of them the run before? I guess anger really was a good fuel.

Another obnoxiously loud blast of the air horn, and I was off again, leaning into the frustration of being held by people who obviously knew more about what I was capable of than they were letting on. I leaned into the anger of the violation of them being in my house, in my *room*, just to show me they were capable of such a thing.

The football I dropped into the basket on this run was a little squishier than the others had been.

The air horn sounded at the end of that run.

"Good," praised Mr. Loudspeaker. "Keep up that pace. Again."

Again. The air horn blared. This place was a maze. Even if my friends and I did escape our hallway, who knew how long it would take us to get from our cells to outside?

So, fine. I'd see how long I could keep running this course.

The air horn at the end of the run had barely ceased as my hands hit the cargo net ramp again. It didn't even sound to signal the start. Which was curious in and of itself, but not curious enough to make me stop.

I ran the course nine more times before I even felt winded. There was no way that was normal. And there was no way I was going to learn what that actually meant.

Five more runs, and the exhaustion started kicking in. My limbs were heavy with the exertion, but I kept going. I wanted to know where my fail point was.

I fell off one of the leap pads this run and was slow to get up. It only hurt because of how tired I was. The mat underneath was remarkably good at absorbing the hit. But it meant I had to go all the way back to the platform before the oblong balls on cables to get back up to where I had been.

I managed not to fall off the balance beam, but I could only lift two of the four lifting walls, and I fell three times trying to get to the blocks from the trapeze bar that released from its catch.

I was so tired, I largely ignored the air horn as I dropped from the last platform after the half-pipe wall. But I pushed myself toward the cargo net ramp anyway.

This run, I fell off the pads twice, and I could only lift the first of the lifting walls. The trapeze bar that released from its catch dropped me five times.

The air horn blew as I made my way back to the platform to start the trapeze bars again.

I furrowed my brow in confusion.

"Enough," said Mr. Loudspeaker.

I was halfway up the side of the platform and pulled myself onto the top to sit for a moment. I wanted to finish the run, but my legs felt like jelly, and my shoulders felt too loose in their sockets.

"Let's get you cleaned up and fed," the nurse called from across the warehouse.

My stomach growled at the mention of food.

And then I realized where I was and looked over my shoulder at the double doors. They were only about ten feet away—an easy dash.

Blondie and Grump and the nurse were still on the other side of the warehouse.

"Still locked and guarded, Ms. Kateri," said Mr. Loudspeaker.

I looked at the lifting walls and remembered what I knew from the bench press. Over four hundred pounds. What lock would hold under four hundred pounds of pressure?

I looked back at the double doors. I couldn't just leave Val and Andy. Even if he *was* crazy, which I definitely wasn't sure he was, he didn't belong here. And if I got out those doors without them—

"Your exit is this way, Ms. Kateri," a deep voice said.

I turned back to see who was speaking.

Grump held a handgun, steady as a rock in his grip.

And it was aimed at me.

TWENTY-TWO

My heart rate spiked as another rivulet of ice drew a frosty finger down my spine and I stilled, controlling my breathing to keep my chest from heaving.

Grump was the one who'd spoken. I remembered his voice from the pickup at Saint Dymphna's. And his golden eyes watched me with implacable grimness.

I swallowed thickly and slowly raised my hands in surrender.

"Down," he said, keeping the gun steady. "Now."

I peeled my eyes from his gun and looked over the edge of the platform. Like nearly every wall in the obstacle course, it was only about seven feet high, but there was no mat on the ground to soften that fall.

"I'll break a leg," I said, proud of myself for keeping the shake out of my voice. I'd never been held at gunpoint before. "Let me climb down." I kept my hands up, but pointed vaguely toward the canvas straps that formed the ladder on the side of this platform.

"You won't," said Mr. Loudspeaker.

Who wasn't intervening here. He'd let Grump take the shot.

"I won't ask again, Naiya," Grump said.

I met his eyes. No one here had called me Naiya before.

Wait. What he'd said before was a question?

No time to contemplate that. If I didn't move, he was almost certainly going to take the shot.

I swallowed thickly again and squeezed my eyes shut as I pushed myself off the top of the platform. I landed and rolled like someone out of an action movie, smoothly coming to my feet with the momentum of the fall and roll.

Holy shit. Turned out years of gymnastics as a kid did pay off.

"This way," Grump said, his gun still aimed at me.

My hands were still up. How the hell were my hands still up? I looked over my shoulder at the platform as I took a step toward Grump. Hell, that whole drop-land-roll thing had been instinct. I turned to look where I was going, stepping around the climbing rope and between the weaving walls and tire mountain.

What the hell was I?

Grump holstered his handgun as I got back over to the starting side of the warehouse.

"Showers are this way," the nurse said, beeping open the door we came in through.

I followed her, but Grump's eyes on the back of my head as he and Blondie took up their usual positions made my neck tingle. As we got farther from the obstacle course, the adrenaline from having a freaking *gun* aimed at me drained from my body, taking the lion's share of my energy with it. I was practically plodding along by the time we got to the showers. I listlessly grabbed clothes and towels from the shelves, and caught a glimpse of my reflection in the full-length mirror at the end of the row of shower stalls. My messy bun hung limply from the back of my head, and my shirt was sweat-darkened around the collar and under my armpits. I hurried into the shower stall to peel it all off me.

I swear I turned to jelly under the spray of hot water and groaned out my appreciation, only to remember that I wasn't the only one in here. Whoops.

And I'd forgotten to try to map the way from the warehouse. Dammit. I thumped my head against the tile wall.

"Ms. Kateri?" The nurse's concern was mild, but there.

"I'm fine," I said, pressing my forehead against the cool tile.

"Lunch is ready when you are," she said.

My stomach growled again at the mention of food. I hurried through the rest of my shower.

"Here," the nurse said, her hand appearing around the edge of the shower curtain as I turned off the water. She held out another small bundle of cloth.

I took it from her. Panties and a bra in my size. Fantastic. I pulled them on along with the sweats and t-shirt, and came out of the shower.

The shoes I'd been wearing had disappeared.

And I finally got it: it's harder to run—harder to escape—if you don't have anything protecting your feet. Gravel parking lots, broken glass from windows, even kicking in a door barefoot would hurt like hell.

Well, at least the shower had renewed me a little. I combed through my hair, adding some of the leave-in conditioner again and pulling a hair tie around my wrist for when my hair was dry.

Blondie opened the door and held it for the nurse and I. Grump joined us once again as the nurse started walking. She took me a different way than she'd taken me last time, after the treadmill. I couldn't be terribly sure of it, though, not in this maze, but it definitely felt different. It was hard to concentrate on the directions with how heavy all of my limbs were. The ache had mostly gone, which was a wonder in and of itself, but my shoulders were still too loose, my legs too heavy.

After a few turns, she beeped open a doorway to a cafeteria. It was a different one than the one she took me to last time, though it was a mirror image of it. There were people bustling about in the kitchen this time, pots and dishes clanging and scraping as they worked.

Lunch was chicken fried steak and mashed potatoes with cream gravy. God, did it ever smell good. My mouth started to water as the nurse gestured to the single place setting at one of the long tables. Grump and Blondie took up seats on the table next to that one, behind and to either side of the place setting.

I sat down slowly, unsure how to feel about Grump being basically within arm's reach of me. I narrowed my eyes as I studied him. His eyes had darkened a bit, or maybe it was just the way the light was hitting them. They definitely had seemed more golden in the warehouse. He still wore his typical scowl, though, and his demeanor seemed largely unchanged from what it had been, outside of the incident on the obstacle course.

"Something wrong?" the nurse asked, placing a cup of water next to the tray.

I jerked my chin toward Grump and addressed him directly. "You pulled a gun on me."

"Tranq gun," he said, his expression flat. His eyes flicked over my head, and he crossed his arms as he leaned back against the table behind him.

"Simply a precaution," the nurse added.

Tranq gun. As in tranquilizer. He'd only have sedated me, not freaking killed me. Not that it made the encounter any less scary because I certainly hadn't known that at the time, but it made it easier to have my back to him again. I rolled my eyes with a sigh and turned around in my seat.

The nurse had already uncovered my plate, but where I had expected to see country fried steak, there was instead a salad of dark leafy greens with grilled chicken strips, cubed hard-boiled egg, slices of avocado, and large chunks of bacon on top. Four cups of dressing sat on the tray next to it: two each of ranch and Italian.

I furrowed my brow. "A salad?"

The nurse pointed over her shoulder as she sat across from me. "Chicken fried steak is dinner," she said.

Honestly? I was too tired and too hungry to care. It was nice to know something ahead of time for once, though.

I poured both cups of Italian dressing onto my salad before tossing it around and mixing it with my fork. As expected, the nurse didn't have any questions for me, and I ate in relative silence, but for the noise of the kitchen staff.

When I was done, the nurse beeped open the door and led the way yet again into the maze of hallways. She left us only a turn or two in, and Blondie took the lead as I tried to remember the path. Down the hall from the cafeteria, second right, keycard door, take the first left … but I lost it after that. I was just too tired. My limbs all hung like lead weights, and I had to concentrate not to trip over my own two feet as we made our way back.

Eventually, Blondie beeped open the door for the hallway where my cell was, and Val and Andy greeted me as I came back. I think I returned their greetings. I'm pretty sure Val had something to say about how tired I looked, but I didn't really process it. Blondie beeped open the door to my cell, and I flopped onto my freshly made bunk before the door had even clicked closed again.

Without moving my head, I looked at the clock on the wall. 1:38 in the afternoon. I'd been gone … hmm … nope, brain wouldn't math at the moment.

The light went off in my room, and I fell into a dreamless sleep.

TWENTY-THREE

SOMETHING SNARLED at me in my sleep, waking me as a soft beep came from somewhere beyond my feet. The light was on. It filtered through my closed eyelids. I squinted my eyes open as someone deposited another covered tray onto my shelf.

Was that Curly? Or Baldy?

I wiped at my face with a quiet groan as I sat up. Nothing ached, but the weariness of exertion was still there. I looked up at the clock. It was just after seven in the evening, and though the light was on in my room, it was still noticeably darker than the hallway.

"You weren't gone all day this time," Andy said as Curly closed the door to his cell.

I heaved myself to my feet and plodded over to the tray as Curly beeped open Val's door.

"They probably expected me to go for longer," I said.

"Doing what?" Val asked.

"Did you ever see that show with the crazy obstacle course in reds and blues?"

"Yeah," she replied. "Something Ninja Warrior, right?"

I nodded and shot a finger gun her way before pulling my tray from the shelf. "That's the one. They put me on something that was three or four times the length of the one on the show and had me run it over and over."

"You managed to get all the way through it?" Andy sounded surprised.

I had been about to sit on the bed with my tray, but his question implied he knew what I was talking about. I stopped and turned toward my window. "They put you on it, too?" It shouldn't have surprised me, given that he'd been on the treadmill and the resistance machine that simulated a benchpress.

He came to his door. "They tried. But I couldn't get from the balls on metal ropes to the platforms after."

I nodded, my gaze losing focus. "I got through the whole thing, except for one of the lifting walls, a number of times."

"In a row?" Val sounded impressed.

I guess she should be. I probably would be if it were her that'd run the course.

"Yeah." I turned back to my bed and sat down as I tried to remember how many times I ran the course. Was it fifteen? Mmm, no. It had to be more than that. "I think it was probably something like twenty or so times I got through it. They kind of all blurred together in the middle."

"Jesus fuck," Val said. It sounded like she'd flopped onto her bed.

"That's quite impressive," Andy said. "You'd make a great adventurer in my world."

I smiled with a quiet little chuckle, my cheeks heating at the compliment. "Thanks."

God, I was like a little schoolgirl! I flopped back onto my bed. Don't even think about trying to hook up here, dumbass. Never mind that there were cameras everywhere, I couldn't even fathom how I'd manage to get out of my own room, let alone this facility.

But if we could, maybe there'd be a spark. Would it be selfish to want both Val and Andy? I tossed the blue ball into the air and caught it, repeating the process again and again as I let my mind wander down that path for a bit.

"Hey Andy," I called, not moving from my bed. "Any idea what else they might try to put me through?"

"I'm not sure," he said. "I'm not like you, so I don't know how much of what they did for me they'll do for you. As I mentioned before, they'd gotten to the point that they largely left me alone but for the occasional wash-up."

"What else did they do to try to learn about you?" Val asked.

"They tried starving me," he said. "That was unpleasant. And they tested my physical capabilities again after some time without food."

"Those pieces of shit," Val said.

"How long?" I asked.

"Four days," he said. "I still had water, though."

Four days without food. I didn't relish the thought of that possibility.

"Here's to hoping they don't try that with me," I said, though I had a sneaking suspicion that was a fruitless hope.

"They also had me lay down inside this machine that made a lot of different sorts of noises," Andy said. "It kind of sounded like a trilling bird sometimes, but there was also something that sounded a bit like a small bellows, like you'd use to blow air on a fire."

I wasn't sure what kind of machine he was talking about. I tossed the ball again as I thought.

"Did they ask you if you had any piercings or jewelry?" Val asked.

"Yes," Andy said. "But I don't."

"Probably an MRI, then," Val said. "I've had one of those. They're basically scanning your physiology."

I nodded, catching the ball and just holding it. "Huh. That's not something I've experienced."

"It's annoying," Val said. "You have to sit still for a long time, and it's noisy."

"I don't have trouble sitting still," Andy said. "I do a lot of meditation."

Well that's interesting, I suppose.

"How come?" I asked.

"It's how I focus," he replied. "A lot of my work at home requires me to have a very ordered mind."

I sat up on the bed, though I couldn't see him from where I sat. "What kind of work?"

"I told you before," he said. "I meddle in the boundaries between planes of existence, studying how they work and how to make travel between them more efficient."

"And that pays the bills?" Val asked.

"I don't really have bills," Andy said. "Not like what I've seen in some of the daytime television shows. I have to gather things to eat and such, but my lifestyle back home is not at all like what I've seen since being here."

"Most people don't live like what's on TV," Val said.

"But it sounds nice and simple," I said. "Certainly quieter than how people live here."

Andy continued to tell us about his home then. It sounded a lot like someone from a fantasy novel might live, down to the travel by horseback or wagon ride and sleeping under a canopy of stars next to a campfire. He talked about the planes of existence too, and how—where he's from—the planes were almost like stacked sheets of paper. He explained that they overlaid each other in some areas, and that you could see it if you know what you're looking for.

It all sounded terribly fantastical.

As the nurse had promised at lunch, dinner was—in fact—chicken fried steak. A pile of mashed potatoes was on the plate too, alongside some steamed broccoli, and all of it was smothered in creamy country gravy. A pair of dinner rolls and a small bowl of baked apples accompanied the meal on the tray.

I swear, the food was the only thing this place had going for it.

And then I remembered Grump's tranq gun.

"Did you know that a tranquilizer gun looks exactly like a handgun?"

"That can't be right," said Val.

I rolled a shoulder as I cut a piece of steak and scooped some mashed potatoes onto the fork with it. "Grump's sure looked like one to me."

"Grump?" Andy asked.

The corner of my mouth pulled up. "No one's given me their name, so I've come up with my own."

"Which one is Grump?" Val asked.

"You know the two who came with the nurse to get me after breakfast?"

"Which one's the nurse?" Andy asked.

"The lady with the bun at the back of her head," I replied. "With the white coat?"

"So is Grump the lady with the ponytail?" Val asked. "Or her partner?"

"Her partner," I said. "The lady with the ponytail is Blondie."

"*Super* original," Val said around a bite of food.

"Who are the men who deliver our meals?" Andy asked.

"Baldy and Curly," I replied.

"So Grump pulled a tranq gun on you?" Val had another bite of food in her mouth.

"Yep." I placed my tray on the bed next to me and stood to refill my cup with water from the sink.

"Why?"

"I think I found an external door. But before you get excited, I couldn't keep track of where it was from here. It was in the warehouse with the obstacle course." I gulped down half the water in the cup and refilled it before sitting back down on the bed.

"And likely heavily guarded," Andy said.

I nodded. "Probably."

"Did you try to leave?" Val's voice was quiet.

I stared at my food for a moment. "I thought about it," I said, just as softly.

"What stopped you?" Andy asked.

I looked across the hall from my vantage point on the bed as Andy came into view. "I couldn't just leave you two here. You guys are keeping me from losing my mind."

Andy blinked.

"Of course you can leave us," Val said. "You should. You can get out and—"

"And what, Val?" I clanked my plastic fork and knife to the tray. "Go get help? From where? Who would believe me?"

"I dunno," Val said with a huff. "You said your parents were rich, right? Maybe they have some contacts."

I shook my head. "I'm not leaving without you, Val." My tone softened. "The only reason you're here is because of me."

"Not me," Andy said, snapping my attention to those too-dark eyes of his.

I shook my head. "No. But you don't belong here anyway. If everything you've said is true—"

His head cocked to the side, and his expression turned quizzical. "You don't believe me?"

I chewed my cheek for a moment. "I think … there's too much I can't explain to dismiss it."

His eyes narrowed. "That's not the same."

"I know." I looked away, back toward my tray in my lap. "I want to believe," I said. "I want there to be another world adjacent to this one where magic is real and …"

"But you don't," Andy said. And the disappointment in his voice made my heart ache.

I looked up as he turned away from his window. "I just wish I could see it."

Andy's tray clanked onto his shelf.

"I don't *not* believe you," I said lamely. And it was true, He had seemed terribly genuine when speaking about it all, and the level of detail he had gone to suggested to me that he wasn't simply making it all up on the fly.

He flopped onto his bed. Or at least, it sounded like he did.

"So, let me get this straight," Val said. "The guy pulled a gun on you for *thinking* about trying to escape? What is he, a mind-reader?"

"I don't think so," I said. "I think he did it because I stared at the door for too long."

I picked at the food on my tray, but I didn't want it anymore.

"I didn't mean to hurt you, Andy," I said softly.

"A girl who turns into a leopard has a hard time believing the guy she's locked in some research facility with is actually from another reality like he says he is," Andy said, his tone wry.

Well, when he put it like that … I mean, I clearly wasn't just a normal human girl, was I?

I placed my tray back on the shelf and moved to stand at the window of my door. Andy was lying on his bunk, his left arm thrown over his eyes. He had three black bands tattooed around the thickest part of his forearm. I hadn't seen them until now.

God, we'd been here how many days now? I leaned back and looked at the clock. Sunday, May

31st. And I'd arrived on Thursday. It had only been four days.

"Will you show me?" I asked him, keeping my voice soft. "If we get out of here?"

I very literally could have heard a pin drop at the far end of the hall in the oppressive silence that followed. But then Andy stirred from the bed.

He stood and came back to his door. "*When* we get out of here." He pressed his tattooed fist to his chest and nodded once, his intense gaze never leaving mine. "It would be my honor."

TWENTY-FOUR

I EVENTUALLY ATE my dinner rolls and baked apples, but that was after another nap that lasted until sometime after the lights had been turned off for the night.

When I went back to sleep after my snack, the leopard stalked me again. It chased me across the grounds of my family's house on Lake Texoma, cornering me on the little dock where my father's boat was moored. I woke with a start as I splashed into the water in my escape attempt.

The hallway was still dark, along with my room, and my cup on the nightstand was empty. I stood to refill it, my steps silent as I listened for Val and Andy. A glance at the clock told me it was nearly three in the morning, so I was sure the two sets of soft rhythmic breaths were them.

The faucet was blessedly quiet, but even so, I didn't turn it on full blast. I didn't want to wake them. It gave me time to think, but that turned fruitless in a hurry.

I had no way of knowing whether my parents were ever coming. I had no way to be sure of what I was actually capable of. I had no way to make sure I even had shoes, so even if I *could* manage to remember a way to an external door, I'd barely get anywhere barefoot.

Cold water splashed over my hand, breaking my train of thought. I quickly turned the faucet off. I grabbed the towel and wrapped it around my wet hand as I took a big gulp from the too-full cup, pacing over to my door with silent steps as I did.

There was a rustle next door, and Val's breathing changed rhythm as she shifted in her sleep. Across the hall, Andy lay on his back with his arm behind his head. Chad, in inanimate crystal form, was placed on his chest. I watched the rise and fall of Andy's breathing for a moment, taking another sip of my water.

He seemed entirely too with it to be crazy. But what he'd said about another world, and the words and language he used like they were as natural to him as breathing—it was just too fantastical to be true. Even if I wanted there to be a world like that, how on Earth could he possibly have come from there? Still, something in my gut told me he wasn't lying.

Making a face, I turned back toward my bed. Whether he was lying or not didn't really matter if we didn't find a way out of this place. I set my cup on the nightstand with a barely audible clunk of plastic on metal, and sat on the bed.

Maybe I could steal a sedative needle from the nurse? Hmm. I'd need at least two. That was the least amount of people I'd seen in our hallway at any given time.

I laid down on the bed and stared into the dark.

Did she always carry three needles like she had that one day? How many needles could I get from her before she noticed and ruined the plan? Not many, I suspected. I'd probably be lucky to get even one.

Dammit.

I was gonna have to be more patient, more aware.

Count the halls and turns, and repeat them as I went. This place had to have fire exits, right? Maybe I could keep an eye out for those. Even if they were only subtly marked, they'd point the way to an exterior door, wouldn't they? They'd have to.

I nodded once to myself and tried to remember any of the paths I'd taken from this hallway. Pass a door and two lefts, then the first right? No. Wait. Two lefts, then a right past a door with a keycard.

I was pretty sure the only way we were getting through a keycard door was by force. There was no way the nurse or Grump or Blondie or any of them would fail to notice their keycard missing.

Did Grump even have one? I didn't think I'd seen him open a door.

Would the doors here even be able to handle the amount of strength I apparently had? If they had obstacles prepped for me like that, what were the odds that this whole facility was designed with someone like me in mind? Probably pretty high. I'd have to try my own door when no one was here. What would they do if I succeeded? Keep me sedated? How could they get any measures from me that way?

At some point, blackness took over as I fell into a dreamless sleep.

I woke to the lights coming back on in my room and glanced at the clock. Eight a.m. My room was still darker than the hallway, but too bright for my liking. I still had the towel wrapped around my hand. I draped it over my eyes and tried to go back to sleep.

I swear I barely blinked and the door at the end of the hall beeped open, followed by the clunk-clunk of the breakfast cart. Something sugary sweet and cinnamon-like wafted on the air along with the usual coffee aroma.

I didn't bother to move until I heard the tray slide onto the shelf and the click of my door shutting.

Then, I peeled the towel from my eyes and squinted at the shelf as I pulled myself to my feet.

Andy nodded to me as I reached the shelf. "Good morning."

I caught a full-body glimpse of him as Baldy delivered his meal. I couldn't be sure how tall he was, but I got the impression he was somehow both skinny and solid. His white tee was snug against his skin, while his dark blue sweatpants were loose.

I grabbed the plastic coffee mug and raised it in greeting. "Mornin'."

I shook off the passing wonder of what his butt looked like as I tore open two of the sugar packets at once and poured them into my coffee, ignoring the little cup of creamer. I tried to convince myself that the watering in my mouth was the anticipation of something other than water to drink, but apparently, the lack of human touch had me thirsty like a desperate chick at the club. Or maybe I just had a thing for guys with tattoos. Maybe that was my type? My cheeks warmed as my brain teased what it would be like to trace the black lines on his hand with my finger, to see where the pattern disappeared off to under his shirt.

Not helpful. Acting on any of that curiosity certainly wasn't going to be a thing here. And if we ever got out, the odds of us all sticking together anyway felt slim.

With a gulp of my coffee, I turned my attention to breakfast. A bowl of oatmeal with banana slices and a little pile of brown sugar sat in the center of my tray. Accompanying it was a little cup of blueberries, a couple of slices of buttered toast, and a small glass of orange juice.

Cup. It was a plastic cup. They didn't do glass drinkware here.

"Did you sleep alright?" Val asked as Baldy beeped open the door to her cell.

I took a sip of my coffee as Curly delivered her tray. "Who are you asking?"

"The only people I give a shit about here," Val replied. "You and Andy."

"I slept fine," Andy said. "I've slept in worse beds."

The door next to mine clicked closed, and the cart rolled back down the hallway, Curly and Baldy in tow.

"It was an uneventful night for me," I said. "I'm pretty sure you'd've heard if it wasn't."

The door at the end of the hall beeped open and, a moment later, clicked shut.

Over breakfast, Andy told us about the more simple things the people here had made him do, though they were largely physical tasks like lifting weights and swimming laps. Apparently, it only took a few days for them to figure out that he was just a regular guy here, cut off from the source of whatever magic he used to be able to do at home. He said it had something to do with there not being ley lines here, not like there were in Arcaniss. But, beyond whatever they thought Chad was, they largely seemed to have written Andy off before Val and I had arrived. It'd been over a week since he'd seen anyone beyond the meal delivery guys.

We played with the blue rubber ball with Chad, trying to see how many bounces we could get in before Chad caught up to it. Andy won the count on that one with a record forty-eight bounces. Val and I could only manage about twenty-five on average, though I did manage to get thirty-seven on one of the throws.

Over lunch—grilled chicken breast and wild rice—Val explained there was a subtle but distinct difference between a handgun and the tranquilizer gun Grump pulled on me. Apparently, if I'd ever seen a handgun anywhere outside of a holster, I'd have noticed the difference.

I wasn't so sure.

The afternoon game of fetch with Chad was about seeing how far we could throw the ball down the hall, trying to get it to make the fewest number of bounces before he caught up to it. Andy won that one too, and I couldn't help but think he had an unfair advantage, given his relationship with Chad.

By the end of the day, the ball was riddled with tiny pinprick holes from where the little crystalline spider had sunk his fangs in to hold it as he brought it back to us. I was impressed the ball hadn't started leaving little blue crumbs all over the place, but as I watched him, I realized that Chad was reusing his previous holes when he could manage it, manipulating the ball in his front legs until he found a set of marks that fit the angle he wanted.

Over dinner—a medium rare steak with a salad and a fully loaded baked potato—Andy told us more about Arcaniss. Aside from the magical creatures he described, which were like something straight out of a high-budget summer blockbuster movie, the world itself sounded a lot like ours was before we started building skyscrapers.

"There are tall buildings back home, too," he said. "Floating ones, too. But they're all made of stone with colored and cut glass in the windows."

"Wait," Val said. "*Floating* castles?"

"Sure," he replied. "For the most part, they are more defensible."

"And there's more than one of them?"

"Uh-huh." He bobbed his head. "There's a wizard near the coast that has a tower out over the water, but the most notable floating structure I'm aware of is the Adamo stronghold. That's where some of the biggest heroes of our time live. It's more like an entire floating city, now that I think on it."

"How does it stay up?" Val asked.

Andy shrugged. "Intricately complex enchantments is my guess. I have to assume they're overlapping and have a lot of redundancies in case someone built up the sort of power it would take to try to break any one of them."

"If I lived there," I said, thinking out loud, "or even *under* that, I think I'd be terrified of something coming along and just breaking all of the enchantments at once."

"I don't think you grasp the size of it," Andy said. "It's easily larger than this building, even with its labyrinthine corridors. I can't think of a single spell with an effective range large enough that it could even cover half of it. Not that I'm terribly well-versed in the way magic works, mind you, but the only one who ever even tried to take down the Adamo stronghold was Luca, and he had an army of spellcasters and dragons at his beck and call."

"What happened to him?" Val asked.

Andy paused a moment before answering. "He was … destroyed, his army routed."

I met his gaze across the hall, certain the curiosity was plain in my expression. "Did he deserve it?"

Andy was quiet another moment, contemplating. And then, in a blink, it was like a mask dropped from his face, anguish suffusing his expression so completely that I couldn't be sure he wasn't in physical pain. His too-dark eyes became endless voids, and he seemed to grow almost gaunt with whatever memory he'd conjured up for himself as he turned away from the window.

I pressed myself against my door, eyes wide. "Andy?"

"He did," he said finally, with a listless nod of his head. "He deserved it."

"What—?"

"Read the room, Val," I said, cutting her off as I relaxed. I wanted to know whatever it was that Andy had just remembered, but I wasn't about to ask him to relive that pain.

"He killed my parents," Andy said quietly, answering the question Val had started, his back still to the door. "My whole family. Right in front of me. He held me captive for …" He shook his head, but didn't look up, and his voice grew gravelly and threatened to crack. "He took countless others in much the same way. His *kenzihoaf levxieriv* twisted her fingers into my brain—"

I threw the ball at his door as hard as I could. The *thok* of it interrupted him, and he turned back to look at me with startlingly wide eyes that were decidedly darker than they'd been earlier in the day. I couldn't make heads or tails of the name of the thing that tortured him, but I understood by the way he spat the words what his meaning was. And I was sure of one other thing …

"He deserved it," I said, eyeing him meaningfully with a slow nod.

Tension released from his shoulders as he returned my nod with a slow heavy sigh.

And if nothing else thus far had convinced me of the truth of his story, that did. Andy was either an *extremely* skilled liar, or everything he'd said about where he came from and how he ended up here was true.

TWENTY-FIVE

We didn't talk for much of the rest of the evening, and I stared into the dark for over an hour after they turned the lights off. When I finally did sleep, I dreamed of impossible floating castles and fantastical creatures. I dreamt of magic and stories and a song just out of reach. I reached for it anyway, falling into fog and darkness where the leopard stalked me. I was sure something else was breathing with me and the predator in the impenetrable mist, but I was as scared to face it as I was to face the leopard.

I was saved by the breakfast cart. Or, at least, the sound of it.

And soon after I finished the breakfast casserole Curly and Baldy delivered, before even Andy or Val had finished theirs, the nurse came by with Grump and Blondie. She didn't have any shoes for me this time; she just asked me to follow her.

With a glance at the clock to note the time—nine o'clock in the morning—I shrugged and went along.

The silence between me and my companions had continued from the night before, but Andy nodded to me as I left my cell, and Val met my eyes as she raised a forkful of casserole in what I had to assume was a gesture of solidarity.

I concentrated on the route this time. Two

hallways down from the door at the end of the hall and a left. Then the first left and another keycard door at the end of the hall. We took a right and followed the hallway around two more rights before another keycard door on the left that opened into a hallway where the ceilings grew higher.

Was that the same hallway I'd been down before? That led to the obstacle course?

I repeated the directions back to myself. Two down and a left. First left. Keycard. Right, right, right, keycard through the last door on the left before the next bend. At the high ceilings, it was a left and then a right and another left, all through keycard doors.

Shit.

I pulled my hair from its tie and raked my fingers through it. There was no way I was going to be able to remember all of this without writing it down. And even if I *could* remember it between now and whenever I got back to my cell, I wouldn't have anything to write it on there aside from my book. Which did me no good because I didn't have anything to write *with*.

Dammit.

I didn't bother trying to repeat anything more. I just chewed on my lip in anticipation as I followed the nurse. I tried not to look over my shoulder at Grump again. He almost certainly didn't have his tranq gun aimed at me, but I could still feel his eyes on the back of my head, and I didn't like it. I pulled my hair back again, flipping it about in a way that would make any regular Joe on the street give me more space. But not Grump. I didn't give him the satisfaction of looking back to see his reaction, but since his quiet clothing rustle didn't even change rhythm, it clearly hadn't fazed him.

Great.

Eighteen or so turns later, the scent of

chlorinated water permeated the hallway before the nurse even opened the door. In the massive room beyond was an Olympic-sized lap pool. We'd come in on the long side, near the corner. There weren't any little diving platforms, nor were there any diving boards, but the lanes were marked with the typical floating blue and white balls on ropes as well as the black tile lines along the bottom of the pool. Despite the high warehouse ceilings with their gym lights buzzing overhead, the room was humid enough that I suspected the pool was at least slightly heated. Little plopping noises of water lapping at the edges of the pool echoed in the space. There was a huge mirror along the opposite long side of the room, with steel panels below it and a standing desk against it. On the desk were a clipboard and pen, along with some other items I couldn't see clearly enough to make out. I suspected at least one of them was a stopwatch.

I sucked my teeth. They were going to have me swim laps. Thank God for the swimming lessons my parents made me go through when my father bought the lake house.

"You'll change into a swimsuit in here," the nurse said, gesturing to one of two more doors along the same side of the room we came in on.

Locker rooms, probably. Or, at least, changing rooms.

I followed her in, with Blondie on my heels, though Grump stayed outside the door. There was a row of four large stalls separated with black curtains that ended a foot or so off the ground. All of the stalls were open, and a white plastic chair sat in each, though the first had a rolled towel with a folded black swimsuit on top.

"Let me guess," I said. "Change, please, and we'll get started? Today is swimming laps." I suppressed the urge to mimic her voice and what few mannerisms she used, but only barely.

"Nope," the nurse said, her expression flat. "It'll be mini-golf today, but we've run out of the proper uniforms, so this'll have to do." She nodded at the bundle.

Funny.

"I was unaware joking was permitted," I said, arching an eyebrow at her. "Are you sure you won't get fired for such unbecoming behavior?"

Her expression remained flat as her dark eyes met mine. "Please get changed, Ms. Kateri. As astute as you are, you should have figured out by now that stalling only delays the inevitable."

I pulled the curtain closed and did as she asked. The swimsuit was a modest one-piece that was a little more snug than I'd like, but not uncomfortably so. I wrapped the towel around me and tried not to be self-conscious of the fact that I hadn't shaved in … well, it'd actually only been a handful of days, hadn't it? What day was it? The first?

I last shaved the day I was discharged from Saint Dymphna's, which was on the 27th of May. That was only five days ago. Mmm, but my pits definitely weren't still smooth. And I definitely wasn't going to get a razor in this damn place.

The nurse gestured back toward the door, and I went. A handful of plastic chairs that matched the ones in the changing room were scattered around the perimeter of the pool, and I tossed my towel over the one next to the ladder at the corner opposite the door. The nurse had followed behind me, and I made a face at the mirror as I climbed into the pool. As I had guessed, the water was comfortably warm. This place must spend a damn fortune on electricity. Grump and Blondie took up positions at opposite ends of the pool, standing near the wall without leaning on it, each with their hands folded behind their backs.

"Please wait at the ladder a moment," the nurse said, continuing on toward the desk.

She looped a stopwatch around her neck and pulled a couple of other small bits from the desk before picking up the clipboard. Then she came over to me, a black wristband made of silicone extended in her hand toward me.

"Sensors to the inside of your wrist," she said.

I looped the black band on and turned it so the little flat silver sensors were on the inside.

She opened the clamp of the pulse oximeter and said, "Finger, please."

I did as she said, and she scribbled down the reading before tucking the instrument back into her pocket.

"Speed is not our concern today," she said. "This is an endurance test. You will swim laps until you can no longer, and you will swim some more beyond that."

I raised an eyebrow at her. "More than I can?"

She sighed and folded her hands across her clipboard. "Were you aware of any of your actual limitations before any of our testing?" Her tone told me she already knew the answer.

I pressed my lips into a line. "No."

"Then it follows that whatever you think you're capable of, you're mistaken. So yes. You will swim more than whatever your definition of 'cannot' is. Because ours is quite different."

"How do you know I can even swim at all?"

She smiled, but there was a feral hint to it. "Then we shall see how you flounder until you figure it out."

"You will start at the sound of the horn," Mr. Loudspeaker said, his voice from overhead making me jump.

I scolded myself for forgetting he would chime in.

The nurse gestured to the wall of the short side of the pool. "Hand on the edge, please." She picked up the stopwatch and placed her thumb on what had to be the start button before nodding once at the mirror.

The same air horn that had blown at the obstacle course sounded again.

I looked around the walls, hoping for a clock to track my time, but they were bare. There wasn't even one of those rescue poles hung on the wall, like you'd see at a commercial pool.

"Tick, tock, Ms. Kateri," Mr. Loudspeaker chided.

Yeah, yeah.

TWENTY-SIX

I SHOULD HAVE KNOWN they wouldn't let me have any indicator of my own progress. I pushed off the wall of the pool and got to swimming at a relatively lazy pace. If this truly was a test of endurance over speed, it would do me no good to use up all my energy right off the bat, right?

And if I wasn't going to be allowed to eyeball a clock now and again to track my progress, then I was going to count my laps. At each end of the pool, I made it part of my turn to tap the ledge before continuing on. I counted taps, but only got to twelve—or maybe that was thirteen?—before I lost count. I evened out my pace and tried to refocus on remembering the numbers as I tapped, repeating which number I was on with each stroke of my arms.

"Good job, Ms Kateri," the nurse said.

And I lost count again. Was that twenty-three? Or twenty-four?

Dammit.

I started counting again. I felt like I remembered the numbers better as I repeated them to myself on the way to the next tap. But trying to remember that and focus on breathing *above* the water got harder and harder with each lap.

I started to lose my rhythm on lap thirty-five, and,

a few—or maybe ten—taps later, I lost track again and had to start over.

"Remember to breathe," said Mr. Loudspeaker.

Goddammit! Was that sixteen? Or seventeen?

I shook my head on the next tap-and-turn and took a deeper breath, pushing the thought that he'd done that on purpose from my head as I started yet another count.

I was only eleven or twelve… maybe thirteen laps in when I lost count yet again.

Focus, Naiya! Don't let them get in your head!

At the next turn, I switched to swimming on my back, sucking in more air and exhaling the noise from my mind. It helped that the change in position and movement eased some of the burning ache that had started in my shoulders, though I hadn't really noticed that was happening until the change. A few more laps later, I switched back.

I alternated then: ten laps forward, ten laps on my back. Mr. Loudspeaker and the nurse didn't seem to mind, since neither scolded me for my choice, and it helped me to keep track better. Working that way, I got all the way up to seventy-eight before I realized I was skipping laps, only adding to the number when I turned on the ladder side of the pool. How long had I been doing that? I grunted and took another deep breath at the turn to clear my head again. And, of course, I started my damn count over again.

"Just relax," the nurse said as I passed her on count number …

Oh shit … thirty-two? Thirty-three?

"If you relax into a rhythm, you'll find you won't struggle as much."

One. Two. Except now, my shoulders and arms were on fire, as were my thighs.

Deep breath in. Slow breath out. Three. Four. Just

keep counting. Or what'd that little forgetful fish from that animated movie say? 'Just keep swimming?'

Five. Six. Not like I really had a choice. Seven.

Oh, but if *that* didn't light a fire in me. Eight. Nine. Ten.

I didn't bother to flip onto my back at the next turn. I just forced myself to keep count. Eleven. Tap. Twelve. Tap.

On and on I went. And when I lost track again, I just started over and kept going. I was slowing, and my muscles burned from the exertion, but I kept going. At the next lost count, I went back to switching every ten laps and managed to get up to fifty-seven when I took a breath and my mouth filled with water. Panic flooded my system as I scrambled for air, coughing and spluttering as I made my way to the ledge.

"Stay in the pool, Ms. Kateri." Mr. Loudspeaker's voice held a warning. "Recover, and keep going."

I tried to compose myself enough to make a face toward the window, but the nurse stepped between me and the reflection, eyeing me as I struggled to take a breath.

She bent down with the pulse oximeter clamp open, and I inserted my finger to let her get her stupid reading while I calmed the last of my coughs and wiped at my burning eyes. With a nod, she took it off and stood to write on her clipboard before picking up her stopwatch.

"Keep moving," she said, placing her thumb over one of the buttons before turning her attention back to me.

"I never swam so much in my entire life! You can't expect me to keep doing this."

"As a matter of fact," Mr. Loudspeaker said as the nurse moved away to stand at the top of the ladder, blocking my exit from the pool, "we *can* expect as much from you. And we do. And more."

One of the panels under the mirror slid out into the room. It reminded me of the kind you see at the drive-through for a pharmacy. The nurse stepped over to it and pulled something from the drawer.

"As has been explained to you," Mr. Loudspeaker continued, "there are consequences for noncompliance, Ms. Kateri."

The nurse held out to me what she'd pulled from the drawer, and my spine turned to ice despite the warmth of the pool. It was a wristwatch with a blocky square face and numbers on rotating belts within the face—a Devon Tread watch, much like my father's. I prayed it wasn't actually his, but as the nurse stepped closer, my heart sank. It was the right colors, and the band looked a little worn.

I steeled my face as I reached for the watch, squeezing my eyes closed as I hoped I wouldn't find what I thought I might when I flipped it over. The ticking of the watch was loud, even over the sounds of the water. And on the back was the familiar engraving: 'To the best father that didn't have to be.' This was not a watch just like my father's—it *was* the one that had been on his wrist every day for the past eight years. I swallowed around a lump in my throat as I closed my fist around the timepiece and brought it to my chest. It reverberated in my hand with each hard tick of the bands' movement inside.

"Consider how we might have come upon this—"

Something twisted in my gut as another layer of ice snaked down my spine, and my eyes snapped open in white-hot fury. "What did you do to him?"

Mr. Loudspeaker tsked at me. "Your father is safe, and if you continue your laps, he'll stay that way."

The nurse reached out a hand, her eyes on my father's watch.

I pulled my fist away and turned my rage-filled gaze on her.

"You *will* return the watch," Mr. Loudspeaker said, "that *we* may return it to its rightful owner."

There was movement across the room as I fought to restrain my rage, not daring to take my eyes from the nurse. Mr. Loudspeaker would have to come through a door to get out from behind the mirror, and Blondie and Grump had likely closed the distance to the pool, ready to sedate me and take the watch by force. But the nurse held my gaze with unwavering stoicism.

Squeezing my eyes shut to fight back the helpless tears that threatened, I let the watch tick a few more seconds in my closed fist before reluctantly handing it back to her.

"Good," praised Mr. Loudspeaker.

As I turned back to move to the head of the lane I'd been swimming in, Blondie and Grump moved back to flank the door after having made it only a step or two from the far edge of the pool. There was a clunk of metal on metal—likely my father's watch into the drawer. I started swimming again, not bothering to count. I was even slower than I had been, but I didn't stop. A handful more laps in, and something tense in my shoulders unwound while something twisted in my gut.

No.

I started counting my laps again.

Not here.

Three. Tap. Four. Tap.

Not now.

Seven. Tap. Eight. Tap.

Not like this.

At ten, I switched to my back again. Another ten, and I switched back. And on and on until my arms and legs shook with the exertion. My movements turned clumsy, and on the next turn, I got another lungful of water.

Again, the nurse put the pulse oximeter on me as I recovered. She did it wordlessly this time, nodding once to the mirror as I slumped against the side of the pool.

"Keep going," said Mr. Loudspeaker.

My whole body was on fire and ached with the exertion. "I can't."

"You're wasting your breath arguing," Mr. Loudspeaker replied.

I glared at the mirror. "If I go any further, I'll drown."

"Or so you think," he said. "But you were wrong on the bench, you were wrong on the treadmill, and you were wrong about the obstacle course."

I maintained my glare and did not move, sucking heaving lungfuls of air in as I clung to the side of the pool. He was right, of course. But whether he was right or not was irrelevant. I did not move.

Mr. Loudspeaker sighed into the microphone, and the nurse stepped over to the panel that had slid open before as it opened once again. "If you expect us to believe that you care not for your father, perhaps you'll care about this."

The nurse pulled something from the drawer and brought it over to me. Once again, the cold shiver of fearful anticipation and anger wrapped around my spine. She held a music box, identical to the one that sat on the nightstand on my mother's side of my parents' bed. It was a silly little thing, chintzy even, in gold-framed cut glass made to look like crystal. My father had brought it home from his business trip to Switzerland. The nurse wound the gear a few clicks, and the familiar tinkling of "The Way You Look Tonight" flooded my ears. It was odd hearing it in such an expansive space when I'd heard it tinkle from my parents' bedroom for as long as I could remember. It was their song—the one they'd danced to at their wedding, the one they played on repeat the day after resolving a fight, and the one my mother fell asleep to every night.

My vision blurred, and my breath hitched in my throat. My parents were so ridiculously in love. My mother must be struggling so hard to sleep without it. How long had these pieces of shit had this?

I slumped from the side of the pool, listlessly dripping back down into the water with only enough movement to keep me afloat.

"You goddamn bastards."

"In case it has not been made *abundantly* clear to you by now," said Mr. Loudspeaker, "you have no power here, Ms. Kateri. The sooner you comply, the sooner you finish the task at hand, the sooner you can get away from us for now and go back to your foolish plans of escape with your friends. Now. *Get. Swimming.*"

I was shaking, and I couldn't tell if it was from the adrenaline flooding my system over fear for the safety of my parents or if it was from the endless laps of the damn pool. I didn't know what these assholes could do to my parents, and I didn't want to find out. If I had to suffer to keep them safe, well, then I just had to suffer.

My limbs were like limp noodles as I made my way back to the lane. I had, at least, caught my breath, so there was that. I poured my anger and frustration and helplessness into the next set of laps, not bothering to count as I simply repeated the mantra I had used on the treadmill: not here, not now, not like this. Stupid as it was, that mantra held the leopard back from trying to take me in my waking life as it did in my dreams.

Eventually, I was alternating limbs doing the work instead of alternating front to back. I couldn't cry the helpless tears that threatened—there wasn't time, and doing so likely would have resulted in more lungfuls of chlorinated water. My parents sure as hell weren't perfect, but they didn't deserve to suffer just because they'd happened to adopt a freakshow of a daughter.

The adrenaline steadily worked its way back out of my system, leaving my limbs heavier than they'd been before with muscles that felt like molten lava. The arm propelling me forward gave out, and my head bobbed under the surface long enough that my next breath was liquid. It jolted more adrenaline into my system as I came up spluttering and scrambling yet again for the edge of the pool.

The nurse took another reading with the pulse oximeter as I pressed my forehead against my free hand on the edge of the pool, refusing to look at her.

"Good," said Mr. Loudspeaker. "Keep going."

I gathered myself, ready to argue, as I lifted my head from my hand.

"If you have energy to argue," the nurse said as I opened my mouth to say something, "then you have the energy for at least one more lap. Go."

God-*dammit!*

She was right. And if I wanted my parents to be okay—and I did—then I had to.

I pushed off the wall and back to my lane, gathering myself a moment at the end before pushing off for more laps.

Not here, not now, not like this. Not here, not now, not like this.

The endless refrain went on and on until the adrenaline drained from me yet again. But this time, my limbs failed all at once. Water filled my mouth and rushed up my nose, and as it hit my lungs and the first cough tried to escape me, all fight went out of me, and I went limp in the water.

There was a splash, and strong arms pulled me from the water as wet coughs tore their way out from my chest. I couldn't get a deep breath in. I couldn't get a small breath in. I couldn't do anything. Blackness loomed at the edges of my vision as my coughs turned weaker. Water or snot or God-only-knows-what dripped from my nose.

Something small pressed against my throat, and I feebly tried to bat away the thing threatening to strangle me, but the sensation was oddly distant, and my fingers had gone numb.

A door banged closed, and Mr. Loudspeaker's voice garbled into my awareness, his voice closer than the overhead speakers. "Time?"

"Six hours, fifty-two minutes, and twelve-point-seven seconds," replied the nurse.

"I had hoped for better."

TWENTY-SEVEN

I JOLTED AWAKE, flailing for a moment before I realized I wasn't underwater. I was covered in fur under a couple of soft blankets that smelled like they'd been freshly laundered. The lights were out in my room, but the light from the hallway slanted in through the door. There were scraps of fabric around me, and as I nosed at one, I realized it was probably a copy of the sweats I'd worn after the obstacle course, and not a swimsuit. It was a wonder I hadn't torn up the blanket.

Still, it meant these people must've changed me while I was out, for all the good it did. Because once again, I'd shredded my clothes and gotten stuck in a body that wasn't mine. Or it was? But not really. My heart started to hammer, but was then immediately calmed, it's rate easing back to normal.

What the hell?

Thank God no one was around when that change happened.

My father's terrified eyes flashed before my mind's eye and I huffed out a quiet whine, which came out like a pathetic little mew.

Something moved in the window of the door, and my ears swiveled toward the movement before I looked. Something about the size of a fist was silhouetted by the hallway light. My eyes adjusted to the contrast, and I realized it was Chad.

"Welcome back," Andy said softly, his voice carrying in the quiet of the hallway.

Oh no.

"Naiya?" Val asked.

"She's a leopard again," Andy said.

"Oh shit," Val whispered.

The little crystal spider tinkled its way into my cell, picking out a path along the wall above my bed and coming onto my bedside table. I scooted back toward my wall as it progressed, my spine curling in a way that felt very much like a fearful alley cat's.

"I don't think I've ever been so close to a leopard before," Andy said.

I shrank into the covers, curling into a tight ball. Of course he hadn't. Who the hell gets themselves into the sorts of situations where you could potentially end up this close to a predatory killing machine? My heart started to pound again before slowing back down yet again. Y'know, unless you're from that show with the crazy guy and his tigers. Or maybe if it's your job, I guess. Someone had to take care of the ones at the zoo, right?

"Is she okay?" Val sounded concerned.

Again, no. At least we were all still locked in our cells. At least I couldn't hurt anyone.

"I think so," Andy replied. "But she's curled under her blanket, and I can only really see her eyes and nose. Naiya, would you come into the light for me? Can I see you?"

He wanted to see me? Chad must be more expendable than I thought. I didn't trust myself like this and shook my head once.

"It's alright," Andy said. "It's just me here."

"Hey!"

My ear swiveled to point at the wall behind me, though the other stayed pointed at Chad.

"And Val too, but she can't see you. Please?"

I huffed. I had no idea how I was going to get back to my regular form, and I certainly didn't know how long it would take before I got there. My heart kicked like a bass drum for a beat or two before calming again.

I didn't like it, but the calm definitely felt better than the fear.

So, I slowly uncurled myself, extricating my limbs from the blankets and scraps of fabric with quick shakes of my paws. Chad backed up as I cautiously stood on the bed, and as I stepped to the ground, I stretched. My limbs were heavy, but I couldn't deny how good the stretch felt, even moving through unfamiliar muscles. The room smelled faintly of antiseptic, though there was an undercurrent of … crisp fresh snow?

Without moving from my spot, I sniffed in the air and traced it to Chad. I gingerly stepped over to where he still stood on my bedside table.

Chad—the crystalline spider—smelled of freshly fallen snow.

"Oh wow," Andy said.

"What?"

"She's bigger than I thought," he replied. "And all black, like midnight on a moonless night."

He couldn't see like I could in the dark. I shook my head at his mistake as I padded over to the sliver of light, and the crystalline spider followed along the wall like a camera on a rail.

"Oh *wow*," Andy said again.

God, I must be truly terrifying, and I squeezed my eyes shut. At least Val couldn't see me for herself. Even if we could get out of here, even if we could be friends after this somehow, there was no way Andy would want to be anywhere near me after seeing me like this.

"What?" Val asked again.

"She has spots," Andy said. "I didn't know that even black leopards have spots."

"How can you tell?"

"She's in the light from her door now," he said. "The spots are … a slightly different shade of black. More brown, perhaps? Or like the rest is a deep rich brown that's almost black, and then there's actual black rings with a deeper brown in the middle."

He didn't sound scared. Why didn't he sound scared?

"Leave it to a guy to not know how to describe colors," Val said.

"Well, I'd show you if I could," Andy said. "But we're all a little locked up right now."

That's why he wasn't scared. Of course. Why be afraid of a thing that is behind a locked door?

"Was that … was that *humor*?" There was a smile in Val's voice, and my ear twitched toward her room.

"Mmm, maybe," Andy said.

I sighed and sat down.

"What's she doing?"

Andy was quiet for a moment. "She's just sitting there."

Not like there was anything else for me to do. My tail whipped from left to right, a move so startling I jumped.

"You've never really moved around at all in that form, have you?" Andy asked.

I shook my head 'no.' Not a lot of opportunity for something like that between the screaming and the hurting people I love.

"You probably move differently than you think you do."

Maybe I did, maybe I didn't. But I was tired, and my tail thrashed from side to side again, more slowly.

"I wish my skills worked here," Andy said, his voice sad. "I could give you a voice to use in that form. Or, at the very least, be a parrot for you." He made a frustrated noise. "I can't understand why *this* works with Chad, but I can't do anything else."

"But you don't question why your spider is anything more than a shiny rock?" Val asked.

"Sure," Andy replied. "But the only thing that makes sense is because he's a part of me. And by that logic, my other skills should work as well, and they don't."

I yawned and instantly regretted it. The feeling of my lips moving over positively giant teeth was unsettling, though the twitching of my whiskers as they brushed against each other when I did was an interestingly novel sensation.

"Wow," Andy said. "Those are some impressive jaws. It's really fascinating to see it so close."

Fascinating. What a nice way to say 'truly frightening.'

"How are you able to see her?" Val asked.

"I'm projecting my consciousness through Chad."

"Yeah, you said that last time, too," Val said. "But what does that mean?"

"I'm … hmm. Well, I'm sitting cross-legged on my bed here, but my eyes are closed to help me concentrate and to reduce nausea—brains don't tend to like conflicting inputs. If I sit very still, I can almost feel Chad's limbs, and I can direct him around and see through his eyes."

"Doesn't his vision work differently than yours?"

I padded back to my bed and climbed onto it.

"It probably would if he were an actual spider. But since he's a crystalline projection of my personality? No. And even if it were different, I suspect my perception would simply filter out the nonsense. I'd probably see worse than through my own two eyes—and probably worse than Chad would on his own, since the way my eyes work is different from the way his do—but I wouldn't be completely blind."

I curled back into a ball and watched the clock tick from 5:07 p.m. to 5:08 p.m. and then to 5:09.

"I wonder what they had her do," Val said.

"I'm sure she'll tell us when she comes back," Andy said as my eyes drifted closed.

I woke to the lights coming on in my room, and scrambled to pull the blanket around my naked form. Thankfully, I had hands again, instead of murder machines.

I hoped my father was okay. I hoped all of my family was okay, Abigail included, but I especially hoped my father was okay.

The dinner cart clunked down the hallway, accompanied by the scent of pork and sweet baked beans, and I squinted in the brightness of my room at the clock. It was a couple of minutes past six, the usual dinnertime.

Except the person who opened my door was the nurse, not Curly or Baldy, though I could see both of them over her shoulder as she entered. She had another bundle with her. I eyed her warily, ignoring the burn in my eyes at the almost intense lighting in my room, as she placed the bundle on the shelf. She retrieved a tray from the cart in the hallway and placed it on the shelf as well.

"You tried to kill me," I said, not bothering to keep my tone calm.

"We did nothing of the sort," she replied coolly as Curly and Baldy continued with their routine meal delivery. "I told you that you'd swim until you couldn't, and then you'd swim some more, and you did just that."

"What have you done to my parents?"

Her rich brown eyes met mine as she retrieved something from her pocket. "How interesting. You readily forget that I won't answer your questions. Or perhaps you are simply hoping I'll make a mistake." Except she sounded bored by the whole thing. She held out her hand, palm up. "Arm, please." She held a needle ready in the other hand.

"If they're hurt—" There was a rumbling snarl to my voice that I hadn't ever heard.

Her demeanor shifted, and the gaze meeting mine hardened. "Choose your words carefully, Ms. Kateri. What power do you truly think you have here?"

Curly and Baldy came into view of the window, but she waved them off with the hand reaching for my arm without so much as a glance over her shoulder.

"Consider that your cooperation could well be the thing that keeps them from getting hurt," she said, her tone as glacial as her now almost golden gaze. "Now, hand me your arm, let me do my job, and we can all stop this ridiculous posturing."

"You bitch."

She actually smirked at me as she took my arm, jerking it toward her. Her gaze didn't leave mine as she pushed the needle into the vein at the crook of my elbow. She didn't blink as she drew my blood, and when she pulled the needle from my skin, she grabbed the hand holding my blanket and pressed the tip of my finger to the spot without a care for the fact that it made me drop the covering from my naked body. Her eyes never left mine.

I tore my arm from her grip as I looked away and hurried to pick up the blanket and wrap it back around me.

"Fresh clothes, there," she said, turning her back to me and waving a dismissive hand at the shelf. "And dinner. Rest up tonight and tomorrow; we'll continue with our testing after."

She beeped open the door and practically sauntered out of my cell and down the hall. The lights stayed annoyingly bright in my cell.

Her eye color had shifted. I was sure of it. One moment, she had dark brown eyes, the next, nearly golden. What the hell did that make her?

TWENTY-EIGHT

"Naiya?" Val said as Baldy and Curly pushed the dinner cart along in the nurse's wake.

"I'm okay." I shuffled over to the bundle of clothes on the shelf and took them behind the curtain to dress. My limbs still felt heavy and perhaps a little stiff, but they didn't ache, and I marveled at it, given the exertion of the hours previous.

"Glad to hear it," Andy said.

The door at the end of the hall beeped open and clicked shut as I pulled my clothes on. But I was still tired, like I could sleep and not wake until the breakfast cart came by.

"These assholes forgot to dim the lights," I grumbled with a sigh as I yanked the black curtain open again. "Hey, jerkoffs! You left the lights on!"

"And after you eat," Mr. Loudspeaker's voice chirped above me, sending ice down my spine, "they'll turn back off."

"Hey, fuck you, dickhead!" Val called.

I flipped the bird to the ceiling as I rolled my eyes. I didn't want to eat; I wanted to sleep. But I was pretty sure I knew how this game went. They'd probably hook me up to an IV with fluids and nutrients if I tried to starve myself. Or maybe they'd just let me and pull a starvation stint like Andy said they had with him.

But the food did smell good, and I'd rather eat now and keep having regular meals than to have them force me onto some starvation diet because I was being a pain in the ass.

So, I refilled my cup with water and plunked it onto my bedside table. I pulled the scraps of my former clothing from the bed and deposited them in a pile on the floor next to the door before grabbing my dinner tray from the shelf. I examined its contents as I sat on my bed. Thick slices of pork loin were arranged alongside a cup of baked beans and a fist-sized ear of corn. There were a couple of dinner rolls as well, and I picked up one to bite into it as I prepped my corn with the little foil-wrapped square of butter. As it melted, I tore open the little packet of salt and sprinkled it over the kernels, turning the ear to dust all around it.

"How long did they have you swim for?" Andy asked around a bite of food.

I'd picked up my utensils to get to work on the pork, but paused at his question and looked to the ceiling, racking my brain for the number I was sure I'd heard as I passed out.

"Six hours, fifty-two minutes, and twelve-point-seven seconds," I said, staring at the spot on the ceiling where I approximated the speaker to be as I did my best impression of the nurse.

"Holy shit," Val said. "Do you swim?"

"I can," I replied. "But I've never been on the swim team or anything."

"That's not a short swim," Andy said.

I nodded. "That's what I thought, too. But apparently, it's underperforming to these folks."

"What makes you say that?"

"Mr. Loudspeaker here apparently hoped I was

capable of more." I looked back up at the ceiling. "Even though I almost *drowned*." For a moment, I could still taste the chlorine in the back of my throat, but I was pretty sure it was psychosomatic.

"That explains why that guy who's always with the nurse and the blonde chick had you slung over his shoulder like a sack of potatoes," Val said.

"Grump," I offered around a bite of pork.

"Yeah," she said. "That guy."

"Well, at least they didn't try to bring me through here in leopard form," I said.

"Do you know what it looks like when you shift?" Andy asked, coming to his door.

I squeezed my eyes shut and repressed a shudder. "No. And I think I'm glad for that, judging by the shredded clothing."

"From what I can see," Andy said, "it's not nearly as violent as you might think. It's like in one breath, you're on two legs, and the next, you're on four. Your clothes kind of puff out and shred as the change happens, but it's not like you rage into that form or anything."

I chewed on the corn as I considered that. It was certainly less aggressive than I had thought, but then it seemed strange that I would tear up my clothes. And then I remembered my father's terrified face as I tore into his arm and shook my head. Not so strange after all.

"What was that the nurse said about your parents?" Val asked.

I made a frustrated noise, drawing it out almost into a growl. "They showed me my dad's watch, the one he's worn every day for years since I gave it to him. And my mom's music box. There's no way my parents just *handed* that shit to them, and they said my father was safe, so I'm hoping that's true for my mother as well. But it means they've snuck these things away from them."

"Unless they were lying," Val said.

"I don't think they were," I said. "I hope they weren't."

"Either way, that's a power play worthy of Luca and his forces," Andy said.

"You really think your parents are okay?" Val asked softly.

"I think as long as I do what I'm told, they will be." I shoveled some more food down, put my tray back on the shelf, and looked at the ceiling, even though I couldn't be sure where they had a camera on me.

"There," I said. "I ate. Now turn—"

The lights went out before I even finished my thought.

"Handy," Andy said.

I rolled a shoulder. "I guess. Not real thrilled to be their little lab rat, though."

"Sure," Val said.

"I need more sleep, guys," I said. "My brain feels like mush, and my limbs are too heavy."

"I'd need sleep too after swimming for so long," Val said.

"We'll work on an escape while you rest," Andy said.

"Don't count on mapping your way outta here," I said as I pulled the blankets over my legs. "I'm pretty sure they're taking me on deliberately confusing routes, and even if they weren't, there's nothing to write it all down on. There's no way I can memorize it."

"Don't give up hope," Andy said. "We'll figure something out. For now, just take it easy and recover."

"Yeah," Val added, "before these assholes decide to take you for even more stupid bullshit."

I smiled at her comment as I curled under the blanket, pulling it up over my head. I was glad to have Val here and wished I'd met her under better circumstances. Andy too, really.

As I expected, I slept like a rock until the breakfast cart in the morning—no dreams, no nightmares, no anything—just sleep. It was almost eerie.

Over breakfast, Andy suggested I take Chad with me any time the staff here take me for testing, and Val agreed it'd be a good idea. I couldn't deny that I liked the thought of having an ally in the room. So, we figured anytime we saw the nurse, that'd be our cue for him to send Chad over, and I would tuck him into my shirt or something—my pants didn't have pockets—and take him along. Andy wasn't sure how far his range would extend here, but he assured me that his range back home was at least the size of a gladiatorial arena, which I figured was about as large as a football stadium here, judging by his description.

We played more games with Chad and the blue ball throughout the day, but boredom was setting in. At their urging, I even agreed to read them my book, but it was slow going, as Andy had so many questions about how creatures here behaved and which ones actually existed.

He was disappointed to learn that the more interesting creatures in the book—the harpy, the manticore, and of course the unicorns—had never actually existed here. I had to explain to him that animals don't talk in our world and that the only thing that even remotely looked like telepathy was animals reading the body language and pheromones off one another.

I finished reading them the story a little before Curly and Baldy brought in the dinner cart. It was lasagne—Andy's favorite—and we had a good laugh about him calling it pasta cake all over again, analyzing which parts were the cake and which were the icing.

And right at the time when I expected the lights to go out, the door at the end of the hall beeped open, and another cart clunk-clunked down the hallway.

Chad went to Andy's window and then made his way across the ceiling into my room, where he plopped onto my bed and curled his legs in on himself. I grabbed the fist-sized crystal as the cart approached and ducked into the corner of my room that pretended to be a bathroom, pulling the black curtain around as I did. I tried putting the crystal between my boobs, but it looked kinda awkward. The same thing happened if I tried putting him underneath a boob, only the awkward there was just that it made that boob look obviously larger.

Someone beeped open my door, and I flushed the toilet as the door clicked closed. I settled on having Chad at the small of my back, tucked into the waistband of my leggings, and opened the curtain to see the nurse with a cart full of machinery and wires. My heart started thumping against my sternum, loud enough that she likely heard it.

"Uh, one moment," I said lamely, taking the single step to the sink to wash my hands.

"Of course," she said, crossing her arms behind her back. "Take your time."

"I thought I was going to be left alone today," I said as I dried my hands.

There was a quiet susurration near her head, like someone whispering in her ear, though we were the only two people in the room. I couldn't make out what was being said, and it was done before I could strain hard enough to focus on it.

She nodded once. "And you have been. Tonight is simply a sleep study."

"A sleep study?"

She arched an eyebrow at me. "I'll place sensors on your temples and a band around your ribcage and another around your wrist. You can move about your room if you'd like, and of course you'll be able to use the facilities should the need arise, but once the sensors have been placed, please do not meddle with them, as doing so will only prolong the study."

I eyed her cart full of instruments. "So, I'm going to have to wheel that around every time I have to pee in the middle of the night."

"Not at all," she said. "There will be sufficient slack on the wires that such movement will be unnecessary."

"Fine," I said with a huff.

She gestured to my bed. "Have a seat, please."

I did as she said and sat still while she glued sensors to my temples, to the pulse points on my throat, and to the middle of my forehead. The band around my ribcage was elastic, held in place by velcro that folded over on itself. The band for my wrist matched the one I'd worn while swimming, and I shook the memory of almost drowning from my mind.

She clamped a pulse oximeter onto my pointer finger and made a note of the reading before taking it back and tucking it into her pocket. She pulled enough slack wire free from the coils on the cart for me to go to the toilet and back to the foot of my bed without even placing tension on the sensors attached to my head. Satisfied, she rolled the cart to the foot of my bed, parking it against the wall and engaging the wheel brakes.

"See you in the morning, Ms. Kateri," she said as she beeped open my door.

Grump and Blondie stood out in the hallway, flanking my door. I hadn't noticed them before, but I'd admittedly been distracted. They took up their usual positions following the nurse down the hall, and —as my cell door clicked closed—the lights in my room went out. As soon as the door at the end of the hall shut, so did those in the hallway.

I pulled Chad from my waistband. "Looks like I'm staying here tonight, Andy." I went over to my door, trailing the wires along behind me, and held the crystal in an outstretched palm toward my window as Andy came into view.

"*Mitne*," Andy said, and the back section of Chad lit up with a pale purple glow as he unfolded himself.

Chad tinked up the wall and across the ceiling as I looked down at the cart. A long, skinny LCD screen glowed faintly and showed a handful of lines that jumped at irregular intervals, largely out of sync. They looked like digital versions of the lie detector tests I'd seen on police procedural TV shows. A little black node next to it had a thick black antenna pointed toward my door. It looked like it came from a wireless router, and a tiny green LED flashed like the CPU indicator on a computer.

"That's handy," Val said.

"I'm surprised it even worked," Andy replied. He was quiet for a moment, and I could practically feel his eyes studying me as I watched the screen.

It wasn't entirely unpleasant.

"That's a lot of wires," Andy said softly.

I looked across the hall at him and gestured to the cart. "It's all connected to this cart she brought. There's a screen here, too. I think it's tracking all the sensors."

"Can you make heads or tails of the readouts?" Val asked.

"No." I shook my head. "I can tell that when I talk, one of the lines on the screen is spiking, but that's probably just a sound sensor to measure whether I snore or something."

"You don't really snore," he said. "But you do sometimes kind of whimper in your sleep."

"Good to know."

"Except for when you change into the leopard," he said. "That's a bit noisier."

"Can't say I'm surprised to learn that." I nodded.

"Do you think you can sleep with all of that attached to you?" Andy asked.

I rolled a shoulder. "I guess we'll find out."

TWENTY-NINE

As it turns out, I could sleep with all that crap attached to me just fine. Though I attributed a large portion of that to the fact that I'd swam for nearly seven hours the day before and thus slept like a rock.

The leopard still stalked me as I slept, but at least this time, it did so through the woods of my parents' lake house and didn't manage to corner me. I woke with a start to the breakfast cart in the hallway, but I was thankful for the intrusion and quickly tucked Chad—who'd come over and become inert on my pillow—into the waistband of my leggings once again.

The lights came up as the nurse beeped open my door. She disconnected me from all of the wires while Curly and Baldy delivered meals, handing me a pack of baby wipes afterward so I could clean the glue residue off my head and neck. When she left, I sent Chad back over to Andy.

The day went largely as expected. No one came to take me to any endurance trials, Curly and Baldy brought meals that were more delicious than a bullshit place like this warranted, and we played ball with Chad to fill time. Val asked me to read my book to them again, and I started on that, though I was only a few chapters in by the time the nurse came to hook me back up to the wires again.

When she left, and the lights went out, I continued reading until I heard the soft, even breathing that told me Val had fallen asleep.

"You see in the dark as well as your alter ego does," Andy observed, keeping his voice low.

"I suppose I do," I replied, bobbing my head once.

"I wonder how much of what you're capable of is due to the leopard part of you."

"I suspect that's what these assholes are trying to figure out." I gestured vaguely around.

"Their methods certainly leave much to be desired," Andy said. "But I can understand the thirst for knowledge."

"Sure," I said. "I just can't understand how knowing exactly what I'm capable of makes it worth it to endanger the lives of people who have nothing to do with any of this beyond being my adoptive parents."

"I can't imagine any knowledge being worth that," Andy said. "Beyond that which would save more lives than it puts in danger."

"Hmm. Something tells me they would argue that's exactly why they're trying to learn what they can about me."

"That sounds like the kind of logic Luca's forces used to make it easier for themselves to sleep at night."

I went over to my door, again trailing a plethora of wires. "Hey, Andy?"

"Yeah?" He came to stand at his window as well.

"If we ... I mean, if you get ... When you're free—"

"What will I do when we get out of here?"

I nodded. "How are you going to find a way home?"

He rolled a shoulder. "I suspect I'll have to figure out how to use your internet."

"How do you …?" I squinted my eyes at him. "The TV at the rehab center you were dropped in. That's how you know about the internet."

Andy gave a rich but quiet chuckle. "People had 'computer time' at that place. I didn't take advantage of it, since I didn't know how it worked, and I looked like a newborn *aurochs* when I asked about it."

I tilted my head to the side. "What's an auroch?"

"*Aurochs*," he corrected. "Always with an S. It's a herd animal from back home. A bit like a cow, but bigger. And stupider. And sometimes meaner."

"So, like a donkey compared to a horse," I said.

He nodded. "Except the size difference goes the other way."

"Well, if we all get out of here together, I'll be happy to show you how a computer and the internet works, so you can find your way home. I'm sure you have people who'll be worried."

"Like I said before, it'll be a long long time before anyone notices I'm gone." A yawn escaped him.

I nodded. "Get some sleep, Andy."

"And you as well, Naiya."

I carefully got into bed, making sure none of the sensors pulled free as I did. I stared into the darkness for a moment, listening to Andy settle into his bunk.

"I'm really glad I have both you and Val," I said quietly. "Waking up to friendly voices, and going to sleep knowing you're here is … well, it's really nice. Not that I'm glad you guys got captured by these assholes too, but just—I can't imagine what this place would be like without you."

"You and Val are a breath of fresh air," Andy replied.

An eerie silence fell after that, where every breath and rustle of blankets or clothes felt like an intrusion. Except for the teeny little whine of the electronics on the cart at the foot of the bed, there was no ticking clock, no hum or quiet whoosh of air conditioning, no sounds of cars driving past on the street, no crickets, no birds, just silence.

I lost track of when the darkness became sleep. When it did, the leopard stalked me through the woods again, but this time, so did Blondie and Grump and the nurse. Mr. Loudspeaker's voice garbled in the air, making wordless sounds that sang 'wrong' into my bones as I tried to get away from my captives. Just when I thought I'd managed to escape, the leopard dropped from a tree above me, and as I turned to flee the other direction, Grump leveled his handgun—or maybe it *was* a tranq gun—at my face.

I startled awake as the door at the end of the hall latched closed a little more forcefully than usual. Or maybe I was just jumpy from the dream. Chad danced into my room, and I tucked him into my leggings once again.

The nurse beeped my door open a moment later and placed my breakfast on the shelf before removing the wires as she had the day before, once again handing me a little packet of baby wipes.

After breakfast, I went back to reading my book to Val and Andy. We only had a handful of chapters left when Curly and Baldy brought lunch through, and instead of finishing the story before dinner, we played some more ball with Chad. The little blue ball was riddled with tiny pinpricks from the crystalline creature's fangs, but it still held together, only dropping one or two blue crumbs along the more vigorous initial bounces of a long toss down the hall.

When dinner came, we all kinda sat with our backs to our doors to eat the chicken curry. They gave us all glasses of milk to help with the spiciness of the dish, and though I didn't have any real trouble with it, Andy insisted it was setting his mouth on fire with each bite.

I finished the book after dinner, and—once again—right at the time they'd normally turn the lights out to sleep, the nurse came by to hook me up to the machines on her cart.

"How many nights are you going to do this anyway?"

She turned her dark eyes to mine. "What makes you think I'll answer that question?"

I rolled my eyes as she checked the last connection to the cart. "Because you're not stupid. You know I'll figure some of this shit out sooner or later, and it's not like I can't count the days."

"Then count them," she said dismissively as she turned on her heel and beeped open my door to leave.

"You know, maybe I'd be more cooperative if you all were even a little bit friendly," I called after her as she shut the door.

She didn't even turn around. "We tried that, Ms. Kateri. You fought. So here is where we find ourselves."

The lights went out in my room as she made her way down the hall, and—as before—so did those in the hallway once the door at the end clicked closed.

I sent Chad back over to Andy and flopped onto my bed.

"Wait," Val said. "So what they started with was supposed to be *friendly*? Sedating you like a fucking wild animal just for trying to get an answer about where you are? Fuck these guys!"

I nodded. "I don't disagree that it's all bullshit, Val. But they have my family. And I don't know if they're holding them hostage here, or if they're just letting them go blindly about their day and plan to ruin it with a sniper shot between the eyes if I don't do whatever they want."

"There's a fucking mental image," she said.

"Exactly." I raked my hands through my hair, careful not to snag the wires. "The Davenports are innocent in this. They didn't know what they adopted."

"I bet they'd do it again, even if they did know," Andy said.

I pressed my lips into a line, trying to ignore the lump in my throat that was making it hard to swallow. "Maybe." I pulled my knees to my chin. "Or maybe they'd have left me where they found me."

Val tsked at me. "Someone would've taken you in. If not the Davenports, then the Department of Children and Families or something."

This was a fruitless line of thought.

"It doesn't matter," I said. "It was the Davenports, and now they're having to suffer for something I can't even control."

"We'll get out of this, Naiya," Andy said, his voice firm. "Trust me."

I wanted to. I really did.

That night, in my dreams, I wandered in an endless black void so thick I swear I could taste it while Mr. Loudspeaker garbled wordless commands at me, the leopard breathing down my neck no matter what I did or which way I turned.

The door beeping open at the end of the hall saved me from the neverending darkness, again triggering the arrival of Chad in my room. I tucked him into his usual spot before the nurse got to me and didn't bother to say anything to her as she delivered my breakfast and disconnected me from her cart. The rest of the day went as the ones before it had, and the boredom was mind-numbing.

In a flash of inspiration—or perhaps idiocy—I tested the integrity of the door to my room. It didn't have a handle, so I pulled on the bars of the window as hard as I could. But they were anchored tremendously well, so all I managed to do was warp them a little before my hands lost their grip entirely on the smooth round metal.

I should have known it wouldn't be that easy.

After dinner, the nurse had a different air about her as she hooked me up to her sensors. There was an extra wire that she connected to each of my temples, and she checked its placement multiple times before she left again and the lights went out again.

That night, I went to sleep with a niggling headache—a mild thing, barely worth noting except for how infrequently I got headaches in the first place.

Between the pain and the growing frustration at my helplessness, I should have expected the leopard to be more aggressive in my dreams. This time, I was alone in my parents' house, moving from room to room as I tried to get away from the predator stalking me. I narrowly avoided being caught a few times, but then the wordless mumbles of Mr. Loudspeaker morphed into a tornado siren, and I took shelter in my parents' walk-in closet like we had when the storms passed through as I was growing up. As a tornado tore my home apart, I heard my parents scream. And then, the leopard pounced on me and I thrashed awake, covered in fur and tearing at the wires and blankets.

I clawed at the sensors and connections with vicious, frantic snarls as I dove off the bed and crawled under it. I bit at the wires like a wild thing caught in a trap until I was finally free of them and could curl into the tightest ball possible in the far corner under the bed.

THIRTY

I don't know how long I stared out into the inky blackness of my cell, but eventually, sleep overtook me again, and I woke, no longer covered in fur but shivering on the tile floor, to the lights coming back up in my room. I tugged on a corner of my shredded blanket, pulling it under the bed to wrap around me as best I could, bits of fluff escaping the seams.

The door to my room beeped open, and someone entered.

"Well, that was quite an interesting result," the nurse said. "Do me a favor, Ms. Kateri. Stay under there for a moment while we clean up your mess."

"Eat shit."

She squatted to look me in the eye. Again, her eyes were decidedly golden, but her tone was dark and even. "Do not test me, girl."

It wasn't like I wanted to come out and be closer to her anyway.

She nodded once at me and straightened as someone else swept a broom around my cell, collecting bits of wire, fluff, and cloth into one of those floor bins like the lobby staff of a movie theater use. When that was done, the sheets of my bed were stripped and replaced with ones that smelled of fresh laundry. The extra set of feet left the room.

"Now, Ms. Kateri," the nurse said, sounding like a mother who'd just finished lecturing her child. "I have fresh clothes for you, and I'd like to dispose of the blanket you've shredded. So be a dear and come exchange your poor excuse of a toga for some proper clothes."

I debated whether to simply comply with her directive. Someone had clearly pissed in her Cheerios this morning, and I wasn't interested in being her scapegoat.

"There are consequences for noncompliance," said Mr. Loudspeaker.

He meant my parents. The asshole. I huffed out a breath and crawled out from under the bed.

The nurse smiled brightly at me, a cheerful lie spread across her face as her eyes seemed to return to their normal shade of brown. "There." She handed me the bundle of clothes and gestured to the corner of my cell with the privacy curtain.

There was no point in fighting it. I didn't want to stay naked or wrapped in a torn-up blanket all day. So, I tugged on my clothes and brought her the mangled coverlet. She beeped open my door just a crack and handed it to … Baldy?

That's a change. Usually, she had Grump and Blondie with her. Was the fact that she needed a cleanup crew the reason for the change? Was Curly in the hall as well?

My door shut again before I could get a look into the hallway, and she stepped between me and the window, pulling an empty needle from her lab coat pocket.

"Arm," she said, holding an expectant hand out to me.

I rolled my eyes and held out my arm so she could draw her vial of blood.

"No vampires at Saint Dymphna's," I said ruefully, "but there sure seem to be some here."

She arched an eyebrow at me, and a smile played over her dark lips. "Such fascination with the undead. Do you read a lot of vampire romance, Ms. Kateri?"

"No," I said, almost by reflex.

The door at the end of the hallway beeped open and clicked closed a moment later as I debated whether to elaborate on my answer.

"Stupid bimbos letting themselves fall for vicious predators hundreds of years older than them?" I said. "How could anyone get into that crap?"

In for a penny, in for a pound, right?

"There are entire cults dedicated to such a thing back home," Andy said.

"How fascinating." The nurse's smile turned into a smirk as she placed the finger of my opposite hand to the spot where her needle had pierced my skin. "See you tonight."

She tucked the vial of my blood into her pocket, along with the syringe, and beeped the door to my cell open again. Grump and Blondie flanked her as she stepped from my room. A moment later, all three were gone through the door at the end of the hall.

With clenched teeth, I growled out my frustration. "God, I hate her!"

"She's a real bitch," Val agreed.

"Sorry for chiming in there," Andy said.

I shook my head and came to the window. "It's fine. It didn't change anything."

"Perhaps." His impossibly dark eyes met mine. "But I prefer not to intrude on already tense situations. And I'd hate to bring more suffering onto you because of it."

I gave him a soft smile. "I appreciate that."

"Y'know," Val said, "it sounds scary as fuck when you shift. One minute, you're whimpering and moving around in your sleep, the next, your whimpers turn to snarls and the sounds of tearing cloth."

I pressed my lips into a line. "Trust me, it's not any better on this end."

"Because of the nightmares?" Andy asked.

I nodded. "It always starts with fear, and I hate that. It's like there's always this *thing* stalking after me, and I can't ever escape it."

"Would you get rid of it?" Val asked. "If you could, I mean?"

My eyebrows knit. "Get rid of the leopard?"

"Yeah."

"God, yes," I replied with a huff, sinking onto the bed. "But considering I don't even know how it's possible that I'm like this, I have no way to know how I would even go about getting rid of it."

"Maybe it's just part of who you are," Andy offered.

"Mmm, I hope that's not true," I said. "It's terrifying."

"Tell me about the nightmares?" Andy asked, and I bolted upright at how eerily similar to Dr. Anderson he sounded.

I came over to the window, my eyes narrowed.

His expression turned quizzical. "What?"

"You sounded like my therapist at the rehab center."

"I'm sorry," he said, deflating a little. "I didn't mean … just … would you tell me about them? Please? Maybe something in them can point to where this all started?"

I turned and thumped my back heavily against the wall. "It's always the leopard stalking me. Well, sometimes I'm the leopard, tearing my parents to shreds and losing any sense of myself." I shook my head. "I hate it. When I was little, I remember having dreams about a leopard too, but they weren't nearly as terrifying."

God, what I wouldn't give to have the nice dreams of the baby leopard back. The playful thing that would chase butterflies and swim into streams darting after shiny fish was a far cry from the snarling, vicious thing that stalked my nightmares these days.

"What changed?" Val asked.

I shrugged and picked at a raw cuticle on my thumb. "I dunno."

Andy's voice was quiet and gentle. "Are you sure they were just dreams when you were little?"

I looked up at him. "Of course they were! My parents weren't so hands-off when I was younger. Hell, they would have seen me like that then if the dreams were real … and they would have believed me when it started happening again."

The door at the end of the hall beeped open, and Curly and Baldy came around with breakfast—waffles, eggs, bacon, sausage, and hash browns, all in absurdly large proportions.

I waited until they left and went over to my door, my tray in hand. "Did they give you guys enough food for three people?"

"Nope," Val said. "One waffle, two slices of bacon, two links of sausage, some eggs, and some hash browns."

"Same," Andy said. "What'd they give you?"

"Two waffles … six, seven, *eight* slices of bacon … five sausage links, and a big pile each of both eggs and hash browns."

"How big?" Val asked.

I balanced the tray on one hand and balled up my fist next to the egg pile for size reference. "About four times the size of my balled fist, for both."

"That's a lot of food," Andy said.

"It's a waste," I replied. "There's no way I'll eat it all."

"Maybe they think you need more because you changed last night?" Val offered.

I nodded and went back to sit on my bed. "Maybe."

I ate as much of the food as I could. It was all really good—the bacon was crispy, the waffles fluffy, the eggs scrambled without being too runny or too firm, the sausage juicy, and the hash browns were well-seasoned with just the right mix of crunch and soft. But I only ate half of one of the waffles, and there were four strips of bacon left when I was done, along with three sausage links and most of the hash browns and eggs.

When I put my tray on the shelf, Andy asked me how I did, and I told him. We spent the rest of the morning playing ball with Chad while we came up with a list of people who would need to eat a breakfast like mine: The Rock, Jason Momoa, sumo wrestlers, marathon runners, and Olympic-level swimmers.

At lunch, the chorizo tacos on my tray were in normal proportions, accompanied by tortilla chips with both a really delicious guacamole that tasted freshly made and a chunky salsa that was good, though slightly spicier than I'd have liked. The three of us puzzled over the change in portion size, but it supported Val's theory that it had something to do with my change at night. Though when I told her they tried to give me monster portions of food after the obstacle course and the treadmill too, she sounded less sure.

It was quiet after lunch, and I'm pretty sure Val and Andy both napped. I dozed a bit myself, but woke to the dinner cart coming in. Dinner was a nice, simple dish of chicken teriyaki and rice, again of normal proportions.

And again, right at about the time the lights went out, the nurse returned to hook me up with all the wires and sensors that connected to her cart.

When I fell asleep, the leopard wasted no time in catching me, and I woke what felt like moments later covered in fur and scrabbling at wires. The little crystal spider came over to me, peering at me under the bed in the darkness. It chittered at me, waving a little purple leg at me. Again my heart rate spiked only to calm a moment later.

"You weren't even asleep for an hour," Andy said. "I don't think they're gonna be happy you tore up the blankets again."

"Hey!" Val's voice was sharp enough that my ears pinned to my head, which was an odd sensation, all told. "Whose side are you on, Andy? Fuck those guys. Ruin the sheets more, Naiya!"

God was I glad they weren't in here with me. I can't imagine what their terrified faces might've looked like if they'd seen me tear everything up. With a rumbled growl, I turned my face into the corner, curling tighter into the ball I'd gotten into under the bed.

"I'm not … look. Yes. Fuck those guys, as you say," Andy said. "I'm just saying that maybe if we cooperate, they'll relax around us, and maybe we can find an opening easier if they're not so hyper-vigilant."

"Well, it's not gonna happen tonight anyway, so leave her alone, and let's get some sleep."

Andy paused a moment before answering. "Okay."

But Chad didn't leave. The little spider tinked closer, climbing onto me with little pricks that made my skin jump—another odd sensation, not entirely unlike a cat being touched too lightly along its spine. Interestingly, the creature still made little tinking noises as it moved, even once it was completely off the tile and into my fur, the sound's most likely source being little legs tapping into one another.

I resisted the urge to uncurl and bat it off me with one of my too-big paws. I didn't want to hurt anyone. Besides, I wanted so badly to be in the same room as someone I cared about that I couldn't help but be happy for some friendly contact, even if it was from a crystalline manifestation of Andy's personality.

So, I let the spider go inert as it curled up on my haunch.

Eventually, I fell back asleep too, only to once again wake cold and shivering to the lights coming on in my room. As yesterday, the nurse asked me to stay under the bed while someone—probably Baldy again, though I didn't see to know for sure—cleaned up the mess of wires, sensors, and cloth.

This time, she held the new blanket open for me as I crawled out from under the bed, keeping her head turned to allow me some semblance of privacy. As I stood, I snatched the blanket from her hands, quickly wrapping it around my body like a towel and tucking the end in before I took the bundle of clothes she'd brought. I ducked into the corner of my cell with the curtain and yanked it closed to get dressed. Once that was done, she took another blood sample and wheeled the cart full of machinery away, Blondie and Grump flanking her as she left the hallway.

And the whole time, she wore a shit-eating smirk that I wanted to tear from her face with my teeth.

THIRTY-ONE

It was over an hour before Curly and Baldy came in with the breakfast cart. It smelled like a similar breakfast to the day before, which seemed odd to me as this place had yet to offer the same meal two days in a row.

Only they started their deliveries with Val and Andy this time, and left without bringing me a meal.

"What the hell?"

"What?" Val asked.

"They didn't give Naiya breakfast," Andy said.

I turned and looked at the ceiling. "What gives? I tear up my sheets a couple nights in a row so I don't get breakfast now?"

"Oh," Andy said, his head dropping back. "I think I know what's going on."

I went over to my window. "What?"

"Remember how I told you they tried starving me?" Andy asked.

I dropped my head back with a heavy sigh as I closed my eyes. "Guess it's my turn."

"Hey, what the fuck, assholes?" Val shouted. "That's inhumane!"

"Here." He handed a couple of strips of bacon to Chad and gestured to my door. "This should help tide you over a bit."

"Please refrain from unauthorized alteration of controlled variables." Mr Loudspeaker's abrupt voice made me jump as Chad maneuvered the crispy bacon through the bars of the window and across the ceiling to deposit the strips into my waiting hand.

"Fuck off!" Val shouted. "You're not starving her just to get your jollies off!"

Chad had lost a couple bits of bacon along the way to me and went back for them

"No no, buddy," I said, directing my voice to him instead of the ceiling. "It's okay. I don't need the bits that hit the floor."

"There are consequences for non-compliance," Mr. Loudspeaker continued.

"Shove it up your ass," Val said.

Andy smirked at her and my heart jumped a little at how striking the expression was on his face.

"Here, Chad," she said, and the little spider skittered over to her. "This too."

Val had really come a long way in making peace with her spider phobia. Or maybe it was just easier for her to think of Chad as some sort of automaton. Either way, I was proud of her.

When Chad came back into view, his fangs were sunk into a biscuit. He managed to get it over to me, but it was in pretty bad shape by the time he did.

Mr. Loudspeaker didn't comment any more, and a cool finger traced down my spine at his silence.

I ate what was left of the poor biscuit and munched on the bacon while Andy and Val had their breakfasts.

I gulped down the rest of the water from my cup and went over to my sink to refill it. "We'll see what no-coffee-Naiya looks like. I can't recall how long it's been since I haven't had a cup to start my day."

"Oh damn," Val said. "That's going to suck. Caffeine withdrawal is no joke."

"Oh, I know," I said. "I gave up caffeine for Lent one year to help my friend Tamara do the same."

"You're Catholic?" Val asked.

I shook my head. "No, but she was."

"There's a lot of that I didn't follow," Andy said.

"Like what?" I leaned against the wall next to the door and crossed my left foot over my right at the ankle.

"Lent, Catholic, caffeine."

"Well, let's see. Caffeine is a chemical in a lot of beverages. Anything brown and fizzy has it, as does coffee and tea. It's a mild stimulant. Helps keep people awake mostly. Catholic is about religion. It's one of the more traditional types of Christianity. Lots of guilt and prayer. And Lent is a thing they celebrate for like a month or so where they give up something as a symbolic mirror of the sacrifice their people had to make way back when."

Andy nodded. "So, how'd it go? When you stopped having caffeine, I mean."

"Lots of headaches," I said. "And, of course, I was tired a lot."

As it turned out, no-coffee-Naiya looked a lot like Naiya-naps-a-lot. I fell back asleep while Andy and Val finished their breakfasts, and napped some more afterward, turning them down when they wanted to throw the ball around the hallway with Chad.

At lunch, Curly and Baldy came down the hallway with the food cart again, and went straight to Val's door, beeping it open.

"What the fuck?" Val said as the tray scraped onto her shelf.

Andy came to his door. "Careful, Val!"

Baldy was holding a gun like Grump had pointed at me, and it was leveled presumably toward Val, though I couldn't see from my angle. She must've rushed at Curly a bit too agressively for Baldy's liking.

"Aw, fuck you guys," she said, spitting the words like poison as her door clicked shut.

I saw the tray Curly gave to Andy. It held a large grey translucent shaker bottle, half-filled with some kind of dark sludge that seemed to be about the consistency of a thick milkshake.

And when he delivered it, he took away Andy's cup.

"Oh, what the hell?" I said as Andy's door clicked shut.

Curly and Baldy wheeled the cart away.

"Consequences for noncompliance," Andy said.

"Protein shakes?" Val said. "Blech!"

"Better than no meal at all," Andy said.

I eyed him. "Mmm, maybe try it first."

"Here, Naiya," Val said. "Lemme see if I can send the bottle over."

Something clunked at the front of her cell.

"Dammit!"

Another clunk, this one more forceful than the last, followed by plastic moving against metal.

"The bottle doesn't fit through the bars," Andy explained, looking at me.

"Of course they thought of that," I said, nodding. "It's okay, Val. I'm not hungry anyway."

Andy popped open the top on his shake and took a swig. "Light the ley lines! That's awful! It's like liquid sand!"

I couldn't help but laugh. "Yeah, I tried to warn you."

"Still think it's better than no meal at all?" Val said. "They're gonna starve all three of us."

I shook my head. "I think you two will resort to those at some point. Better than an empty stomach."

Mine growled at me then and I sighed. This was going to suck. I grabbed my cup and gulped down some water, which thankfully stopped my stomach from making such a racket.

"Was that gun the shaved-head guy had the same as the one the other guy had at the obstacle course?" Val asked.

I nodded, and then remembered she couldn't see me. "Yeah."

"Tranq gun. A handgun will have more heft to the barrel."

"Good to know." I shot finger guns in her direction and then blew out a breath at the hilarity of the gesture.

Andy caught my eye and smiled at me too. "At least they didn't take your cup."

I raised my cup. "Mm, there is that." I took a sip. "I saw they took yours."

"Fuckin' bastards," Val muttered.

"Look," I said, "if you want water so bad, you could dump your shake into your sink and rinse out the bottle to refill it with water."

There was a wet plopping sound, and then the toilet flushed.

"Not a bad call," Val said.

I napped a lot the rest of that day, and when dinnertime came, Curly and Baldy once again came around with protein shakes for Val and Andy, and nothing for me. I knew those shakes would be disgusting, but my stomach growled anyway and I gulped down more water to help quiet its complaints.

Next door, Val gulped something down. "Fucking disgusting."

"At least it's a different flavor than the one earlier," Andy said.

"You can sugarcoat a shit all you want," Val said, "but it's still shit."

"Sounds like the jello from Saint Dymphna's," I said.

"Eeuuugh," Val said with an audible shudder.

When it came time for lights out, I expected the nurse to come back to hook me up to her machines again. But she didn't, and when I slept, I dreamt of the leopard hunting things other than myself.

The next day went largely the same, as did the next, and the one after that. In fact, it was a full week before the pattern finally changed.

That was the morning the nurse came to get me. At the sight of her coming through the door—with Grump and Blondie trailing her, as usual—Andy sent Chad over, and I tucked him once again into the waistband of my leggings.

The leggings I had been wearing for a full week.

I'd washed my face and my pits in the intervening time, but I hadn't been provided with the opportunity for a proper shower or change of clothes. I raked a hand through my greasy hair and tried not to think about it as my door beeped open.

"Please give Mr. Kjelliho back his companion, Ms. Kateri," the nurse said, offering me a pair of slip-on shoes as she entered.

"I gave it to her," Andy said, coming into view of his window as I slid my feet into the shoes. "It's hers now."

I knew it wasn't true, but it still felt incredibly sweet for him to say so.

The nurse, however, tsked at him as Grump leveled his tranq gun at Andy.

"You know better than to lie to us, Mr. Kjelliho," she said, not even turning to look at him. "Now, Ms. Kateri, you can either send the crystal spider back to him, or we will take it from you and return it to him ourselves. But you are not leaving this hallway with it in any scenario."

I held her gaze, which remained impassive as she

waited for me to comply. And when I didn't right away, she arched an eyebrow at me.

"Perhaps you'd like a reminder of the consequences of noncompliance?" Her gaze flicked out my window and back to mine.

Blondie had a tranq gun too. And it was leveled at me.

Called my bluff. Not that I actually thought she wouldn't. But still. Damn.

I reached behind me, under my shirt, and pulled Chad from his spot at the small of my back. I moved slowly over to the shelf next to the door, where I placed him down. I glanced up at the clock. It was 9:37 a.m. on Monday, June 15th.

Andy whistled, sharp and quick, and Chad unfolded himself from my shelf and skittered back across the hall. No one moved while he did so—not Grump, not Blondie, and certainly not the nurse.

"Now, come with me, please." She turned on her heel and beeped my door open, holding it wide and gesturing out into the hallway.

THIRTY-TWO

I followed the nurse out into the maze of hallways again, Grump and Blondie at my back. My brain was foggy from the lack of food, and my stomach started complaining as we walked. I didn't bother trying to memorize turns. Instead, I focused on the way the nurse moved. She didn't limp or anything, but she definitely favored the left side of the hallway, which seemed odd. And she did sort of lean as we got to an intersection, telling with her body language where she was going before she actually started the motion.

The next beeped-open door was the little gym I had come to during my first foray into the labyrinth of this place. The place where I learned I could run for twelve hours or more and could bench over four hundred pounds. The wires and tubes were still draped over the rail of the treadmill, and the digital resistance machine still had its display turned toward the large two-way mirror.

"We'll start again at the bench press," said the nurse, gesturing as Grump and Blondie took up their positions on either side of the door.

I folded my arms across my chest. "You already know these numbers."

The corner of her mouth twitched upward, but she controlled the movement before it could turn into a smirk or a snarl. "Irrelevant. The bench press, please."

"No. Not until I get something to eat." The words spilled out as I thought them, but they felt right and good. "Not until I know my family is safe."

"Comply and they will be," said Mr. Loudspeaker.

I shook my head. "Show me they're safe, and I'll comply."

There was a long silence, and then a quiet susurration at her ear.

"Very well," the nurse said, stepping past me to go beep open the door. "This way."

I narrowed my eyes at her. "Where are we going?"

"You've asked for proof of life," Mr. Loudspeaker said. "And proof you shall have."

I didn't like the way he said that. I didn't like the way this felt. Something about all of them screamed trap.

My gut twisted and I shook my head once.

No. Not here. Not now. Not. Like. This.

"Why now?" I asked.

"I hardly think that matters, Ms. Kateri," Mr. Loudspeaker said. "You currently have two choices. Either get moving, or start lifting."

I eyed the nurse and the door. Proof of life. That meant they had it, didn't they? I had a chance to find out for sure what was going on. A chance to learn whether these assholes were full of shit.

I stepped over to the door and followed the nurse out into the hallway. Grump and Blondie took up their usual positions behind me yet again as she guided me down a few passages. I couldn't even focus on the directions. This had the potential to be the biggest mistake I could have made.

The nurse beeped a door open to my right and gestured inside. "Have a seat."

I turned to survey the room she'd opened. It

looked like a small interrogation room plucked straight from a police procedural. There was a metal table in the center of the room and a metal chair with its back to the door. There was no chair on the other side of the table. Instead, there was simply the large, two-way mirror.

"Ms. Kateri," Mr. Loudspeaker's firm voice called from inside the room. "Sit."

I was really starting to dislike the way he said my name all the time. I took a breath and stepped into the room. The nurse followed me in, as did Grump and Blondie. As I sat down, the nurse stepped around the table to the far left corner of the room, and the other two took up positions in the corners behind me. A panel in the wall pulled into the room beneath the two-way mirror. Another drawer. The nurse pulled out a large tablet and handed it to me, a shit-eating smirk on her face.

There was a video playing but the screen was black. My brow furrowed in confusion. A moment later, a light came on, revealing an interrogation room, much like this one. An LCD clock on the wall proclaimed it to be 9:53 a.m. on June 15th. Today. I left my room at a little after nine-thirty, which meant this was happening right now, more or less.

"Have a seat," a man said off-camera.

An older man with ruddy skin and dark hair came into view of the camera, bringing his badge into focus. He was a TSA agent named Robert Mendoza, and as he moved away from the camera, revealing the person he had spoken to a moment ago, my blood turned to ice in my veins.

Abigail was seated at the table, concern and anxiety pulling at her features.

Agent Mendoza sat down across from her and proceeded to grill her about her travel plans, noting that today would make her fifth visit to Cincinnati in the past six months. Cincinnati was where her sister lived. Abigail wouldn't talk much about it, not even to Agent Mendoza here, but her sister was sick enough that Abigail took the opportunity to visit nearly every time my parents and I traveled.

And if Abigail was traveling to see her sister, that meant my parents were out of town.

"What a shame that Abigail's ID matches the known alias of another individual on the no-fly list," Mr. Loudspeaker said. "I wonder if she'll ever be able to see her sister again."

"You goddamn pieces of shit," I said, placing the tablet deliberately down on the table so that I didn't smash it.

"I take that to mean you'll cooperate now?" Mr. Loudspeaker's voice was smug.

"Fine," I said, standing.

"Sit, Ms. Kateri," Mr. Loudspeaker ordered. "Your proof of life is incomplete."

In the video feed on the tablet, a phone rang and the TSA agent stepped out of frame, the door to the interrogation room opening and then closing again as he answered it. Abigail ran a hand through her hair and fidgeted nervously until he returned a moment later.

"It seems there was simply a mixup with your ID, Ms. Davis," Agent Mendoza told her. "You're free to go. If you hurry, you'll still make your flight. The ground crew is holding the plane for you, though they have to leave in ten or they lose their departure window."

The nurse came over and paused the video before picking up the tablet.

"Do not underestimate the reach we have," Mr. Loudspeaker said. "Further acts of noncompliance will force an escalation of consequences."

The nurse placed the tablet back into the drawer

under the two-way mirror, and the panel slid closed. She stepped around the table and beeped open the door behind me.

"This way please," she said.

I slowly stood from the table and numbly followed her back to the room with the digital resistance machine and the treadmill.

Grump and Blondie once again took up positions on either side of the door, and the nurse went over to the display facing the two-way mirror. I laid down on the bench as she input the first number, and just started pulling on the spongy foam handles when I was prompted.

I don't know how many reps I did on that damn machine, and I didn't bother trying to see the number of the weight I got up to. It didn't matter. I just knew I needed to get the hell out of this place and make sure my family was safe. Abigail and the Davenports didn't deserve to have this bullshit shoveled into their lives because of me. But there was nothing I could come up with that didn't end up with me taking a surprise nap. No one came to see us alone, and they never had more than one door open at once in our hallway, which meant that only one of us could ever hope to get out at once, and any aggressive action toward any one of their staff would result in sedation by the other one in the hallway.

I did, eventually, run out of steam. There was only so much I could do on multiple days' worth of an empty stomach. When I couldn't move the next weight, the nurse beeped something on the machine and prompted me to try again. I did, it didn't move, and she beeped something again. This happened twice more before I was able to move the next weight. I was pretty sure she was making it incrementally easier, in order to find that exact number somewhere between the one I'd last successfully lifted and the one I couldn't.

And then she had me move over to the treadmill. She gave me a sip of water before hooking me up to all of her sensors and airflow, but then I was off.

"Just keep it steady," she said. "We're not interested in your top speed."

So I tried to pace myself, but I didn't have the mental focus to keep any kind of rhythm. At least, not at first. Not until I started singing a stupid song from that one Disney animated movie about the girl who fights the Huns—the song about how the general is gonna turn all the new recruits into fighters.

It was a dumb song to suddenly pop into my head, but it worked, and I ran with it endlessly repeating in my brain. At least, until my limbs started to feel heavy, my legs burning with the effort on a too-long-empty stomach. I stumbled once, and started the verse over to get back into the rhythm. But I stumbled again. And again. And again.

As I started racking my brain for a different song, my legs gave out altogether, and my vision clouded.

Fingers snapped in front of my face. "Stay with us, Ms. Kateri. Unless you intend to let the leopard finish this run for you."

"Not a chance in hell," I mumbled into the mask. Well, it's what I tried to say. Thanks to my fatigue level, I'm pretty sure it came out unintelligible.

But it changed my rhythm, and gave me something to use in place of a song.

Not here.

Not now.

Not like this.

It wasn't like I thought I might actually change, but I certainly didn't want to give them the satisfaction of pushing me that far. So I kept the mantra going like a silent prayer.

But my limbs were like lead weights, and my legs felt like molten jelly. My vision abruptly tunneled and I lost a step. And then another. And when I tried to recover from the one after that, the world went fuzzy and dark. I was vaguely aware of the treadmill coming to a stop, but I wasn't standing on it when it did.

Or maybe I was? It was hard to tell. I couldn't see. It smelled like Grump as the world went black.

THIRTY-THREE

I blearily came awake in the dark, yet again covered in fur—yet again a leopard. I was on the tile floor under my bed, back in my cell.

How long had I been out? How the hell had I managed to not only get back to my cell, but also have a bad enough night terror that I'd shifted into this vicious predator yet again, all without having even a flash of recollection of it?

Chad tinkled into my field of view, peering at me with crystalline eyes before tinkling back off.

"She seems to be okay," Andy said.

"Those fuckers," Val said. "Good."

A few moments later, just as I was starting to doze off again, the door at the end of the hall beeped open. A moment after that, so did mine, though it only opened a crack.

Oh no.

No one needed to come in here right now. I'd probably try to maul them like I did my father. I pressed myself into the corner.

A tray with three raw steaks piled on it slid in on the floor, and my door clicked shut again.

I didn't hesitate. Or maybe the leopard didn't? Either way, the steaks were gone in seconds and I curled back under the bed and fell asleep once more.

I woke sometime later to the door of my room beeping open. I was, once again, shivering and naked under the bed.

The nurse stepped into the room, and pulled the blanket from my bed to hold it open for me. "I have yet another change of clothes for you Ms. Kateri. And, of course, I'll need another blood sample."

"Why am I not surprised?" I grumbled, as I crawled out from under the bed.

I took the proffered blanket and tucked it around me like a towel again before taking the bundle of clothes to change into.

"How are you feeling?" Her tone was conversational.

"Empty, but fine."

"Empty," she said, more to herself. "So the steaks did nothing to help?"

I finished pulling on my shirt. "Sure, they filled my stomach."

"Ah," she said, as understanding flooded her face. "But you feel empty complying with what we ask of you due to your attachment to Ms. Davis and Mr. and Mrs. Davenport."

"You assholes are monsters," I spat.

She cocked her head to the side, considering me for a moment. "Some would certainly think so. Arm."

I held out my arm for her to draw her vial of blood. She pulled my finger to the spot again when she was done and turned to beep open the door.

When the door at the end of the hall clicked closed, Andy came over to his window. "Sorry, Naiya. For the whole Chad thing yesterday."

I rolled a shoulder. "It was worth a shot."

"We'll have to just watch for our moment." He pushed his tattooed hand through his hair.

"They can't be perfect all the time," Val added.

Andy nodded. "Even the slightest slip on their part has to be exploited immediately."

"Exactly," I said. "Because if we don't, we'll just be stuck here waiting for another chance that may never come."

"Oh, it'll come," Val said. "They can't stay on high alert forever. But who the fuck knows how long it'll take?"

I nodded. "Better to take any advantage we can get as soon as we get it."

"When you aren't fed love on a spoon," Val said, "you learn to lick it off knives."

"Jesus, that's dark, Val!"

Andy shrugged. "She's not wrong, though."

It was nearly an hour longer before Curly and Baldy came down the hallway with the breakfast cart. And they didn't skip me today. The meal was oatmeal with strawberries and bananas, with a side of toast.

"Where'd they take you, anyway?" Val asked.

I rolled my eyes as I shoveled oatmeal into my mouth. "Mmm." I swallowed and took a sip of my coffee. "They had me lift weights and run again."

"How'd you do?"

"I don't know. It was hard to focus after I found out these assholes are also willing to use Abigail and *her* family to coerce my cooperation." I didn't bother to keep the seething anger from my voice, and shoveled another spoonful of oatmeal into my mouth to punctuate the whole thing.

"Abigail is your former nanny," Val said, "right?"

"Yep," I said, nodding.

"Holy fuck," she breathed.

"Do you think they've hurt them already?" Andy asked, his voice quiet, his tone gentle..

I shook my head as I swallowed more oatmeal. "I don't know. They just delayed her for her flight, and then told me that they could escalate from there."

"Wait," Val said. "How'd they delay her?"

"Apparently these assholes have connections in the TSA," I replied, waving my spoon vaguely in the air. "They pulled her aside for questioning for her flight yesterday and then released her, all while I watched on a live video feed."

"Just damn," Val said. "We have to get out of here."

"Yep," I said. "We do. Except everything I can think of ends with a surprise nap, because no one here travels alone."

"And they only ever have one door open at a time," Andy said.

"Exactly," I replied.

The rest of breakfast was quiet. I finished everything on my plate, including my little cup of orange juice and my coffee.

We then settled into another game of ball with Chad. Today's game was bouncing the ball off the ceiling from farther and farther away. Andy won, but only by a hair.

Afterward, Andy asked me to read to them again, only this time, he tried to explain all the ways that it was similar to where he came from—similar to Arcaniss. As it turned out, nearly everything in the book was something that could have feasibly happened there, down to the talking butterfly and King Haggard trapping the unicorns in the waves. He explained that the Red Bull was likely either a bull pulled from a lower plane of existence—like an actual version of hell—or it was a dire bull, which basically just meant it was a bigger, stronger, angrier version of a regular bull. He even talked about how the dark circus, with its manticore and harpy and illusions, would have been almost common in some of the less savory reaches of the world. I was torn between longing for a world where such magical things were possible, and uncomfortable with the idea of living alongside such casually dangerous things.

We didn't get back to reading before lunch came, and I wasted no time with the fried chicken strips and the rice with black beans. I had it all down in short order, just in time for the nurse to come down the hall.

Instead of Grump and Blondie flanking her, however, she had two other ladies. Both looked lean and moved with the same quiet and deliberate steps Grump and Blondie took, but they were a little bulkier —like they lifted weights and did squats where Blondie likely focused on pilates and yoga. The one on the left—whose whole demeanor screamed 'try me'—had curly blonde hair that was styled into a poofy mohawk on the top of her head, with curls that brushed her eyebrows, while the sides were shaved short. Her pale skin was almost the same color as her hair, and she had blue eyes with a little upturned nose. Her partner, on the other hand, was less pale, with a straight brown bob that brushed her shoulders and cheekbones that could cut glass. They both wore white tank tops and black leggings, and they both had hand—no, *tranq* guns tucked into brown leather shoulder holsters over their tank tops.

The nurse stopped before she got to my door, however. Which, aside from her change in companions, also surprised me. This close, her companions had the same wild tinge to their scent that Grump and Blondie had, though they also smelled of sweat and … maybe sawdust?

The nurse beeped open Val's door. "Ms. Jenkins. If you'll come with me, please."

"Not a fucking chance," Val said. "Who are you going to leverage against me? My parents are well and out of the picture."

"I assure you, no harm will come to you."

Something niggled at me about the way she said it, and I came to the window in my door.

"I don't buy it," I said, but I wasn't sure why.

"Your input is unwelcome at this juncture, Ms. Kateri," the nurse said. "We'll come gather you momentarily."

"Looking forward to it," I said, pouring as much sarcasm into the words as I possibly could.

"Please do not make us sedate you, Ms. Jenkins," the nurse said. "It will be better if you come on your own."

"The naps are cold," I said. "But they don't suck that bad."

"I will not ask you to refrain from commentary again, Ms. Kateri," the nurse chided.

The blonde one—Mohawk, I decided—came into view, her tranq gun leveled at me. I put my hands up in surrender and pressed my lips into a line as I held her gaze, trying *not* to focus on the tranq gun pointed at me, even if it did look a little more like a proper gun than I felt strictly comfortable about.

"Careful, Naiya," Andy said.

I nodded once.

"Just go with them, Val," Andy said. "Can't be perfect all the time."

She sighed with a groan. "Fine. Lead the way."

The nurse came back into view in the hallway. Val trailed after her, and Mohawk's companion—Bob, I decided—took up position behind Val. Mohawk watched me for a moment before following along as well, tucking the tranq gun back into her holster. I put my hands down as she left.

The door at the end of the hall beeped open and clicked shut.

I looked across the hall to Andy. "Other than that first time back when we first got here, have they ever taken Val?"

"We've both been taken for showers and clean clothes," he said. "But those have all happened while you were gone, and done before you returned."

That was news to me. Why wouldn't Val have mentioned that? Why wouldn't Andy?

"I've said something wrong," he said, studying me from across the hall. Again, his accent made me unsure whether he was asking a question or making a statement.

"I just … didn't know you'd gone anywhere."

"It was largely irrelevant," Andy said.

"I wish you'd told me," I said meeting his eyes.

"It was never my intention to hide it from you," he said. "It simply never seemed relevant to the topic at hand. They do not take me the same path every time, but I always end up at the same place. There's a chip in the tile next to the handle in the second shower stall. It's small, but that it is always there tells me they have taken me to the same spot."

"Do they take you at the same time?"

He shook his head. "No. And there is no pattern to who they take first. Sometimes it is Val, other times it is me."

I took that in. "Okay. So beyond that, have they taken Val for any kind of testing that maybe she came back from ragged enough that she might not have wanted to talk about it?"

He shook his head again. "Not unless they've done so in the middle of the night."

"Are those two the ones that came to take her the first time?"

"They are," he said. "But the nurse is different."

"Well, then the odds seem slimmer than I thought that whatever they have planned now is okay."

I refilled my cup from the sink and took a long slow sip, thinking. I couldn't push my brain into making words of it, but something about the way the nurse had said she wasn't going to hurt Val felt off.

"Did it seem like she was lying to you?" I asked Andy.

"When? Who?"

"The nurse," I said. "When she said she wouldn't hurt Val."

"Well," Andy said, "I wouldn't believe her. But I don't think they mean to do anything worse to her than they've done to you or me. She's not a wereleopard."

A wereleopard.

I mean, it was true, wasn't it? That's what I was. A wereleopard. It felt like such a cheesy term, even if it was exactly the right word for it.

I slumped onto my bed. "She's just a girl."

"Then she'll be fine … I think."

"And I'm a wereleopard."

Andy nodded. "You know the word?"

I sighed. "No. But I know werewolf."

"Ooh," he said, wincing. "Those are worse."

I put my cup down on the side table and looked across the hall. "So they're on some kind of ranking system where you come from?"

Andy shook his head. "No. Well … now that you mention it, you could argue that it is a ranking system, but perhaps not the way you mean. Werewolves are evil and destructive. Wereleopards are no more evil and destructive than their mundane counterparts. And werebears are typically good and almost kind. There are other werecreatures too that I have heard of, like wererats and weresharks, but I have only heard of them in passing."

I blinked at him. "I don't think we have any of those here."

"Mmm, if wereleopards are a part of your world

—and they clearly are—then it follows that you'd have other werecreatures as well."

I raked both hands through my hair and held my head, squeezing ever so slightly with my fingertips. That could only be true if the foil-hat-wearing conspiracy theorists were right about certain things that had been showing up online lately—like vampires and werewolves.

"God, I hope you're wrong," I said.

THIRTY-FOUR

A FEW MOMENTS of silence later, the nurse came back with Blondie and Grump in tow. I stood as she got to my door.

"Follow me," she said, beeping open my door and holding another pair of slip-on shoes out for me.

I folded my arms across my chest and didn't move. "Where's Valerie?"

"I'll take you to her."

I narrowed my eyes at her, but snatched the shoes from her hand and pulled them on. I nodded once to Andy as I stepped out into the hallway.

"She had better be okay," I said.

"Yes, yes," the nurse said, waving a hand. "Keep your idle threats to yourself."

I set my jaw and followed her, with Grump and Blondie flanking me like usual. She took me through the hallways and security doors with her usual confidence, though I was relatively certain that I was again in an unfamiliar section of the complex. The air smelled more like chemicals here, and though the ceiling vaulted up as high as the warehouse space that held the obstacle course, it didn't smell the same.

And I just couldn't put my finger on that scent. Maybe it was like industrial fertilizer?

The next door she beeped open made my jaw drop.

We were in a truly expansive warehouse space, but the ceiling was open like a stadium's retractable roof. In the center of the space was a two-story house, complete with a wraparound porch, swing, and curtains. It smelled like metal and dust and fresh construction and … something else. Something biting. Almost like that polish remover scent in nail salons. It tickled my nose and made my eyes water a little. But worse, it just felt *wrong*.

"As I'm sure you're aware," said Mr. Loudspeaker, "Ms. Jenkins is just a regular human."

I narrowed my eyes and looked around the space, looking for Val. I couldn't be sure whether I was hoping she was there and okay, or that she was being held here against her will and I could get her out, or something. I just knew I didn't want to learn she was working *with* these assholes.

"She's hidden somewhere in that house," continued Mr. Loudspeaker. "Restrained and without escape."

The air horn sounded once again, and the house burst into flames.

My eyes went wide as the flames licked up the walls and took hold almost immediately. The sharp smell was some kind of accelerant, I was sure of it. And if Val was in there, she was going to die if I didn't do something.

I jolted forward, only to find two sets of arms holding me back with vice-like grips on my biceps. Grump and Blondie held me with impassive masks set firmly on their faces.

"Let me go!" My voice was barely louder than the roaring flames.

I struggled against them for a few moments, watching helplessly as windows burst open, spraying shards of broken glass, from the mounting heat inside. The swing on the porch came alive with fire, and thick black smoke that glowed with embers billowed from the top of the house.

An eternity later, Mr. Loudspeaker's voice sounded again, barely audible over the sounds of breaking glass and the crackle of burning wood. "Save her before she dies."

Blondie and Grump's grips loosened, and I tore off toward the house, shouldering through the smoldering front door without even a passing concern for how hurt I might get in the process. I did the same with every door I encountered in the house. I had never seen a house so closed and compartmentalized. Even the dining room had pocket doors that closed the room off from the great room and the kitchen. All of the rooms were on fire, the thick black smoke rolling along the ceiling, and all of the doors were smoldering. I had to push through. After forcing my way through every door on the bottom floor, including a door to a walk-in pantry off the kitchen, and a small bedroom to the left of the back door, I realized something that turned the sweat running down my back to ice.

Why wasn't Val screaming?

With blurred vision but renewed vigor, I retraced my steps and darted up the stairs. They were losing their structural integrity—a smoldering hole had already formed right in the middle of the flight—and I stumbled once, catching my weight on the utilitarian wrought iron banister that had grown so hot it burned my hand. I coughed out a scream of pain, but I didn't have time to focus on it.

I had to keep moving—had to find my friend.

The doors up here had largely fallen from their frames, and after searching two rooms, I finally found Val tied to a chair on the floor of the closet in the third bedroom.

"Val!" My voice barely worked. I might as well have been whispering.

Her eyes were closed, and though she was still breathing, her breaths seemed shallow.

I sucked in what air I could and shouted, "VAL!" It tore a racking cough from my chest.

She stirred a little at her name, her eyes fluttering open for a moment before closing again.

"No no no, come on, Val, stay with me!" I patted her cheek as I coughed again, and her eyes fluttered open and back closed.

I didn't have time for this. We were both going to die if I didn't get us out of here.

I slung her over my shoulder like a sack of potatoes and darted from the room. I was off-balance with the dead weight and stumbled into the wall in the hallway, only for it to crumble at the sudden weight. My shoulder glanced off a smoldering stud in the wall before I fell.

Only I fell through the floor and onto the hot springs of the burnt-out husk of a mattress and had to get Val off it quick. I rolled her body onto the floor as I pulled myself to my feet again, coughing as more thick black smoke filled my lungs.

There was a blown-out window in this room. It wasn't huge, but it was large enough.

I hefted Val back up onto my shoulder and jumped through the window frame, landing on the concrete floor of the warehouse without losing my grip on Val's weight.

Well, good.

I coughed some of the smoke from my lungs. The air was cooler and cleaner here, but I had to get Val clear.

The nurse wheeled a stretcher over to me.

"Here," she said, and I laid Val down on it.

Val's eyes fluttered open again, and she reached

for me, her fingers only a couple of shades lighter than the rose on the back of her hand. But her arm fell limp before I could grab it and her eyes rolled back into her head.

"VAL!"

Grump and Blondie grabbed me again as the nurse wheeled her away.

"Let me go!" I coughed more smoke from my lungs and felt like I was finally able to take a deep breath.

"I can assure you," said Mr. Loudspeaker, "Ms. Jenkins will make a full and speedy recovery."

There were people on the far side of the warehouse, Mohawk and Bob, and a lanky guy in a lab coat. The guy in the lab coat stepped toward the nurse and took control of the stretcher. He pressed fingers to the inside of Val's wrist and clamped a pulse oximeter on her as the nurse came back to me.

"This way, please, Ms. Kateri." She gestured back to the door we'd come in through. "We'll take care of your friend. In the meantime, let's get you cleaned up."

"She had better be okay!"

The nurse arched an eyebrow at me. "More idle threats? Let me assure you, Ms. Kateri, she is in far better care here than she would be at the best hospital in the country. Now. Shower." She stepped back toward the door, making a wide circle around the still-smoldering house.

Beams from the roof collapsed, sending a shower of sparks and roiling orange-and-black smoke up through the open warehouse ceiling, and I was relatively certain that nothing in the house was up to proper building codes. But then, I suspected it didn't need to be if they were only going to set it on fire and destroy it as soon as it was built. There hadn't been anything on the shelves of the pantry, and though there had been curtains on fire down in the great room, it was like all of the furnishings that had been in there were just staged. Like they'd burnt down something that a realtor would have used to stage a model home.

"I will kill you myself if she dies." Something feral danced through my deep tone as my hands closed into tight fists.

The nurse stopped in her tracks and turned back to me. Her eyes had gone golden again.

Something hit my neck, like a burning ember floating on the breeze. My limbs grew heavy all at once.

A tranq dart. Of course.

I crumbled to the floor as blackness took me.

When I woke, I was back in my cell, clean and in fresh clothes. My hair was still very wet, though it had only soaked the towel on top of the pillow. Which meant I couldn't have been lying there for long.

"Val?" I bolted from the bed and went to my door.

"She's not back yet," Andy said.

My heart pounded in my chest. "They tied her up, hid her in a house, and then set the house on fire."

"Light the ley lines! Is she okay?"

I shook my head as my vision blurred. "I don't know."

Andy's hand came out his window as he reached for me. "Oh, Naiya. I'm sorry."

I thunked my head against the bars of the window. "They said they had good medical staff here. They said she'd be okay."

Chad skittered up the wall, across the ceiling, and came to rest on my shoulder, nuzzling into my neck.

"I wish I could tell you that I'm sure that's true," Andy said. "But I don't want to lie to you. I do not know this place, and I cannot be sure of their intentions. I only know that they have never tried to kill me."

"She was unconscious," I said. "Probably from the smoke, but I think they may have sedated her, too."

The door at the end of the hallway beeped open, and the nurse came in, again flanked by Mohawk and Bob.

"Valerie?" I straightened and moved to try to get a better vantage point to see down the hall, pressing my cheek against the cool metal wall as Chad scrambled over to my other shoulder.

She was limp in Mohawk's arms.

"*VALERIE!*"

The nurse beeped open Val's cell and stepped into my view, her eyes golden. "She's unconscious, not dead. And in either case, she can't hear you."

Red seeped into the edges of my vision, and my hands curled into tight fists. My stomach twisted, and I slammed one of my fists into the wall next to my head as Val's door clicked closed.

Not. *Here!*

Chad poked sharply at the spot where my neck met my shoulder, startling me.

I tilted my head away from him, and he skittered down my arm. When he got to my still tightly closed fist, he paused and poked it sharply, like he had my neck. I furrowed my brow at him, and he pointed with a leg toward my window.

I uncurled my hand and held him up as burning tears of anger and helplessness trailed down my face. My friend had gotten hurt in the name of testing me. These *motherfuckers* hurt my friend just to find out what I was capable of.

Chad poked my hand and pointed again, this time directly across the hall.

I looked across to Andy, who held my gaze and

nodded once, slowly. I swallowed thickly, the red fading from my vision.

The door at the end of the hall beeped open, clicking closed a moment later.

"We're going to get out of here, Naiya." His gaze still hadn't left mine. "It's only a matter of time." He sounded so earnest, and his heart was in his eyes.

Chad tinkled back up my arm and nuzzled into my neck as a fresh round of tears pulled me to my knees, my forehead pressed against the cool metal of my door.

"I really, *really* hope that's true."

"I wish there was more I could do," Andy said. His tone turned angry at the end and something hit the wall in his cell. "I hate being so powerless!"

Chad nuzzled me once more and then tinked up my door and across the hall.

I cried silent tears then. For my friend, for my endangered family, for Abigail, for my own immense powerlessness, and for my absolutely monumental anger that anyone at all had to suffer because of me.

And sometime later, when the tears had subsided, and I was just a limp, hopeless shell, a small cough came from the room next to mine. It gathered strength and grew louder as Val sucked in fresh air and purged the smoke from her lungs.

"VALERIE!"

"I'm—" Another cough. "I'm okay, Naiya." But her voice sounded like a chain-smoking toad who had swallowed sandstones.

The water turned on in her room, her cup refilled, and she audibly gulped it down before refilling and draining it three more times.

"It'll take more than a burning building to kill me," she said, her voice sounding stronger now. "At least, more than that as long as you're around. Thanks for saving me."

"Don't thank me!" I was incredulous. "I wasn't about to let you die in there. These people are fucking *monsters* to think I ever could!"

"Well, all the same," she said, "thank you."

I sucked in a long deep breath. "You're welcome."

THIRTY-FIVE

Val napped the rest of the day, and Andy and I kept quiet so we didn't disturb her. It was pretty easy, since I napped as well. Curly and Baldy eventually brought us some classic shepherd's pie for dinner. Val sounded better after eating, which led me to believe that the nurse, for all her bitchiness, at least hadn't lied to us about the medical care available here.

Not that there was much I was going to be able to do about it if she had.

My nightmares that night were visceral and terrifying. The leopard stalked me through the burning house while my parents screamed at me from beneath the floorboards, Abigail screamed at me from between the sheets of drywall, and Val and Andy screamed at me from where they were contorted between the steps of the staircase.

Every time the leopard got too close, I had to jump out a window to get enough clean air into my system to go back in. And every time I rescued someone, I'd take them outside only for them to disappear as I turned back for the next one, their screams suddenly rejoining the chorus of those still inside, but from a different location than I'd first found them.

Eventually, the whole house collapsed in on me, trapping me under burning embers.

I jolted awake in my bunk and snatched the water cup from my bedside table, gulping down half its contents just to keep from screaming before setting it back down.

It was half past five in the morning. The lights were still out in the hallway, and Andy and Val were still asleep.

But I didn't want to go back to sleep and allow the leopard more chances to stalk me. So, I started reading again, trying to imagine what it would be like to live in a world where the things in my book were real and possible.

My eyes grew heavy, but then the lights flickered on in the hallway with a quiet hum of electricity, startling me enough that I could keep reading without falling asleep. When my eyes grew heavy once more, so did the book, which dropped on my face. I shook my head and rubbed my nose as I sat up in the bed, leaning against the wall to go back to reading.

I blinked, and the door at the end of the hallway beeped open, again followed by the clunk clunk of the breakfast cart. Baldy dropped off my breakfast first before continuing to the others, and I waved good morning to Andy as I stood to retrieve my tray.

He waved back and then placed the first finger of his tattooed hand to his lips before pointing across the way toward Val's window.

I mouthed, "Is she sleeping?" and put my hands palms together against the side of my face, tilting my head like I was lying down.

Andy nodded, and I did the same before grabbing my tray from the shelf and sitting on the bed with it. Today's breakfast was omelets with bacon and toast. And again, it was hard to find a complaint about the food here.

"Mrrngh," came Val's voice from her room as I stood to put my tray back on the shelf.

"Good morning," Andy said, his voice almost tauntingly cheerful.

I grabbed the ball from where it sat on the floor in the corner next to the door and pushed it through the bars to throw it at Andy's door.

It *thoked* against the metal well after Val's "fuck you" sounded, and he looked at me with a playful grin. It was … actually really nice.

I shook my head. "No one likes the bright-eyed squirrel."

Andy shrugged.

"How ya feeling, Val?" I asked.

"Mmrrrnnngh, these assholes fucking suck." Things bounced against her metal breakfast tray as she sat heavily on her bed.

"Yeah, but the food's still good."

"Hmmph."

The door at the end of the hallway beeped open, and the nurse came in, flanked again by Blondie and Grump. She beeped open my door and gestured out into the hallway.

"Please follow me, Ms. Kateri."

She sounded a little more chipper than usual, and I narrowed my eyes at her, but followed. Blondie and Grump took up their usual positions, and I sighed as we traveled the maze of hallways.

"I'd ask you how many of these stupid tests you have for me," I started.

"But you already know I won't answer," said the nurse.

"Leaves room for nothing but awkward silence."

She didn't answer me, letting the quiet close in around us. The only sound that even indicated we were moving was the rustling of our clothes.

Eventually, we came to a heavy metal door with a

big square window. When the nurse beeped it open, it gave a little hiss, like a seal being broken, and I furrowed my brow. The little square room within, which was barely larger than a walk-in closet, smelled of antiseptic, and while there was a desk and another two-way mirror, those were the only furnishings in the otherwise steel-lined room.

Grump and Blondie took up positions outside the door in the hallway.

"I'll be back," the nurse said, heading out the door and closing it behind her.

There was something ominous about the sound of it, but I couldn't put my finger on what.

"We'd like to see your change to leopard, Ms. Kateri," Mr. Loudspeaker said.

"And I'd like to not ever see the leopard again," I replied. "So, someone's sure walking out of here disappointed."

"As a courtesy, I will remind you once more that there are consequences for noncompliance, and that they will escalate from our previous demonstration."

Ice danced down my spine. I didn't want to think about what escalation meant for that. Would they arrest Abigail? Would they keep my parents from returning home from wherever they'd traveled to?

Focus, Naiya. He wants to see the change.

Not that I thought that would ever be a good idea, but at least there was no one in the room with me.

Though, I wasn't even sure I'd feel bad hurting any of them.

"Look," I said, "if I had any clue how to make it happen, I'd show you."

"I don't believe you," Mr. Loudspeaker said.

I raked my fingers through my hair and then spun in a circle once, my arms out at my sides. I had to think of something. What was he going to do to my parents? To Abigail?

But I couldn't do it. I'd never done it. It was never a thing that I had any sort of control over.

I groaned out my frustration. "I can't just do it on command!"

Silence.

Real silence.

Not even the hum of the lights overhead. I heard my own blood rushing through my veins, and could hear my heartbeat when I concentrated. It was eerie.

And then there was a tiny, quiet hissing all around me.

I didn't like the sound of it. It felt like a trap.

I spun in a circle to locate the sound's source, scanning the walls. I found slim vents near the ceiling along all four walls.

The air felt thinner. It was like I'd gone on a hike at a high altitude or something. I tried to suck in a deeper breath, my face crumpling in frustration, but I couldn't get enough air. Was this a panic attack? And at that, my heart kicked into high gear, but it was definitely getting increasingly hard to breathe.

I pressed a hand to my chest. "What the hell are you doing to me?"

"It will get easier to breathe when you show us the leopard," said Mr. Loudspeaker.

My eyes were starting to water, and I swallowed hard as I tried to suck in a deeper breath. My lungs felt half-empty, and I could envision them as deflated balloons. But I couldn't get more air into them. In fact, every attempt to get more air seemed to make them deflate more.

"I can't," I said, my voice cracking as the panic set in. "I don't know how!"

There was no response.

I pulled at the desk, trying to pull it from the wall to see if there was another of those drawers like they'd had in the previous rooms, something that would lead to whatever room this asshole was in. There had to be air there. But there was no drawer, and the desk didn't move. Abandoning it as the air grew thinner still, I went back to the door I'd come in through, scratching at it with my fingertips until I broke every nail I had trying to break the seal.

"Let me out of here! You're killing me!"

"Show us the leopard, and the air comes back." Mr. Loudspeaker's voice was calm and collected—a stark contrast to my heart pounding in my chest.

I went to the two-way mirror and hammered a fist against it, but it didn't budge. I pulled back for another, and another, and yet another, but the strength was leaving my limbs.

"I can't do what you ask! I'm not capable!" Tears ran down my face, and the congestion in my sinuses from the unwanted tears made it even harder to breathe.

"You are," Mr. Loudspeaker asserted. "Now do it."

The hissing grew louder, and the next breath I tried to take in did nothing.

My heart flew in my chest like a rabbit from a pack of dogs. And my gut didn't even so much as jump.

"I can't *breathe*." I tried to shout it, but it came out weak and powerless as I sank to my knees in the middle of the room. There was no air left, I was sure of it.

Blackness seeped into the edges of my vision.

"Show us the leopard, and the air comes back," said Mr. Loudspeaker once again.

"I … can't."

My cheek hit the cool tile of the floor as the blackness tunneled in, and I almost smiled at the smoothness of the floor as I closed my eyes. My heart sped even faster, pounding against my sternum like a heavy metal drummer with two pedals for his kick drums. My lungs were on fire, my whole body begging for just half a breath of air to stop this. Tears pooled on the tile under me.

The hissing stopped as my awareness drifted away from me.

A moment—or an eternity—later, I pulled in a gasping breath, my eyes fluttering open before something sharp hit the side of my neck and the world went black yet again.

THIRTY-SIX

I GASPED awake in my cell. The lights were dimmed but not off, and the hallway was still blindingly bright, so I couldn't have been out too long, right?

"Naiya?" Val called.

I nodded. "I'm alright. They tried to suffocate me."

"What the fuck?"

I grabbed the cup on my bedside table and heaved myself to my feet to refill it. "They wanted to force me to change into the leopard."

"Did you?" Andy asked.

I filled my cup with water from the sink and gulped down the entirety of it before refilling it. "No."

"Why the hell not, Naiya?" Val asked, her voice incredulous. "They've got your family by the balls!"

I gingerly placed the cup down in the sink so I wouldn't try to crush it, though my hand was shaking. "I *know*! But I also have *no idea* how to make it happen on purpose. It always just takes me. Usually, when I'm sleeping. I don't have any actual control over it."

My spine went cold. What the hell were they going to do to my family because I simply couldn't do what they asked? What was going to happen to Abigail?

I tried to hold back the sob that took me then, but

it hit me so hard, so quickly, that I had nothing. I crumpled to the floor in tears.

"Naiya?" Andy's weight hit his door, judging by the sound, but it was hard to tell over the sounds caused by the ache in my chest.

"What happened?" Val asked, her voice sharp with worry.

"She just cr—"

"My *family*," I cried.

"Oh, shit." Val's voice softened.

"What are they gonna do to my *family*?" I hammered my fists against the floor and left them there as my forehead came to rest against the cool tile. Sobs wracked through my body in convulsing movements.

"They have to give you credit for trying, Naiya," Andy said.

Chad tinkled under my arm and pressed cool sharp facets against my cheek. Odd as that was, it was also kind of comforting.

"My parents don't deserve this," I squeaked out through my tears, curling my elbows up so my hands rested on the back of my head, their weight pressing my forehead harder into the tile. "They should have just left me in New York where they found me."

"Waitascecond," Val said. "Your parents found you in *New York* as a child and just took you with them back to Texas?"

I sucked in a breath, trying to calm myself enough to explain. "They stayed in New York for months trying to find my birth parents. When they couldn't, they took me home—but I'm pretty sure they kept up the search."

"How the hell did they even get you on a plane?"

"Private jet?" I said. "I dunno for sure, I can't remember it. I'm not even sure how old I was."

"Maybe this 'New York' place had a portal to Arcaniss open up and dump you there," Andy offered.

Val laughed.

I sat up, wiping tears from my cheek and sniffling. "That's an odd theory. Let's hear it."

Chad clambered onto my knee and looked up at me. I reached down and stroked his back with my pointer finger.

"It was Luca's favorite way to dispose of enemies," Andy said. "And there *have* been a lot of anomalies here, right? Enough to make your news? It can't be that far-fetched for one to have opened up there."

"But the anomalies haven't been happening since I was a kid, Andy," I said patiently.

"Oh," he said.

"Shitty parents abandon their kids all the time," Val said. "Public places aren't exactly at the top of the list—usually they pick fire stations or churches—but it's not unheard of."

"Oh," Andy said again. "Sorry, it just seemed like … well, I mean … if you've never seen a wereleopard, and they're not exactly uncommon all over Arcaniss, and this world and that are connected by these random portals, then it kind of … well, it follows, doesn't it?"

I raked my hands through my hair, resting them on top of my head. "I mean, I guess I could see how the logic of that works. It just falls apart when you know the portals haven't been happening for that long."

"What if they were?" Val asked.

I frowned and gave the wall adjoining our rooms an incredulous look. "What?"

"I mean, come on," she said. "What if the whackjob conspiracy theorists are right? What if there *is* more than what we can find on the news and with official government statements?"

"I thought you told me *not* to join the ranks of the foil hat wearers."

"I did," she said, laughter in her voice. "I'm fucking with you."

I furrowed my brow, because something in the way she said it didn't feel right.

"She is smirking," Andy said as Val started snickering. "I'll show you. Come to your door."

Brow still furrowed, I went over to my door as Chad crawled up onto my shoulder. Andy's face was screwed up in some weird smirk-frown expression.

"She looks like this," he mumbled, trying not to let his mouth move with the words.

Val's giggles grew into full-blown laughter, and I burst into giggles despite myself.

"What the hell is *that*, Andy?!"

He stopped making the face and gestured toward Val's door. "It's the face she was making."

"Fuckin' rude," Val managed through her laughter.

I wiped at my eyes again and sobered. "But it doesn't change that I can't be sure my parents and Abigail aren't already paying the price for my inability to do as they ask."

"Then we force the issue," Andy said, "and go now. Naiya, you attack the next person that beeps open your door. Get their badge and beep open my door, then Chad can take the badge and get Val out while I help you take them down."

"No way," Val said. "It wouldn't work."

I nodded. "She's right. I'd likely get sedated before I even made it out of my room. Besides, if we try now and fail, my parents could get even more hurt than they may already be right now, and Abigail could end up more stuck."

"That's only likely to get worse the longer we wait," Andy said.

"Still," I insisted, "we can't chance it. *I* can't chance it. Not right now."

Andy nodded, his eyes meeting mine. "Okay. Alright. Then we wait."

The door at the end of the hallway beeped open, and I checked the clock on my wall. It was lunchtime, and the food on their cart smelled of toast and tomatoes. Baldy started the deliveries with me, as usual, and I found out it was tomato basil soup with grilled cheese sandwiches. Even better, there were multiple types of cheese in the sandwiches, all melted together in a deliciously gooey mess that lent itself well to dipping in the soup.

"God, at least the food here is good," Val said around a bite of her food.

I nodded as I tried not to slurp the soup. "True."

When we all finished, we tried playing ball, but I was feeling listless. It didn't matter whether Andy won or whether Val made any progress getting over her nervousness of Chad. I kept thinking about my parents and Abigail. Crying had gotten the worst of those feelings out of me, but what had happened to Abigail with the TSA was my fault. And anything further that could happen, or had already happened, or was happening right now would *also* be my fault.

The ball *thoked* against my door. Startled, I looked up to find Andy studying me.

"There is nothing to be done for them while you're here," he said.

I sighed and sluggishly bobbed my head once.

The door at the end of the hall beeped open.

"Interesting," Andy said a moment later.

"What?" I asked.

And then Grump and Blondie came into view. *Just* Grump and Blondie. That was weird enough, but on top of that, their demeanor seemed … well, wrong.

Blondie beeped open the door to my cell and

rushed in, not waiting for the door to close behind her. Without a word, she threw a fist toward my face, landing against my cheekbone, which crunched softly from the blow. My eyes filled with tears as pain shot up and over my skull, and my hand flew to the spot where she'd connected. Andy called my name, but I was only vaguely aware of it. My ears rang from the hit, and my heart kicked into high gear as adrenaline flooded my system.

"Naiya!" Andy called.

"Wha—?" I looked up at her as I pulled my hand from my cheek. My fingertips had blood on them. I gingerly searched for the cut and found my aching cheek had been split by the blow. "Why—?"

Blondie's fist connected with my mouth, splitting my lip on my teeth and knocking me back onto the bed. My heart slammed against my sternum like a wild thing caged, and my hands shook from the shock of the blows.

"Hey assholes," Val shouted, "leave her alone!"

The door clicked shut as I sat up. Grump had circled around to my right. There was a small tinkling sound as Chad clambered in through my window.

I put my hands up. "Stop! Please! Just lemme try again, okay? There has to be some—"

Blondie's fist connected with my stomach, knocking the breath from my words. I doubled over, and she balled a fist against the back of my head, tugging on my hair as she lifted me back up.

Her other hand was already pulled back for another swing, and I swatted at her chest with all I had. She stumbled back toward the sink with fresh welts seeping blood into her white tank top.

Holy shit, I had scratched her? With just my hand and my broken nails?

But then there was the sound of cracking joints as Blondie's body convulsed and doubled over. Her arms extended with the sound of breaking bones, and her legs changed proportions, the length of her feet growing—tearing out of her shoes—as her shins shortened. The meaty snaps made my stomach turn, and I couldn't help but watch as she turned into a giant wolf right before my eyes. She was still wearing her white tank and grey sweats, though the latter fell from her furred hips, and she kicked out of the legs. She was colored like a coyote, all in browns and tans, except her belly and paws, which were creamy white.

There had just been a person standing there, and then her body broke before it became … *this*.

"What the hell?" My eyes were wide and unblinking, my eyebrows trying to join my hairline as the pounding of my heart kicked into a truly breakneck pace. My stomach twisted.

Oh no.

Grump lunged at me, and my spine turned to ice as I inhaled, only to warm on the exhale as I roared and launched myself off the bed. The sound deepened in tone as I connected against him, reversing his momentum until I was on top of him on the ground. My paws—

Paws? Holy shit. I'd had *hands* half a breath ago.

But he meant to hurt me, and I meant to stop that. So, I raked and gnawed at the arm holding my jaws away from his throat, dripping blood and saliva onto Grump's face as his other hand reached toward his hip.

"There it is," he said, his voice decidedly calmer than I felt.

There was a soft popping sound as something sharp hit my belly. My limbs grew heavy, my bites and scratches sluggish, as I realized what had happened.

He'd shot me. With a tranq dart.

Dammit.

Blackness swallowed me yet again.

THIRTY-SEVEN

I DIDN'T DREAM, but I didn't wake with a start either. I just sort of drifted back to awareness as the breakfast cart made its way down to us. Which meant I'd been out at least long enough that I missed dinner entirely.

And then I remembered what happened. Grump. And Blondie. My face screwed up in horror at the realization, and I slapped my hands over my mouth to keep from saying anything with Curly and Baldy delivering meals. Not that Mr. Loudspeaker wasn't listening anyway, but still.

I was wearing clothes. Someone had dressed me while I was unconscious. I tried not to think about what else they could have done while I was out. I stilled as Curly opened my door and delivered my breakfast—biscuits and creamy country-style sausage gravy. I didn't move again until the door at the end of the hallway clicked closed.

"Oh God," I exclaimed, jumping to my feet. "I would have killed him! I'm a goddamn monster!"

"Naiya!" Val said.

"Mmm, no," Andy said. "That's probably why he sedated you. And you're not a monster; you were defending yourself."

"The important bit is that you *didn't* kill anyone," Val said. "They threw the first punch."

"And the last," Andy added.

I washed my face in the sink, drying it with the towel on the rack. "Okay, but what the hell was …?" I caught my reflection. "Holy shit." There were no cuts on my face, no bruising where I'd been punched, no split lip, *nothing* that indicated I'd been in a fight. I opened my jaw wide and tilted my head from side to side. Nothing ached. It was like the fight had never happened.

What the hell?

"What?" Val asked.

I went over to my window, catching Andy's eye as I gestured to my face, and he nodded knowingly.

"Your cuts and bruises are healed already," he said.

"Huh," Val said. Only she didn't sound surprised.

"How is that possible?" I asked. "What *was* she?"

"She looked like a giant wolf," Andy said. "Like a werewolf."

Val's voice was quiet and resigned. "That's because she was—*is*—a werewolf."

My brow furrowed in confusion. "What? How?"

"You know those conspiracy videos that keep popping up online? The ones that claim to prove vampires and werewolves are real?"

"The foil hat wearers are right … at least about the werewolves," I said, voicing my thoughts aloud as they came to me. "That's why you thought I was serious about the staff of Saint Dymphna's being vampires!"

"What do you mean by 'foil hat?'" Andy asked. "You mentioned them yesterday too."

Val sighed. "Wow, you really *aren't* from around here, are you?"

Andy shook his head as I raked a hand through my hair.

How the hell was I supposed to explain a euphemism two or three levels deep?

"Okay," I said. "So, you get the concept of a conspiracy theorist, right?"

Andy nodded. "Someone who has crazy ideas about how something works."

"Right," I said. "Some conspiracy theorists think that aliens from outer space can read your mind, but that aluminum foil blocks the signal. So, they make hats out of foil to keep the aliens out of their brains."

Andy gave a little half chuckle. "I have been known to read minds through steel helmets. Someone ought to tell those guys they're wrong."

I tilted my head to the side. "Are you telling me you're from outer space?"

Andy's chuckle deepened to a laugh. "Hardly! I'm just saying that if there are other creatures out there that can read minds, foil won't stop them." He contemplated for a moment. "That said, Arcaniss *is* another world, so perhaps I really *am* from this 'outer space' of yours." He winked at me.

"Wait," Val said, "you can read minds?"

Andy looked at her door with a rueful smile. "Normally, yes. But I have to concentrate, and I haven't been able to activate it since I got stuck on this side of the rifts. In your world."

I turned to take my breakfast tray over to sit on my bed. "Why?"

"I'm not exactly sure," Andy said. "Well … hmm … I think it's like gravity."

"Gravity?" Val said. "How?"

"Well, here, gravity is a centrifugal force and is affected by the mass of the planet and how far it is from your sun." He sounded like he was reciting from a textbook. "But where I'm from, gravity works because of the magic within everything being pulled toward the core of my world and the nexus of magic contained therein."

I swallowed the bite I was chewing and took a sip of coffee. "How is gravity like telepathy?"

"It's not," Andy said. "But it's the best comparison I can make. The fundamental rules of existence in your world are different than the ones of mine, which makes it harder for me to exert my will over them."

"Okay," Val said. "But how do you know anything at all about our gravity?"

"I was at a place called the Lamb of Hope Recovery Institute for a handful of days before these people picked me up. They had some basic science books there, along with some other books too. There was a really sad story about a boy whose dog gets rabies, and another about some really vicious rabbits."

"*Old Yeller*," I said, "and *Watership Down*, by the sound of it."

"You've read them?" Andy said. "They seemed kind of neglected."

"I had to read them in school." I took another bite of gravy-covered biscuit, but then put my fork down on the tray. "Wait. You can read? How?"

"I think it's part of the translation magic that gave me your common tongue when I came through the rift," Andy said. "I can read and write several languages back home, so I guess it translated the common one here. I really wish I understood how it worked better. It will be one of the key things I look into when I get home."

"Did the rehab center ever put on Telemundo?" Val asked. "Could you understand that, too?"

"They did sometimes have something on that was in a language I couldn't understand," he replied, "but I don't know if it was what you're asking about. Not for sure, I mean."

"Well, to get back to the foil hat term," I said. "The people shielding their thoughts from aliens aren't the only ones who have crazy-sounding conspiracy theories. There just happen to be probably more of them than any others."

"Or they're the most vocal," Val said.

"That's probably true," I conceded. "Anyway, 'foil hat wearer' kind of became the catch-all term for someone with really wild conspiracy theories."

"I see," Andy said.

It fell quiet for a moment as we all ate.

"The nurse came and drew your blood while you were out," Andy said. "Once you were human again. But I think she sedated you again afterward, because you didn't even wake up to dinner."

I nodded. "I'm guessing she's the one that put me in clothes."

"Yes," Andy said.

A thought occurred to me then, and my cheeks heated at it. "You didn't watch, did you?"

"Uh, I mean, I *did*," Andy said. "But that guy, Grump, put you in bed under your blanket before he left. So when you turned back, there was nothing to see."

"Good to know."

"It's an interesting dichotomy," he said.

"What is?"

"Your change to leopard," he said. "It's nothing like the werewolf woman's. I saw, through Chad, how her body contorted and wrenched itself into strange angles to accommodate the change as it happened. It's so much slower for her. Your change is much smoother. It's like in one breath you're on two legs, and the next, you're on four."

"That's almost exactly how it happened," I said. And then something clicked for me. "Wait. Val. You said she *is* a werewolf. Like you're sure of it."

Val sighed. "I am."

"How do you know that?" I asked.

She was quiet for a moment. We all were.

"I … I knew …" She blew out a breath and stopped.

I put my tray down and came to my window. "How. Did. You. *Know*?"

"I knew … because … well, I used to be one."

Andy's eyebrows shot up. "'Used to?'"

"You used to be a …" God, could I even say it like I was serious? "A werewolf?"

The foil hat wearers were right? Andy was right! I looked across the hall at him. He met my eyes with an almost apologetic smile and then looked back at Val.

Val took a deep breath in and let it out slowly. "Yeah." There was a sound of fabric moving, and I was pretty sure it was her rubbing at the scars on her stomach.

"And you're not now?" I wasn't sure how to take that it could even be possible.

"Yep." More fabric moving. She was definitely rubbing at those scars. "Sometimes, when a person gets turned, it goes bad … *they* go bad."

"Only sometimes?" Andy said. "Where werewolves are concerned, that's always true in my world."

"Well," Val continued, "it went bad for me."

A light bulb lit in my brain. "The scars on your stomach."

Four parallel scars about a finger-width apart. The scratches I'd put on Blondie would likely leave similar scars. Val had known this whole time?

"The scars on my stomach," Val confirmed with a sigh. "Look, Naiya. I'll tell you more. And you too, Andy. I will. I promise. But not until we get out of here, okay?"

"Someone cured you?" Andy asked.

"Not here, Andy," Val said. "They're always listening."

"Val—" I started, not even sure what I was going to say or ask.

Her voice was firm. "Not. Here."

THIRTY-EIGHT

A LITTLE AFTER BREAKFAST, the door at the end of the hallway beeped open. I stood up and went to my door. I'd gotten the routine of this place down by now—at least as it pertained to taking me for whatever test or trial they had next.

The nurse came into view, flanked by Blondie and Grump. Blondie had a tight t-shirt on today, a departure from her usual tank top, and Grump's left forearm had a bandage around it.

From me. Because of me.

My hands started to shake, and there was a small twist in my gut.

Shit.

It wasn't enough that I thought I might change, but I also wasn't sure what he was going to do.

The nurse beeped open my door and gestured out into the hall. "This way, Ms. Kateri."

I eyed Blondie and Grump. Their demeanor was different than yesterday. Back to their usual stoicism, I suppose. I didn't relish the idea of having someone whom I'd tried to kill—and someone who'd thrown an unprovoked punch—following along behind me, but I didn't see much of an option. I pressed my lips into a line with a sigh and stepped out into the hallway.

Andy pushed his hand through the window of his door, almost like he was reaching for me. Blondie stepped between me and his hand.

I met his eyes over her shoulder and nodded once as he did the same.

"Be careful, Naiya," Val said.

I nodded to her too, as I fell into step behind the nurse. Blondie and Grump took their usual positions, and the four of us set to wandering the labyrinth of halls yet again.

After a few turns and a few more security doors, we arrived in a hallway not entirely unlike the one where I'd played dodgeball with the machines. There were three doors on either side, offset from one another so that none were directly across from each other, with big wide windows in each door. There was another door with a smaller window at the end of the hallway. We hadn't gone into the high-ceiling area of the building, but the walls here were darker than the hallway my cell was in.

I glanced in the windows of the first rooms—they were small and empty. No furniture or people. Or werewolves, I suppose. I was still wrapping my head around how that was even possible.

The nurse beeped open the middle door to my left and gestured for me to head inside. It was a small room, like the ones we'd passed, but something felt … not quite okay.

The door clicked closed behind me, and I couldn't shake the ominous feeling. It didn't help that no one had come into the tiny space with me.

The hairs on the back of my neck prickled. The walls of this room were almost *too* close. Like the angles were wrong? I couldn't put my finger on it. There wasn't a two-way mirror in the room, but the wall directly opposite the door had two barred openings near the ceiling, each about six inches tall by about two feet wide. As I visually traced the lines of the wall, I noticed the little seams right where the floor met the wall. It was like the flooring was off by less than a quarter of an inch.

As I puzzled at it, there was the high-pitched whine like a TV that's just been turned on, and then a heavy, but still quiet, click followed by the smooth hum of the wall retracting into the floor.

Beyond the now-retracted wall was a space about the same size as the one I had entered. In the middle of that was a clear plastic box almost the size of the other half of the room. Its walls were easily a couple of inches thick. And inside the box were two gaunt and greasy-looking goth kids.

They were maybe in their early twenties, but so pale and haggard, it looked like they hadn't seen the light of day in years. I don't think they'd seen a shower in any recent time frame either. One was taller than the other, with blond hair that hung past his shoulders, and the other was shorter, his hair so black I was relatively certain he dyed it. Both wore black jeans, though the taller had a red t-shirt on with his, while the one with the black hair paired his with a black button-down shirt that was open at the collar. They watched me with sunken too-dark eyes and stepped side-to-side within their box, their movements almost hypnotically matched. I didn't like it.

My gut twisted like a warning klaxon.

Wrong, kill it!

No. Not here.

But the hairs on the back of my neck were standing up even straighter than they had a moment ago, my fingers curling into fists and releasing.

The front panel of the box was almost like a door, with round bits of metal evenly spaced around the seams. With another barely audible whine and another click, that panel swung open, and the two guys burst toward me as the scent of something very much not okay filled my nose. It was like rotting garbage, maybe? Or raw meat? I couldn't place it.

And I didn't have time to.

The shorter of the two goths lunged at me. My stomach twisted as I dodged away from him, my perspective on the world shifting as I landed on four black paws. Red seeped into my vision as my heart rate spiked for a beat or two.

Shit.

Well, it didn't matter now. The tall blond one's knee slammed into my chin, knocking me backward as my jaws clicked closed. My heartbeat returned to normal as I twisted in the air, rebounding off the back wall and leaping onto him. He held my weight for a moment before finally tossing me aside. The shorter one followed my movements, his hands reaching for me as I landed. Except I didn't land. I bounced again off the wall and grabbed the back of his neck with my jaws as I came down, shaking my head. There was a meaty snap as I did, and he stopped moving.

But his pal was too close by then. He scraped a solid gouge along my side with clawed fingers until I released my hold on the shorter one. Pain and warmth blossomed momentarily from the wound, but even as I became aware of it, it was fading. I grabbed the remaining one's arm then with my jaws, snapping the bone easily as I pulled the guy away from my side. He yelled something, but I didn't hear it. I was still in motion, just as he was. He lunged at me again, but I ducked under him and spun around quickly to pounce on him from behind, once again grabbing the back of his neck and shaking until there was another meaty snap, and he stopped moving.

It was over in a matter of seconds.

I checked them where they lay, nosing their bodies and making sure they were not inclined to get back up and continue the fight. Their teeth were too sharp, too long in their mouths, and still bared, though their eyes were vacant. Globs of too-thick black-red blood were spattered around them.

The door I'd come in through beeped open, and a black blanket flew in, unfolding from its bundle as it fell.

I grabbed it with my teeth and curled into the corner farthest from the two wrong things that were very much dead on the ground.

Dead.

They were dead. And I had killed them. I hadn't even known I'd wanted to, hadn't even known I could. But it had all happened so quickly.

I curled into a ball in the corner, but was almost instantly back to two legs again as I did. Holy shit, I'd just been along for the ride as the leopard killed them. I wrapped the blanket tightly around me and tried to keep my breakfast down.

I didn't succeed. But at least I managed not to be sick on the blanket.

The nurse opened the door then. She stepped around the two greasy goth kids on the floor and over to me, pulling a needle from her pocket as she reached for my arm.

My heart slammed against my sternum, and I clutched the blanket tighter to me in one closed fist.

"Arm, please, Ms. Kateri," she said patiently.

I didn't move, I just looked at her with wide, wild eyes. "What the hell were those things?!"

She didn't move; she just stared at me implacably.

I ran a hand through my hair and forced my breathing to slow. Why should she start answering my questions now? I thrust my arm out for her to get her stupid sample.

"There," she said when she was done. "Now, let's get you cleaned up and into fresh clothes."

I sullenly followed her from the room, edging around the walls to stay as far from the dead bodies as I could. The walk to the bathroom was even more awkward with nothing but a blanket to cover myself. I tried to ignore the feeling of Grump and Blondie's eyes on the back of my head as we made our way through the halls.

I took a long shower. Longer than I'd ever taken at this place. I tried to hold back the flood of tears at the fear for my parents, and the disgust with myself for having killed those guys, even if they were trying to kill me. And when I remembered that I'd been raked along my side by the taller one, I checked the skin only to find that the wound had already healed.

God, I was like something straight out of a superhero movie. Only one of those with the questionable morality types. Because no actual good guy superhero killed their enemies in their movies. No good guys hurt the people they loved. But the morally grey ones did it all the time. And they did it with the same mindlessly efficient ruthlessness that I had just deployed.

Oh God, I really *was* a monster!

At some point, I finished my shower, put on the clothes that were provided, and brushed through my hair. I plodded along, going through the motions as I followed the nurse most of the way back to my cell before she peeled off, and I was left with just Blondie and Grump. My anxiety ratcheted up a notch then, but they didn't make any move to say or do anything to me. They simply kept walking, so I kept following, my thoughts swirling incoherently.

Blondie beeped open the door at the end of the hall to let me in, and Grump beeped open the door to my cell as one thing became clear: the foil hat wearers were definitely on to something.

"Are you okay, Naiya?" Andy asked as my door clicked shut.

I waited until the door at the end of the hallway was closed before saying anything. Those guys had had big long teeth and their fingers ended in claws. That's just not how people work.

"Vampires are real, too," I said. "Aren't they, Val?"

Shock painted Andy's face. "You have vampires here?"

"I didn't think they did," I said. "But they just made me fight a couple of them."

Made me *kill* a couple of them.

Val sucked in a breath between her teeth. "Ffluck, how'd you do?"

Their lifeless eyes and the wrong angles of their heads flashed through my mind, but I wouldn't let the images stay. "I killed them both."

"They weren't human, Naiya," Val said quickly. "They would have killed you."

I thunked my head against the bars of my window. "How do you know about this stuff, Val?"

"I picked it up along the way," she said. "I can't really say more here. I don't know who these guys are … or who they work for. Any info they hear me give you is essentially me giving it to them, and that could hurt people I care about."

I lifted my head and pinched the bridge of my nose, squeezing my eyes shut. Except the last bit was a mistake—I saw their lifeless, unfocused gaze every time I closed my eyes.

"When we get out of here, then," Andy said.

"Absolutely," Val agreed.

I blew out a breath. "Fine. Do you at least know how to tell which of these people is a werewolf *before* they go all wolf?"

"Well," Val said, "not entirely. But I can be pretty sure."

I nodded. "Okay. So, who else are you *sure* is a werewolf?"

"Best I can tell? All of them."

I took a step back from my door. "No way."

"Well, you know that girl who was just here—Blondie—is," Val said. "But her friend—"

"Grump," I supplied.

"Yeah, Grump is too. You can tell by the golden eyes."

"Which means so is Baldy," I said. "And the nurse's eyes go gold sometimes."

"So, she's one too," Val said. "And the odds that the other guy who delivers the meals—"

"Curly," I supplied.

"The odds are high that he's one too," she said. "If he's paired with Baldy."

"What about those two that came to get you the other day, Val?" Andy asked.

"Mohawk," I said, "and Bob."

Val snickered. "Pretty sure they are, yeah, but I'm not as sure about them as I am the others."

I went back to the door as a thought hit me. "What do you think the odds are that the entire staff is full of werewolves, all the way up the chain to Mr. Loudspeaker himself?"

"Mmm," Andy said, meeting my gaze. "I don't think he is."

"Why?"

"If he was, you'd likely have seen him by now. There'd be no reason to hide like he does."

I cocked my head to the side. "That's a good point."

"Yeah," Val said. "But you're probably right about the rest, Naiya. This whole place is likely to be full of werewolves. There are too many to keep it a secret from whoever else they have on staff here."

"So, tell me about vampires then," I said.

"They're real," she said. "They're dangerous. They look like people, but they're not. They're the *real* monsters. They'll kill a person as soon as talk to them, and they hate werewolves as much as werewolves hate them. It's a wonder these assholes managed to keep any alive without killing them."

"Sounds a lot like the vampires from Arcaniss," Andy said.

"It's still better if I don't detail out everything that I know for them," Val said. "The less they know I know, the better. But I can tell you this: killing them was the best thing you could have done. For you, for them, for your family, for the staff here, for *everyone*."

I nodded with another sigh and let the topic drop.

THIRTY-NINE

The rest of the day passed in an almost mindless routine. Curly and Baldy brought us taco salad for lunch. We played a few quiet rounds of ball with Chad before I peeled off to read my book again. I started to doze, but every time I started to drift, I saw the faces of the dead things I'd killed and snapped back awake. Monster or not, I didn't like killing things that looked like people.

Eventually, Curly and Baldy brought us chicken parmesan for dinner. And when the lights went out at their usual time, I stared into the dark, jolting awake as I started to doze, until I finally lost awareness sometime well after Andy and Val had fallen asleep.

A loud *shkunk*, like someone had thrown the breaker for the lights of a football stadium, woke me —saved me, really—from my usual nightmares. It was still dark in my room and the hallway beyond, and I looked at the clock on the wall.

Except I couldn't find it. The spot where it was had gone black.

I threw the blanket off me and stood, moving slowly and quietly toward my door as I listened for Andy and Val's breathing.

It didn't sound like they were sleeping, and Chad was tinkling around in Andy's cell.

"Val? Andy?"

"Yep," Val said, her clothing rustling as she moved around in her cell. "I think the power went out."

"It did," Andy said. "*Mitne.*"

The little pale purple glow that came from Chad's backend lit up in Andy's cell.

I tried my door, pushing against it to see if I could get the lock to disengage, but it didn't budge.

There was a little iridescent glow in Andy's room followed by a click of the latch of his door and … he pushed it open.

Holy shit. He was out.

Little purple, green, and orange geometric shapes quickly faded from the air like silently popping bubbles. They reminded me of his tattooed arm. Chad sat on his shoulder, his back legs were extended to hold his butt as high off Andy's shoulder as he could manage, while his front legs were hooked firmly into Andy's shirt.

"Holy shit, Andy," Val breathed, echoing my thoughts.

I met his eyes in the dark and glanced at my door, but he already had his hand extended toward the box on the wall that the staff used to beep it open. A spray of those same geometric shapes as before shot out the sides of the mechanism as a tiny breeze brushed the scent of freshly fallen snow across my face and the latch clicked. I pushed open the door and threw my arms around him in a hug. He was only a couple of inches taller than I was, though that still put him at six feet tall, easy.

"Thank you," I whispered in his ear.

He wrapped both of his arms around me and squeezed me tight to him, his hand brushing along the hair at the back of my head as he pressed his cheek against me. He also smelled vaguely like the crisp frost of freshly fallen snow, but I didn't try to pin down the other notes. It was enough just to have the friendly contact of another person. Chad tinkled up over my head and then up over Andy's, coming to rest on his other shoulder, chittering happily. Tears stung at my eyes, and I held him for just a moment longer before letting him go.

"Val," I said.

He nodded and turned for her door.

"You don't have time to get me out too," Val said. "There's no way these guys aren't already on their way to secure these cells."

I didn't know what had made her hide being a former werewolf from me, or what made her hide that she'd gone for showers and things while I was gone, but if I left her here, I'd never know. Besides, she'd been with me through my stay at Saint Dymphna's as well as everything here, and the friendship we'd built wasn't worth just idly throwing away.

"I'm not leaving without you," I said.

Andy's hand was already extended toward the black keycard sensor next to her door, his brow furrowed in concentration while Chad danced from side to side on top of his head. A moment later, the box shot more iridescent shapes from either side with a little puff of a snow-scented breeze as the latch clicked.

I yanked open Val's door and wrapped her in a hug too, which she returned just as heartily.

"You tried to warn me about these guys when they brought me here from Saint Dymphna's," I said into her faded rainbow hair. "Which is probably what landed you here in the first place, and you've helped keep me grounded, so I didn't completely lose my shit here. You're coming with us."

I started toward the door at the end of the hall, my heartbeat in my throat.

"Wait!" Andy said, grabbing my hand and tugging in the other direction. "They always come in from that door. There's another door at the other end."

I nodded and turned. "Good call."

"Andy," Val said, gesturing to Chad. "That thing is gonna give us away. I don't like not being able to see where we're going, but I'm way less interested in getting caught."

"I can see without the light," I said.

Andy nodded. "*Whedab*."

The light went out on Chad's backend and we were left with only the miniscule amount of moonlight from the skylight above us.

"I can use Chad's vision," Andy said, closing his own eyes. "It's not perfect, but it's better than nothing."

"We don't have time for this," Val said. "If we're going, let's go. Quickly and *quietly*."

I grabbed her hand. "I'll try to guide you."

"And I'll guide you to the end of the hall here," Andy said, squeezing my hand once as he passed me.

I wasn't sure I liked the thought of following someone who literally had their eyes closed, but I had to hope Chad's vision was good. Though, realistically, I didn't need to trust Chad's vision anyway, since I could see just fine.

"If we hear anyone, we have to turn around immediately and find a different path," Val said. "If I'm right, and they're all werewolves, they can hear your heartbeat."

"Holy shit," I whispered.

Andy led the way around a bend to a door at the other end of the hall, where he broke the lock the same way he had on our cells. The door opened into the hall, and we paused to listen before we stepped through.

The hallway beyond was so quiet my ears rang.

Val and Andy and I sounded like winded horses by comparison. But, since we didn't hear any movement, I poked my head into the space.

The hallway stretched in front of me for a handful of yards before splitting in a wide Y. There were doors to the left and right along the way, all with keycard locks.

"Keycards probably mean people," Val whispered.

I nodded. "I'll take point, since I don't need assistance to see."

Andy nodded and let me pull Val past him as I stepped out into the hall. We ducked as we passed the doors, since they all had windows in them. I suspected that from the inside, those windows were two-way mirrors—especially if what Val said about werewolves was true. They wouldn't need to see what's on the other side of the door if they could just hear it.

When we got to the Y intersection, I paused to look down each side, leaning to see as far as I could. The fork to the left bent around further to the left after a ways, while the right side ended in a T. I looked back at Andy, whose eyes were still closed.

He shrugged and whispered, "Your guess is as good as mine."

I nodded once and went toward the T to the right since it seemed like that would give us more options. If it weren't for my clothes rustling, I would have been damn near silent, though Val was noisier, as was Andy. But at least Chad didn't move from where he was anchored to Andy's shoulder. As we got to the T, we paused so I could listen. There was something coming from the right, but it was quiet enough that I was relatively certain it was around the bend. Still, it likely meant people, so I turned left and followed the hallway around until it took a sharp left turn. There was a keycard door at the turn too, though there was a window in the door that I peeked through. The hallway continued beyond, but Val was likely right about keycards leading to people, so I followed the sharp left. A little ways down, there were voices coming from one of the doors on the right side of the hall. I stopped to listen.

"The generators *are* running," said one voice, agitated. He sounded a little like Grump.

"Then why don't we have power?" A female voice. Maybe Blondie?

"I don't know," the guy who sounded like Grump said. "Comms are down, and cell service is out, too."

Something heavy slammed against one of the doors.

Shit. Time to go.

Val tugged on my arm. Andy jerked his head back the way we came.

I nodded and we turned back.

We got around the bend and crouched to hold still for a moment. I didn't like the thought of going back the way we came, and nothing else slammed against a door.

I reached across Val and tapped Andy's knee. He looked up and blinked before closing his eyes again. He pointed to Chad.

I nodded and pointed at the keycard lock of the door across the hall—the one the hallway extended beyond—and back to Andy before making a motion with my hands like I was breaking a stick.

He nodded and stood to creep past me. He held his hand up to the lock and focused on it until more iridescent shapes spewed from the sides with another little gust of wind scented with snow. I pushed the door open, tugging Val along behind me. Andy closed the door gently and quietly behind us and then put his hand to the spot where the latch went into the frame and focused until the shapes shot out again.

I arched an eyebrow at him as the scent of snow

fluttered past my face, hoping the question was plain enough in my expression that he could see it in the dark through Chad's eyes.

"So it's harder for them to follow," he whispered.

I nodded and turned to head back down the hall. We passed a hallway to the left, but kept going straight, following the hall around a gentle bend to the left until we came to a wide four-way intersection. I paused to listen. It sounded like there were people far ahead of us, but I couldn't be sure if they were moving, and the hallway to our right was quiet, so we turned right. We passed another quiet hallway to our right, but then I heard something ahead of us and we had to double back to hide in the hallway.

Val tugged my arm as I focused to hear where the movement was going. I turned to see her pointing at a little glow-in-the-dark arrow at the far edge of the furthest ceiling tile in the intersection. It pointed back the way we came.

That had to be fire exit directions.

Or, at least, I hoped it was.

And following them was better than casting about blindly in this maze.

The movement in the hallway we'd been in sounded now like it was moving away from us. So, I guided us back into the hall, doubling back the way we came as I watched along the ceiling for more arrows.

We followed them all back to the door I was sure Andy had broken the lock of. It still vaguely smelled like snow here.

Andy leaned close to my ear, bonking his head against mine once as he did. "I just broke this lock," he breathed.

I nodded. "Gonna need you to break it back so we can get out."

Val tapped both of us and thrust her first finger against her lips.

Andy nodded with a shrug and turned back to the lock, holding his hand out to the spot where the latch met the frame. It took longer, and he had to bring his other hand up to focus harder, but it eventually burst into little iridescent shapes and Andy pulled it open as the snow-scented breeze wafted past me.

We kept following the arrows, taking a left at the Y intersection ahead until we hit another door with a keycard lock. Up in the top right corner of the door was a tiny little glowing word: "EXIT."

Holy shit.

Andy held his hand toward the lock and opened it. The scent of snow was quickly overpowered by the fresh heat and humidity of a summer night in Texas.

My eyes filled with tears as I stilled.

Val tugged my hand. "We have to *go*."

I nodded and stepped from the door onto concrete that had cooled from the day's sun as my heart returned to pounding in my ears. Andy shoved the door closed behind us with a click of heavy finality, and I sucked in a lungful of warm night air as he held his hand to the latch until a tiny spray of geometry flew from it.

Free.

I was finally *free*.

FORTY

We didn't have time for celebration. We had to get out of eyesight of the building. We had to get *away*.

"Can you see?" Andy asked Val.

She nodded. "Yeah, better than I could before."

"There are lights beyond the trees, over that way," Andy said, pointing to the left. Chad danced on his shoulder, his facets catching the moonlight so that he sparkled as he chittered.

It was probably a shopping center, or at least a gas station. Getting somewhere public, somewhere they couldn't take us *back* without making a scene, sounded like a *real* good idea, even if there was a rather thick amount of underbrush and trees between us and whatever civilization was there.

"Let's go," I said.

Andy took off at a jog, Val joining him, and I realized they both had shoes. And I was still barefoot. Dammit.

No time to worry about that now. I shook my head and started jogging into the scrub and grass beyond the edges of the base's concrete slab to catch up, hoping some sharp rock didn't slow me down. There was a bit of clearing between us and the underbrush, though it gradually got thicker, turning to patchy, waist-high grass and weeds before the trees finally took over.

I looked over my shoulder as I caught up with Val and Andy. There was a faint sound of motors running on the far side of the building—probably the generators I'd heard about. Despite that, the whole building was eerily dark. There wasn't a search light or even those little red indicator lights to show where the top of the building was. Though, I supposed they only used those for skyscrapers, didn't they? Still, it was eerie that not a single light indicated the building was even there.

Andy said something I didn't understand, though his tone clearly indicated it was an epithet.

"What?" I asked, turning back around.

Andy pointed at a dark spot just at the edge of the trees, a little more than a hundred yards away in the tall grass. It was an inky black tall oval, ringed in purple, green, and orange.

"What the hell is *that*?" Val asked, squinting her eyes.

"That," Andy said, "is a rift."

Something impossibly black moved between us and it. Two somethings, actually, one larger than the other. And I was pretty sure they were moving toward us.

"Okay," I said, pointing. "And then what the hell are those?"

"Rift cats," he replied, setting his jaw and taking a step in front of me as a long, thin sword just ... manifested in his hand. It looked like a fancy fencing weapon, like out of an old swashbuckling movie.

Except he hadn't been carrying a sword.

My eyes were wide. "How the—?"

"You'll probably stand a better chance against them in leopard form, Naiya," he said. "They are *very* dangerous."

"I don't have any control over when it happens," I said, my heart rate spiking. "And even if I did, I can't be sure I wouldn't end up hurting you or Val!"

Andy turned to me then, placing a hand on my shoulder as he met my gaze. Even in the moonlight, his eyes were a deep dark blue with pupils that were a void-black field of stars.

"I trust you, Naiya," he said. "You're not gonna hurt us."

I took a shaky breath and swallowed a lump of anxiety. "Do you know your pupils are huge and full of stars?"

The corner of his mouth pulled up. "Good to know getting stuck here didn't get rid of that, at least." He kissed me on the forehead before turning back toward the rift.

Chad tucked himself into the pocket of Andy's sweats, and then Andy broke into a run. I didn't like how the black things stalking toward us moved. They were like living shadows that moved wrong and were hard to track. As Andy came close to one of the impossibly black shapes, he slashed at it. These things were faster than him, though, and it was gone from the space he swung into before he'd even committed to the motion. The other one circled around him.

As Andy spun to try to keep both of the things in his field of view, Val found a thorny bush off to our right and pulled a branch of it off. It didn't come easily, and she had to put most of her weight into tugging it free. When it did, she stumbled a few steps before recovering and brandishing it like a baseball bat.

She moved in a wide circle, like she was trying to get into the treeline beyond the portal, keeping the thorny branch between her and the things Andy had named rift cats.

And I was helpless unless I could get into that

nightmare form of mine. Hell, I didn't even have shoes! Even if I did, I certainly couldn't just abandon my friends, not when one of them was the whole reason I'd even managed to escape in the first place.

Besides, the shadowy creatures were too close for me to get past them.

As I thought it, the one Andy had slashed at leaped into the air with claws out for a positively lethal-looking pounce. Andy cried out as it tore into his shoulder and my gut twisted at the sound.

Oh no! Andy! I clapped one hand to my mouth to keep from shouting and calling attention to myself, and the other pressed hard against the twisting feeling in my stomach.

The other creature had peeled off and was stalking toward Val, who made nervous little squeaks as she stumbled and regained her footing.

I had to help them. I didn't know how to do it, but I had to. My gut twisted again, harder this time, and I tried to lean into it, doubling over the hand pressed to my gut as I tried to just let the leopard take over.

But I was still so scared that I'd hurt my friends too.

"Naiya!" Andy called. His call was followed by a hard grunt of pain as the creature swiped a claw across his side.

One of the black shapes was stalking toward me. There had been three of them and I just hadn't been able to track them all the way they'd been grouped up.

Oh no. I had nothing. At least the leopard had claws and teeth. How do I let it out?

My gut twisted hard again, pulling me to my knees, and my perspective shifted from one breath to the next as my body launched into motion at the thing coming at me. I snarled and growled like the wild thing I'd just unleashed. I pounced on top of the creature as it tried to dodge under me, but my jaws snapped on empty air. It was like it was made from the very shadows of the night, as inky and incorporeal as a midday shadow on the pavement.

Chad had come out of Andy's pocket and was poking at his wounds.

Val brandished the thorny branch at the other of the two things, but when it heard me snarl, it turned its attention to me as well.

Great.

Still, her hand went to her stomach, her mouth moving as she closed her eyes.

I turned my attention back to the thing—the rift cat—who stalked around me with movements that were difficult to track. So, I closed my eyes to listen for it, paying attention to the way the air moved against my whiskers. I managed to catch it as it leaped at me. As my claws found meat, I opened my eyes. I'd got it in the throat, just under its jaw. Replacing my clawed paw with the teeth Andy had called impressive, I tore out its throat, spraying black metallic-tasting ichor in an arc around me as I shook my head.

One down. Two to go.

The other paused, but then leaped at me. It scraped a claw across my face, and I tasted my own blood in my mouth, but I rolled and launched it over me, slamming it into a nearby tree trunk. It yelped out a rasping noise like shrieking metal as it hit, and I winced at the sound, lashing out with a paw to make it stop. It leaped at me again, and I caught its front leg in my jaws, snapping the bone as the rift cat crashed to the ground. Another yelp of shrieking metal, and I batted my paw into its jaw, gouging out an eye with my claw and tearing open the creature's face. It tried to stand then, but I grabbed the back of its skull in my mouth and shook violently side-to-side. Like the goth—no, *vampires*—there was a meaty snap, and the thing fell limply to the ground as I released it.

Two down. One to go.

Another shrieking yelp and the third went limp over top of Andy, impaled through the chest on his sword.

I stepped over the bodies of the creatures I'd killed, which were dissipating into the night air with wisps of inky black smoke that trailed back to the open rift. Andy was still on the ground, and Val had her back to a tree. She whispered something about me not being mooncrazed over and over to herself like a mantra.

Andy dropped his sword as the creature dissipated into the wind and held a hand to the wound at his side. Chad tinked over to the injury, poking Andy's fingers until he let go. Andy did, flourishing his hand limply. The sword turned into a tiny spray of pale iridescent geometry that fluttered back to the inside of his wrist and was gone. Andy's hand dropped to the ground like dead weight.

Chad made a little squeaking sort of shriek and dug his legs in on either side of the gaping wound on Andy's side, pressing his little body down as he pulled his legs together. His body gently pulsed with a dimmer version of the glow Andy had activated in him earlier. There was a lot of blood, and the breeze turned metallic as I pinned my ears back against my head. My tail thrashed side to side.

Val stepped closer, edging around to the far side of Andy with wide eyes that darted between me and Andy. "Andy! Oh no!"

With a little hiss, the rift closed, leaving behind a wisp or two of quickly dissipating inky black shadow.

Val looked up at me, back at the building, and then down at Andy, whose eyes had closed. "We're going to have to leave him here, Naiya." Her voice shook, and she only glanced at me once or twice as she said it.

A snarl escaped me and she jumped at the sound.

"No," she said shakily, wincing and turning her face from mine. "No. Look. I know. But if we take him, those guys are way more likely to catch up to us."

I didn't want to scare her, but I wasn't leaving anyone behind.

I took a step closer and snarled again.

She squeaked in fear and squeezed her eyes shut as she ducked her head further toward Andy.

"Naiya," she whimpered. "Please."

I stared at the top of her head, unmoving. She glanced up once and then looked back away. Her face was almost exactly what my mother's had looked like before the screaming started and guilt pooled in my stomach for a fraction of a second before a strange certainty washed through me.

"Fine! Fine." Val lifted Andy's arm—the one closest to her. "Andy, if you can hear me, I need your help." She looped the arm around her neck and shoulder and grabbed his far arm to get him to sit up. "We have to go. C'mon." She leveraged herself to get him the rest of the way to his feet.

And Andy held his own weight. Kinda. He shook on his feet, and his head was limp.

"Need you to bring me 'long." Andy's words were slurred, his voice weak. "Steer me. Chad's working."

Val took a deep, shaky breath and looked at me. "If we get caught again, it'll be your fault."

A leopard's smile is not nearly as friendly as a human's. Val squeaked and looked away when she saw mine, pulling Andy along for a step or two.

She restarted her mantra in a quiet whisper. "Naiya is not mooncrazed. Naiya is not mooncrazed."

I had no idea what the hell it meant, but it seemed

to help her. Some of the tension left her posture, though she didn't look at me as she steered Andy toward the treeline. Once we got far enough in that we couldn't readily see the door we'd come out of, she paused, setting Andy gently down.

"Andy," she said. "I can't do this, I don't have the kind of strength it takes."

Andy's head bobbed once and I made a wide circle around them, watching and listening back toward the building. It sounded like the generators were still running, but I could only just barely make out the outline of the building against the night sky through the trees. They still didn't have power yet, as far as I could tell.

"Give me … a minute," Andy said, his breathing heavy. "Let me … lean on you."

I didn't like it. But there was nothing I could do. Val sat on the ground, her back against his, keeping him upright. He looked too pale, and I hoped it was just the moonlight doing that.

He got very still then, and his eyes closed as I paced around. I tried to keep both the two of them and the building in my view, since I was entirely too antsy to feel like we were safe. Andy's breathing slowly evened out. Chad's pulsing light slowed and matched Andy's breathing. His legs pulled away from the cut one by one, and then they started to gently poke from one side to the other. As they did, the spot would almost regrow to connect to the other side of the wound and close up, leaving fresh pink skin.

Andy nodded once as Chad finished basically knitting the wound closed. "That should help, but it's not finished." His voice sounded stronger, but it still wavered a bit. He reached back and tapped Val as he leaned forward, taking his weight off her back.

She turned as she stood, eyeing the spot under

Chad's glowing body. It wasn't even scabbed over, it just looked like a fresh scar.

"Holy shit," she said. "You can heal just about anything that way."

Chad clung onto Andy's side and pressed his body against the fresh scar.

Andy shook his head once and squinted his eyes shut. "No … anything more would've done me in."

I stilled then. He meant he almost died. A quiet snarl escaped me.

"Holy shit," Val breathed.

He looked at me and nodded once before turning to Val. "We have to keep moving."

Val gestured to me. "People are going to notice her like that! No one here just walks the streets with a leopard."

I skulked off behind a tree as Andy tried to pull himself to his feet. Val hurried in to help him.

"That may be true," he said as Val looped one of his arms over her shoulder again, "but we should still keep moving toward those lights. We'll stop before we get out of the trees until Naiya changes back to two legs."

Val looked at me and rubbed her scarred stomach. When she spoke, her voice was barely more than a whisper. "Please come back to us."

FORTY-ONE

WE'D ONLY BEEN MOVING through the trees for maybe ten minutes when I collapsed to the ground, shaking and shivering as my fur became skin again. We had finally gotten far enough in that the building wasn't in sight, and the lights of whatever civilization lay beyond the trees were like a beacon of hope. Still, I curled into a ball, trying to cover my nakedness while I shivered, despite the warmth in the air, and refused to make eye contact with Val or Andy. There was a bruise on my knee that faded even as I sat there, and there was a dull ache that indicated a bruise on the opposite hip, though it was fading as well. I touched my lip where it had been scraped by the claw of one of those things, only to find it had already healed closed.

"Naiya!" Val's voice sounded relieved, but I shrank against my knees all the same.

"Here." With a grunt, Andy peeled off his shirt and offered it to me.

When I didn't move, he bent down with another grunt and guided me into it. I let him, not meeting his eyes as he gently unfolded me from myself and pulled my arms through each of the sleeves of his black t-shirt. Somehow, it wasn't nearly as bloody as I thought, though it did have a big hole in the side.

Most of the blood from his wound must've gone into the dirt. I took a breath that wracked a sob through me, and tears leaked down my cheeks.

He could have died!

Andy just wrapped me in his arms, and I clung to him as he brushed a hand over my hair and made little shushing noises.

"It's okay," he said softly. "You're okay. We're okay."

Beneath the soap and shampoo they had at the facility, Andy's scent was like dark chocolate and honey, edged with that crispness of freshly fallen snow.

Pull yourself together, Naiya! We're not in the clear yet.

"We're not," he said softly. "But we're almost there."

I blinked and released him, looking up as I wiped the trail of tears from my cheek.

His expression turned quizzical. "What?"

"I … I didn't say that out loud," I said slowly.

"Didn't say what?" Val asked.

"That we weren't in the clear yet."

"Oh, uh …" Andy scratched at the back of his head as his expression turned guilty. He wavered a bit on his feet and I caught him. "Sorry. It's … hard to filter."

"What is?" Val asked.

"You can read my mind," I said, holding him steady.

He tilted his head one way and the other, but then winced. "Mmm. That makes the world spin a little." He took a deep, steadying breath. "I did mention I could do that. But like I said then, I haven't been able to activate it since I got here." He studied me for a moment before dropping his hand to his side. "I got used to it not working. I'm sorry."

"What does it mean that it's working again?" I asked him, an eyebrow raised.

He gestured back the way we came. "Probably that the rift back there could have led me back home."

I smacked his chest. "Andy! You should have gone!"

"Ow!" He screwed his face up as he wavered again and I had to catch him. "And leave you two here to fend off the rift cats? I don't think so!"

"Well," Val said, "with an ability like that, I bet you're *super* popular back home."

Andy shook his head. "I'm not. I usually can parse out one voice from the next and tune out those that aren't likely to appreciate the intrusion, but it takes effort on my part."

"Hmm," I said. "So … most people in Arcaniss *can't* read minds, then."

He looked at me. "No. And most people don't have the patience to hang around while I figure out which mental voice is theirs. It doesn't usually match your speaking voice, actually. Most people just want me out of their head."

"I'm sure you don't do it on purpose," I said.

"Oh no," Andy said. "I definitely do sometimes. It's just that I'm typically much more targeted about it when I do it on purpose. The accidental stuff usually happens while I'm getting to know people."

I couldn't be sure, but I think there was color in his cheeks as he said that, like he was blushing. I was just glad to see him looking a little less pale.

"You don't even have underwear," Val said, peeling off her leggings. "Here."

"Val!"

"Look," she said, "at least I have panties, and I've worn less to clubs. They're probably gonna be short on you anyway, but at least they'll cover your ass if a strong breeze comes through."

I sheepishly took them from her and pulled them on. They were a little tighter than I liked, and they were almost like longer capris, but I pulled the bottom of them up to just under my knees and found it much more comfortable than being bare-assed to the wind.

"We have to keep moving," she said. "Those guys aren't going to let us go that easy."

"Civilization, Naiya," Andy said. "If Val's right, we need to get around people."

I looked over my shoulder. A light flickered to life back the direction we came from as I watched. With a sharp inhale, I nodded.

I looked at Andy. "I'll help you from here."

He nodded once and winced. I pulled the arm of his uninjured side over my shoulder and pulled him tight to me as we continued toward the lights Andy had first seen at a quickened pace.

"I need a cell phone," I said as we made our way through the brush and trees. "I can call Abigail and get us out of here."

"What's a cell phone?" Andy asked.

"You seriously didn't see any commercials for those at your rehab place?" Val's voice was incredulous. "But you know what a treadmill is."

Andy shrugged and then winced again.

"It's a communication device," I said. "I'll show you when we get somewhere."

As we started moving, Val moved around to my side. She looked down at my feet and then watched my face as we went along.

I arched an eyebrow at her, glancing her way before focusing back on picking my way through the underbrush. "What?"

"How is it not completely sucking for you to be

walking barefoot through all these brambles?" she asked.

"I dunno." I shrugged. "But I'm glad it doesn't. I thought not having shoes would slow me down for sure."

It was only about ten minutes more of walking through the scrub and trees before the wilderness opened up again onto a highway. To the left was a truck stop, its huge sign and well-lit parking lot declaring that it was 4:37 in the morning, and that there was overnight parking available. Not that many truckers would be stopping for their overnight parking right now. If anything, they'd be getting ready to start their day.

We were approaching the red brick convenience store from the big rig parking lot, which worked out nicely to help us keep a low profile.

"There are people here that are gonna ask questions about you supporting him like that," Val said, pointing at Andy as she kept her voice down.

"Give me a few minutes with Chad in the shadows there," Andy said quietly, pointing at the fenced-in dumpster on this side of the lot. "Then I'll be able to carry my own weight."

I nodded and took him around the far side of the fence, away from sight of both the trucks and the highway. I helped keep him steady as he lowered himself to sit cross-legged on the concrete. Chad was still glowing in time with Andy's breathing, and the pulses slowed once again as Andy closed his eyes. He looked like he was meditating, and I turned to keep an eye out for anyone who may be clearing trash from their rig.

The clock on the truck stop sign read 4:41 before Chad finally tinkled off Andy's side as Andy pulled himself to his feet.

I looked at him. "Good?"

He nodded. "Good."

We crept back toward the trucks, sneaking around them to keep out of sight of the highway. As we came around the front of one truck, the driver put a paper-wrapped sub sandwich on the front bumper before he opened the door to grab something out of the cab.

Val snatched his sandwich before he got back out the door and ushered us around to the next truck, stopping next to the wheel as the guy exclaimed about his lost sandwich.

And then, as luck would have it, a raccoon tottered out from around the back of the truck next to him.

"Dammit," the guy said. "You prolly took it back to your friends'n'shit, din'tcha?"

The raccoon ignored him and continued on.

"Damn things gettin' too friendly-like with folks," he muttered to himself as he headed back toward the convenience store.

"Whew," I said.

Andy smiled.

In the light, I got a good look at his tattoos. They were complex geometric shapes that sprawled up and around his right arm, crawling onto his neck before spilling across his toned chest and smooth stomach as they trailed off somewhere toward his left hip. Three black bands circled his left forearm—one thin, one wide, and one about twice the width of the thin one. They seemed to color shift like the iridescent black of grackle feathers, pulsing in subtle rhythmic waves of color. I was pretty sure they were pulsing in time with his heartbeat, but it was hard to tell for sure over the sound of one of the big rigs idling. I was also pretty sure they *hadn't* been doing that while we were in our cells.

Andy caught me visually tracing the lines and smiled at me. He leaned his right shoulder down and turned slightly to show me how the shapes crawled across and onto his back.

Though my cheeks heated at getting caught, I couldn't help but trace a shape or two with my finger. His skin erupted into goosebumps at the touch, and the pulsing colors changed tempo ever so slightly.

"Here," Val said, elbowing me as she handed me half of the now-unwrapped sandwich. "Shifting takes a lot of calories."

As I took it from her, she handed the other half to Andy.

"Aren't you going to eat some?"

She pointed to herself. "Human." She pointed to me. "Wereleopard." She pointed to Andy. "Something else entirely. Of the three of us, I still have a little bit of dinner in my belly."

Andy smiled gently at her as he tore his section in half and handed her one of the pieces. "So do I."

She smiled as she took a bite and then looked at me. "Why call Abigail? Shouldn't you call your parents?"

I shrugged and shook my head. "My parents won't answer a number they don't recognize. I'm pretty sure Abigail will. And she'll have access to my car."

Another trucker walked past the line of big rigs, talking to someone on a cell phone.

"Ooh," I said. "Andy, see that guy?"

He nodded.

"A cell phone is the little black thing he's holding to his ear."

Andy nodded again and shoved the last bite of his sandwich into his mouth. "Be right back."

He brushed crumbs from his hands and crept off to follow the guy, making sure his steps were quieter than the idling of one truck or another as he went.

"Those tattoos are mesmerizing," Val whispered

to me. She was staring after Andy. "He's a little skinnier than I normally like, but—"

"Val!" I thwapped her bicep with the back of my hand.

"What? It's been a while!"

"We're not even in the clear yet!"

"Yeah, but once we are …" She waggled her eyebrows at me and winked.

The trucker finally finished his call and hit the button on the side of the phone to turn off the screen. When he tucked the phone into the back pocket of his jeans, Andy extended a hand toward him, fingers splayed.

The cell phone actually *floated* out of the trucker's pocket and into Andy's waiting hand, where he tucked it into the pocket of his sweats before quickly creeping back toward us.

"How did you do that?" I whisper-shouted at him, my eyes wide.

"I told you," he said, keeping his voice low as he handed me the phone. "I'm from the other side of those rifts. Arcaniss is absolutely overflowing with magic. That's why those people were studying me."

"Let's move to the other side of the convenience store," Val whispered. "In case that guy notices his phone's gone."

I nodded, and we crept around the back of the building to the far side, where the gas pumps were. There, I pressed the button on the side of the phone, lighting up the screen. The poor guy hadn't even set up a lock on his phone. One swipe and I was at his home screen, which was a mess of unorganized icons. It took a bit of poking around to get to the full list of the phone's apps, but I finally found the maps app as I finished the last bite of my sandwich.

"Midlothian? Really?"

"What's Midlothian?" Andy asked.

"The city we're in," I replied. "Maybe it's a township? Anyway, it looks like there's a Walmart nearby and a Starbucks. But the Starbucks won't be open for another thirty minutes, and it'll be an hour and a half before the Walmart is open."

"And we can't call the cops," Val said, "or we'll end up in another psych ward—"

"And right back there," I finished.

She nodded. "So what do we do?"

I shrugged. "We wait for something to be open and call Abigail. She's gonna have too many questions I don't want to answer as it is. No need to make more by having her come this way before things are even open. Especially not with the two of you looking like you do."

"Well," Andy said, nudging Val with his elbow, "you *are* shorter than I expected."

Val made a face and looked up at him. "Yeah? You're skinnier."

I blew out a little laugh. "I mean you're both nakeder than you need to be. People are gonna notice."

"The convenience store probably has sweatpants and t-shirts." Val eyed my bare feet. "Odds are good they'll have flip flops, too. And since none of us have any cash—"

"I got this," Andy said as he nodded and turned toward the front of the store.

"Wait," Val said.

He stopped and looked at her.

"Most places require you to wear a shirt," she said.

"Ooh," I said. "Right. No shoes, no shirt, no service."

"Oh," he said.

She peeled off her shirt, leaving herself in just a

sports bra and panties. "Naiya, put this one on and give Andy back his shirt."

I stood and looked at her for a moment. She was definitely out of my league hot, and—for just a moment—I really wished she wasn't. Heat rose in my cheeks, and I quickly turned my back to them. I peeled off Andy's shirt, replacing it with hers, which was much tighter. As I turned back around, I held out Andy's shirt, the heat rising in my cheeks once again as I watched the iridescence chase along his tattoos.

Andy took the torn shirt from me with a little smile.

I took a breath and brushed a hand through my hair, trying to clear my head as he pulled his shirt on. That done, he went back around and into the store, leaving Val and I alone behind the building.

FORTY-TWO

Val sat down on the concrete. Uncomfortable with the way standing left me absolutely towering over her, I sat down too, my thigh pressed against hers. Like the concrete outside the door of the facility, the ground here had cooled during the night. She leaned her head on my shoulder and sighed heavily. She smelled like ripe juicy apples under the soap and shampoo of the facility.

It hadn't been as scary when the leopard took over before. It had scared Val, for sure, and I still felt almost like I'd been puppeted through the fight with the rift cats. But the time afterward, traveling through the trees, was almost like I was myself but in that body. It made me kind of uncomfortable to think about. And a relatively safe time with the leopard out once was a fluke, wasn't it? It didn't trump all the times I'd hurt people.

"Sorry for scaring you," I said lamely.

She shrugged. "I get it. You didn't want to leave Andy behind."

I nodded. "We wouldn't even be out if it wasn't for him."

She nodded, her cheek rubbing my shoulder. "He set us free."

"He did."

We were free ... mostly. Just a phone call away from safety. Just thirty minutes to pass.

"Still," I said. "You were just trying to keep us free."

She nodded again. "It's alright, Naiya. I know what you are. I might not like the leopard much, but it comes with the territory."

I leaned my cheek against the top of her head, putting an arm around her and rubbing the bare shoulder of her tattooed arm. Her skin was soft and smooth, the colors of her vine and chain vibrant against her skin. The lacework tattoo on her right thigh—the one pressed against mine—caught my eye, with its rainbow gem so well done it was mesmerizing, and I reached out a finger to brush along it, lifting my cheek from her head as I did.

"It's pretty," I said, kinda lamely.

She nodded and hooked a faded rainbow strand of hair behind her ear before looking up at me with a soft smile. "Thanks." She readjusted the way she sat, so she didn't have to crane her neck at an odd angle and brushed a hand on my cheek, her fingertips dancing along my cheekbone. "Your eyes are so pretty, Naiya. I've never seen that shade of green fuckin' *anywhere*."

I couldn't help but smile at her. "Thanks, I get it from my mom ... or my dad. Hard to know for sure, really."

Her lustrous brown eyes were focused on my mouth, which suddenly went dry as she ran a feather-light thumb across my bottom lip, leaving tingles of ghost touch in its wake.

"One of those, for sure," she said with an almost pouty nod.

Well, now I was watching her mouth, which had closed most of the distance between us. I saw what was coming and leaned toward her as her lips tentatively brushed mine. Her lips were soft and pillowy, and my arm curled around her, pulling her to me as my eyes fluttered closed. She deepened the kiss between us, her pierced tongue finding mine, and heat started to build between us.

Someone cleared their throat next to us, and I about jumped out of my skin as my cheeks went red hot with embarrassment.

Moment successfully broken, that was for sure.

Andy just gave me a lopsided smile as he handed me a pair of flip-flops and held out a pair of black sweatpants to Val.

Val leaned close to me and whispered, "I've wanted to do that for a while now."

I nodded and pulled my bottom lip between my teeth, wishing for just a moment longer with her lips pressed against mine.

She jumped up and pulled Andy down to place a light kiss on his cheek. "Thanks!"

Andy nodded with a chuckle and waited for Val to put on the sweatpants he'd grabbed. They were too big, of course, but they had a drawstring that she pulled tight, so they didn't fall off her narrow hips.

"How …?" I thought better of the question I wanted to ask. "Nevermind."

Andy handed Val a grey t-shirt that said 'Don't Mess With Texas' on it with a big Texas flag. "How'd I manage to get these out of the store without a hassle?"

"I don't want to know," I said.

"The clerk thinks—"

I put my fingers in my ears. "La la la, I'm not listening."

He smiled and pulled on my arms. "Alright, alright. I won't tell you."

"Do you have Abigail's phone number

memorized?" Val asked. "I didn't think anyone bothered with that kind of thing anymore."

I shook my head. "I remember it starts with 817, but I can't remember beyond that. But I *do* know my email login, and her email signature has her phone number in it."

"Nice," Val said.

I checked the time on the borrowed cell. "I should probably wait until something more reasonable than six a.m. to call, right?"

Val looked back the way we had come and shook her head. "I think that'd be a terrible idea."

"Is Abigail going to be mad about the early phone call?" Andy asked.

"No," I said. "But she's going to have a lot of questions."

"You don't have to answer them, Naiya," Val said. "Take a page from the nurse's book and just tell her you can't answer all of her questions."

"And maybe," Andy added, "there won't be as many questions as you think there will."

I nodded. "Okay."

And as dawn lit up the horizon, I checked my email for Abigail's phone number and called her just after six a.m.

She yawned as she answered. "Hullo?"

"Hey Abigail," I said. "It's Naiya."

She brightened immediately. "Aww Naiya, honey, good to hear from you! How're you doin'?"

I smiled at the delight in her tone and blew out a breath of relief. "I'm alright. Sorry for calling so early, but I need a really huge favor."

"It's no problem, honey," Abigail replied. "I was getting up in about thirty minutes anyway to make breakfast. What d'you need?"

I bit my lip. "Can you bring my car to me? I'm at

the … Starbucks in Midlothian. I'll text you the location?"

"I thought you were at Saint Dymphna's?" she said.

I couldn't get her caught up in this, but her question told me that what I'd feared was true: my family had been fed a lie about where I was. They wouldn't have ever tried to come save me.

"I finished my program early," I said. "They cleared me for release, so I took a cab with a friend to the Starbucks."

"Well, alright, hun," Abigail said. "I didn't know they did that. You sound tired, though. Why don't I just take you home?"

"Mmm, I'm not … I just … I could really just use some peace and quiet," I said, thinking quickly. "So, I'm going to the lake house for some fresh air."

"Good time to break some old habits," Abigail said, her tone sure. "Lemme get Tommy up and moving so he can follow me in my car, and I'll be there in … maybe an hour or so?"

"Sounds great, Abigail," I said. "Thank you."

"See you soon, hun," she said, and the line went dead.

"Well, that was less messy than I expected," I said as I made sure to log out and delete the web browser history.

"Sure," Val said. "She trusts you."

I nodded.

"Let's go over to the Starbucks," Andy said, "so we can get eyes on a good pickup spot."

"Sure," I said, nodding.

It wasn't a long walk to the Starbucks, but stepping into such an open space as the truck stop parking lot and going to the crosswalk where we had to stand on a median to wait for the indicator light all felt entirely too exposed for my liking. I couldn't help but keep looking over my shoulder, praying there wasn't anyone tailing us.

If there was, they were damn good at hiding themselves.

The flip-flops Andy got me were only a size or two too large, and though they still did their job without tripping me, I was definitely going to have to kick them off if something—or someone—started chasing us.

At the Starbucks, Andy, Val, and I took up one of the empty patio tables outside to wait, and right around 7:30, my pretty little blue four-door Mini Cooper with black racing stripes and black convertible top pulled up, followed by Abigail's white Honda Accord.

I stood to meet Abigail, a lump in my throat and tears in my eyes to see her safe. She wrapped me in a tight hug and handed me the keyring for my car as well as her key to the lake house.

"Your mom and dad are out of the country again," Abigail said.

"Of course they are," I replied. "I'm an embarrassment, after all."

"Not at all, hun! Someone from Saint Dymphna's called just a few days after you were admitted and said you had to stay for a full six-week treatment."

Val clapped a hand over her mouth.

That meant those assholes had been meaning to take me since before I was even discharged. I did some quick math, I was at Saint Dymphna's for two weeks, and then I'd been locked at that facility for at least three past that.

"Yeah, but I was only a few days shy of that anyway, and the staff said I was doing really well." I pressed my lips into a line. I didn't like lying to her. "Thanks for coming, Abigail. And for your help."

"Of course," she replied. "I'm glad I could help. Your mom and dad aren't due back till late next week, so you should have plenty of time to yourself out at the lake house."

"Thanks."

She nodded and then jerked her chin toward Andy and Val. "Your friends there got rides coming too?"

I looked back over my shoulder at Val and Andy and then turned back to her. "They do."

She nodded again and wrapped me in another hug. When she released me, she pulled me down to place a light kiss on my forehead. "You be careful, little one. There's clearly more to this story than you want to tell me right now, and that's fine, as long as you're being careful."

Another lump formed in my throat as I nodded. "I will. I am. Thanks, Abigail."

I waved to her husband in the Accord as she got in, watching them drive away before I turned back to Andy and Val with a deep sigh.

We were almost in the clear.

I hit the button to unlock the doors of my Mini. "Ready to go?"

Val climbed into the backseat, leaving the front passenger seat open for Andy. I got in and showed him the lever he could pull to move the seat back to accommodate his longer legs before showing him how the seatbelt worked.

"You gotta keep that on every time you're in the car," I said, thwapping it against his chest. "It'll keep you from getting killed if we have an accident, and it'll keep me from getting stopped by a cop. You too, Val."

"Yeah, yeah." She waved a dismissive hand at me, but clicked her seatbelt in as I walked around to the driver's side.

I pulled up the navigation to get the first handful of steps on the way to my parents' lake house, committing them to memory. I knew the way once we were on the tollway, and I knew how to get over to 75 if the tollway backed up.

Val looked over my shoulder at the map. "Make sure you're not using toll roads, those are easy to track."

I nodded and shot a finger gun her direction with a click of my tongue. "Good call." I tapped the screen to get to the option to avoid tolls and studied the route again. It was pretty much a straight shot up 75 anyway, even if it was a little slower.

Once I was sure I had the route figured out, I stood from the car and threw the phone as hard and as far as I possibly could in a direction completely different—but not opposite—the way we were going.

"Here's to hoping we don't get lost," Val said, leaning forward between the front seats to look at me.

"Can't chance them tracing that after the call to Abigail," I said.

"True." She nodded, and sat back.

I got in and started the engine.

"Can they track your car?" Andy asked.

"Sure," I said. "But that's a bit more involved, and not nearly as easy as tracking a cell phone."

Val crossed her fingers, meeting my eyes in the rearview mirror with a little wink.

And with that, we headed out.

I tried to remember not to have a lead foot, tried to remember that this was the middle of the morning rush hour for the metroplex, and tried to remember that all of the slowdowns were just because of regular folks trying to get to their normal, boring, nine-to-five jobs. I couldn't help but wonder if I would ever know the safety and security of such a life.

Andy placed a gentle hand on my knee, quieting my worries and drawing me back to the present.

Get to the lake house.

We could plan our next steps from there.

FORTY-THREE

Traffic cleared more the closer to the lake house we got, though it had been annoying with long stretches of stop-and-go that slowly unwound as we got north of Addison and the George Bush Turnpike. Thanks to that, we didn't reach the winding road through the trees surrounding Lake Texoma until nearly ten in the morning. I was just glad I had a small, easily maneuvered car that could dart around the slow-pokes who didn't know where they were going or how a highway works.

Something unwound in me as soon as the house came into view. It was covered in windows and had a porch around the front with the back deck leading toward the little boat dock, just barely visible as I pulled into the driveway.

"Wow," Val said as I cut the engine. "When you said your family was rich, I didn't know you meant 'owns a McMansion on a lake for funsies' rich. I'm surprised there's not a gate."

"No need," I said, opening the door and standing. "No one really comes out here by accident."

"It doesn't look like anyone comes out here at all," Val said.

I shrugged as I walked toward the front door. "We do, at least in the summers, and my father brings his clients out here sometimes." I unlocked the door and swung it wide open. "But it otherwise sits empty most of the year, except for the day the cleaning lady comes to dust." I gestured inside with a grin. "Welcome to the Davenport lake house."

"It's June," Val said as she passed me. "Aren't you nervous your parents will show up?"

"Sure," I said. "But Abigail said they're out of the country right now, so even if they call and find out I'm here—which is unlikely—we probably have at least a couple of days before they'd arrive."

"At least a couple of days of peace, then," Andy said.

I clicked my tongue and shot a finger gun at him, following the two of them into the house. I kicked off my too-large flip-flops as soon as I got inside. Val and Andy did the same with their slip-on shoes from the facility.

The ground floor was tiled with irregular slate-grey flooring, and the living room had vaulted ceilings with industrial metal supports crossing overhead, with a loft overhanging the open-concept kitchen. A huge leather sectional sofa dominated the living room, facing the stone fireplace in the middle of the outer wall, with a giant wall-mounted TV above the mantle. In the middle of the floor space between the sofa and the hearth was a wrought iron and glass coffee table. Past the short side of the sofa was a pair of round dining room tables in the same wrought iron and glass as the coffee table, both with four chairs each set around them. There was an office off to the left of the kitchen, and a pool table with an accompanying bar off to the right.

And thanks to the floor-to-ceiling storm windows, which stood in the place of virtually all of the exterior walls, the whole house was well-lit even on a cloudy day like today. I didn't like how exposed it made me feel, but at least I'd be able to see anyone coming. Thankfully, the bedrooms upstairs had a little more privacy, though that was mostly achieved with floor-length curtains.

I let out a gentle sigh. It was good to be on familiar territory in any case.

"Do you play?" Val asked, pointing at the pool table.

"Nah," I said. "I only ever played when I was out here. But my mom is an absolute shark. She'll lure you in with her 'I'm not even sure I know all the rules' play, and then run the table on you."

Val whistled. "Smart."

Andy placed Chad down on the ground, where the little creature promptly skittered off.

I arched an eyebrow. "He's not gonna get lost, is he?"

Andy shrugged. "He probably will, but I like to let him explore."

"How do you get up there?" Val pointed at the loft.

"This way," I said, gesturing for her to follow. "There's a set of stairs behind the office."

"Holy shit, that deck," she said, stopping in her tracks as she came around the kitchen island. "Is that a fire pit?"

"Yep," I nodded. "There's a walkway down to the boat dock over that way, with a rinse-off shower right there, so you don't have to come into the house smelling like Lake Texoma."

"Nice!" She nodded in approval.

"C'mon Andy," I said. "I'll show you where my father has some clothes you can borrow if you'd like to get out of the facility's sweats. He's a little wider than you, but about the same height, so it shouldn't be too hard to find something that'll work."

"You sure he won't mind?" Andy sounded skeptical.

"It'll be fine," I said, climbing the stairs. "He probably doesn't even remember the stuff he's got out here. And Val, I'll show you to my room. I'm sure I have some clothes that'll fit you, and probably be more your style than truck stop apparel."

"Thanks," she said, following Andy up the stairs.

"The master bedroom's this way," I said, "above the office."

Upstairs, the floors had thick white high-pile carpet to reduce noise. I showed Andy to the master bedroom, where there was a king-size black-upholstered sleigh bed with a fluffy pillow-top mattress and plush white linens. There was a floor-standing full-length mirror just to the side of the door, reflecting the views of the giant picture windows with their gauzy white curtains. The wide, low dresser was in grey-stained pine with black bar drawer pulls, which matched the nightstands on either side of the bed. In the corner, next to the entrance to the ensuite bath, was a plush armchair with the same upholstery as the head- and footboards of the bed.

I pointed to the dresser. "Feel free to go rooting around in there for something that fits. There's also a closet in the bathroom through that door, but it's probably mostly empty except for a suit or two."

Andy gave me a grin. "Thanks!"

I grabbed Val's hand. "C'mon, my room's this way."

Wow. I really just said that like I was eight years old. I rolled my eyes at myself as I showed her to my room.

My parents had indulged me a little, letting me have a giant ornate four-poster bed in white with a gauzy grey canopy and a matching dresser and nightstand. The bed was made up in rich purples, and I had an armchair of my own in plush black velvet with a creamy white woven throw draped over the back next to a modern black floor-standing full-length mirror. There were a few books stacked on top of the dresser opposite the wall of picture windows with their tall grey blackout curtains, and my ensuite bathroom was all crisp marble and sparkly chrome.

"Jesus," Val breathed. "Your bedroom is bigger than my dad's entire apartment."

"Oh wow," I said. "Well … uh … I should have a bunch of clothes in the dresser. There's a couple of sundresses in the closet over there next to the bathroom, if that's more your style?"

Val pressed her lips into a line. "Mmm, not really the sundress type."

I went to the dresser and pulled out a pair of black skinny jeans from the bottom drawer on the left. "Hmm, I don't think these will fit you so well, you're skinnier than me. But I do have some leggings. And the drawer … here?" I pulled open the middle drawer on the left. "Yes. There's tank tops here in lots of different colors. And I *should* have some undies … here?" I pulled open the top left drawer, which was filled with socks. "No. Here?" I pulled open the top right drawer. "Here. Help yourself to whatever you'd like."

While Val considered her options, I grabbed a grey tank top from the drawer to go with the black skinny jeans and peeled off my borrowed clothes. After pulling on some panties and hooking a bra behind my back, I threw on the tank top and shimmied into the jeans.

By then, she'd settled on what she wanted. "I'm actually gonna go ahead and take a shower while I have access to hot water."

I nodded. "I'll go check on Andy."

She padded over to the bathroom and shut the door as I left the room.

Down the hall, Andy had managed to get into a pair of my father's jeans—which looked decidedly better on him than they did on my dad—though his belt was a mess. He was shrugging into a white button-down shirt as I leaned against the doorway, his iridescent black tattoos peeking out above the collar.

I sucked on my bottom lip for a moment and jerked my chin at him. "You missed a couple of loops with the belt in the back."

He gave me a lopsided smile and stopped buttoning his shirt at only the second button from the bottom. "Can't say that's surprising. Help me out?"

I was taken aback by the request. "Uh … Sure."

My breath caught as I got closer to him. He was not an unattractive man—lanky and slim, with hints of muscle definition. I liked his unruly tuft of brown hair and the way his mouth formed words. It definitely did *not* have anything to do with his lyrical accent. With a deliberate huff, I shook my head, blinking to clear it as I reached for the belt buckle.

It wasn't like this was a sexual thing he was asking for. He wasn't from here. He clearly just didn't have a lot of practice with belts and belt loops.

The iridescent waves of his tattoos sped up a little as I pulled the belt from the loops until I got to the first missed loop. His dark eyes were intent on me as I brushed my fingers across his hips, straightening the belt, which had apparently *also* gotten twisted.

It's not sexual, Naiya. He's just a guy who's not from around here. Maybe you shared a shit-pile of meaningful glances across the hall, but being this close is different.

But his skin lit up with goosebumps once again at my touch, and he lightly gripped my wrist as I went to buckle the now-fixed belt. Startled, I stopped what

I was doing and looked up, only to realize his face was much closer than I'd thought it was. With a quiet gasp and a quick readjustment of my posture, I managed not to headbutt him in the nose, but only just.

"I … I didn't know you two were involved," he said, his gaze intense as it searched my face.

Who …?

I blinked. "Valerie?"

He nodded.

"We're not involved." I probably said that too quickly.

He raised an eyebrow at me.

I shook my hair back from my face. "Well, we're not. I've only known her a couple of weeks longer than I've known you."

"Hmm." He brushed a hand through my hair, and I leaned into it, glad for the connection. For a moment, I let myself drift and get lost in the starfield of his eyes.

Except then I remembered something.

"Wait," I said. "You're not trying to read my mind right now, are you?"

He laughed then, an almost musical sound that was more free than anything I'd heard from him. "Should I?" His expression turned conspiratorial as his laugh faded. "What might I find in there if I did, Lady Kateri?" There was definitely a note of something dark and tempting in his tone.

Wait.

'Lady?' He called me *Lady* Kateri?

I blinked. "I think … I'd like it best if you didn't. Maybe just ask me instead?"

His lips brushed my forehead, so feather-light I almost thought I imagined it. "I can do that."

But there was something about the way he'd said my last name. The way he pronounced it … it sounded better coming from his mouth than it ever had coming from anyone else's.

He released my hands as the water turned on in the bathroom down the hall, but he didn't button his shirt, and he didn't move from where he stood. Something was definitely charged in the air between us, and I couldn't deny that I wanted more than just a gentle kiss on the forehead.

"What are you thinking, Lady Kateri?" he whispered, the sound barely louder than Val's shower.

I bit my lip and met his eyes again. "I'm thinking you could be a lot of trouble for me."

The corner of his mouth pulled up. "Funny. I was just thinking the same thing about you. What else?"

The heat rushed to my cheeks … and elsewhere. "I'm … wondering why you haven't buttoned the rest of your shirt."

He cocked his head to the side as curiosity flooded his expression. "Mmm, that's not quite it, is it?"

I raked a hand through my hair. "More like I'd like to unbutton it the rest of the way and trace my fingers along every line of your tattoos." The words came out in a rush, but they were true.

He met my eyes as he unfastened the two buttons at the bottom of his shirt and pulled it off, dropping it to the floor beside him. He took my hand in his and pulled me along as he sat on the bed, where his gaze left mine as he manipulated my hand into a fist with just my first finger extended and pushed it gently against the bottom-most line of the shapes on his right hand.

"There's as good a place as any to start," he said.

I swallowed thickly and started tracing the lines.

FORTY-FOUR

The faint shimmer of iridescence through his tattoos sped up ever-so-slightly at my touch, and goosebumps spread across his skin once again. He moved his fingers as I traced the lines there, rolling his wrist over so I could continue the line that passed across the soft skin over his pulse point.

His heart was pounding. I blinked.

"What is it?" he asked at my change in expression.

"I can … hear your heart beating. It's … pounding, actually."

He nodded once, slowly. "Interesting. What do you make of that?"

I left my finger where it was against the inside of his wrist and met his intense gaze. "I'm not sure just yet."

He gave me another conspiratorial smile. "Let me know when you have it puzzled out."

I looked down at his wrist. There, cleverly hidden among the geometric shapes, was an artist's rendition of the sword I'd seen him use against the rift cats.

"Your sword," I said.

He flipped over his hand, and I pulled my own away. With a flourish, he was holding the sword once more.

"It's called a rapier," he said. "It … stores there."

My eyes were wide with the magic of it. "How?!"

He took a deep breath and scratched at the back of his head with his free hand as he turned the blade over. "Uh … I'm not really sure how to explain it. Think of it like a pocket, maybe? But one that only exists theoretically, perhaps. It doesn't take up any actual space in my arm or anything, but I can certainly feel when it's there versus when it's not."

I reached out to run a finger along the cool metal. I didn't know what I was expecting, but it definitely had a sharp edge and was as solid as a sword should be. The swept hilt and wirework basket had an understated elegance to it—an interesting contrast to the hard lines of geometry on his arm.

"How do you … access it? Or … bring it out, I guess?"

"Mmm, I just assume it's in my hand, and then it is."

"And when you want to put it away?"

"The same thing, but in reverse."

He flourished his hand in the reverse direction, and the blade flashed into pale iridescent glitter that flowed toward the image on his wrist before disappearing into his skin.

I reached for his hand with both of mine, turning it over front to back as I examined the shapes.

"Ah-ah," he said, taking my hand and manipulating it back into a fist with the first finger extended once again. "You were tracing lines."

I arched an eyebrow at him, but smiled. "So I was."

I traced over and then across the sword, pressing a little harder as I did.

He studied my face. "Do you feel it in there?"

I shook my head. "I'm pretty sure it's just the tendons I'm feeling."

He smiled. "It's handy, back home. Most people

overlook the tattoo entirely, and even when they do identify that there's magic to it, my whole arm lights up."

"So, it's like a forest for the trees sort of thing."

He cocked his head at me.

"It's a saying we have here: 'can't see the forest for the trees.' It's basically the concept of needing to step back and look at the whole picture … hmm. The analogy falls to pieces now that I try to explain it."

His smile returned. "I see where you're going with it, it's just reversed. Can't see the tree for the forest. Spend too long looking at the big picture, and you're likely to miss the details."

"Hmm." I returned my focus to the lines on his skin.

He turned his hand over as I followed a line back over his elbow and up his bicep. He didn't try to flex the muscle or anything under my touch, which I couldn't help but find interesting. He didn't need to try to impress me? Or perhaps he assumed he already had, and would continue to, so there was no need for such an overt attempt.

"There's an interesting thought," he said.

I raised an eyebrow at him.

"Whatever that was that crossed your mind just now told its tale on your face," he explained. "Though I'm not nearly familiar enough with you to know what that expression was."

I cocked my head to match my raised eyebrow. "You're good at boundaries."

"Exceedingly."

I took a breath and sucked on the corner of my lip as I considered whether to tell him at all, and what words to use if I *was* going to say something.

"I find it interesting that you aren't trying to impress me with your physique," I said finally. "Most men I know would be flexing under the wandering finger of a relative stranger."

"I'd hardly call you a stranger, Lady Kateri."

There it was again. My name from his mouth. With the word 'Lady' in front of it to boot.

I took a breath and went back to tracing lines, letting my hair fall to hide the heat rising in my cheeks. He had no such luxury—the pulsing iridescence along his tattoo lines increased in tempo once again, and his heart pounded even harder than it had been. Not faster, per se, just harder.

At his shoulder, I had a choice: trace the lines across his chest and down to his stomach, or follow the shapes to their end up near his jawline. He angled his head away from me, practically making my choice for me.

If I'd been as spicy as Val, I suspect I'd have moved down across his chest simply due to his body language.

But I wasn't Val—who was taking as long a shower as I typically did.

He stilled as I traced the lines across his throat, pausing at the vein pumping strongly under the skin. He closed his eyes as I followed one shape and the next, his jaw tilting upward as I circled the outer edges of the forwardmost octagonal form, which almost reached his Adam's apple, before following the lines down onto his pec.

There wasn't a shape that crossed over his heart, but it didn't stop me from flattening my palm against the center of his chest to feel it beat. I leaned close to him then, propping my weight on the bed with a knee as I did.

"And if I were to ask you what *your* thoughts were," I whispered against his ear as another wave of goosebumps passed across his body, "would you tell me?"

His heartbeat thundered under my palm as his arm curled around my back, pinning my hand between his body and mine as he held me in place.

"I would," he said, and then dropped his voice to a whisper as he leaned close to my ear. "I'd tell you that I've never met anyone whose touch continually does to me what yours does. I'd tell you that I'd like to make your skin light up the same way. And I'd tell you that there is a not-insignificant part of me that would like very much to get a taste of you."

An undeniable heat surged to life between my thighs, adding to the otherwise gentle warmth that had already been building there. I leaned back to meet his eyes, which had darkened a shade or two with desire, and glanced at his lips as I bent my head toward them. I very much wanted to get a taste of him as well. I closed my eyes as I closed the distance between us, and when his lips brushed mine, the air went out of the room.

He tasted as sweet as he smelled, and I brought my other knee up to straddle him on the bed as I kissed him, my other hand coming to trace his jawline. He made a throaty little noise and deepened the kiss, his tongue dancing with mine as a considerable length of hardness formed in his lap.

Holy shit. I swear the warmth between my legs tripled.

Well, now I have to see it.

"Something's surprised you," he whispered against my lips as I took a breath.

I blinked my eyes open then, studying his face for a moment as I pressed my hips into his lap, grinding them a little against him to be sure he understood.

He got it.

His eyes fluttered closed. "*Suiaerl mitne,* Naiya."

I didn't know what that meant, but I didn't have the time—nor the inclination, at the moment—to contemplate it. His mouth closed against mine again, but I had already started peeling off my shirt. He broke the kiss momentarily as I pulled the tank over my head and dropped it to the floor. And then his hands were on my waist, climbing my sides as my mouth found his once more. A wave of goosebumps passed over my skin as his hands grazed the bottom of my black satin bra. I pressed closer to him, and he lowered himself back onto the bed, taking me with him as our tongues continued to dance.

That was clearly all the invitation either of us needed. I unbuckled his belt, and unbuttoned and unzipped the fly of his pants.

Holy shit … he hadn't bothered with underwear.

More heat gathered between my legs, turning me absolutely molten, and I sat up.

"Problem?" He raised an eyebrow at me.

I met his eyes as a sultry smile pulled my lip from between my teeth. "There will be when you try to peel these pants off me."

He leaned up on his elbow and rubbed at my thigh. "How so?"

I leaned down to kiss him once more before standing. "Try it and find out."

He sat up eagerly then, heedless of the porn-star-sized erection that escaped his pants as he did.

"Watch where you point that thing," I said, the words out of my mouth before I'd even considered them.

His cheeks colored as he reached for the fly of my jeans, a smile playing at the lips I already missed the taste of. "Sorry."

He tugged the top of my jeans down over my hips, turning them inside out as he peeled them down my legs. I took a step closer to him as he did, to help him get more reach on my long legs, and he pressed a number of kisses to my soft belly, nipping at my hipbone once as he hooked a finger under the side of my underwear.

He looked up at me then, his eyebrow raised once more. "May I?"

My jeans weren't even completely off me, but *God*, did I ever want more of his hands against my skin, more of my flesh pressed against his.

And—more than anything—I wanted to wrap myself around that magnificent dick until I had him moaning and twitching with ecstasy.

FORTY-FIVE

I BENT to finish the job of getting my jeans off and then leaned my hip toward him, where he once again hooked a finger under the side of my underwear and peeled downward. Another wave of heat rushed through me, and I reached up behind my back to unhook my bra, dropping it to the floor as he guided my feet out of my underwear.

"Light the ley lines," he breathed. "You are a truly exquisite creature of beauty, Lady Kateri."

I didn't bother to say anything then; I simply straddled his lap once again and kissed him, aching to taste my name on his lips. He lifted me to drop the borrowed pants to the floor and put me down on the bed. The geometry that tapered off across his chest and down his stomach picked back up again into a cluster of pulsating iridescence on his left hip and thigh.

He looked wildly around, a suddenly lost expression taking his face. "I … uh …"

I furrowed my brow at him. "What are you looking for?"

"Do you take herbs?" he asked, moving his hands in too vague a gesture for me to grasp the meaning. "Or is there …?"

I arched an eyebrow as I sat up, feeling as lost as

he looked. "Herbs?"

"So you don't conceive."

"Ah." I nodded slowly with understanding. "I have an IUD … an implant. No babies."

No sooner were the words off my tongue before his mouth crashed against mine, pushing me back to the plush white linens as the air left the room once again.

"Good," he said, between desperate breaths as he stood back up and held his dick in his hand, its tip already slick with precum as he lined himself up with my positively drenched entrance.

And the feeling of him stretching and filling me as he eased his way inside me sent another wave of goosebumps across my skin, and I made a deeply appreciative noise in my throat. There was no question that he easily had the longest cock of all the guys I'd slept with—not that that was a particularly high number—but holy *God*, was I not expecting how good it would feel to have him inside of me.

He slowly slid in and out a few times, gripping the back of my knees as he held my ass on the edge of the bed. I worked my hips against him with what little leverage I had, trying to get more of him inside me. Thrust by thrust, he increased speed and depth until I swore I could practically feel him in my throat. I tried to stay quiet so that Val wouldn't hear us over her shower, but he felt so good, and my cries grew increasingly louder as his cock edged deeper into me. My whole body wound tight as he buried himself in me over and over like a jackhammer until—finally—my orgasm crashed hard into me, and my hips bucked against his with wild abandon as my cries rang through the house. He came too then, his own moans of appreciation a delicious harmony to mine.

"*Suiaerl mitne,*" he said breathlessly.

I still didn't know what that meant, but he

sounded impressed.

Well, good. Lord knows I was.

As the waves of ecstasy tapered off, Val appeared in the doorway, wrapped in a white towel, her rainbow hair a shade or two darker with wetness.

I threw an arm across my breasts as my cheeks practically sizzled with embarrassment.

Her brown eyes were positively lustrous as she looked between the two of us with a pouty smirk. "Is there room for one more?"

Andy looked at me. His cock was still inside me, my legs still spread in his hands. Modesty seemed an entirely moot point, so I dropped my arm.

Val let her towel fall to the carpet. As I expected, she was naked underneath.

I wanted to lick a line from her navel to her neck. And I wanted to do it while Andy made her scream his name.

I met Andy's eyes and nodded once.

His cock twitched inside of me as he returned the nod.

I reached a hand toward Val. She sauntered over and bent to kiss me, caressing my body as I ran a featherlight touch along the swell of her ass and over the curve of her hip. I sat up as Andy pulled out of me, but as I whined with the emptiness he left behind, Val plunged the fingers of her rose-tattooed hand into me. I gasped and then cried out in pleasure at the suddenness of it. She kissed my jawline and up to my mouth as I pawed at her clumsily, shifting on the bed to give her better access.

It had been a while since I'd been with a woman, and Val was an entirely different creature than the girl I'd given my v-card to.

She tangled her other hand in my hair as her thumb circled my clit, her fingers dancing inside me in rhythm with her thumb. She tugged my head back and licked my exposed throat, placing tiny kisses along my jawline as I moaned my enjoyment at her touch.

A sharp gasp escaped her and her grip on my head loosened as her eyes fluttered closed. There was no resistance as I looked to see where Andy had gone. He was on the floor beneath her, his back against the foot of the bed as his mouth pressed against her shaved mound, his fist around his cock. I leaned over to watch him lap at her entrance, his tongue circling her clit as he slowly jacked his hand up and down his dick, bringing it to full attention once more.

God, he could put two of his fists along the length of his shaft and still have room for a third. If he was the standard for all the men in Arcaniss, maybe I'd want to live there, if only for the dick I could get.

Val's hand against me fell into rhythm with his mouth against her. She bent to lick my dark nipple, flicking her tongue across the tip in time with her thumb on my clit, and I gripped the vine-and-chain-inked arm tightly, holding her hand in place against me. She increased speed and intensity again, presumably as Andy did on her, and her legs went rigid as her orgasm built. When it crashed into her a moment later, she shook with the waves of ecstasy rolling through her, her cries just as loud as mine had been in the end, and Andy sucked greedily at the juiciness that dripped from her as she shuddered through her orgasm.

"Birth control?" I asked her.

"Pill," she replied breathlessly, her hand falling away from my body.

I pulled my knees under me and crawled toward the footboard, looking down to meet Andy's impossibly dark eyes. "No babies."

He wiped his mouth with a smirk and nodded.

I pulled Val around and over to the side of the bed so that she didn't have to finger me over the footboard, and Andy followed. I guided her up onto the bed and took her mouth in mine, noting that she tasted ever-so-slightly metallic compared to Andy, what with her tongue piercing and all.

Mmm. New plan.

"What're you thinking, Naiya?" Andy was studying my face again.

I smiled at him as I tangled my hand in Val's still-damp rainbow hair and leaned close to her ear, dropping my voice to a whisper. "I'm thinking I'd like your mouth to finish what your fingers started."

She made a throaty little noise and looked over her shoulder, eyeing Andy's erection before looking up at him through her lashes. "Only if you'll fuck me while I do."

He met my eyes, the question plain on his face.

Damn, he was good at boundaries.

The corner of my mouth quirked upward. "As long as you try your hardest to break her concentration."

His smile could have lit the world for years, and he bowed his head just a fraction. "As you wish, Lady Kateri."

Val made another throaty little noise as Andy's tattooed hand reached between her legs. The lines were pulsing wildly with the iridescence that chased across his chest to his hip. Even the black bands on his left forearm shimmered as she moaned her appreciation at his touch. She kissed me once more before blazing a trail of kisses and nips down to where her hand had been just moments before. As her mouth closed on my clit, my eyes rolled back with pleasure. She fell into a steady, insistent rhythm, punctuated by her moans of appreciation at what Andy was doing with his fingers. Her piercing flicked against my clit almost as often as the tip of her tongue, the sensation of something hard versus something softer winding me tighter and tighter with each touch.

Her rhythm faltered for just a moment as he plunged into her, though it quickly resumed, keeping time with Andy's wet thrusts into her dripping folds. He changed rhythm, pounding harder—deeper—into her small frame until every cry she started, she finished against my clit, thrusting her tongue inside of me as her cries became more intense. And then she came again, her body quivering and shaking as she screamed her ecstacy against me until my orgasm tore through my body. She rolled my ultra-sensitive pearl between her lips and tongue as she moaned against me, making me shudder and buck with every electric touch.

Andy came only a moment later as he thrust against Val, his thrusts punctuating his moans until he languidly pulled himself free.

As the waves of ecstasy subsided in us all, we curled under the blankets of the king-size bed. Val got up a moment later, padding off to use the bathroom. When she returned, I did the same.

Andy wrapped his arm around me when I came back to bed.

"We're finally free," I whispered.

"Free," Andy said, pulling me closer to him and placing a slow kiss on the back of my neck.

Val just made a pleased little noise and curled onto her side against me as well.

As Val and Andy dozed off, I lazily traced the vine and chain of Val's arm while taking immeasurable solace in Andy's warm breath on my neck. There may not be magic in this world like there was in Andy's Arcaniss, but there was magic in that sleepy moment.

We were free. Maybe not permanently. But we were free. And in that moment, I would have died to ensure we were never locked up again.

FORTY-SIX

When I slept, the leopard ran alongside me in my dreams instead of stalking me—something that had never happened in my adult life. And while I couldn't for the life of me understand why, I simply reveled in the simple joy of it. That joy was compounded by the fact that, instead of wind rushing past my ears, someone hummed a song that felt so familiar to me, but I couldn't recall ever hearing it in my waking life. I recognized it as the same song from the dreams I'd had when Andy told me about the floating castles of Arcaniss, but the tune fled from me as soon as I woke.

It was still bright outside, but only Andy was in bed with me, his arm draped across my waist like that was where it had always belonged. He pulled me closer to him as I looked around the room for Val, pressing a slow kiss to the back of my shoulder. I briefly considered another round with him, but I didn't see my friend—or was she my friend with benefits now? I closed my eyes and listened. The telltale tinkling of Chad's movements came from somewhere down the hall, but beyond that, someone was moving around downstairs.

"Unngh," Andy protested as I sat up. "Stay."

I gave him a gentle smile and kissed him, though he tangled his hand in my hair and deepened the kiss, easing me back down as he did. It spread warmth through me as the log between his legs came to attention once again. I wrapped a hand around it and slid along its length, kissing his throat as he threw his head back in pleasure at the touch.

"More later," I said, nipping at his Adam's apple. "I wanna see what Val's—mmm."

His fingers found the sensitive spot between my legs and went to work. "I haven't enjoyed anything in my life quite as much as I enjoyed being responsible for the sounds you made earlier." He punctuated his words with thumbed circles around my clit as I panted against his neck and pumped his dick in sync with each circle. "I can't help but wonder what other sounds I could be responsible for. Help me find out quickly, and I'll happily go anywhere you ask."

"Mmmm, you have a deal," I said between breaths, my hand still on his cock.

He tangled his hand in my hair, pulling me tight against him as he made an appreciative noise in his throat. "And just one more thing." He thumbed more circles around my clit as I ground my hips into his hand. "Let these be just for me?"

I nodded my head once, but moaned softly into his neck as he edged me closer to ecstasy.

His hand stopped. "Quiet, now, or no deal."

I bit my lip and ground my hips greedily against his hand, but he simply cupped my mound and refused the contact I ached for. My hand on his dick, however, gripped him harder and kept pumping as his hips gently bucked along.

He arched a brow at me. "Do we have a deal?"

I kissed him, reveling in the taste of him on my tongue.

"Deal," I whispered.

His hand resumed its prior work and, in short order, left me shuddering and gasping into his neck, biting my lip hard enough that it bled just to keep from crying out as my orgasm crashed over me.

But my hand hadn't stopped on his dick, and he came soon after, spilling his seed mostly against my belly and onto the sheets, though some did get on my fingers. I brought the glistening fingers up to my mouth, meeting his eye as I licked them clean.

He held my face and kissed me then, deeply, before pulling back. "You are going to be so very much trouble for me."

The corner of my mouth lifted once more as I kissed him again. "Mmm, at least you're likely to be the same for me."

I threw my legs over the side of the bed and stood to gather all the discarded clothes. I handed Andy his borrowed shirt and jeans before stepping into my panties and pulling them up over my hips. I then shimmied into my jeans and threw my tank top on as Andy stood to pull on his jeans.

I padded out of the room and down the stairs.

Val was pacing in the kitchen, a wild expression on her face and her hands buried in her hair as she muttered to herself. She had on a pair of my tight-fitting black athletic shorts and an electric purple sports bra, but she'd also grabbed one of my father's white button-down shirts, the tails tied at her waist instead of buttoned up.

"I'm on my own here," she said, making another lap of the kitchen. "*Fuck.*"

She pounded once on the kitchen island with the side of a closed fist.

On her own? But she wasn't. Not at all.

I furrowed my brow as Andy descended the stairs behind me. "We're here, Val. It's okay." I reached for her shoulder to comfort her.

She jolted away from me, and I dropped my hand, but her expression softened as soon as she focused on me. "Sorry. I'm just …" She huffed out a breath and then looked over my shoulder at Andy. "How did you manage to break the locks of the facility, anyway?"

"These shimmered to life." He held out his arms. "So I checked for my rapier. When it was there, I figured I could do what I've been able to do back home—I can sort of dismantle small mechanical things and break lesser enchantments. I haven't been able to do that since I arrived here. I think the rifts may allow some of the energy and power of Arcaniss through." He turned to me. "Isn't there anything you can do now that you haven't been able to do before?"

I blinked and shook my head. "What do you mean?"

He cocked his head at me. "I … hmm … I thought my meaning was clear. Is there something that you are now capable of that hadn't been true before encountering the rift?"

"Why would there be?"

"Because it must have poured some of the magic of that world into this one," he said. "At least enough to power someone whose own abilities stem from there."

Oh I see.

"You think she's from Arcaniss?" Val asked.

She took the question right out of my mouth. I placed my hand on top of hers on the counter and squeezed. She glanced at me and smiled gently, hooking her thumb over the side of my hand and rubbing.

"I'm not from there, Andy," I said, shaking my head.

"But …" His brow furrowed in confusion. "Your shift is different from theirs. You're much more like the lycanthropes or druids of my world than you are like the creatures that attacked you at the facility."

Val pulled her hand out from under mine so she

could rub at the scars hidden behind the knot of my father's button-down.

I stilled. "I'm a what?"

"A lycanthrope," he said. "It just means you can shift between human and an animal—a leopard, in your case."

"I mean, yeah. That's why they wanted to research me." I still didn't move. "But you think, based on that, it means I am from the other side of those rifts?"

Chad tinkled over to him, and he bent to pick up the little purple spider. "Well … they wanted to research me after I'd come through a rift, and they put you in the same hall as me. That place was clearly large enough that they could have separated us, so why put you there if you aren't somewhat like me?"

His logic was sound, actually. Except …

"They could have put me there just because they knew you weren't going to tell them any more without someone friendly to draw information from you." I raked a hand through my hair and softened my tone as I reached for Andy's hand, squeezing it. "You may be from that other world, Andy, but I'm definitely from this one. Besides, none of that explains why they took Val."

She was still rubbing at her scars. I reached out and placed my hand gently over hers, drawing her close in a hug.

"I'm just glad your shift doesn't take long," she said into my shoulder as her arms curled around my back. "And that you don't sit around in it for too long."

"I know," I said quietly. "It scares you."

She nodded. It wasn't like I didn't already know it, she'd said as much at the truck stop, hadn't she? But it didn't hurt any less to have it confirmed … again.

"I'm sorry," I said. "If I could do anything—wait, Val?"

She pulled back and looked up at me.

I met her brown eyes. "You said you used to be a werewolf, right?"

"Yeah, but those assholes didn't know any of that until I talked to you about it."

"No," I said. "But you said you're not anymore."

"Right."

"Which means I can get rid of being a wereleopard too, right?"

Andy raised a hand in protest. "Wait."

Val rolled a shoulder. "Theoretically."

"So, how did you get cured?"

Val glanced at Andy before looking back at me. "Why don't I just take you to her?"

I arched an eyebrow. "'Her?'"

She nodded. "There's a woman who can do it. She's kind of amazing, actually."

Andy put a hand on Val's shoulder. "Wait. Just wait." He met my eyes. "Why try to stop being a wereleopard at all? Why change who you are?"

I raked a hand through my hair. "I just … I don't want to keep scaring everyone. And the nightmares? No, thank you." I crossed my arms over my stomach. "I'd like to stop being afraid of losing control and hurting people I care about."

Andy turned and pulled me into a hug. "You may not have to get rid of the leopard to do all that."

"Well, we gotta get away from here either way," Val said.

Andy blinked. "What?"

"Why?" I said.

Val eyed us both. "Do you really think those guys won't come here to look for you? For all of us? If they have things from your house, and can just detain your nanny—"

"House manager," I corrected.

"Whatever," she said, waving her hand dismissively. "If they can do all that, they almost certainly know about this place even if they *aren't* tracking your car, which honestly seems like a long shot anyway."

Andy sighed. "She's right. It makes sense that those people would want to reacquire what they lost, and if they don't find you at home or at Abigail's, this would be the next place they'd look."

Shit. He was right. They both were. I took a few steps backward and sank onto the second-to-lowest step of the stairs.

Dammit.

"The woman who cured me is part of a pack," Val said. "Even if you decide *not* to try to stop being a wereleopard, her pack could probably help you figure out how to get some better control."

I blinked up at her. "Do you really think she could cure me?"

"She made me human again after I'd been a snarling creature of violence," she replied with a shrug. "I'd say it's at least worth a shot."

"The leopard could be a great asset to you if you gain some control and lose some of the fear surrounding it," Andy said. "Just look at what you did to those rift cats."

"Mmm, but it's also pretty terrifying." Val started rubbing at her scars again. "Having something so primal as part of you? And no telling how close or far from the surface it is? I was glad to be rid of it. I bet you will be too."

I sighed and held my head in my hands, staring vacantly at the ground. "Okay ... well ... let's at least try getting to her—or them?"

"Them," Val said. "You can tell them who you are

—*what* you are—and they have a wolf there who should be able to help you."

I nodded. "Let's try getting to them, then."

"Wait," Andy said, putting a hand out toward me, palm down, as he looked at Val. "I want to make sure I understand. Werewolves here aren't evil?"

Val shook her head, her now-dry faded rainbow hair flying into dizzying motion. "Generally not the ones on two legs, at least."

"Well, then you can think about it on the way," Andy said.

"It's not like you won't have time," Val added.

I looked up at her again, one eyebrow raised.

"Well," she said, "they're in Colorado Springs. It's kind of a long drive."

I sighed with a nod and heaved myself to my feet. "I'll go pack a bag."

FORTY-SEVEN

I found a large black duffle bag on the top shelf of the linen closet. It had a little bit of dust on it, but was otherwise in good shape. I took it to my room and shoved most of my clothes from my dresser into it. I grabbed a pair of closed-toe hiking sandals in purple and grey with black soles from my closet and slipped them on before grabbing one of my old backpacks and slinging it onto a shoulder. Moving over to the master bedroom, I added a few pairs of jeans and a handful of folded white shirts to the duffle. I grabbed a couple of my father's white v-neck undershirts, too.

I took the duffle and empty backpack downstairs into the office, dropping the duffle by the door. Val and Andy had slipped on their shoes while I was grabbing clothes, and they followed me. A large desk with smokey grey-black glass and black powder-coated steel legs and drawers sat in the middle of the room on a plush faux-fur rug.

I shook my head and sighed, remembering my mother's animal activism phase and the way she'd insisted upon the faux-fur version of the rug despite the giant leather couches in the living room. I pulled open the top drawer of the desk as I sat in the black mesh computer chair. Val and Andy sat in smokey grey acrylic chairs on the other side of the desk.

"There's not a cell phone here that we can take," I said, "but there is a laptop."

"Better than nothing," Val said, a nervous bounce starting in her leg.

I unplugged the laptop from its charger and pulled it from the drawer. Setting it on the desk and opening it up, I let it boot as I traced the wire back to where it met a power strip mounted to the back of the drawer and unplugged it. I wound up the wire as I straightened. The laptop only had my father's profile on it, but he never kept anything secure on this thing anyway since it was cloud-based. Which, thankfully, meant he'd shared the password with me, so I keyed it in before opening up a browser window and turning the laptop to Val.

"Pull up a map of where we're headed?"

"Sure," she said and started typing as I put the cord in my backpack. "I don't know the exact address, but I know the general area, and can show you once we get there."

Andy's eyes went wide. "Does that say eleven hours and thirteen minutes?"

Val pressed her lips into a line and nodded. "Yup." She turned the laptop around to me.

I zoomed in on the first section of the route. "Looks like I need to head south to pick up 82 west."

A shadow outside caught my eye.

"There's someone out there," Andy said, standing and taking a step toward the door to the office. "They went around the back."

My heart kicked into high gear as the rapier materialized in Andy's hand.

"Shit," I said, snapping the laptop closed.

"I hate that I was right about this," Val said, jumping to her feet as well.

She grabbed the duffle bag as I shoved the laptop into the backpack and zipped it closed. The door to the back deck slammed open as I snagged my keys from the kitchen island on the way toward the front door.

"RUN!" I yelled, doing just that.

I got there first, but Andy and Val were right behind me as I pulled the front door open.

"Trouble!" Andy called as soon as he was outside, Val hot on his heels.

He wasn't wrong. Two giant black SUVs had blocked in my little Mini in the driveway. I slammed the front door behind me as Val rushed to throw the duffle in the car. I got in the driver's seat and slammed the car door too as Andy buckled his seatbelt. I started the car as Val climbed in the backseat.

"How are you getting out of here?" Her voice was frantic as she slammed the door and buckled her seatbelt.

I put the Mini in reverse, so the backup camera came on. I backed up, cutting hard to get around the edge of the house, when I spotted my opening. There was just enough space between the back SUV and the treeline for my Mini to make it.

Backing up further to point my nose at the SUVs, two guys in black with rifles on their shoulders burst through the front door.

"Hold on!" I shouted as I put the Mini into drive and floored it.

The tires squealed as I tore out of my spot toward the back bumper of the far SUV. I swerved at the last moment, narrowly avoiding the considerably larger vehicle, only to find that the spot I thought I had was smaller than I thought, thanks to the shrubs that lined the edges of the driveway.

Still, I managed it, only crushing the first of the line of shrubs.

I sped as fast as I could on the winding lane, back

toward the main road that ran through the trees around the lake.

Thankfully, the guys assaulting the lake house hadn't bothered to shut down the main road. I sped through the trees as fast as I dared, trying to put as much distance as I could between us and them as I headed south to get to highway 82.

"Andy," I said as we pulled out onto the two-lane highway. "Are you familiar with our money?"

"I know it comes in little green papers," he replied.

I nodded and reached over to open the glove box. "There should be some cash in there. Hand it to Val so she can tell me how much I have?"

There were four folded packets of bills, along with a pair of sunglasses, a keychain flashlight, a small hairbrush with a hair tie around the handle, and a bunch of valet ticket receipts. He passed the folded cash back to Val, who started counting, muttering numbers to herself.

"Jesus, Naiya," Val said. "You have a hundred and ninety seven dollars here!"

I nodded. "My dad said I should always keep cash in the car for valet."

"Smart guy," she said. "But this is a lot more than a single tip."

I shrugged. "Sure. But I don't usually carry cash, so when I have some, I just shove it in there."

"What is a valet?" Andy asked.

"They're guys who park your car for you at nicer restaurants, dance clubs, and hotels," I explained. "You drive your car up to the front door like you're dropping someone off, only you get out and they drive your car to their designated parking area and hand you a claim ticket. When you get done with whatever you're doing—whether it's eating, dancing, or checking out of the hotel—you go back outside, give the guy your claim ticket, and they bring you your car."

"It saves time," Val said. "And it saves you the headache of trying to find a parking spot downtown."

I kept the speed up until we hit 82 west, where I had to slow down some because of traffic.

Val looked out the back window, watching the road behind us for a bit. "I don't think anyone is following us, Naiya."

I furrowed my brow as I looked at the back of her head in the rearview mirror. "Really?"

I sped up again and dodged around a few cars on the highway, quickly changing lanes as I did to see if anyone would do the same to keep up.

Val turned back around and met my eyes in the mirror. "No one's on our tail."

"Good." I slowed back down to a reasonable speed and tried to blend in with the traffic again. "We can't really afford to get stopped right now. I don't have my license on me, and tipping off a cop might ping whatever systems they have to track us."

Wind rushed into the car, making my ears ache with the sudden pressure change, as Val rolled down her window. She leaned her head out and looked up and around for a moment before pulling her head back inside and rolling up the window again.

"If they have the resources to follow us with a helicopter," she said. "They aren't using it."

Andy looked over his shoulder at Val. "Why would they stop following us?"

Val rolled a shoulder. "Don't look a gift horse in the mouth?"

"We haven't seen any horses," he said.

Val sighed.

I snorted as I tried not to laugh at him. "It's a turn of phrase. It's basically a reminder to take the blessings you're given without looking for flaws."

Andy nodded. "Sage advice."

I pressed my lips into a line as I contemplated why the guys in the SUVs wouldn't be following us.

"Maybe they know where we're headed?"

"We took the laptop with us," Val said. "So unless they're hacking your family's accounts, I doubt it."

"Considering what they have on my family," I said, "I wouldn't put it past them."

Andy placed a hand on my shoulder, squeezing it gently.

FORTY-EIGHT

Just outside of Wichita Falls, US82 West merged with US287 North, which was kind of a misnomer as US287 ran more west than it did north there. But shortly after the merge point, the road curved gently until it ran more northwest. When we hit Memphis, Texas, right around nine at night, we stopped for some food and gas.

"I didn't even know there *was* a Memphis, Texas," Val said, stretching her arms above her head.

"Sure there is," I replied. "Memphis, Paris, Athens, Palestine, Atlanta … they're all right here in Texas. Everyone else just wishes they were this cool."

"Or Texas has a mighty big head under that hat and wishes it could be as cool as all those other places," Val replied.

I laughed. "That probably makes more sense, all things considered."

After eating, I used the rest stop's wifi to check where we were headed next. Val bought a notebook and a couple of pens from the convenience store to write the directions down as I pulled it up. The next bit had us traveling some really off-the-beaten-path roads, and I couldn't help but think this was not a commonly traversed route. With the directions written down (and a screenshot taken for the rest of the drive, so we didn't have to rely on the slow-as-hell public wifi from a rest stop), we got back on the road, and I tuned the radio to one of the satellite rock music channels to stay awake as Andy dozed in the seat next to me.

Just outside of Amarillo, we had to shift from US287 to I-40, but then it was a tangle of doglegs and interchanges before we were back to a proper highway. Though, even that was just US385—a tiny little two-lane highway. Still, at least that was a long stretch before it merged into US87, and the music from the radio helped.

Val turned sideways in the back and stretched her legs across the seat, but she kept shifting to try to get comfortable.

She leaned between the front seats, keeping her voice down so she didn't wake Andy. "Any chance we can stop to grab a blanket or a pillow or something? This backseat is not built for long drives."

"Sure," I said. "I'll keep an eye out."

But it was late, and finding a twenty-four-hour convenience store was a chore. I didn't manage to find one before Texline, a little town right on the border of Texas and New Mexico. It was midnight by then, and I was struggling to stay alert, even with the radio.

We stopped at a 24-hour truck stop and grabbed a couple of throw blankets and three of those U-shaped pillows people take on flights. Val took over driving, which was easy as we were finally at the part of the directions where it was just 'follow US87 north for 142 miles until it hits I-25.'

But she only made it about forty-five minutes down the road before she reached back to tap my knee and wake me—just long enough for me to doze and wake up even more tired than I had been before I'd slept.

"What's wrong?" I asked.

"Naiya, I can't," she said. "I'm tired too."

"How come you didn't sleep before?" I tried to keep the annoyance from my tone. Tired Naiya is not always the nicest Naiya on the planet.

"I can't really sleep with the motion of a car," she explained. "If I close my eyes, my stomach starts to feel like it's filled with worms."

"You're both exhausted," Andy observed, stating the obvious like we didn't already know, "and I don't have the skills to pilot this machine. Isn't there somewhere we can rest?"

"I don't remember seeing a lot of options for that on the map," I said. "But as long as we haven't gotten to the other side of Des Moines, New Mexico, we should be okay. I think I saw a town there, but there's a whole lot of *nothing* past that till we're into Colorado."

"There," Val said, pointing to the sign as we passed it.

"I'll take your word for it," I said.

She pulled off the road and into a rest stop parking lot. "We probably still have around three hours of driving left to go."

I glanced at the clock; it was just after one in the morning. "I don't really wanna show up on anyone's doorstep at four in the morning, anyway."

Val nodded in agreement. "Definitely a rude time to ring a doorbell."

We parked under one of the light poles, making sure there was plenty of open space around us so we could get some kind of warning if someone approached.

Andy put Chad on the steering wheel. "Keep watch for us, alright? Wake me up if you see someone come toward us."

"A lot of things are likely to come toward us, Andy," I said. "Birds, raccoons, rest stop security. How … smart is he?"

The corner of his mouth quirked up. I was really getting to like that expression on his face.

"He's not quite as smart as I am," Andy said. "But as an extension of me, he definitely understands my meaning better than he understands my words."

I nodded as Val yawned. And then I yawned. And then Andy did. Because yawns are contagious. I showed Andy how to recline his seat, though I didn't let him put it back too far, or I wouldn't have any room in the backseat. Val put a pillow on the center console and turned sideways in the seat, crossing her legs and arms before laying forward on the pillow. I locked the doors and set the alarm for the car, just in case. I put one of the U-shaped pillows between my head and the window and tried to go to sleep in the relatively cramped space.

Considering we'd literally started the day running and fighting, it shouldn't have surprised me when we didn't wake up till nearly nine in the morning. The sun was climbing in the sky as we roused, and Val moved the car closer to the rest stop bathrooms, which we all made use of before I drove us over to top off the gas tank.

Val pulled open the laptop while I went inside the convenience store to prepay.

"Shit," she said quietly as I came back to the car.

I put the nozzle in the tank and started the flow. "Everything okay?"

Val ran a hand through her now-faded rainbow hair, her dark roots more pronounced than they'd been when I first met her, the color clearly needing a touch-up. "It's fine. Here we go. I found the address." More key taps. "It looks like we keep heading west until we hit I-25, which we then take north to Colorado Springs. When we get to the Springs, we wanna exit like we're going to the Garden of the

Gods." A few more key taps. "I got us a screenshot of the rest of the way from there."

"Sounds good," I said, letting the pump click itself off before I hung up the nozzle.

"I'm gonna go get some coffee," Val said as she closed the laptop. "You guys want one?"

"Sure," I said, handing her a twenty.

Andy nodded. "That would be nice, thanks."

She wasn't gone long, since the rest stop and convenience store were practically deserted. This *really* wasn't a popular road trip route. When she returned, we all piled into the Mini Cooper and got back on the road.

"What are werewolves capable of, anyway?" I asked, glancing up at the rearview mirror to meet Val's eyes.

She pressed her lips into a line. "Mmm, a lot of things. Why do you ask?"

"Well, if there's a chance this leopard thing could be an asset to me like you say, Andy," I glanced over at him and back to Val, "then it would make sense for me to try to understand how that could be possible."

Val ran a finger across her stomach and took a deep breath. "Well, lemme see. Do you smell things that people don't normally smell?"

"How would I know that?"

"Uh … do you smell me? Even though I'm not next to you?" She sniffed at her armpit and made a face. "We should find another convenience store once we hit the Springs and clean up a little before we meet them."

I arched my eyebrow and inhaled. "I … can. I can smell you. You still smell like my coconut conditioner, but under it, there's this smell that reminds me of fresh juicy apples. I can smell you too, Andy, but that makes more sense since you're right next to me."

He turned a little in his seat to face me better. "What do I smell like to you?"

I took another slow deep inhale, smiling softly as I picked out what I already knew. "Dark chocolate with a hint of honey, but with a crisp edge to it, like freshly fallen snow."

"How do you even know what snow smells like?" Val asked.

"It's not like it doesn't snow in Texas, Val," I said. "But it doesn't compare to the powder most places further north get. My family took ski trips when I was younger. I never really wanted to do any skiing, so I just stayed in the lodge and drank hot cocoa. I did play in the snow, and there was a certain beauty to the peacefulness of a night sleeping by a crackling fireplace, but I always suspected my parents wanted me to be more active than I was."

"Hmm," Val said. "Well, what about hearing?"

"Do I hear things people shouldn't?"

She nodded.

"Sometimes." I shrugged a shoulder. "I sometimes can hear your heart beating, even from this distance. But not always."

I took a slow breath to focus, and my first finger started tapping on the steering wheel in time with Val's heartbeat.

"Yours?" Andy asked.

I shook my head once. "Val's."

My taps increased in tempo a bit as she ran her finger along her stomach again and looked away from me in the mirror.

I shook my head and listened for Andy's instead. "Yours." I started tapping a different beat.

Val leaned forward and turned up the radio. "See how long you can keep track of it?"

I nodded once, focusing my eyes on the road as I listened past the bassline and guitar riffs. Rock music had heavy drum beats that would certainly make things a challenge. Still, my finger kept tapping.

Val turned up the music little by little. It was nearly blasting by the time I started to lose the rhythm.

"No," she said. "That's mine."

Shit. She's right. I had switched. But that pace …

"What are you afraid of, Val?" I asked, sure that the pounding in her chest meant just that.

FORTY-NINE

SHE TURNED down the music and sat back in her seat, biting her lip for a moment. "Did you want to kill those vampires when you saw them?"

I angled my head to the side, remembering as I glanced up to meet her eyes in the mirror. "Not at first. But something inside me screamed that they were wrong."

"They are," Val said quickly. "They're evil, and they prey on the weak and lonely."

She went quiet then, something haunting her eyes.

"You have firsthand experience with their evil," Andy said.

Val nodded, rubbing at her scars again. "Yep."

"Val?" I kept glancing between her and the road until she finally met my eyes. "Why didn't you tell me about vampires and werewolves from the start?"

"Would you have even believed me without any proof? Even though you're a wereleopard? Hell, you didn't even mention that until after we were locked up." She sounded kind of frantic, her words rushing over each other.

I pressed my lips into a line and huffed out a breath. "No ... I guess that's fair."

"And I couldn't let those assholes know how much

I knew," she said. "What if they'd tried half the shit they did to you on me? It would have killed me."

I nodded. "Yeah, I don't think you could swim for however long like I did."

"Most of the lycanthropes back home don't mention it either," Andy said. "It tends to go poorly—they get run out of towns and publicly humiliated, and that's when the people they tell are particularly civilized."

I raked a hand through my hair. "Is that why the rest of the world doesn't know they're real?"

Val rolled a shoulder. "You really think that'd go well if they tried to go public?"

"I'm just saying that, with cell phones everywhere with their amazing camera resolutions, it must be hard for them to stay hidden."

"Sure," Val said. "But have you noticed lately that there's been an uptick in reports of animal attacks and people who are entirely too strong fighting outside of clubs?"

I nodded. "I don't really watch the news, but I've heard it."

"And you know how there seems to always be someone hot on the heels of those reports to debunk the 'breaking news?'" She put air quotes around the last bit.

I nodded again. "Werewolves and vampires?"

"It's all propaganda," she said, leaning forward between the seats again. "Between the vampires and the werewolves, virtually everything you think you know about them is because that's what they decided was okay for humans to know. Movies, TV shows, books—they're all just propaganda. These things have been around for nearly two thousand years."

"Holy shit," I said.

"That's … a long time to stay hidden," Andy said.

"It is," Val said, sitting back in her seat. "And

when you know, I feel like you gotta respect it. Werewolves are the good guys in the fight, but they're also the kind that completely change form into something that—especially here in America—people instinctively assume is evil and vicious. Here, humans have been hunting wolves and blaming them for livestock incidents since we first started colonizing."

I chewed the inside of my cheek. Maybe the only reason I assumed the leopard was a vicious monster was because of what I knew about lions and tigers: they were predators, built for the hunt.

Wait.

"Werewolves are the good guys?" Andy asked, saying aloud the thought I literally just had.

I arched an eyebrow at him.

"They are," Val said. "They protect people from the vampires."

I looked at her again in the rearview. "But they scare you."

Something didn't add up. How could good guys be so terrifying?

"What about the guys at the facility? If they're all werewolves, what are they doing testing people like they are?"

"I don't know," Val said. "But however dangerous they clearly are, I don't think they would have done anything to actually kill you or me, or even you, Andy."

"How can you be sure? If I hadn't been able to find you in that burning house, you would have died."

"With all those other werewolves in there? There's no way they'd have let that happen." She sounded so confident, but she was rubbing her scars in earnest now.

"They attacked me," I said, a note of anger threading through my tone.

Andy placed his hand on my knee.

"I know," Val said, slumping back in her seat again. "Which is the thing I'm having trouble reconciling. I don't know why they'd want to hurt you."

"He said 'there it is,'" Andy said.

I glanced at him. "What?"

"Grump," Andy explained. "He said 'there it is' before he sedated you, but *after* you'd changed into a leopard."

"You think they were just trying to get me to shift," I said. Saying it out loud made me sure he was right.

Andy nodded. "I do."

It made sense. They were trying to get me to shift when I nearly suffocated in that room, and they were ready for my shift when they threw me in with the vampires. Vampires which were very much real, as were werewolves. I killed a pair of vampires, and I would have killed a pair of werewolves if they hadn't sedated me.

"Do vampires have a reflection?" I asked. "I feel like I should have been paying closer attention to that."

"I haven't exactly been up close and personal with one in a while," Val said, "but I'm pretty sure they do. Particularly since all the stories say they don't."

"What about that whole drinking blood thing?"

She nodded. "That's true. Vampires can't process food."

"Does silver do anything to werewolves?" Andy asked.

"Nothing more than steel or iron would," she said. "They're tough motherfuckers."

"Interesting," Andy said. "That hurts the ones back home."

I blinked once at him and then glanced back at Val. "And they aren't just wild killing machines?"

"Well," she hedged. "They *are* killing machines, but any you've seen on two legs are generally much more likely to help you change a flat tire than they are to attack you on sight."

"And the ones on four legs?" Andy asked.

"If you've only ever seen them on four legs," she said, folding her arms across her stomach, "it's a toss-up. Mooncrazed wolves are insanely violent and dangerous. They don't have rational thought, just instincts to kill."

"You were mooncrazed," Andy said. It wasn't a question.

Val nodded and rubbed at her scars again, her heart starting to pound. "I told you. I got attacked and turned, and it went real bad for me. I was stuck in the form of this slavering thing that only wanted death and destruction. I was shoved into a cage that I chewed and fought against so hard I would bleed, only for those wounds to close up so they could be reopened again. There was no *me* left when I was like that. So, I'm taking you to the person that took that thing out of me."

I nodded. "And you're hoping that when I turn into a leopard, that's not me."

She glanced up and met my eyes furtively before looking away. She seemed so much smaller in the backseat than she had a moment ago.

Andy turned in his seat to look at her. "Are any of their capabilities still left with you?"

Val looked up at him and ran a hand through her hair. "Not really. I can't smell you guys unless you're, like, hugging me or if you're all sweaty and gross. I can't hear your heartbeat. I'm not strong like they are."

"Wait," I said. "Super strength is a thing for them?"

She nodded. "Yep."

"So four hundred pounds or more would be right in line for them."

"It's probably on the weak end," she said.

"And I'm guessing they can probably run for hours and hours without stopping."

She shrugged. "Maybe? They don't usually need to, but I'm pretty sure they could. And if they can, that's certainly not something I can do anymore. But I do still get a sense of when someone is lying."

I furrowed my brow. "Don't most people?"

"Mmm, not like that," Val said. "I dunno how to explain it exactly, but a werewolf can smell a lie—or hear it?—as soon as it's said. Can't you?"

"I don't think I can do that," I said.

"The sky is yellow," Andy said.

"No, it's not," I said.

"And that's not how it works," Val said. "It's more like … if I tried to tell you that I grew up rich too, you'd just know it wasn't true. Not because of my clothes or my hair or the way I talked or whatever, you'd just instinctively know that the words were a lie."

"I'm not sure I can do that," I said.

She was quiet for a moment.

"I grew up on a farm, with my aunt and uncle, and never knew my parents," Andy said, raising an eyebrow at me.

But there was something about the way he said it.

"No … you didn't," I said, and I was just as sure of that as I was that Grump and Blondie had been trying to get me to shift when they attacked me.

Holy shit. I clapped a hand over my mouth, which had gone slack.

"I think you can do that," Val said quietly.

"No," Andy said, "I didn't. I grew up in the city. My father was a philosopher of sorts, and though he wasn't from our plane of existence, he was a hopeless romantic who fell for my mother. She was a wizardess who specialized in transportation magic."

"Well," I said, "at least that means you come by the wandering honestly."

He nodded. "Indeed. It's no wonder I am fascinated by the threads of the fabric holding all of our realities in place."

Well. That was something.

I knew a lie when I heard it. Which made me look at the serial relationships I'd had among my social circle in a whole new light. No wonder I always thought so many of them were fake.

But it also meant one other thing that was a lot more harrowing to me.

I gripped the steering wheel with both hands to keep them steady. "Does that mean that everything those people told me when we were locked up was true?"

"I think it does," Andy said, turning to face the front as he placed a gentle hand on my knee again.

I took a deep breath as I processed that, laying my hand down on top of Andy's. That means they never thought any of those tests would kill me. They really were just trying to gauge my capabilities. And they really were willing to hurt my family to get me to do it.

"Ow," Andy said, jerking his hand from my grip.

Blinking, I let him go. "Sorry."

He shook his hand and put it back down on my knee. "I'm alright."

That's not a rabbit hole I could let my mind go wandering down right now. We were trying to see if getting rid of the leopard was possible. If it was, that would keep my family safe.

"So Val," I said, forcing a change of topic. "Why call the people who actually have this whole vampire-werewolf thing figured out foil-hat-wearers?"

"Because most of them are," she said. "There are a lot of werewolves in the world, sure—and even more vampires—but there's not nearly as many as those conspiracy theorists would have you believe. Besides, a *lot* of what they have is actually doctored footage."

"Hmm. Does that mean the people 'debunking' the videos are doctoring the footage themselves to hide their existence?"

Val nodded. "Pretty fucked up, huh? And all because people are 'shoot first, ask questions later' when it comes to the things they fear."

"Yeah," I agreed. "And people fear what they don't understand."

Because fear is what caused my parents to dump me at Saint Dymphna's. And if I had to guess, fear was also why everyone at the research facility was working so hard to find out exactly what I was capable of.

I ran a hand through my hair. "I'm really glad I have you guys." I glanced over and Andy and met his eyes before meeting Val's in the rearview. "You've been there every morning when I woke and every evening as I went to sleep."

"Minus the times you were unconscious," Val said, her tone playful.

"Val," Andy chided, looking over his shoulder at her.

She threw up her hands in mock surrender. "I'm just saying!"

"Well," I said. "I'm glad that you two were the first and last people I had contact with every day. And I'm glad we're out, and *together*."

Andy squeezed my knee. "Me too."

FIFTY

Val and Andy fell quiet again after that, though Andy's hand stayed where it was on my knee. We merged onto I-25 just a few minutes later, which meant we still had about two and a half hours of driving before we got to Colorado Springs.

Val had become increasingly twitchy and fidgety during the drive, constantly shifting around in the backseat like she couldn't get comfortable and twirling bits of hair around her finger while she rubbed at her scars.

I met her eyes in the rearview. "You okay?"

She froze and then ran a hand through her hair. "It's been about a day and a half since my last dose of the meds the doctors at Saint Dymphna's put me on. Going cold turkey off them isn't great."

"Cold turkey?" Andy asked.

I patted his hand. "Hmm. I'm not even sure where the phrase comes from, actually, but it's what it's called when someone quits a substance all at once without weaning off it first. Like quitting smoking or eliminating alcohol. It usually results in some pretty nasty side effects while you level out."

Val shook her head. "It's not bad. We can't stop and track down refills, or they'll know where we're going. I'll have to call Saint Dymphna's and figure out a way to get it refilled when we get to Colorado Springs."

Andy turned to look at her. "Is there anything we can do?"

"Mmm, maybe? Take the next exit and lemme grab a bag of hard candy?"

I nodded. "Sure."

She already had a piece of yellow candy clacking against her tongue ring as she slumped back into the car after our stop, the scent of sugary lemon filling the car.

I stopped to fill up again somewhere just south of Colorado Springs, where we also grabbed deodorant. Since I hadn't had a shower in a couple of days, I brushed my hair and pulled it into a high ponytail, regretting that I hadn't grabbed any toiletries while prepping to leave the lake house.

With another piece of candy rattling around in her mouth, Val directed me to a neighborhood where the houses were spread widely apart, each one with sizable yards to either side. The whole neighborhood looked like it had been here for a while, what with the giant trees and bushes.

Except for one house, which had new siding and a stack of drywall and lumber in the open garage.

"Strange that there's just this one new construction house in the middle of all these others," I said.

"That used to be the pack's house," Val said. "Take the next left."

I followed her directions. "Used to be?"

"Vampires burned it down last year," she said.

"Aren't they scared they'll burn down this one too?"

"Nah," Val said. "They're … uh … well-off. If the vamps burn this one down, they'll just move again.

Hard to get attached to stuff when you're effectively immortal."

"Waitaminute." I stopped the car between houses. "Immortal?"

"Nearly, yeah," Val said, nodding. "It'd be hard for them to fight vampires if they weren't."

"Do you think—?" My vision lost focus as my brain finished the question I'd started.

Does that mean I might be immortal too? As in, never going to grow old and die?

Andy squeezed my knee. "The face you're making makes me want to poke around in your head."

I blinked and refocused, looking at him before glancing up to meet Val's eyes in the rearview.

"Am I immortal too?" I asked quietly.

Val shrugged. "Hell if I know. But if you are, getting rid of the leopard will definitely change that."

"Will they know?"

"I dunno." She shrugged again. "I don't think anyone's ever seen a wereleopard before, Naiya. I don't think anyone knows what to expect from you."

Which means no one will have any answers as to how I'm even like this.

Shit.

"Come on," Andy said. "We can at least see what they know."

"I still think you should just get them to take the leopard out of you," Val said. "It would simplify everything and give you some normalcy."

Normalcy.

A normal life.

I took a deep breath as I chewed the inside of my cheek again.

I turned in my seat to look at Val. "Does it hurt?" My voice shook a little.

She shook her head. "No, she just kind of touched me and I was me again."

I sighed in relief and Andy rubbed my knee.

"It's just up here on the right," she said. "The one with all the cars in front of it and the black Dodge Ram in the driveway."

I nodded and started us moving again. The house she indicated had blocky modern architecture with nearly as many windows as my parents' lake house. Thick shrubs blocked the view of the house from the street. There was a motorcycle in the driveway next to the pickup, along with an old red muscle car with black racing stripes and a white Mercedes SUV. Parked along the street, on either side of the driveway, were a little purple two-person car with the top down and a blue Mustang that was almost the same shade as my Mini.

I glanced at the clock in my car. It was just after noon.

I pulled up behind the little purple car. "You're sure this is the place?"

"Yep," she said, opening her door. "Let's go introduce ourselves."

I stretched as I stood before going around to the back hatch and grabbing the backpack. I threw it over my shoulder as I came around the car. Andy stepped closer to me, pulling my arm into his—a gesture of support I was more than grateful for.

We followed Val up to the front door, where she rang the doorbell.

A linebacker of a guy in his late thirties or early forties answered the door before the bell had even finished ringing. He had sandy blond hair that brushed his shoulders and golden eyes that were friendly and warm. He wore a black v-neck shirt with blue jeans, though he was barefoot. The scent of roasted chicken and potatoes wafted out to us, carrying the gentle warmth of his scent as well. My mouth watered at the thought of food, and my stomach replied with a hungry little gurgle. Behind him, beyond the couches in the living room, people were seated around a giant black dining table.

The man at the door furrowed his brow as his head angled in an unasked question. He seemed to fill more and more space from one breath to the next, though I couldn't explain how or why I felt that way.

"Uh … hi," Val said lamely.

An athletic-looking woman in her early twenties came up beside him. She had wavy dark hair to about the middle of her back, with stormy blue-grey eyes that had a hint of gold in them. She wore a long white sleeveless tunic top with brown leggings. She put a hand on the larger man's shoulder, and he stepped to the side to make room for her.

"Hayley?" She virtually ignored Andy and I to talk to Val. "What are you doing here? I thought you were with General Buckheim?"

The eyes of everyone at the table landed on us. It made me uneasy.

General who? And who the hell was Hayley?

Val's tattooed hand went to her belly, where she idly rubbed at the scars behind the knotted tails of my father's button-down. "It's Valerie, actually. Or Val. And … well … I need your help."

The man narrowed his eyes at her.

She grabbed my arm and pulled me into his field of vision, although, being as tall as I am, I couldn't see how he could have possibly missed me.

"Well," she said. "*She* does, actually."

My eyes went wide.

Shit.

This was where I was supposed to say something, wasn't I?

"I … uh … yeah." I swallowed thickly and started again, extending my arm for a handshake. "I'm Naiya. Valerie says you can help me?"

Something heavy and deep rang through me, like a big heavy wind chime ringing in the distance. I felt it more than I heard it. Neither the man nor the lady took my hand, and I dropped it sheepishly.

He crossed his arms and leaned against the doorframe. "Does she now?"

A waifish woman in her early thirties with platinum blonde hair hurried out of the kitchen and toward the door, throwing a white kitchen towel over the shoulder of her pale blue sundress. "C'mon now, Shep, don't mess with th' poor girl!" She looked at me with crystal blue eyes. "Help is what we *do*, honey."

The man glanced at her and then met my eyes. "And what help is it, exactly, that you're hoping for?"

There was movement behind the three people already at the door.

"She's *consanguinea*," a deep smoky voice said. There was an accent to it that I couldn't quite place.

The three parted to make room for him—the women to the right and the beefy man to the left—revealing a man even more bulky than the blond guy, though he was shorter by a couple of inches. He had unruly curly hair to his chest, and the muscles of his arms strained at the light grey t-shirt he wore with loose black linen pants.

The deep clang of a distant wind chime thrummed through me again, with a sparkle of lighter chimes dancing along my skin as he met my gaze with honey-gold eyes. There was a faint hum, like someone was playing a Tibetan prayer bowl somewhere in the house, only I was certain now that none of the sounds were actually audible.

I wasn't sure I liked it.

"And … somewhat else it seems," the shorter man said. Though, despite his height, his presence was certainly larger than the others that had come to the door in a way that I couldn't quite put my finger on.

I blinked at him in curiosity. He definitely had some flavor of European accent. But I could not for the life of me place it. Moreover, it felt like the chime along my muscles connected to him.

He was still looking at me expectantly. I supposed he wanted me to confirm whatever else I was for him.

"Leopard," I said. "Which is the problem, really."

Because it was. It was the leopard that was endangering everyone I knew and loved. So it was the leopard I needed gone.

The blond man furrowed his brow at me and then turned to the stockier one. "*Consanguinea*? You're sure?"

The dark-haired man nodded once. "I'm certain, Alpha. Are you really telling me you can't smell it on her?"

"I can," he said. "But it makes no sense."

"I'm still right here," I said. But I might as well have been talking to the wind.

Another man's voice joined the conversation. "What does that make him?"

Another muscular blond, this one a little more hard-edged than the first, came up beside the dark-haired man. The two were of a height, but the newcomer had a horribly scarred face. His left eye was milky, while the other was clear brown. He jutted his chin toward Andy.

"Oh!" I grabbed his arm and pulled him up beside me. "Uh … that's Andy."

Andy waved an arm. "I'm just a guy."

Something rumbled in the chest of the one with the scarred face. Did he just growl?

"You can't lie to a werewolf, Andy," Val whispered, nudging him with her arm.

He turned to her. "But it's true. I am just a guy. I'm just not from around here."

"Hmmm," said the one who answered the door.

The dark-haired guy tapped the chest of the taller blond with the back of his hand. "Between me and you and the rest of the pack, I'm sure we can take care of it if he becomes a problem."

There was definitely an implied threat there, and —if I truly was staring at no less than five werewolves —I didn't like our odds.

Andy put his hands up. "Not necessary. There won't be a problem." He placed his hands on my shoulders. "Naiya just needs your help."

The waifish blonde woman smacked the chest of the one with the scarred face as she brushed the others out of the doorway and gestured into the house. "Well, don' jus' stand 'ere jabberjawin'! Come! Sit 'n eat, y'all! There's plenty t'go aroun'. Chas, grab a couple chairs from the garage."

A freckled redhead with long curls disappeared down a hallway as the blonde woman gestured at the man with the sandy blond hair. "'At's Sheppard." She gestured to the dark-haired man. "'N' Kristos." She waved a hand in the direction of the dark-haired girl who had called Val 'Hayley.' "'At's Lynn. The scarred one is Matt."

Matt grumbled as he went to sit back down at the giant black table.

The waifish blonde continued gesturing around the table. "Jonathan, Jamie, Ian, and Daniel." She kissed the last one on the top of his head.

The redhead came back with three white folding chairs—the nice wooden kind with padded seats. She unfolded them and placed them at the end of the table closest to the front door as everyone else shifted their seats around to make space.

"Chastity's th' one wi' th' chairs," she continued. "'N' I'm Kaylah."

We still hadn't moved from the doorway.

"C'mon! Sit! Sit!" She gestured to the table with

both hands before putting her fists on her hips and looking at the one who'd opened the door—Sheppard, I think. "Shep, tell 'em!"

He pressed his lips into a line and dropped his chin, though there was mirth in his expression.

"Come on in," he said, gesturing to the empty folding chairs. "Have a seat. Let's talk over lunch."

FIFTY-ONE

I CAME into the house and chose the center seat of the three open spots at the end of the black granite table, leaning my backpack against the side of the couch on my way. There were flecks of iridescence in the table's surface, the bits catching the light in a brighter, flashier version of the soft iridescence of Andy's tattoos. As I sank into the chair, Andy took the seat to my right, and Val the one to my left.

"There's no way I'm gonna remember all those names," I whispered to Andy.

He grabbed my hand and squeezed it. "I think I got it. I'll help you."

The one called Sheppard—hadn't that burly guy also called him Alpha?—pulled a chicken leg onto his plate as the rest of the people around the table followed suit. He eyed the dark-haired guy—Kristos—and then looked at me.

"What's your full name?" Sheppard asked.

"Naiya Kateri," I said.

His brow furrowed deeper. "I don't remember a Kateri on the chart." He sucked a bit of roasted chicken from the tip of his thumb as he pulled his phone from his back pocket. With a swipe, Sheppard opened his screen.

Kristos shrugged as he spooned a heap of peach

cobbler onto his plate and passed the dish along to Andy. "I don't know anything about your chart, but *that one's* definitely of the blood." He nodded toward me and the inaudible chime thrummed lightly along my skin.

"'Of the blood?'"

"*Consanguinea*," Sheppard said, not looking up from his phone as he swiped a finger across the screen.

Kristos met my gaze. "The lineage of the children of Mary."

Andy leaned close to me and whispered, "Who's Mary?"

Sheppard looked up and cocked his head at Andy, his expression as quizzical as it had been when he opened the door.

The rest of the people at the table—the rest of the pack, if I understood correctly—seemed to pause, some with bits of food on their forks.

"Mother to Jesus of Nazareth," the athletic woman who'd come to the door—Lynn—said.

"Have some, hun," said Kaylah, nodding to the bowl of roasted potatoes in front of Val.

Val scooped a few onto her plate and passed the bowl to me.

"Waitaminute." The serving spoon clattered from my grip, but at least it landed in the bowl. "You're trying to tell me I'm related to the Son of God himself?"

I knew Jesus had actually lived. There were historical documents that supported such a fact. But if I understood what they were saying, they thought I was part of his bloodline.

"What?" Andy looked bewildered and lost.

I squinted and turned to him, pinching the bridge of my nose for a moment as the deep wind chime sounded along my muscles once again.

"One of the predominant religions here is Christianity," I explained. "A faith based on the belief in a single God who sent his son to die for all of humanity's sins."

"Okay," Andy said slowly. "And who's Mary to that God?"

"Ugh, this guy!" Val shoved a bite of potato in her mouth.

I shot her a look.

"Mary is the woman on Earth who God chose to carry His son to term," Kristos said around a bite of chicken.

"But Jesus wasn't an only child. He had siblings." The redhead with the long curly hair bit into her corn on the cob.

Sheppard was still swiping around on his phone. "And if Kristos here is right—"

"I am," Kristos said.

Sheppard looked up then, blinking before looking at me. "Then it means you can trace your lineage all the way back in an unbroken line to one of those siblings. Except you're not on the chart." He gestured to his phone.

Kristos held out his hand, eyeing the phone and arching an eyebrow at Sheppard, who passed over the device and finally took a bite of potato from his otherwise untouched lunch.

The rest of the people at the table ate quietly as Kristos swiped a finger over and over on the screen.

"Oh, easy," he said finally. "You're missing one of the sisters."

I bit into my chicken. It was as tender and juicy and flavorful as it looked.

Sheppard shook his head. "No, no. The lost sister is a myth. The church debunked it decades ago."

Kristos pressed his lips into a firm line as he handed the phone back to Sheppard. "I'm telling you,

Alpha. There was one more. I was barely more than a child, but I recall when she disappeared. They were still looking for her when Peter created the bears."

Holy shit. Wait. What? This guy was alive when Jesus' siblings were still around? That would mean he was close to two thousand years old!

"That would certainly explain it though," Lynn said, scooping some cobbler onto her spoon. "Wouldn't it?"

"It would." Sheppard nodded. "But then why would the church lie about it?"

Kristos gave a rueful chuckle. The deep thrum of the wind chime rumbled with it as a shimmer of the tinkly high chimes flickered against my skin. It was an entirely odd sensation to feel a sound more than I heard it, but it was not entirely unpleasant.

"You really think they would be completely forthcoming about losing an entire section of the bloodline of Mary?" Kristos' laugh deepened. "Did they tell you about us bears, too?"

Sheppard smiled at him, catching some of the other man's mirth. "*Touché.*"

I sighed. One thing just became brutally clear: even if I was a child of the bloodline of Mary …

"Sounds like I won't ever know what my birth parents were like." I took a sip of the water in front of me, my hand shaking, and the chime thrummed a hollow note.

Andy brushed a hand on my knee as Val leaned against my shoulder.

"Maybe not," Lynn said. "But it does make you a distant cousin of mine."

My eyes snapped up to hers as the hum of the prayer bowl I'd felt earlier deepened and intensified.

I looked between Kristos and Lynn, my gaze meeting each of theirs in turn. "How are you doing that?"

Lynn furrowed her brow. "What?"

"The chime, the song, the … note? It started when I got here—when I first saw you." I gestured toward Kristos. "But you have one, too." I nodded my head at Lynn. "So, how are you doing it?"

Lynn looked at Kristos. "That's you."

Kristos shook his head. "It's not, really."

The chime clanged in harmony with the prayer bowl tone while the little chimes tinkled along my skin again.

"That," I said. "How are you doing that?"

"It's a thing," the guy seated next to Lynn said, gesturing toward Kristos. I think that was Jonathan? Or maybe it was Jamie. "Connected to him. It's part of his whole protector schtick."

I met Kristos' eyes. He blinked and looked at the one who spoke.

"You hear it?" He asked.

The guy shook his head, his long, wavy brown hair brushing his shoulders as he did. "No, but pack doesn't keep secrets." He gestured vaguely around the table. "We all know. Now would you answer her already?" He jerked his chin toward me. "She's getting antsy."

Andy placed a hand on mine, and I realized I'd shredded my paper napkin.

Kristos took a breath and turned back to me, meeting my eyes. "I couldn't tell you how or why, but it's a connection I have to *consanguinea*. I can tell when one is nearby. I know whether they're hurt or frightened or … well, other things."

Lynn's cheeks colored at the last bit, but she quickly pressed her face against the shoulder of the guy with the wavy hair, who's expression immediately reminded me of trouble.

I narrowed my eyes at Kristos. "How am I

connected to you when I've never met you before in my life?"

"I really wish I knew," he said.

"Confirm my suspicion for me, if you would, please, Naiya," Sheppard said around a bite of chicken. "You're here because you're hoping Lynn can help you stop being …"

"A wereleopard," I provided. "And yes. That. Exactly."

Sheppard cocked his head at me and then looked at Kristos, a question on his face.

Kristos met his gaze and shook his head.

I was pretty sure that meant that neither of them knew anything about what I was. I sighed as another hollow note sang through the big wind chimes.

"I told you," Val said quietly. "I don't think anyone's ever heard of a wereleopard before."

I kept my voice quiet too. "Then that pretty much settles it, doesn't it?"

No one was going to be able to tell me anything more than I already knew, aside from Mr. Loudspeaker and his lackeys, and they sure as hell weren't going to tell me anything. Besides, even they didn't know anything beyond what they'd learned from me.

I chewed my cheek and turned to Lynn, who was poking the last of her potatoes with her fork.

"Do you think … That is, can you help?"

Andy squeezed my knee again.

She studied me for a moment, glancing between me and Val a couple of times like she was deciding how much to tell me. "Well, I've done it a few times for the General already. And though they were mooncrazed creatures of violence, the concept's the same, right?" She looked at Kristos. "Even if she is a leopard?"

Kristos shrugged. "Theoretically, sure. There's not

likely to be any surviving documentation on how the last *purgatum* did *anything*."

"And even if there was," the redhead chimed in, swallowing a bite of peach cobbler, "it's unlikely we could even hope to have access to it."

"Don't be so sure," said one of the other guys—Jamie? Ian, maybe? He was slim, but not quite lanky, and had short brown hair with sapphire blue eyes.

"We're not hacking into church databases on a whim, Ian," Sheppard said.

Got it. So that was Ian.

"Spoilsport," said the guy who'd spoken earlier. The one who'd talked about the chimes with Kristos. His green eyes sparkled with mischief.

Sheppard just smiled and shook his head at him.

"*Purgatum?*" Andy asked.

"Apparently, that's what I am," Lynn said, gesturing vaguely at herself. "With this ability I have."

"It means 'purified' in Latin," Kristos said, polishing off his cobbler. "Since she can pull the affliction from werewolves and vampires alike, the church decided that's what she's doing: purifying the blood."

Andy leaned close and whispered, "Who speaks Latin?"

Chastity didn't hesitate. "No one anymore—other than church sermons, at least. Some scholars still know the language, and a lot of doctor types learn it to help with their work."

I looked at Andy and gestured to Kristos. "And, of course, that guy, apparently."

Lynn cocked her head to the side. "Why do you want to have this leopard taken out of you?"

I swallowed another bite of chicken. "It's … putting people I care about in danger. I already hurt my—" I stopped myself and took a breath. These people didn't need my life story. "I've hurt people I care about and I can't let that happen again. And if that wasn't bad enough, there are people who have clearly never seen this before, and they're threatening my family because of what I am."

Andy rubbed my knee.

"Are they holding your family hostage?" Sheppard asked, a simmering danger in his tone.

"Not in any way they know about," I said. "At least, I don't think so. My parents are out of the country right now, but our house manager—who is as close to me as a second mother—isn't."

"C'n we see th' leopard, hun?" Kaylah asked.

My heart rate spiked, and the thrum of wind chimes responded, soothing in their deep tones. "I … that's part of the problem. I don't have any control over it."

Everyone paused and sat back in their seats.

Val put a hand on my arm and looked at Sheppard. "She's not mooncrazed."

"She just doesn't know how any of it works," Andy said.

I brushed a stray hair back toward my ponytail with a huff, though I tried to keep my tone civil. "She can speak for herself."

Everyone around the table slowly resumed eating.

"It just doesn't matter," I said. "Whether I understand how it works or whether I can ever learn control, it just *doesn't matter*. It's been stalking me for too long—giving me nightmares for too long—and the fact that it's a part of me is putting too many people I care about in danger."

I squeezed Andy's hand, and he squeezed back before leaning close to my ear.

"Are you sure?" Andy whispered, pulling back to look at me, his eyes searching mine.

I brought my other hand to his cheek and kissed him, and he melted against me. "I'm sure."

FIFTY-TWO

I WAS SITTING at the table among an actual werewolf pack. It was like joining in on some family's holiday dinner. We were welcome, sure, but we weren't quite a part of it.

It was hard to get food down, though it was truly delicious. I was antsy to know whether Lynn could help me, and nervous to know if she'd simply have to touch me to make it happen, like Val said had happened with her.

The thrumming of the big deep wind chime and the ringing of the prayer bowl changed pitch as dinner went on, winding tighter in a way that I couldn't explain, but certainly felt.

But by the end of it, I had a pretty good feel for everyone's names. Andy kept leaning over when someone was speaking, whispering their name in my ear.

"How do you remember it all so quickly like that?" I asked him.

He shrugged. "I've always been good at things like that. Names, numbers, diagrams, maps. Anything memorization could feasibly help with, really."

I couldn't help but notice Lynn kept looking at Andy's tattoos. Not that I could blame her, really. I was actually surprised more of the pack weren't gawking or asking about them. Matt kept eyeing Val, though, with his one good eye, almost like he didn't trust her—but he didn't say anything.

After lunch, a bunch of the pack went out into the backyard and started tossing around a football, while Sheppard, Lynn, and Kristos stayed seated around the dining room table. The one with the green eyes and mischief in his features—Jonathan—kissed Lynn before heading out, and she watched his departure like a puppy looking after a beloved toy.

"Y'all take that business to th' office," Kaylah said, making a shooing motion. "I gotta wipe down th' table!"

Sheppard nodded and stood, gesturing to a hallway off to the left. "The office is in the basement."

I wasn't sure I liked that. Something thrummed through the deep heavy wind chime.

"Why don't we sit in the living room instead?" Kristos said, standing and stepping over to one of the couches, arms spread wide. "Less closed in, easy escape."

Lynn nodded as she moved to join him. "And less creepy vibes." She looked at me. "The basement is fully finished and well lit, but there's no way you could know that."

"And you're strangers to her," Val said.

Kristos nodded. "That we are."

The three of them sat on one couch, leaving the other one for Val and Andy and I.

"I don't want to waste your time," I said as I sat down. "If you don't want to help, or you can't, just let me know, and we'll get out of your hair."

Andy placed a hand on my knee as he sat down on my left, closer to the others. Val plopped down on my right, kicking off her shoes so she could sit cross-legged next to me. She leaned against my shoulder, and I pressed my cheek to the top of her head for a moment.

"If I can help," Lynn said, "I want to. You're clearly spooked by what's within you, and while I usually do this for those who are stuck in their other form, I should be able to help you anyway."

"Should be like clearing a vamp," Kristos said, patting her knee once, "minus the desiccating and the dust."

Lynn bobbed her head. "That should make it easier."

Sheppard studied Val and then looked at me. "What Lynn can do. It's not a temporary thing. This isn't something you can change your mind on later."

Lynn put a hand on his arm. "You're not a wolf. I can smell that. But I can't even guarantee that I could take this leopard from you, and then maybe you could somehow be a wolf later." She eyed Val, something unspoken going between them.

"I can't think of any reason I'd try to undo getting rid of it," I said. "I need those people to leave me and my family alone. And I need to know I won't hurt anyone."

Sheppard narrowed his eyes. "You've mentioned a couple of times that you're doing this to keep your family safe. You have people chasing you?"

I nodded. "I don't think they know I'm here, but it can't be long before they track something of mine down and find me again. But if I'm just a regular human, they won't have a reason to throw me back into a cell and study my capabilities."

"We know of ways to get people off the radar," Sheppard said.

"Unless you have the kind of connections that can do that for two whole families at the same time, including an extremely successful businessman and his wildly popular graphic design wife," I said, "I think you'll find the assholes tailing me are quite tenacious."

The chime thrummed deeply, something ominous in its tone.

My parents would *never* believe what'd happened to me at the research facility. They'd never believe this pack was real, along with vampires and werewolves. And hell, if they did, it'd probably put them at even more risk. Better that I just become the mundane. Just a silver-spoon rich kid learning to take over her father's business.

"You're certain this is the path you want?" Lynn asked, meeting my eyes. "I need you to be certain."

I stood and turned to look at Val and Andy. The movement out back caught my eye as the guys all tumbled together into a pile.

"You don't have to do this," Andy said, "if you aren't sure."

"But if you do," Val said, "you definitely won't have to worry about whether you'll hurt someone in that other form ever again."

The deep heavy chime thrummed again.

"Let her choose," Sheppard said, his tone heavy with finality.

I took a deep breath as my throat started to close, tears stinging my eyes. I didn't know if the leopard was really part of me, like Andy had tried to imply, but I couldn't keep this part of me if it was. My parents … Abigail … they'd never know peace if I didn't get rid of this. And I couldn't stomach if I ever hurt anyone again like I'd hurt my father. I closed my eyes as a tear spilled over, and Andy wrapped his arms around me. I turned into his embrace as another tear made its way down my cheek.

"You could come with me to Arcaniss," Andy whispered against my ear, his words more breath and quiet air than voice. "I'll figure out a way. I'm sure someone there can help you."

I shook my head as I buried my face into his neck. "I can't. Abigail. And the Davenports."

He made shushing noises as he rubbed my back. "Okay, okay."

I gathered myself and turned to Lynn, who'd stood while I was crying.

"Do it," I said. "I'm certain."

She held out a hand to me. I wiped at my eyes and pulled away from Andy as I stood and took her hand. It was so warm. She placed her other hand atop mine and closed her eyes, her breathing deepening and then changing rhythm until it matched mine. I closed my eyes as well because … well, it simply made sense to do.

The deep chime thrummed, and the prayer bowl sang along my spine and out to the tips of my fingers and toes. The air filled with the scent of crisp fresh snow, and it was suddenly like there were claws digging into the backs of my hands, rending at my flesh. I cried out and pulled my hands from hers, opening my eyes and flipping my hands over to see the damage.

But there was none. My hands were untouched, unscathed. There was only the lingering warmth of where her hand had lain overtop of mine.

The pain had been exactly what I imagined my father had felt when the leopard's claws tore into him.

"What the hell was that?" Andy demanded, wrapping his arms around me and pulling me back down to the couch.

The chime thrummed an angry tone, and Kristos got to his feet, stepping once toward Lynn.

"No," she said, stopping the burly man with just a word. "I don't know what that was, and I don't know what happened. But … Naiya, if you'll let me, I'd like to try again."

The confusion was plain on her face. She didn't know what had happened any more than I did.

"It's okay, Andy." I gently pulled myself loose from his grip. "I don't think it was her hurting me. It was like claws tearing into my hand. I think … I think it was the leopard fighting back."

"She's not letting you go without a fight," Sheppard said.

Lynn snapped her attention to him, and something passed between them like an inside joke before she turned back to me. "If you and I can try to breathe together, I might be able to make it work." She turned to Kristos as she held out both hands toward me. "It doesn't feel like anything I've done for General Buckheim, or anything I've done otherwise." She looked back at me. But I'm not ready to give up yet. Let me try once more?"

I pressed my lips into a line as I swallowed thickly and stood, reaching for her hands.

Again, she closed her eyes, and I did the same. Once again, she matched her breathing to mine. And once again, the deep chime thrummed, and the prayer bowl sang along my spine as the scent of fresh snow filled the air.

I was ready when the claws dug into my hands. Ready as they rent and tore at the flesh there. I opened my eyes to force my mind to see that it was not actually happening. No. The leopard had to go. It was the only way to keep everyone I loved safe. Only my vision was going red, and something jumped and twisted in my gut as Lynn trembled with the exertion.

She cried out this time as she pulled her hands from mine, but I still rubbed at the spots where I'd felt the claws digging in. I was a little light-headed and swayed on my feet.

Andy guided me back to sit on the couch.

"I … I don't think I can do it," Lynn said, her voice quieter than a gentle mouse.

My heart sank.

The note of the prayer bowl shifted lower, more solemn, as the deep chime thrummed along my muscles again.

FIFTY-THREE

Why did I let myself think it could be that easy? Just come to some stranger and get rid of the leopard. Never see Grump or Blondie or the nurse ever again. Never get taunted by Mr. Loudspeaker.

It could never have been that easy.

Ice formed along my spine, so thick and heavy it resonated with the thrumming of the chime and the humming of the prayer bowl, and my heart pounded in my ears.

Lynn looked at Kristos, rubbing her hands as she held them to her chest. "Maybe because she's a leopard?"

Kristos shook his head. "More likely because she's *consanguinea*."

"I'm not sure it's because of either," said Sheppard.

"Well, whatever it is," I said, "I need it gone. I can't chance hurting someone else I love and I sure as hell am not going back into some off-the-grid facility where they can run more tests and try to kill me some more. Three weeks is more than long enough."

My voice was rising in pitch as the frantic words built upon themselves. I stood from the couch as tears stung at my eyes enough to blur my vision, though they didn't spill over. Panic found a foothold in my chest and spread roots throughout my limbs, and there was nothing I could do to stop it. Just like there was nothing I could do to keep those I loved safe. I was powerless. Helpless. I might as well have been a newborn kitten.

The chime thrummed, and a single lonely note responded.

"Oh, bless your heart!" Kaylah hurried out of the kitchen.

I hadn't even realised she was still there, but she threw her arms around me. I stilled at her touch, uncomfortable with the thought of hugging her back. She was shorter than me, and my nose was in her hair. She smelled sweet and flowery.

"They held you captive for three whole *weeks*?" She turned her attention to Sheppard. "We gotta help her, Shep!"

He nodded as he stood, fishing his phone from his back pocket. "Agreed. I'll need to make a call." He glared at Val as he thumbed open his phone.

She winced and looked away from him. Why was he angry with her?

He looked at me. "There are a couple of loose ends to tie up before we can help you the way you need."

He started for the hallway, and I pushed away from Kaylah, who still had her arms around me. "Wait, who said I wanted your help with anything else? You couldn't help get rid of the leopard, you *definitely* can't help with the assholes from that facility! There's only like ten of you and way more of them." The power went out of my voice as a lump the size of Texas formed in my throat. "They're gonna come and take me again."

The lonely note sounded again, but it was Chastity's voice that stopped my movement. "Where else are you gonna go?"

A tear seared a path down my cheek, and I wiped at it with more fierceness than I felt as my heart pounded in my chest. I was pretty sure virtually everyone in the house could hear it now, including Val and Andy.

"I … dunno," I said lamely. "Maybe I'll … go back to the lake house and … see if I can get in touch with some of my parents' contacts overseas?"

God, I sounded like a little kid who'd just been told not to play with the only toys they had in front of them.

Andy stood and placed a hand on my shoulder. "The lake house just got overrun with their guys, remember? That's why we had to leave."

My pounding heart raced as hard as my mind. But there were no productive thoughts to be found, no words to the panic taking over me.

The low deep chime thrummed eerily, the note raising in pitch as it traveled along my muscles.

I bobbed my head as I brushed a stray hair back toward my ponytail. "Yeah. I know. But … maybe they'll stay gone since we left."

"Or maybe," Val said, "they set up surveillance so they can know the instant you return. Maybe they're waiting there to grab us all if we go back."

The air felt thinner, and the edges of my vision tunneled in.

She was right.

The thrumming chime cracked the ice around my spine, only to cover it with a new sheet of even colder frost. My tenuous hold on my panic slipped. There wasn't enough air, and my fingers started to tingle.

The people from that facility were going to find me no matter what I did or where I went. My stomach twisted as I remembered my father's watch, my mother's music box, and Abigail's face as she sat in the TSA interrogation room.

My parents.

Abigail.

They didn't deserve to suffer because of what I was—even if they didn't know, even if they didn't *believe*. As long as I was still able to turn into a leopard, no matter how much or little control I had over it, the people from that facility would find me. They'd lock me up again, only this time they'd throw away the key and make sure I'd never escape again.

My vision went red as adrenaline and fear flooded my system. I doubled over as my stomach tried to invert itself.

And then, my perspective on the world shifted, and I could breathe again.

I was lower to the ground, covered in fur, draped in scraps of clothing, surrounded on three sides by strangers, who all made various noises of surprise.

People came in from the backyard.

I backed into someone's legs.

Andy.

He dodged around me as I backed into a corner. A growl rumbled in my throat, tickling my nose with its quiet warning to stay away. I didn't want to hurt any of these people, but I also wasn't sure I could trust myself not to.

"Give her space!" Andy's voice held a bold authority as he threw an arm out between me and the rest of them.

Something warm pulsed in the air, and the pack turned to Sheppard, who tucked his phone into his back pocket, his eyes on me.

I pushed backward, my rump hitting the wall as I held his gaze. Something tickled along the length of my tail, a decidedly odd sensation. The end flicked into my peripheral vision, puffed up and fluffy like a cat's when it's scared.

Sheppard nodded once without looking away from me.

"Do it," he said, his voice steady and calm.

All of the people—the pack—backed up, a few stepping into the hallway and around the dining room table to allow space for the others.

"No one's going to hurt you here, Naiya," Sheppard said.

I couldn't be sure it was true, though I was relatively certain he wasn't lying.

Kristos hadn't backed off with the rest of them. He stepped around Andy, kneeling and leaning low next to me. His head was on level with my own as his honey-gold eyes met mine.

The low chime thrummed along my muscles as my lips curled from my teeth in an entirely involuntary expression. The growl in my throat intensified as I pushed deeper into the corner.

He held my gaze and made a shushing noise as the deep note sounded once more, thrumming through me more powerfully than it had a moment ago.

"We'll keep you safe, Naiya," he said, his voice flat, quiet, and almost devoid of emotion. But there was a confidence to his words that flowed through the note dancing along my muscles.

I wanted to believe him.

There was a simple, serene truth to Kristos' words that slowed the panic swirling in my head.

We'll keep you safe.

I held his gaze and slowly filled my lungs with the cacophony of scents of those around me. With that came a strange sort of peace. My heart rate slowed, and the rumbling growl from my throat quieted before stopping altogether.

He reached a hand toward me, and I squeezed my eyes shut, trying to focus on the deep, resonant calm of the low note singing between him and me. I hoped that focus was enough to keep myself from trying to hurt him. I wanted it to be enough. I knew he was trying to help. My father's face flashed in my vision and I shook my head once, opening my eyes and focusing on nothing to keep from watching a replay of the night my parents found me.

His voice rumbled again, his tone more firm than it had been, but still just as calm as his hand drew closer. "I swear to you, Kitten. We will keep you safe."

Sheppard nodded behind him. Lynn did as well.

I wanted to believe him—believe them.

His fingers brushed the fur of my ear, and his hand came to rest solidly against the top of my head. "For as long as I draw breath, *I* will keep you safe." The words were barely more than a whisper. The chime thrummed through me like a plucked bass string, answered by the prayer bowl tone.

And I believed him.

I met his eyes.

He nodded to me, his honey-hued gaze intense as he pulled his hand away.

Jonathan's voice was quiet from just behind Sheppard's left shoulder. "He kept Lynn safe from an enemy that nearly killed us all."

"Mostl—" Jamie's word was cut off by a swift jab of Jonathan's elbow.

"Dude," Ian said, gesturing toward me with an open palm. "Read the room."

Something I still couldn't name pulsed through the air again, and a hush fell over the room. Val and Andy looked at each other and then back to me. Valerie rubbed a finger along the scars under her shirt.

Sheppard turned back to me and nodded. "When you're ready, Naiya, come back to us, and we'll talk."

I huffed out a breath. Yeah, if I had any clue how to do that, I would.

"Whether we find a way to get rid of this," Kristos said, keeping his eyes on mine, "or *control* it, I'm not letting them hurt you anymore."

Andy looked at me. I glanced pointedly at Sheppard and then held his gaze.

Realization lit his face.

"She doesn't have enough control to choose when she comes back," Andy said.

Sheppard nodded. "I have an idea." He moved closer to me, looking me in the eyes as he knelt next to Kristos. "You're not exactly pack, so I'm not sure if this will work."

I shrank away from him, lifting the paw closest to him from the ground as I did. As he reached for me, I closed my eyes.

He put a hand on my shoulder, and the skin along my back twitched. He said something that sounded like what a priest in church might say—some sort of prayer, maybe?—but I couldn't put proper words to it. Power washed over me, but left me unchanged.

Somewhere off to my left, the front door opened and closed.

Andy pulled the throw blanket from the back of the couch and draped it around me, over Sheppard's hand on my shoulder.

"So you don't have to be naked in front of strangers," he said softly as I opened my eyes again.

A little of the tension in me unwound itself.

Kristos looked to Sheppard. "You're right. She's not pack, but *I* might be able to help."

Sheppard pulled his hand away, and Kristos pulled the blanket together at my chest and held it in one hand. He placed his other palm against my sternum and took a deep breath, concentration clouding his face as he closed his eyes.

I closed mine as well and matched his breathing.

The pressure of his palm increased for half a breath, and the rich deep wind chime tone rang in my head.

And then … well, then I was me again. Naked but for the throw blanket.

Kristos moved his hand away quickly, and I took over his hold on the blanket.

The front door opened and closed again.

Andy wrapped me in a hug as I stood. I buried my face into his shoulder to hide the hot embarrassment I was certain was coloring my face.

Someone moved close behind him. They smelled like ripe apples and a hint of outside.

"Fresh clothes," Val said, pressing a bundle against my side. She squeezed my fingers as I took it from her.

As I pulled my face from Andy's shoulder, he tucked an errant strand of hair behind my ear. He held my gaze, his expression questioning. I nodded once to let him know I was alright before I tore myself away from the starfield in his eyes.

I turned to Sheppard. "Um … is there a bathroom?"

Kaylah pushed her way toward me and gestured down the hall. "This way, hun."

FIFTY-FOUR

I followed Kaylah down the hall to a bathroom that would have fit right in at my parents' lake house with all the grey and chrome. I took stock of the clothes Val had picked for me: a sleeveless black crop top with black bra and olive green palazzo pants. It was a little more revealing than I would have picked, but it wasn't like they hadn't all just seen me scurry off with only a throw blanket for coverage. Besides, the clothes I'd come in certainly weren't an option anymore.

Which sucked because I happened to like the jeans I'd just shredded with that shift.

I'd felt more like myself when I was in that form again than I had even when we were in the brush beyond the facility. I wasn't really in control of what had happened, but I also didn't feel like I'd been puppeted around this time either.

Maybe being around these people helped me, even if they couldn't get the leopard to go away. Maybe, if I let them help me figure out how to get Mr. Loudspeaker off my ass, they could help me learn more about myself.

I ran a hand through my hair. Pfft. Yeah right, Naiya. And maybe they'll make unicorns real too, while they're at it.

I got dressed and came back to the living room,

where the pack was sprawled around on the couches and floor. Andy and Val had resumed sitting in the folding chairs.

Sheppard's voice came from somewhere off the hall, perhaps from the basement? I forced myself not to eavesdrop.

I couldn't get rid of the leopard. I couldn't protect my parents or Abigail. But … maybe I *could* protect Andy … sort of. He had to go home sometime, didn't he? And if he went home, if I never saw him again, he'd be free.

He'd be free, and I would still be trapped.

The deep chime thrummed through me, its tone almost mournful. I raked a hand through my hair as I took a shaky breath, trying to ignore the way my throat tried to close around the thought.

Andy would be *free*.

"Okay," I said. "If I can't go back to the lake house, then I can't go back to the lake house."

Andy stood and put an arm around me.

"But the only way you're truly safe from them is if we get you home." I huffed out a breath, pulling away to look at him. "I can't … they can't take you again if you're not here to take."

"Where're you from?" Jonathan asked, straightening to look at us.

Andy started to say something in his musical language, but he stopped and said, "Not anywhere you've heard of."

I looked at Jonathan and studied the rest of the pack, trying to figure out if any of them could even possibly be the sort who could believe where Andy was actually from. And if they didn't know about the rifts? Forget it.

"He's … not from around here," I said finally.

Val put a hand on my arm. "It's alright. I told you—they're safe."

I pressed my lips into a line. Kristos nodded at me, as did Lynn and Sheppard.

"It's still going to sound dumb," I said.

Val cocked her head to the side and speared me with a look.

"Fine!" I threw my hands up as I turned to the pack, keeping my voice low. "He's ... from another world."

Matt scrunched up the scarred side of his face. "So he's an alien?"

Andy took a breath to say something.

"They're immigrants, ass," said the tall, lanky one —Jamie—interrupting Andy.

"Not *those* aliens," the other, shorter lanky one—Ian—said. "The ones from another planet."

Andy took a step forward. "No—"

Lynn and Jonathan were laughing, and the prayer bowl sang a mirthful note.

Jamie furrowed his brow. "Aren't those guys supposed to be grey with big black eyes?"

I went still, waiting them all out.

Kristos raised an eyebrow at me, and when he spoke, his voice was a low rumble. "The rifts we've been seeing."

Lynn and Jonathan sobered, and the rest of the pack went quiet.

Andy nodded. "Yeah."

Sheppard came out of one of the three other doors in the hallway that *didn't* lead to the bathroom. He furrowed his brow as he looked around at everyone having gone quiet.

"Andy's from the other side of the rifts," I said lamely.

His mouth opened in a silent 'ah,' and he nodded once before pointing at me. "Well, Buckheim denies knowing anything about you, and he wasn't lying, which means …" He looked at Val. "You and I need to have a chat."

Buckheim? The guy Lynn helps sometimes? I furrowed my brow in confusion as I looked between the two.

Val glanced at me and put up her hands as she shook her head. "Mmm, no no. This isn't my rodeo."

Sheppard's demeanor changed and something charged through the air. "It wasn't a question, *Valerie*." He gestured toward the basement. "This way."

Val crossed her arms over her stomach, a pinky finger tracing the topmost of the lines as she followed him.

The quiet lasted only half a breath after the door to the basement shut behind them.

Chastity's hazel eyes met mine. "How long have you been a leopard—?"

"A *were*leopard," Ian corrected.

"I'm not sure," I said.

"Probably your whole life," Andy said. "Unless you were attacked by a leopard at some point?"

"What?" My eyes were wide. "No!"

"That's apparently how most people get to be werewolves," Lynn said. "Unless you're born to it."

"Were you born a wereleopard, then?" Jamie asked.

"I don't know," I said. "I don't remember my birth parents."

"Oh, you poor thing!" Kaylah pressed a hand to her heart as she placed her other hand on the knee of the dark-haired man next to her—Daniel.

"It's fine," I said, shrugging as I slumped into a chair. "The Davenports, my adoptive parents, are good people."

"Your shift happens so much faster than ours," Lynn said, awe in her voice. "Does it hurt?"

I shook my head. "No. It just twists my stomach."

"Who held you captive?" Kristos asked.

"I don't know. But they threatened violence to my parents and had TSA detain my house manager—who used to be my nanny—for questioning to get me to cooperate."

"I'm certain they were capable of worse," Andy said.

I pressed my lips into a line and nodded. And then an utterly random thought hit me. "Wait, Kristos." I met his gaze. "Are you Kristos of Athens Couture?"

His expression lit up, and the tinkling of the tiny wind chimes danced across my skin again. "You know my work."

"My mother—well, my adopted mother …" It seemed only right to clarify since we'd recently been talking about bloodlines, and I certainly didn't know hers. "She has a pair of your earrings—the amethyst ear climbers. She wears them to all of my father's events."

He smiled then, though his face didn't look like it was well-versed in such an expression. "I'm glad to hear they are bringing joy."

"They are," I said. "She loves them."

"Are you strong and fast like us?" Matt asked, eyeing me with his one good eye. It was kind of uncomfortable to look at him. His scars looked like they still hurt.

"I think so," I said. "Maybe not as strong, but I don't know for sure. They never let me see any of the measures they took."

"Except the one," Andy said. "You can lift over four *bis*—"

"Over four hundred pounds," I said, interrupting him to avoid a repeat of the *biskyt* conversation he and Val and I had had at the facility. "There is that."

"And you ran a treadmill for hours," he pointed out.

I shot him a finger gun as I clicked my tongue. "That too."

"How do your tattoos do that?" Lynn asked, leaning forward as she gestured to Andy's arm.

Andy shrugged. "I'm not sure. It's just what they've always done back home, though they went solid black for a time here."

The man sitting next to Kaylah—Daniel—sat forward, leaning his elbows on his knees. "Have you ever seen a vampire?"

I nodded. "Yeah."

"Did you kill it?" Matt asked.

"I did. Both of them."

He folded his arms and sat back.

"What do you know about the people who were holding you captive?" Kristos asked.

I shook my head. "Not much. They were secretive, organized, methodical. They seem to know what I should be capable of better than I do—certainly better than I did."

"Didn't you know they were lying to you?" Jamie asked, his eyes wide.

I went still as the deep chime thrummed an eerie note, and ice trailed along my spine.

Andy put a hand on my shoulder. "I don't think they ever actually lied. They were careful with how they worded things, but I cannot recall them ever telling an outright lie."

"You don't smell like a werewolf," Lynn said, studying Andy. "But you don't quite smell human either. What are you?"

Not quite human? What, just because he's not from here?

He nodded toward her. "A … uh … well, a scholar of sorts, a meddler in the fabric that holds worlds together."

"You're familiar with the rifts," Kristos said.

He rubbed at the back of his neck with his tattooed hand. "Yes and no. I've seen them before. I'm passingly familiar with the sort of magic that creates them, though I haven't yet mastered it myself."

"What do you know about them?" Matt asked.

Andy shook his head. "Not as much as I would like, unfortunately. I didn't know they were popping up at all. Where I come from, word doesn't seem to travel as fast as it does here. I don't know how long it's been happening, but it may be related to a war that happened in my world. A powerful evil force was looking to tear apart the boundaries that held realities separate from one another."

"Whoa," said Ian.

Lynn was practically gawking at Andy.

Sheppard came back with his hand on Val's shoulder. "The General is on his way for a pickup."

"A pickup?" I furrowed my brow. "Val? What's going on? Who is the General?"

Val wouldn't meet my eyes. She just held her arms folded tightly across her belly with her shoulders slumped.

"General Buckheim's good people," Sheppard said. "But he has his rules, and Valerie should know better than to cross them."

Val's eyes flicked up to mine. "Things weren't supposed to go like this." Her voice was quiet and low.

A rivulet of ice traced down my spine, and I stilled yet again, my eyes narrowing at her. "Like what?"

She took her arms away from her stomach and reached for my hand. "I didn't know they would take you and lock you up like that."

Her fingers interlocked with mine as pieces fell into place.

She hadn't told me she was a former werewolf

until I learned that werewolves were more than just folklore.

They're not who you think they are.

She'd known the people from Saint Dymphna's were wrong from the start.

I'm on my own here.

She was freaking out at the lake house.

She hadn't wanted to tell me the truth about why she was even at Saint Dymphna's in the first place.

And like a slap in the face with a block of ice, it hit me.

Val had never been my friend.

I tore my hand from hers as the chime sounded a furious note, but my voice was deadly quiet. "You were a plant."

FIFTY-FIVE

Val looked away from me and sank onto a folding chair next to Sheppard, her arms crossing tightly over her stomach. It all but confirmed it.

Again, the heavy wind chime thrummed an angry note along my muscles. It was so loud that I couldn't even hear the sparkling tinkle of the smaller chimes, nor the humming almost-whine of the prayer bowl tone.

Andy drew close to me, his face uncomprehending. "A plant?"

I looked over at him with a huff, and he leaned away from me a fraction at the expression on my face. I closed my eyes and forced calm into my voice.

"A spy," I said, spitting the words as I opened my eyes to glare at Val. And then the deadly quiet returned. "They threatened my family, invaded our privacy, and tried to kill me, Valerie. Multiple times. Were those threats even real?"

"I don't know," she whispered, too quickly for my liking.

"Were you ever in any real danger?"

"I don't know," she mumbled.

"Were you working with them from the start? Back at Saint Dymphna's?"

"No!" she said.

But something in it was a lie.

"You lie!"

"No! Please, Naiya, I didn't know!" Tears poured down her cheeks. "I was just supposed to get information and get you here. To them. To *her*." She thrust her hand, palm up, toward Lynn. "She's a *purgatum*, Naiya! She's supposed to be able to cure you of the leopard."

"Except she clearly can't!"

"I didn't know that. You have to believe me!"

"No wonder you wanted to know if I instinctively knew when people were lying! Did they even *do* anything to you other than use you as bait, Valerie? Is that even your name?"

An arm wrapped around my waist—Andy's—alerting me to how I'd closed the distance between Val and myself. She'd shrunk back in her chair like a child being scolded.

Something dribbled down my cheek, and I wiped away the wetness with the heel of my hand. "Was *any* of it true?"

Sheppard put a placating hand out toward me. "She's not lying, Naiya. She didn't know." But his voice was hard with reproach as he looked back at Val.

The rumble of a deep chime, steady and true, thrummed along my muscles as Kristos came into my field of view. "And Lynn certainly didn't know she couldn't help you the way the both of you hoped she could."

Sheppard gestured to the empty seats around the dining table. "Let's all have a seat and talk this out."

I looked over my shoulder at Andy, then pointedly down at the arm around my waist and back up at him. "There's nothing to talk about."

Andy nodded once as he released me, and I stormed toward the front door of the house.

I needed to be outside. Trees. Fresh air. Anything but to breathe the same air as *her*. The traitorous bitch. The charlatan parading as my friend. The one making a fool of me.

No one got in my way as I yanked the door open and—

"They wanted me to tell you your parents were dead," came Val's small voice.

I stilled, my hand on the handle of the now wide-open door. I would not turn to face her. I would not give her the satisfaction of witnessing the pain of her betrayal.

"But they weren't ... and I refused." Her voice cracked. "I wouldn't lie to you. I knew I couldn't, but I didn't want to anyway. And I haven't. The kiss. The sex. How I feel about *you*. That's all real. It's *true*. When Lynn turned me human again, the military ... Buckheim ... he gave me a new identity—a new life. What I told you about my childhood is true. My parents never gave a shit about me." Her voice cracked again. "But you did. Even when you didn't have to. Even when it would have been better for you not to. I never wanted to hurt you, Naiya."

I didn't give her the satisfaction of a reply. She wasn't lying, I was sure of that. But she hadn't told me the truth from the start. And a lie of omission is still a lie. I shook hair out of my face and stepped into the afternoon breeze, resisting the urge to slam the door behind me.

Clouds blanketed the sky like rain was going to come, but the scent of the change in the wind hadn't happened yet, so it was likely to be some time yet before rain fell from these clouds.

Something hot and wet rolled down my cheek, and I rubbed it away angrily as I stomped toward my Mini Cooper.

"Naiya!" Andy came outside. "Wait!"

I stopped walking.

"Don't go," he said. "Please."

I turned and met his impossibly dark eyes as he walked toward me. "There's nowhere *to* go, Andy. But … I can't be in there anymore. Not with her betrayal."

He put his hands up in a placating gesture, slowing his steps as he reached me. "No. No, of course not. I only mean … don't leave me in there with them?" His voice dropped to low conspiratorial tones. "Are they really all werewolves?"

I shook my head. "I don't know."

He pulled me into a tight hug, his fingers in my hair, their tips rubbing at the scalp at the base of my neck. It felt truly very, *very* nice.

"They are," Kristos said, startling me into looking up at him as he leaned against a pillar outside the front door, his arms crossed.

Andy released me and turned to step between Kristos and myself. I put a hand on his shoulder and took a step to stand next to him.

I jutted my chin at Kristos. "Are you?"

The corner of his mouth quirked upward. "Bear, actually."

Andy's shoulders relaxed as I narrowed my eyes at Kristos. "Bear?"

He nodded and looked past me, eyeing the houses in the neighborhood meaningfully. "I'd show you, but the neighbors might be watching."

"Okay." I sighed. "Uh … well, do you happen to know any way to track the rifts?"

Andy scratched at the back of his head with a black-tattooed hand.

"Waitaminute." I cocked my head to the side and grabbed Andy's geometry-covered arm.

"What are you doing?" Andy said, letting me have his arm.

Chad poked out from under his collar as I traced a finger along the lines of his tattoos, which had stopped pulsing with iridescence.

"They were shiny before," I said.

"My tattoos?"

I nodded. "But they're black again now."

Andy gently pulled his arm from my grip as he flexed his fingers and flourished his hand. "Aaaand my rapier's stuck again. By the ley lines, next time, I'm just leaving it out."

"With any luck," I said, "next time, you can get home."

Andy sobered and met my eyes as his voice went quiet, intimate. "I like it here."

I pressed my lips into a line, and though I didn't roll my eyes, my head followed the motion. "Andy …" He closed his eyes as I put a hand to his cheek. "Look, you don't belong here. Everything that is *you* doesn't work here."

He opened his eyes, and I fell into their starfield once again.

"And if you stay," I said. "They will never stop chasing you."

He pressed his forehead against mine. "But they're not going to stop chasing you either, Naiya."

I bit my lip. He wasn't wrong, but I didn't have an answer to that bit readily at hand.

"That's going to have to be a problem for tomorrow-Naiya. Today-Naiya needs to get you back to where I know you'll be safe from them."

Even if it means I never see you again.

Though I really hoped that wasn't going to be the case.

I swallowed around the lump in my throat.

"Sheppard might be able to reach out to some of the other pack alphas he knows," Kristos offered. "See if they have any way to help."

My jaw dropped. "There are *even more* werewolves?"

Kristos scoffed. "More? There are *loads* of werewolves all over the world, Kitten." He pushed off the pillar he was leaning against and gestured toward the door. "Let's head back inside before the General gets here—unless you're keen to answer even more questions?"

I shook my head and took a step toward the house. "I'd rather not."

Andy grabbed my hand, and when I turned to him, he kissed me. I melted against him as I deepened the kiss, listening to his heart pounding in his chest.

"I don't want to have to say goodbye to you," he whispered against my lips. "Not yet."

I bit my lip and swallowed around the lump in my throat. "Let's go inside."

He nodded once and kissed my forehead.

We followed Kristos back into the house to find the pack was still largely sprawled around the living room. Except Val sat slumped in one of the folding chairs in the dining room, and Sheppard was still standing next to her. She'd always seemed kind of small to me, but she looked even tinier as she shrank in the chair at the sight of me.

The chime sounded, and a little pang of sympathy for her went through me, but it was then completely overshadowed by fury at her betrayal. I'd trusted her, told her everything about myself, and let her get close to me. I wasn't one who usually kept people at arm's length, but she made me want to start.

"Naiya," Val said.

That bitch had some goddamn nerve to try to talk to me now. I glared at her.

She pushed a contacts case across the dining room table in my direction.

"What the hell is that?" I demanded, picking up the white and blue plastic.

She met my eyes. Hers were blue. I crushed the contacts case as my fist closed tightly around it. Another fucking lie. The chime hit a furious note answered by a somewhat more calming one from the prayer bowl.

"They were my mask," she said, swallowing thickly, "the only one I had. It was the only way I could even make it okay for myself. I am sorry. I wish I had met you under different circumstances."

I set my jaw and turned away from her. Andy put an arm around me and kissed my temple.

"Do you have a way to get the word out to find if there's any rhyme or reason to these rifts?" Kristos asked Sheppard.

Sheppard nodded. "I can send an email to the alphas I'm friendly with, see if they know anything. Why?"

"I need to get Andy back home," I said, squeezing his hand. "The people chasing me are also chasing him."

"They aren't likely to come here," Val said. "Not with Buckheim and Sheppard here. Not if they're smart."

I had *so* many distasteful words for her. I reminded myself that wishing bad things on others only set karma up to bite you in the ass. Even if they did deserve it.

Andy pressed his lips into a line.

The 'ah' expression crossed Sheppard's face again as he pulled the phone out of his pocket and started tapping out a message with his thumbs. "I'll email as many as I can to ask, of course, but I get a lot of bouncebacks these days. I'm not sure who, if anyone, will reply."

"With the surge of conspiracy theories online,"

Ian said, "and the fact that we're showing up on news networks, they're probably locking down their accounts."

"Smart of them, really," Chastity asserted.

Matt snorted. "Yeah, but it likely feeds right into the vampires' plan. If we're isolated from one another, we can't communicate their patterns and movements as well."

A car pulled up to the front curb, one of those nondescript black SUVs.

"Buckheim," Lynn said.

FIFTY-SIX

I don't know what I expected of General Buckheim, but a stocky man who was shorter than me by a couple of inches wasn't really it. He had an imposing presence though, and looked weathered, with his tanned leather skin and salt and pepper hair. His brown eyes were kind, but his expression and demeanor were all no-nonsense. Sheppard greeted him at the door with an old deference, Val at his side. The rest of the pack stayed where they were as Buckheim put an arm around her shoulders and ushered her out onto the porch.

"I'm looking forward to your debriefing, Ms. Jenkins," he said.

She slumped, shrinking into herself a little more at his words.

The General turned back to look at Sheppard, but nodded toward me. "And yours."

"Absolutely, sir." Sheppard nodded, leaning against the doorframe. "I look forward to *yours* as well."

The General turned his attention to Lynn. "Another set of recruits coming through this month. I'll call if you're needed."

"I'd expect nothing less, General," she replied, her

tone friendly and warm as she waved a hand. "Thank you."

He turned toward the nondescript black SUV, Val following after him. She looked over her shoulder once at me, but Sheppard was already closing the door.

And when the latch clicked on their exit, I couldn't help but feel it was symbolic. Lord knows I never wanted to talk to her again. The 'why?' didn't even matter anymore.

A more relaxed air washed around the pack as the car outside pulled away.

"Welp," Kaylah said, patting Daniel's knee as she stood. "Time t' git dinner goin'." She walked through the kitchen on her way out the back door. Chastity got up and went to the kitchen as well.

"So, Naiya," Sheppard said, turning his golden eyes to me. They were just like Grump's, and Baldy's. I stilled.

No. Theirs were like his. I had to frame it that way. Werewolves weren't evil. Whatever Val had done, what she had said about them rang true.

Sheppard took a sip from the glass of water he had at the table. "How much do you know about your abilities?"

I sat heavily in one of the folding chairs. "Not nearly as much as I'd like." And I didn't like where this line of questioning was likely to lead. It was frustrating to know so little about myself.

"I ask because getting your friend to a rift so he can go back where he belongs may involve a fight," he said. "So, I'd like to know if you have experience with that."

The scent of grill smoke wafted into the house as Kaylah came back into the kitchen to prep food. She was cutting potatoes, by the smell, though the scent of ground beef and garlic and barbeque sauce came from the kitchen as well.

"She can fight once she's a leopard," Andy said, "but she's better at sneaking."

"And she's capable of answering for herself," I said.

Andy put his hands up in surrender. "Okay. I just thought you might end up lying to this guy by accident. Taking out a couple of rift cats is nothing to sneeze at."

"Rift cats?" Kristos said, the question plain on his weathered face.

I nodded. "They're nasty things. Too many teeth and a weird mix of … iridescent black scales and impossibly black fur that almost drinks in the light. They aren't always where you think they are, like they're too fast to be, and they move wrong. It's hard to keep your eyes on them, but if you stop and use more than just your eyes, you can track them with sound and smell and get 'em."

Wow. The fight itself was a blur, but I definitely recalled more of their appearance in retrospect than I knew when I was fighting them.

"They move on an adjacent plane of existence," Andy said, placing a hand on my shoulder. "They phase in and out between this reality and the one they came from. They feed off the rift energy and whatever prey they can take down when a rift opens."

Lynn had turned from where she was sitting on the couch to look at Andy, her mouth agape. "It's like you're straight out of a fantasy novel."

Andy furrowed his brow and turned to look at her. "What?"

"Next, you'll tell me you've walked alongside dragons and elves and fairies," she said.

"I have," he said. "Well, elves at least. I try to stay clear of the dragons. They can be fickle and quick to anger. Fairies too, though they're more likely to kill you with the tricks they play."

She leaned back against Jonathan, whining, "You're not even making that up."

Another wave of grill smoke wafted in the house as Kaylah went out back again.

Andy cocked his head to the side. "Why would I make that up?"

I placed a hand against his thigh, and he looked down at me. "Like I said back at the facility. Dragons, fairies, elves. None of those exist here."

He nodded as he sank into the chair next to me. "This world is so …"

"Mundane?" I finished for him.

He turned to me. "You know, I thought that at first, but no. It's the wrong word. The patterns are different here, harder to see, but there's still a magic to this place. The way you shift is definitely magic. The way the wolves that attacked you shifted is a different kind of magic, but it's still magic. *Their* temperament, once they changed, is much more what I expected of lycanthropes—much more like what I've seen."

"No one calls them 'lycanthropes' here," Lynn said. "Not outside of books and movies."

"They used to," Chastity called from the kitchen, where she was cutting up apples and drizzling them with honey and cinnamon. "But once the word hit a level of familiarity among the general populace, it seemed to fall out of use. As the geeky types have gotten more vocal in recent years, there's been a bit of a resurgence. You can watch the trend on the search engines online. It's really interesting to see."

I bet it is.

Kaylah came back inside, bringing more of the grill smoke scent in with her.

Sheppard met my eyes again. "Have you ever been in control of your change?"

"No." I shook my head. "It scares me. It usually happens in my sleep, and it hasn't ever worked when I've tried to make it happen."

Change form, and the air comes back.

The chime thrummed deeply, and I squeezed my eyes shut, forcing a deep breath into my lungs as my heart rate spiked at the memory.

Something lightly clunked onto the table. I opened my eyes. I had a glass of water in front of me, and Kaylah delivered another to Andy as I took a sip.

"So, it don't hurt, breakin' n' rearrangin' 'at fast?" She made a vague gesture with her hands, rolling them over each other.

"No," I replied. "I've only ever done it a handful of times when I was awake. It … I think it might be triggered by fear."

Matt stood from the couch and cracked his knuckles. "Cool. I got this."

I stilled, my vision focusing on his fists as I assessed what he could do to me. He was bigger than me and likely a skilled fighter—or at least an experienced one, judging by the nasty scars on his face.

The chimes clanged through me, like they'd been haphazardly struck.

"Matthew." Sheppard's voice held a warning.

But the back of Kristos' hand hit Matt's chest, stopping his progress toward me. When Matt turned his attention to him, Kristos shook his head just once.

He folded his arms across his chest and sighed as he sank back onto the couch next to Daniel. "Fine. Your way then."

Kaylah breezed back into the kitchen, grabbing trays of things on her way out back. When she opened the door, the scent of potatoes roasting on the grill wafted in. It was quiet for a moment before she came back in.

"When you shift," Lynn said, "you said it itches? Or tickles? And it doesn't hurt?"

"Yeah." I nodded. "Yours does?"

She bobbed her head. "Yes, it's like tearing and breaking apart only to come back together again, but it's over quick. Not as quick as yours, but quick."

"Mine's more like breathing … or … sneezing is probably more accurate," I said. "One moment, I'm on two legs, and the next? Well … you saw."

Sheppard leaned forward in his chair. "Always snarling like that?"

I nodded again and swallowed thickly as the chimes tinkled faintly along my skin, the thrumming so low and deep that I was barely even aware of their eerie note.

"It's terrifying," I said, forcing my tone to be even. "I hardly ever feel like myself. It's like I'm watching while the leopard just kind of does things. But I can calm down. I've laid curled in a big black ball for hours, praying for sleep to take me. I'm usually asleep by the time I come back to myself."

Something resolved on Sheppard's face as he took a deep breath. "Do your parents know, Naiya?"

I pressed my lips into a line. "They didn't believe me even when they saw me, and had me committed. Abigail thought I got it from some wild story I'd read."

Kaylah clucked her tongue and sat down next to me, placing her warm hand on top of mine. "Oh, bless your heart!"

It was odd to be comforted by someone I'd only just met. Odd that they would want to. Odd that it would feel … actually kind of okay.

The chime along my muscles changed tone, brightening some.

Mmm. But it was still too odd for my comfort. I

gently pulled my hand out from under hers and placed it in my lap.

Kristos studied me with serious eyes. "Abigail?"

Kaylah patted my shoulder once as she stood up to head back to the kitchen. "S'alright, hun. Nuthin' 'ere's gonna hurtcha."

I looked at Kristos. "Our house manager … though she was my nanny until I turned eighteen."

Jamie sat up straighter to look at me over the couches. "How old are you, Naiya?"

Kaylah balled up her towel and threw it at him, but towels aren't exactly the best projectiles on the planet, so it fluttered uselessly to the floor well short of him. "Ya don' ask a lady her age, ya silly goose. S not p'lite!"

I smiled over my shoulder at her and looked back at Jamie. "It's alright. I'm twenty."

Kaylah headed outside again.

Chastity brought a basket of rolls and another full of burger buns to the table. "Do you still live with your parents? Or where are they?"

"I do still live with my parents," I said. "We live in Dallas. But my parents are out of the country right now and don't know everything that's happened since they dropped me in rehab."

A warmth shimmered in the air, and the pack went still. The thrumming chime turned peaceful, along with the singing prayer bowl tone. The air seemed less oppressive than it had a moment ago, and I hadn't even noticed that my heart was racing at all of the questions.

Sheppard eyed each of the pack in turn before meeting my gaze. "I'd like for you to come and stay with us, Naiya. At least for now. I think we can help you gain at least some control over your changes."

"And your best bet for protection is right there,"

said Jonathan, pointing to Kristos, who sat a little straighter in his chair next to Sheppard.

I blinked. "What?"

"He's sworn to protect *consanguinea*," Lynn explained. "That's you." She pointed at me. "And me." She pointed at herself.

Protect *consanguinea*. Protect … me.

The chime thrummed along my muscles, harmonizing with the prayer bowl tone.

Kristos' honey-gold gaze met mine. "It's true."

He wasn't lying. I was sure of that. I swallowed thickly and reached for Andy's knee under the table. He placed his hand atop mine and squeezed.

Still, protector or not, I didn't know Kristos. This wind chime tone thrumming along my muscles definitely connected me to him, but how the hell could that help against Mr. Loudspeaker's assholes? Even if he *was* a bear … a werebear? Whatever. He may be sworn to protect *consanguinea*, but protecting two of us would mean splitting his attention, likely making him less effective than he'd normally be, even if only one of us was in any actual danger. And if Sheppard and them couldn't get Mr. Loudspeaker off my ass—off my *family's* ass—then it didn't matter what they thought they could teach me.

Kristos looked at Sheppard. "Except you're leaving Colorado Springs soon."

"We are," Sheppard said. "But we're all staying together, because that's what pack does. And *all* of us can help."

Andy leaned closer to me, still holding my hand. "It might be nice for you to be around people who know about this stuff, Ny."

I blinked at the nickname, and the corner of his mouth pulled up.

I thunked my forehead against his shoulder. Maybe he was right. If they wanted to help me learn to control this … well, why shouldn't I let them while they're trying to help me get clear of the facility's guys? And hadn't Kaylah said that help is what they do?

It didn't change that I wanted to keep Andy safe by sending him home. But maybe the pack and I could figure out a way to get the people from that facility off my case, and then I could find one of the rifts and maybe find him?

I took a deep breath, inhaling the dark chocolate and honey scent of him. Who was I kidding? If I sent Andy through a rift, I'd never see him again.

FIFTY-SEVEN

Kaylah came in a few moments later with grilled burger patties and ribs on a platter. The pack all wandered off to wash their hands before gathering at the table, so I did the same, showing Andy where the bathroom was that I'd used earlier.

I flicked off the lights as I left the bathroom, even though Andy was still in there.

"Hey!" Andy caught my arm and pulled me to him, and I giggled at the game. "You may be able to see in the dark …" He kissed me, and I reveled in his smile against my mouth.

"But there's not enough light in here for you?" I arched my eyebrow at him.

He crowded me against the wall, and warmth gathered between my legs as his mouth crashed against mine again.

"I don't need light to find you, Lady Kateri," he whispered against my mouth.

I reached for the back of his head and pulled him to me again. I definitely ached for his touch on my skin and arched my back toward him to press my body against his—but now was not the time.

A breathless moment or two later, we got back to the table, where everyone had already started eating.

"Dig in, y'all," Kaylah said, gesturing to the two seats at the end of the table.

The third had been folded up and was leaning against the wall out of the way.

Should've just thrown the whole chair away, really.

Aside from the burgers and ribs and rolls, there were grilled cut potatoes, baked apples, corn on the cob, and asparagus spears with garlic and butter.

I grabbed a few of the remaining ribs along with some baked apples and asparagus. Compared to the others at the table, mine and Andy's portions looked like children's plates, and we didn't eat nearly as quickly as they did.

But the ribs were delicious. Everything was, really. And by the time the rest of them were done eating, I was still picking at the remnants of my baked apples.

"You don't eat like a werewolf," Kristos said, eyeing my mostly empty plate.

I arched an eyebrow at him. "People keep saying that."

"It takes a lot of calories to fuel shifting back and forth," Lynn said, giving Jonathan a half-smile before looking back at me.

"And a starving wolf is an angry wolf," Sheppard said.

"Except I'm not a wolf," I said. "And I've never really eaten a lot, not any more than any normal person."

"I think," Andy said, "there's something about you being a wereleopard that works differently than the werewolves of your world."

Sheppard nodded. "That would make about as much sense as anything else."

Kristos looked at Lynn. "Are you and Jonathan staying here tonight?"

She looked to Jonathan, who shrugged at her.

"Might be a good idea to," he said.

Sheppard looked at me. "They'll probably take one of the upstairs bedrooms, while Kaylah and Daniel will likely take the other. Kristos usually sleeps on the sectional in the loft, while Matt and Chastity take one of the two other bedrooms on this level. Jamie and Ian usually have some contest or another going for the other bedroom down here, but there are a couple of couches in the basement for you."

Jamie looked at Ian. "Let the newcomers have the bed?"

The thought of a night in a soft bed instead of on a firm bunk probably lit my face with more hope than I intended. And while I definitely enjoyed my nap in the bed at the lake house, that had only been a few hours before we'd had to go.

Ian looked at me and then Andy before looking back at Jamie. "Sure."

Chastity and Kaylah stood to start clearing the table.

"The boys are all gonna go play some woofball before bed," Lynn said, hooking a thumb toward the backyard. "It's a fun game. Wanna play?"

"Mmm. Maybe I'll just watch," I said, scooping up the last bit of my baked apples before handing my plate to Chastity.

As it turned out, woofball was actually pretty entertaining, and the pack was endearing. Kaylah and Chastity came to join in as soon as they were done cleaning up in the kitchen. It was interesting to see how the game was played, even after the rules were explained to me. Getting rid of the ball and keeping it off the ground weren't the real challenge. The *real* challenge was not letting the bear get the ball. Because when he did, they had to work together to get him down.

"They build teamwork that way," Andy said.

I nodded, watching as they took Kristos to the ground.

The ball landed near my toe, and Andy nudged me with his elbow.

"Show 'em how it's done," he whispered to me with a wink.

"What?" My eyes were wide. "No!"

"Throw the ball or run, Kitten," Kristos said.

"Do it." Andy picked up the ball and held it out to me. "I'm not strong like they are, like you are; they'd crush me."

I took the ball with a huff. "Fine."

If I could do the obstacle course, I could do this, right?

I danced around in a half-circle, trying to figure out where to throw the dang ball as the pack edged closer. So, I taunted them, teased them closer before finally throwing it to the far corner of the yard where there was no one to catch it.

Daniel had been biding his time at the back of the pack, so he quickly redirected and caught it before it hit the ground.

As the game progressed from there, I didn't do any tackling until Jonathan ran into me on his way to tackling Kaylah. When I went down into the dogpile —literally—I hopped back up almost as soon as I'd landed, though Jonathan was laughing like a hyena.

Andy giggled too, and I stuck out my tongue at him.

"Heads up," he said.

And, once again, I had the ball.

Shit.

Well … fine then. Catch me if you can, suckers.

And catch me they could *not*, as it turned out.

They had to regroup and box me in to stop me from dodging away, and though they managed to take me down, they only managed it at the very last second when I'd finally launched the ball to Chastity.

"New rule," Matt called. "Don't let the cat have the ball, either!"

"You're just mad you couldn't catch her," Jonathan said.

"Yeah, I'm not playing by that rule," Lynn said, catching the ball and tossing it to me.

I didn't let them get a pincer move set up on me this time. Instead, I dodged toward them as they went to tackle me. Over Jamie, under Sheppard, around Matt, under Kaylah and Jonathan, over Daniel.

And then I hit a wall.

Well, a wall that was shorter than me by a couple of inches but distinctly more solid.

Kristos.

Before I could conceptualize what was happening, he'd swept my legs out from under me, which popped the ball into the air so he could catch it.

"I'd suggest moving if you don't wanna be under the dogpile, Kitten," he said, turning his back to me as the pack rushed him.

I scrambled to do as he said, pushing into a handstand and kicking over like I'd done a handspring. More tumbling that I hadn't done since middle school. It felt good. It felt really good.

The pack slammed into Kristos hard enough that I jumped back and squeaked my alarm. But he didn't go down right away. He looked over his shoulder and winked at me, lifting the ball over his head as the pack worked at his legs.

He was shorter than me. If I jumped for it, I could get the ball away from him.

Did I even *want* the ball?

Screw it.

I jumped at his lifted hand, nabbing the ball from

his thick fingers. I rolled when I hit the ground, and a sharp whistle blew from behind me.

The pack paused.

"Aren't you only supposed to take me down if I have the ball?" Kristos asked, looking pointedly at me.

I tossed the football from one hand to the other as the pack turned their attention to me, except I bobbled the catch and had to scramble for it.

Only Matt snatched it from my hands before I could get a grip on it. Up close, his scar looked even more painful than I'd initially thought. But his milky eye moved like he could still see *something* out of it.

"C'mon, kitty kitty," he said, his tone taunting. "Let's play."

I didn't think I was strong enough to take his legs out from under him, but as Lynn crept around behind him, I got an idea. I launched myself at his arm, grabbing his wrist as I yanked him hard backward. He lost his footing, thanks to Lynn, and then flipped over himself like something out of a martial arts movie, landing flat on his back.

Andy and Jonathan both burst into laughter as he hit the ground.

I gingerly took the ball from his other arm, where he'd tucked it as soon as I'd moved. He let me have it.

"You alright?" I asked him, arching an eyebrow as I looked down at his face.

He was grinning from ear to ear—a strange sight amongst the scars. "That was magnificent!" He started laughing too.

"Woofball," I said with a smile. "Because you're all dogs. Clever."

"'Cept fer the bear," Kaylah said, hooking her thumb at Kristos.

"Well, if kitty cat here joins us too," Jonathan said, "then we might have to give it a new name."

Kitten. Kitty. Kitty cat.

I kinda liked the nicknames. But the ones from Andy were better.

Lady Kateri. Ny.

I looked over at him. He'd caught the infectious laughter of the pack, and it was joyous music that harmonized beautifully with the deep bass chime.

Wait. If I joined them?

Lynn hooked an arm around my shoulder, thunking the side of her head into mine. "Nice!" Her voice dropped into conspiratorial tones. "Way better than my first time with these guys."

I smiled at her. "Thanks."

She released me as Andy came over to give me a hug.

"That was really interesting to watch," he said. "I'm glad I didn't try to play."

"We could go easy on you," Jamie said, tapping a hand on Andy's bicep.

"No, we couldn't," Ian said. "We'd try, but then we'd lose focus and end up turning him wolf just to keep him from dying."

"Ooh, good point," Jamie agreed.

"Pretty sure you'd end up with a pissed off leopard if you tried it," Daniel said, jerking his head toward me.

"Pretty sure I don't want to know who wins the fight when wolf meets leopard," Ian said.

"It'd be bear," Kristos said, stepping between me and them.

Protector.

"*Touché*," Jamie said.

Sheppard turned to me. "If you wanna shower between now and when you go to bed, you'll wanna use the one at the end of the hall downstairs."

Which made me realize there was a duffle bag full of clothes in the car.

"Thanks," I said.

"With any luck," he said, putting a hand on my shoulder, "someone will get back to me by the morning, and we can get your friend back where he came from."

I nodded as Sheppard squeezed my shoulder once and let go.

I wasn't really the type to have a big circle of friends, but if I did, these guys probably wouldn't be a poor choice.

Not that I was sure I even wanted to be friends with them. I mean, I didn't even really know any of them. Hell, I barely had their names down. Still, if I was going to lose Andy—and I was certain that was going to happen—it might be good to have someone around that actually knows about all the things that go bump in the night.

FIFTY-EIGHT

Sheppard showed me and Andy to the room we'd be in for the night. The walls were a stark white, and there was a simple king-sized bed with a black-tufted head and footboard made up with teal linens and a fluffy black comforter under a wide short rectangle of a window that spanned the whole wall. There was only one side table, and it was ornately carved and finished with gold leaf. I placed my backpack on the floor next to it. There was a black leather armchair in the corner of the room, with a creamy knit throw folded neatly over its back.

I grabbed the duffle bag from the back of my Mini and took Sheppard up on his offer for a shower. I tried not to make it an inordinately long one, but it did feel really nice to just be there, knowing no one was standing outside the shower stall waiting for me to get done so they could poke and prod at me some more. Chastity had a curl-care leave-in conditioner that was better than nothing for brushing my hair when I finally got out of the water, and the deodorant I'd picked up at our last rest stop ensured I wouldn't end up smelling like the wild animal I sometimes was.

I tried not to curl my lip at the thought of that, even if it *had* felt good to run and play with the pack.

All the clothes that I'd brought from the lake

house were just basic pieces, even if there were a fair amount of them. But it left me with only basic choices: the grey tank or the blue one, the stonewash skinny jeans or the black leggings, the black bra or the nude one. I mean, sure, there were a couple of breezy palazzo pants too, but I'd just had a pair of those on.

The black leggings reminded me too much of the facility we'd been locked in, so those were out and the stonewash skinny jeans were in. That was a fairly easy choice. But then I had to find a different tank because the grey was too close in tone to the stonewash, and the blue tank wasn't really great for jeans. So I opted for an emerald green tank—which meant the nude bra so it wouldn't show through—and applauded my choice when I looked in the mirror, because the top definitely brought out the bright green of my eyes.

And then I chided myself for bothering with any of it. The bedroom was just down the hall, and I was literally just going to go to bed, so a damn t-shirt would have been fine.

Hell, just a towel would have been fine.

Because I knew what I was doing.

I wanted to look nice for Andy. I wanted him to want me. I didn't want to have to say goodbye.

Which made me chide myself all over again because I *had* to in order to keep him safe. He *had* to go home. Splitting my focus between getting both my parents and Abigail and her family safe from those assholes was going to be hard enough without adding Andy to the mix.

Because all they'd have to do was capture and separate us, and I'd do anything they wanted to keep him safe.

Shit. I had it bad for him.

I peeled off the tank and jeans, folding them together so I could wear them tomorrow.

I ditched the bra and panties too, and just

wrapped the towel around me. If I was going to say goodbye to him, I was at least going to keep him up all night, giving us both something to remember each other by.

The deep chime thrummed a dark note, answered by a harmonizing tone from the prayer bowl, and I swallowed down the tears that stung my eyes.

I took a deep breath to collect myself, checked that the towel wouldn't fall as I walked, and headed out of the bathroom.

The people I'd met here—the pack—had largely retreated to their rooms, though their voices came from all over the house. I passed Matt and Chastity's room on my way down the hall, but stopped myself from eavesdropping on them.

When I got back to the room Sheppard had offered us, Andy was sitting on the edge of the bed in fresh clothes. By all appearances, he hadn't even managed to miss a belt loop or twist the belt as he added it to these dark wash jeans, and the shirt he wore was a pale pastel green that was only a shade or two away from white. It reminded me of Easter baskets, and I tried to etch the image into my mind.

Maybe I'd have to say goodbye, but I would *never* let myself forget him.

"Kinda presumptuous that we'd prefer the one bed over the two couches, isn't it?" The left corner of his mouth quirked up. God, I loved that expression on him.

I laughed as I shut the door and put my clothes down on top of the duffle next to the chair. "Maybe." I dropped the towel. "But is it an incorrect presumption?"

"*Suiaerl mitne*," he breathed, his eyes roaming over my naked body like a caress. "No."

He stood to reach for me then, but I was already closing the distance between us.

His hair was wet, and though he smelled like soap, the scent of dark chocolate, honey, and fresh snow—the scent of *him*—still clung to his skin.

"You showered too," I said.

His hands landed on my hips as he cocked his head to the side, eyebrow raised. "Should I not have? Do you like your men musky and unwashed?"

I laughed. "No. Definitely not. Clean is better."

He pulled my hips to his lap. "Then do not try to pretend you are not pleased." His tone was playful, and he gently nipped once at my chin.

I smiled as I put a knee on either side of his hips, draping my arms around his shoulders to kiss him. I wanted to memorize the taste of him. His hands glided up my body and I focused on remembering exactly the way they felt brushing along my skin. He was already hard under me, which told me that I wasn't the only one who'd thought to make it a night to remember. I deepened the kiss, my tongue finding his as I breathed in his honey and dark chocolate scent. I pressed my body against his chest as his hands roamed along either side of my ribcage until his thumbs reached the dark tips of my breasts, which were already hard from the friction against his shirt.

"You are overdressed, sir," I whispered against his mouth.

He flicked his thumbs across my nipples, drawing a pleased sound from me as his tongue danced with mine before pulling away.

"Had I been informed of the dress code, Lady Kateri," he said, his lips brushing against mine, "I could have adjusted my attire accordingly."

Lady Kateri. I never wanted anyone else to ever call me that. I never wanted to forget the way he said it.

His hands returned to my hips, where they put pressure to lift me from his lap. I stood, and as his hands went to the buttons of his shirt, I reached for the buckle of his pants.

Once again, he hadn't bothered with underwear, which I was beginning to think meant he never wore any.

Well, that could be handy to know.

And then a pang of jealousy that other women would get to unwrap his impressive cock made me yank his pants to the floor a little harder than I meant to. I blinked and pushed the thought from my head. Maybe there would be other women; maybe there wouldn't. Either way, I'd make it hard for them to measure up to the memory of me.

I wrapped a hand around the hard shaft bobbing between his legs and dropped to my knees to close my mouth around its head.

"Light the ley lines," he murmured, an appreciative noise coming from his throat.

He'd managed to get the shirt fully unbuttoned by then, and as I pulled him deep into my mouth, his hands tangled in my hair. They clenched into tight fists as I drew him out and back in, going deeper and deeper every time as he moaned his appreciation.

I put a hand on the shaft and slid up and down his length as I pulled him from my mouth.

"Careful now," I said quietly. "Apparently, werewolves have even better hearing than I do, and the house is full of them."

He reached for my elbow and tugged me to my feet, where he kissed me once before his hands found the warm wet spot between my legs, eliciting another pleased sound from me.

"Let them hear," he said against my mouth. And his hand went to work, the fingers of his tattooed hand burying themselves deep within me as his thumb circled and flicked at my clit.

I tried to keep a rhythm with my hand on his dick,

but with everything swirling in my head as I tried to memorize everything, it was all I could do to let myself get lost in his touch. As he drove me closer to the edge of my orgasm, winding me tighter than a guitar string, I moaned against his neck and leaned against him. He stopped just before I crashed over, a mischievous smile on his face.

"Not just yet," he murmured, nipping at my bottom lip as he pulled his hand from me. He patted my mound once, making my whole body jerk at the impact.

He peeled off his shirt and dropped it to the floor before kneeling in front of me, his warm breath teasing my dripping wet folds. He slid a hand up my leg and gripped the thigh, spreading me open as he guided my knee to rest on the edge of the bed.

"I have been aching to taste you since you kissed me earlier," he said, and his tongue flicked out to run a feather-light line along my folds as he closed a fist around his dick.

I squirmed toward him as he did, trying to get more contact with him again. "Then don't keep a girl waiting," I whined.

The corner of his mouth pulled up again. "As you wish."

My breath hitched as his tongue parted my folds and his mouth pressed against me. Goosebumps spread across my skin as his hand cupped my ass, holding me to him as he lapped and sucked at my core. His tongue fell into a rhythm that he matched with the fist pumping his cock, driving me once again closer and closer to the edge of my orgasm.

And, once again, he left me teetering on the brink of ecstasy, kissing a line up the side of my body as he pushed me down onto the bed. I whined at the cessation of his touch.

He climbed up on the bed, kneeling as his dick

twitched, the head pointed toward my entrance. He wrapped his hand around it, jacking it once as I licked my lips.

"Tell me what you want, Lady Kateri," he said, running a finger lightly along the inside of my thigh.

"All of you." The words were out of my mouth before I'd even properly thought of them, and I didn't care.

He bobbed his head and lowered himself on top of me, pressing into me in one deliciously long stroke that made my back arch and eyes roll back in my head with a needy little sound deep in my throat. His hand came up to rest on my collarbone, his thumb brushing my pulse point as he started slow, deliberate thrusts into me. Once again, I was completely taken with how amazingly good he felt inside of me—too taken to think about the noise I was making—and I ground my hips against him with every stroke.

"Light the ley lines, you are exquisite," he said, watching the rolling of my hips with his absolutely lustrous blue-black gaze.

"I could say the same for you," I breathlessly managed.

As I approached the edge of my orgasm once again, I hooked a leg around his and switched places with him. He gave me a gruff laugh for the trouble, and he sat up, wrapping an arm around me as the movement of my hips drove him deep enough inside me that I swore I could feel him in my throat yet again as I rode him.

When my orgasm finally crashed into me, it was like coming up for air after drowning for hours. The chime rang a deep resonant note that thrummed along my muscles and danced with tinkling small chimes. His mouth crashed into me as I rode the waves of my ecstasy until, with increasing moans of his own, he came as well.

And I immediately came again as he did, the absolutely electric euphoria doubling me over as the chime thrummed another note, and he fell back onto the bed.

Holy shit. I'd never had multiple orgasms like that.

He closed his mouth against mine and pulled me close to him, his massive cock still twitching inside of me with the aftershocks of my orgasm.

God, did he ever feel good … and taste good … and smell good.

Damn. I had it *bad* for him.

"You are a truly breathtaking creature, Lady Kateri," he said.

I propped my chin on my hand, which rested above his thundering heart, and wriggled my hips just enough to watch the pleasure of it cross his face, memorizing the way his mouth quirked up at the corner as it did. "I am indescribably pleased you think so."

FIFTY-NINE

One quick, towel-wrapped trip to the bathroom later, and I was snuggled under the blankets with Andy once again, our foreheads lightly pressed against each other as I lazily traced a finger along his tattoos.

"I liked how they were lit up before," I told him.

He smiled ruefully. "They had power then."

"They don't now?"

He shook his head. "No."

I pulled back to study how the tattoo that covered his arm spread across his chest and down to his thigh. "Tattoos powered by magic. Specifically, the magic of your homeland."

He nodded, watching my finger as it traced the trailing shapes over his stomach.

"How do you get magical tattoos like that?"

"You spend a lot of time with mages," he said. "And even longer on a table or bed as they force the effective energy of the incantations to lie under your skin."

I looked up at him. "So what, exactly, do powered tattoos do?"

He propped his head on his hand and showed me the inside of his other wrist. "Well, you know what the sword does."

I nodded.

"This one—" He flipped his arm over to indicate all of the geometry, "—is like armor. And this one—" He pointed to the bands on the arm propping up his head, "—helps me not need to eat."

"Why on Earth would you do that?"

"Because when you meddle with transportation magic—and you meddle with the boundaries between planes—you sometimes end up places where 'food' is a subjective term. And I'd rather not starve because I got stuck on the elemental plane of fire."

"There's an elemental plane of fire?"

He nodded. "There is. It's attached to Arcaniss, but I wouldn't be surprised if it somehow touched here as well—perhaps in your biggest, most active volcano?"

"It sounds like eating or drinking there would be the least of your worries."

"Not if you were stuck there for days before successfully reverse-engineering the magic that put you there in the first place."

"Sounds like you speak from personal experience."

"It's a mistake you only make once," he said.

"But your tattoos worked there—on the elemental plane of fire—and they don't work here unless you've recently been near a rift?"

He nodded.

"So, when those assholes at the facility tried to starve you, not even your tattoo could help, huh?"

"It was more than a little frustrating, yes."

"Why would they work there, then? On the 'elemental plane of fire?'"

His eyes unfocused as he thought. "I'm not sure exactly. Broadly speaking, that plane is connected to Arcaniss. Its connection is woven into the very fabric of that world, while this world is essentially cut off entirely from the magic there. I'm not certain on the how or the why, so I cannot work around such limitations."

"Hmm," I said, turning my attention to the lines on his thigh.

"It's very distracting to have your hands on me like this."

I arched an eyebrow at him. "Distracting?" I pushed his shoulder, putting him on his back, and laid my head on his chest. "Better?"

He nodded once. "Better … for now. Easier to answer your questions, at least, without wanting more of your intoxicating moans."

I kissed him once. "I'm happy to give you more of those whenever you're ready for them."

His fingers wandered toward my folds.

"What, now?"

He chuckled, the sound reverberating in his chest. "Perhaps a break is wise."

I was quiet for a moment, listening to his heartbeat as it pounded beneath his ribs.

"Teach me to say it?"

"Say what?"

I sat up and looked at him. "Your name. Teach me to say it the way you do?"

He smiled and sat up as well, folding a leg in front of him while he extended the other beside me. "Sure. Andrezmes Kjelliho. And-*raze*-mess K-yell-*ee*-ho. Emphasis on the long 'ay' sound and the long 'ee' sound."

I draped a hand on his thigh as I sounded it out slowly. "An-*dray*-zz-mess Kyell-*ee-ho*."

"Close," he said. "But only put the emphasis on the long 'ee' at the end. It helps if you lilt my first name up at the end and my surname down at the end." He gestured with his hand to indicate his meaning and then repeated his name with the gesture.

"And-*raze*-mess." I gestured my hand up. "K-yell-*ee*-ho." I gestured it down.

"Yes!" His smile lit up his face. "That's it."

"Andrezmes Kjelliho," I said, my hand making the same gestures as before.

He kissed me.

"Perfect," he murmured against my lips.

"Teach me the other thing? The one you said earlier. Something meet nay?"

"*Suiaerl mitne*?"

I nodded.

His smile lit up his face again. "It's like an expletive."

"I gathered that much," I said. "What's it actually mean?"

"The literal translation would probably be 'arcane light,'" he said. "And in spellcasting, that's exactly what it means. But it's more like a general exclamation outside of spellcasting."

"Like how you say 'light the ley lines.'"

He chuckled. "Well, that one is more … emphatic than *suiaerl mitne*."

"Teach me to say that one too?"

He nodded. "Soo-ee-*air*-l meet-nay"

"*Swear*-l meet-nay."

"Slow it down a bit," he said. "Soo-ee-*air*-l."

"Soo-ee-*air*-l meet-nay."

"There you go, now the lilt on that goes down on the first bit and then up on the second." He emphasized with his hand.

"*Suiaerl mitne*," I said.

And he kissed me again. "You're a natural."

My heart filled with the praise, and the light tinkling of wind chimes danced along my skin.

I kissed him, and we fell back on the pillows. He tangled a hand in my hair as our tongues found each other, reveling in the taste of one another yet again.

When we broke the kiss, I resettled against his chest as his fingers rubbed my scalp for a long, quiet, magical moment.

"Andy," I said. "Andrezmes."

"Mmm, I like my name from your lips."

I nodded against his chest. "I … when we find out where these rifts happen …" His fingers stilled. "I need you to get yourself back home and stay put, okay? You can't go looking for portals or anomalies or strange weather events or anything."

"You know how I ended up here, though, right?" He sighed. "I meddle in rift magic, Ny. It's what I do. It's part of who I am. Remember, I'm not exactly going to be missed back home. I'm known to disappear for long stretches." His voice softened, a hint of sadness creeping in. "I've spent months away from anything I was even passingly familiar with, only to find no one had even questioned my absence upon returning." He squeezed me tightly to him and sighed. "Staying here a little longer, with you, is not going to cause anyone any issues back home. No one will even care."

The lump in my throat was back, and I wrapped an arm around his waist, holding him just as tightly as he held me.

"But you have to," I said. "I need you to. You go, and you stay safe."

He put a finger under my chin, tilting my face up as he looked down along his chest at me, his expression incredulous. "Safe? There are literal dragons and avatars of deities that just walk around Arcaniss like it's a walk in the park for them. And it is. And that's not even including what happens when I end up on different planes."

"But—"

"Naiya," he said, interrupting me. "There *is* no safe for me."

I shook my head, pulling my chin from his hold as the deep low note of the wind chime sounded.

"There is," I said emphatically. "At least you can do something there—you aren't cut off from your abilities. No one in Arcaniss is going to lock you in a facility and throw away the key. No one there is going to take Chad and chip away at him until you show them exactly how you do what you do. No one there is going to try to kill you just to see where your limits are."

My voice cracked, and tears spilled onto his chest as the wind chime thrummed a dark depressed note. Chad chittered over on the nightstand.

"Ny …" His voice was pleading.

"No," I wailed. "Don't you see? I can't risk that happening to you again. I can't lose *you* to *them*!"

"But if I leave—"

"Then you're free! And, more importantly, you're safe."

The tears were flowing freely now, the sobs wracking my chest as Andy held me. He waited for the storm to pass, holding me tight to him and sitting up with me, so I had an easier time breathing.

As the sobs turned to sniffles, he took a deep breath.

"Except then you've let them win," he said softly, wiping tears from my face with gentle hands.

"Fine," I mumbled with a sniff. "Then they win. If that's what it takes for you to go home and be *safe* … then let them win."

I looked up at him, searching the starfield of his eyes for any other answer that made sense.

There wasn't one.

"Hate me for letting them win," I said, defeat in every word. "If you'll just … please …"

The sobs stole my words again, but his mouth crashed against mine, his tongue dancing in my mouth for a long, long moment as the fight fled from my bones.

"Never," he said, "in my entire life would I be able to hate you. The ley lines themselves would grow dark and still long before such a thing was possible."

He held me as I sobbed, crying out my tears at the loss of him yet to come, at the frustration and fear for my parents and Abigail, and at the gut-wrenching betrayal of Val.

Eventually, I was cried out, left as a limp shell in Andy's arms as he kissed my forehead and nose. He kissed my cheek, and then his mouth found mine once again.

"Come with me," he whispered against my lips. "Please."

Like I hadn't already considered that and dismissed it just as readily. It wouldn't save my family.

"That's not my home, Andy. I don't belong there."

"I'll show you everything you could possibly need," he said, growing more excited as he spoke. "The people from the facility won't be able to get you, even if they knew that's where you went."

He held both of my hands in his, his eyes searching my face for even a shred of hope.

Hope I wanted to give him, but knew I couldn't.

I kissed the back of each of his hands.

"I want you to be right," I said, squeezing against his grip. "I really do. But to find out that's where I'd gone? They'd probably do all sorts of awful things I can't even imagine to my parents and Abigail and probably this pack, too. I can't just leave everyone to their mercy."

It hadn't even really occurred to me until now that I may have also been putting this pack in danger. Shit. I'd just been following the only option I thought I'd had. And even that turned out to be fruitless.

"Then I will stay with you, Naiya," he said, his voice firm. "I'll help you to get free of them."

The tears were falling again, some as yet untapped reservoir deep in me welling up and spilling over. "Andy ... you can't. I couldn't stand it if they took you again. You're only in this mess by accident. You don't belong here, and as much as I am so glad to have met you and known you, and as much as I appreciate your presence, I just ... you can't stay."

"I can't just leave you," he said, pressing kisses to my forehead.

"You *have* to," I managed through my tears. "If I can get clear of them—if I can get them to leave my family alone—maybe then I can find a way back to you."

The deep thrumming tone sang along my listless muscles. I wanted so bad for that last bit to be true, but couldn't see any possible way it could be.

"I'll be counting the days," Andy said, holding me tight to him as I cried some more.

Exhaustion started to set in then, and sleep finally swept in to do its job. The house had gone quiet, and Andy's breathing and heartbeat had both evened out, though he stroked my hair over and over as I laid there.

In that last moment of drowsy wakefulness, I could have sworn I heard him whisper, "I love you."

And as sleep swept me away, I tried to whisper it back to him.

Because it was true. I loved him. And I was *still* going to have to say goodbye.

SIXTY

IN MY DREAM, someone hummed a song. I was sure it was the same one I'd heard in my dreams the night Andy told me about the floating castles of Arcaniss, though the melody was gone by the time I woke.

In my dream, there was a woman humming it, and it made me feel warm. But then the melody twisted, turning dark and cold, as a flash of black fur dashed past me. It circled around me, and it was as if there were multiple leopards pouncing on me at once.

I woke snarling and covered in fur.

Andy jumped back and rolled off the bed, but his voice was calm. "Easy, Ny."

It was a good thing I hadn't managed to put on any clothes, and that I'd fallen asleep with the blanket just loosely draped over me.

I shrank into myself, embarrassed to be in this form again.

"Easy," Andy said again, putting a hand out toward me. "Nothing here will hurt you. You're safe."

Safe. Yeah, right. Safe until someone burst through that door and tried to shoo me out the way my father had after my mother screamed.

He slowly, gingerly crawled back onto the bed and patted the pillow. "Let's just lay down and go back to sleep." His heart thudded hard in his chest, a stark contrast to the soft voice he was using to speak to me.

Some deep rumbling noise came from my chest, and I blinked.

"It's alright," he said, meeting my eyes. "I'm not afraid of you."

The rumbling softened, and I sat down.

"I never was," he said, his soft voice calm and even. "And I never will be."

Never.

Never is a really long time.

His heart still pounded, though. I thought it meant he was afraid, but his words rang true. He wasn't afraid.

His hand brushed the top of my head, and I pressed into his touch.

"There, see?"

It was truly embarrassing to be caught like this, to be stuck in a form that couldn't speak. I curled into a ball on the bed, trying not to touch him. I didn't want to make him have to touch me more than he already had.

"It's alright, Ny," he said, pressing his side against me. "I'm here."

Something moved outside the door, and my ears swiveled toward the sound as the deep chime thrummed. The rumbling started again in my chest.

"No one is going to bother us," Andy said, pointedly looking at me and then toward the door. "It's just you and me. I got you."

He ran a hand down my side.

The rumbling stopped again and I blinked.

He wasn't shrinking away from me.

He carefully, gingerly pressed a kiss to the top of my furred head.

Holy shit.

"I got you," he whispered.

We lay there for God only knew how long before I finally fell asleep again.

When I woke, I was curled against Andy, and daylight streamed in through the window over the headboard. His honey and dark chocolate scent, however, was overshadowed by the smells of breakfast on the air.

He kissed the top of my head as I stirred. "Good morning."

I looked up at him. "How long have you been awake?"

He shrugged a shoulder. "Not long. Everyone moving around the house woke me."

"Back home, you live alone, don't you?"

"Other than Chad," he said, "yes."

I nodded. No wonder movement in the house woke him. And why no one would miss him for a long while if he disappeared.

He leaned close to my ear. "Do you know, Lady Kateri, that we both appear to be without clothes?"

I smiled and hooked a leg over his hip, straddling him as he lay back on the pillow, his hard length laying along his stomach under me. "It hadn't escaped my notice."

Much like it hadn't escaped my notice how hard he was—a fact which spread warmth all through me, particularly between my legs.

Or how amazing he'd been when I'd woken from my nightmare last night. Which I very much wanted to thank him for. I was beginning to think that so long as everyone stayed calm around me when I shifted forms, no one would get hurt. And if it weren't for him, I might never have learned such a thing.

I reached down and gripped his dick, leaning down to kiss him as I pressed him against my folds, sliding just the tip inside.

His head fell back with an appreciative moan as I rolled my hips to slide more of him into me.

I nipped at his Adam's apple. "Quiet now, or the whole pack will hear."

The corner of his mouth quirked up in that delightful lopsided smile of his as he pulled his head up to look at me. "Only if you'll do the same."

He thrust his hips up, the rest of his length sliding into me, so that once again, I was sure I could feel him in my throat.

I sat up and threw my head back with a gasp of pleasure and bit my lip on the moan that tried to escape me as he pulled his hips down for another thrust.

Pressing my hands to his waistline, I rolled my hips along his length, matching his rhythm as I drove both of us closer to the edge of ecstasy. He sat up to hold me against him, his hand gripping my thigh as the other pressed against my back. His breath started to come in ragged gasps. His lips brushed my shoulder, my neck, my chin in time with his thrusts, and I closed my mouth against his.

His thrusts grew more forceful, and I gently bit his lip as a reminder of our deal, keeping pace with his thrusts as I ground my hips against him.

But when my orgasm finally crashed into me, I moaned my ecstasy into his mouth as the deep chime resonated through me. His hand tangled in my hair, and he pressed me to his neck, where I closed my mouth on his collarbone, gasping, kissing, and licking him there as the aftershocks took me.

When he came a moment later—as had happened last night—I came again even harder than my first as the wind chime rang another note. It left me shuddering against him, and if it weren't for his hold on me, my boneless body would have fallen listlessly to the sheets.

"I have never had that happen before you," I whispered breathlessly, regaining control of myself.

He kissed my forehead. "Never what?"

"Y'know … twice like that. One right after the other." I traced one of the shapes on his chest.

"I feel like a 'you're welcome' is in order," he said, running a hand up my back.

I kissed him. "Mmm, that wouldn't be the only thing I'd be thanking you for."

"Well, you're welcome for all of the rest of it as well then," he said, kissing my jawline. "Now, what do you say we go see if the wolves have left us anything for breakfast?"

My cheeks heated at the thought of going and facing the pack right away.

"Ooh, Lady Kateri," he said, ducking his head into my field of vision as he hooked a finger under my chin. "What mischievous thought was that?"

"I was just thinking how there's no way any of them don't know what we were doing either last night or just now."

"Do you think they don't do that?"

"No," I said. "I'm sure they do."

"Do you think they care?"

"No," I said. "But I kinda do."

"Why?"

"Um …" I bit my lip. "Maybe they'll judge me for it?"

"And if they do, are they the type of people you want around you?"

Shit. He had a point.

"No."

He patted my ass gently. "Then let's get dressed and go eat."

So, I got dressed and made a quick bathroom detour before heading to the dining room, where there was organized chaos at the table. Everyone had plates of eggs and sausage and waffles. There were bowls of berries scattered around the table, the largest of which was in front of Kristos, and everyone was talking about where to go next.

"I'd recommend steering clear of the Midlothian area," I said as I sat down. "It's just south of the DFW metroplex in Texas, and it's where those assholes were holding me captive."

Kaylah came out of the kitchen and placed a hand on my shoulder. "How d'ya like yer eggs?"

I looked up at her. "Sunny side up?"

"Sure." She nodded and looked at Andy. "How 'bout you, hun?"

Andy looked a little like a deer in the headlights. "Uh …"

I placed a hand on his knee. "How about just scrambled with cheese?"

He looked at me and then back at Kaylah. "Actually … um. I saw omelets on a show at the Lamb of Hope?"

Kaylah clucked her tongue. "'At I can do. Onions, cheese, and bacon okay? I got tomatoes, too?"

"Oh, that all sounds good," Andy said.

"You got it." And she was off, back to the kitchen.

Chastity came out a moment later with coffee mugs for the both of us. "Honey and milk are there." She pointed to a little honey pot and a small pitcher of milk across the table. "Matt. Pass 'em down."

He did as she said, though I didn't bother with either in my coffee.

Andy leaned over to me. "What's the honey for?"

"Your coffee," Lynn explained, spearing a couple of sausages with her fork. "I thought it was strange too, but try it."

"I mean, I guess it would work like sugar," I said with a shrug.

"It does," she said.

Andy put a couple of spoonfuls in and stirred before adding a few drops of milk and taking a sip. "It *is* good." He sounded surprised.

"See?" Lynn said.

He raised his mug to her and took another big gulp as the potatoes and waffles were passed down our way. There wasn't much sausage left, not that I was surprised.

As we started to dig in, Kaylah brought us both plates with our eggs, and I watched Andy try his omelet.

"Light the ley lines," he said. "That's delicious."

Kaylah kissed the top of his head. "Ain't you sweet?"

Daniel leaned forward to look down the table at me. "So Midlothian is out, huh?"

I nodded. "Unless you wanna run into a bunch of asshole werewolves."

Matt took a sip of his orange juice and looked at Sheppard. "Sounds like a church pack."

Sheppard nodded and turned to Andy. "What's Lamb of Hope? Is that a recovery center?"

"I think so," Andy said, taking another bite of his omelet.

I nodded. "It is."

"It's a ways away from where we were imprisoned, though," Andy said as he cut off another piece of his omelet. "It took a few hours to drive from there to the facility."

"Do you know what city that was?" I asked. "Or maybe what it said on the cop cars?"

"Oh," Andy said and closed his eyes for a moment. "Selma Police."

"That's down near San Antonio, I think," I said. "I didn't know they transported you that far."

"It never seemed relevant," Andy said with a shrug.

"Isn't there a pack out that way?" Matt asked.

Sheppard nodded as he swallowed the bite of sausage he'd just taken. "There is. And it's not a church pack."

"Bet they'd be pretty pissed to find the Church meddling on their territory," Matt said as he cut up a syrup-soaked waffle.

"Church?" I said around a bite of potato. "What's a church got to do with anything?"

"Werewolves were created by the Catholic Church," Kristos said, popping a handful of blueberries into his mouth.

Holy shit. He said it so casually. Like it shouldn't be a shock to anyone. And … I didn't think he was lying.

Sheppard sighed and met my eyes. "Yes. And there are a fair number of packs that are part of the Catholic Church that work here in America, though most of the packs here are not church packs."

"By the sounds of it," I said, "you don't get along all that great with church packs."

"Dogmatics," Lynn said, cutting up her syrup-soaked waffle.

Sheppard nodded. "Correct. They fight the same good fight, but their methods … leave much to be desired."

"So, the people at the facility are likely a church pack?" My voice was small, and I balled a hand into a tight fist. A church held me captive like a wild animal?

"By the sound of it," Sheppard said, "almost certainly. Where were you before they captured you?"

"Saint Dymphna's Institute of Behavioral Health," I said. "It's in Dallas."

"Likely Church-run," Ian said.

Sheppard nodded as he took a sip of his coffee.

"So, we should just steer clear of the metroplex in general then?" Lynn asked.

"Wait," I said. "So there's a church pack in Midlothian holding people captive to see what they're capable of, and you guys are just going to steer clear of them?"

The deep resonant chime thrummed through my muscles, quiet anger in the tone. The prayer bowl rang in response.

"The Church has jurisdiction there," Sheppard said. "To go there, to confront their methods, would start a fight that could very easily turn into a war."

"A war the Church has already lost once," Kristos said, lifting a dry waffle to take a bite of it like it was a piece of toast.

"That was more than two centuries ago," Sheppard said. "Vampires didn't have the kind of foothold here that they do now. If we started that fight—"

"It'd be just what the vampires wanted," Matt said, his fist hitting the table. "Fighting amongst ourselves."

Sheppard looked at me. "You don't have to like it. You shouldn't. *I* don't like it. But it's not a fight we want to start. Not without a more egregious trespass."

"More egregious than holding people captive?"

"Holding people who are not quite human," Sheppard said, meeting my gaze with an almost uncomfortable intensity. "Like I said, I don't like it. I can't like it. But it isn't out of line. They're trying to protect humanity. They didn't kill you. Or Valerie."

"They tried!" I bent my fork over itself in my white-knuckled grip.

Andy's hand covered mine, gripping it tightly.

Kaylah stood and breezed into the kitchen.

"They didn't," Andy said gently. "They just walked up to that line."

"But my family—"

"They've only implied harm to them," Andy said. "Abigail was fine."

Tears spilled down my face as the wind chime rang through me so hard I was shaking. Or maybe it was the anger.

"How can you defend them?"

Andy's entire demeanor shifted, stiffening as he sat taller in his seat. "I wouldn't *dream* of defending those monsters. Least of all to you. They may not have killed you or me or anyone else they've ever held captive, but they are still monsters. The problem is that they're monsters that apparently play by rules—which is arguably the *worst* kind of monster. As one who has been held captive by such monsters before, I understand why you have to have everything *perfect* when you're ready to take them down." He kissed my forehead and softened. "I have no doubt that you and this pack will find a way to stop them. You just have to wait and prepare for the perfect moment."

I looked around the table at the pack, barely containing my fury.

"We'll get them, Kitten," Kristos said, another note singing through the wind chime.

Sheppard was still focused on me. "We just have to be smart about it."

Kaylah gingerly slid a new fork across the table to me and sat down.

"And we should make sure your family is safe first," Lynn said, a harmonizing note from the prayer bowl joining the thrum along my muscles.

She was right. It took the wind right out of my sails, the intensity out of my anger. If we did anything at all to the people of that facility, it would need to be *after* I knew for sure that my parents and Abigail and her family were untouchable.

SIXTY-ONE

"So, Andy," Sheppard said. "You came through a rift somewhere, and then they took you to Lamb of Hope before taking you to the facility in Midlothian, right?"

Andy nodded. "Right."

"And Naiya, you were at a recovery center in Dallas before they took you to Midlothian?"

"Right."

"Oh, you poor thing!" Kaylah reached for my arm. "I di'n't even think about it! Were y'all sheep?"

I blinked. "Sheep?"

"Being fed on by vampires," Matt explained. "Humans that vampires keep to feed on are called sheep."

"That's horrible," I said and shook my head. "No. I was there because my parents thought I drugged them."

"Did you?" Chastity asked.

"What? No! They just found that an easier explanation than me being able to turn into a leopard."

"That's dumb," Ian said.

"'N' you?" She looked at Andy.

"Oh … uh … they said I was delusional, likely schizophrenic," Andy said.

"Jesus," Lynn said.

"Well, look," Sheppard said as Kaylah and Chastity stood to clear the breakfast plates. "Until I hear back from the other packs, we'll have to work on what we know and do some research. Ian, do you think you and Chastity can track down and map the spots where the rifts have happened? Maybe there are recurring locations."

Ian nodded. "It shouldn't be hard to map the ones that have hit the news."

Chastity nodded. "We can probably map it down to the city-level, at least. I doubt the exact addresses or coordinates will be readily available."

"It's a start," Sheppard said.

"We'll wanna start by searching the headlines for each individual state and hope we get some hits," Ian said.

"I can help too," I said, standing to grab the laptop and cord from my backpack in the bedroom. "Worst case, we know one happened near San Antonio, and another in Midlothian."

Kristos jutted his chin our way. "And one more about an hour south of here on I-70. Happened toward the end of last year."

A few minutes later, Chastity, Ian, and I all had our laptops open while Andy drew little X's on a US map that Sheppard brought up from the basement. I had to show him where to put the X's, which slowed down my part of the research. But if he was as good with maps as he was with names, like he said, then seeing the map and where all of these places were would increase his chances of being able to find me if he ever came back.

It was such a stupid hope, though.

He really needed to *not* do that, because I certainly wasn't going to have a way to get word to him that it was safe for him to come back this way, even if I *did* succeed in getting Mr. Loudspeaker and his team of assholes off my family's back. And there was no telling how long something like that could even take.

"So Naiya," Ian said, "where'd you grow up?"

"Dallas," I said.

"Any siblings?" Jamie asked from where he'd sat on the rug to play some battle-royale-style video game.

I shook my head. "No. My parents couldn't have children. So they adopted."

"Are the records sealed?" Daniel asked as I pointed to New York for Andy to add an X to the three that were already there. He sounded like he already knew the answer.

"Yep." I shot finger guns at him as I clicked my tongue. Is it really so damn common for adoption records to be sealed? I sighed and focused on the task at hand.

As we went on, we found that most of the rifts ran in a sort of diagonal line from New York City down to Corpus Christi, though the occurrences were spread wide across that line, and there had definitely been other locations as well.

"There are fifty-seven X's on this map," Andy said.

I put my hand on my hip as I stood. I hadn't even been counting.

"That's a lot of rift openings," Chastity said.

"Well," I hedged, "that's assuming everything we found actually is a rift and not some plausible weather event. It'd be hard to see which of these are from reputable sources without redoing the whole thing and color-coding."

"I think I can put together a program to scrape news sites and put it all on a digital map for us," Ian said. "And that *could* feasibly color code for reputable versus questionable sources. But while I could get it up and running in maybe a couple of hours, it would take forever to get the data looking like we need it to. And with all of the news reports going up on every news outlet all over the country, it's probably not going to ping fast enough. But I could set it up to at least email new articles that we can put on the map."

"Let's do that," Chastity said.

Ian nodded. "Lemme get to work then."

It took him until lunch to get it up and running, and he set up a separate email address just for those pings, writing down the password for me and handing a copy to Sheppard, who took a picture of the post-it note. Kaylah had made a truly ridiculous amount of tuna salad and pulled chicken to have on sandwiches for lunch.

Sheppard's phone buzzed as Chastity started to clear the table. He thumbed it open and studied the screen for a bit before turning to me and Andy.

"Looks like we're headed to San Antonio," he said. "Jessica's pack has had a recurring rift in their territory for the past few weeks. She said it's been growing in size recently."

I sighed. "Oh yay, another road trip."

The resonance clanged a deep thrumming note.

Andy's eyes sparkled as he looked at me. "That was sarcasm, wasn't it?"

I nodded. "That, it most certainly was."

My time with Andy was almost over. I chided myself as a lump filled my throat. This was always coming. He had to leave.

"No need," Daniel said. "I can get IDs set up so the two of you can fly."

Kristos shook his head. "No, no. I don't trust the flying caves."

"That's rather pedantic," Chastity said.

"We can't fly," I said, remembering Abigail's face in the interrogation room. "They have pull in the TSA."

"So that's out," Lynn said, nodding.

"Probably for the best anyway," I said, looking at Andy. "I'm not sure how Chad would get through security."

Jonathan looked up, furrowing his brow. "Chad?"

Andy pulled Chad from his pocket, and the little crystalline creature unfolded itself, to various levels of surprised noises around the table.

"Chadmahrazhalorne," Andy explained. "He's a crystalline manifestation of a fragment of my psyche. An … extension of my personality, if you will."

I memorized the way he said it. *A crystalline manifestation of a fragment of my psyche.* I didn't want to forget the sound of his voice.

"Mmmhmm," Kaylah said, standing to help Chastity clear plates. "You keep 'at spider off my cookin' surfaces 'n' we'll be jus' fine."

"I think he's cute," Lynn said as Chad tinkled across the table to her.

"Sounds like driving is our best option," Sheppard said.

"Neither of our trucks holds four," Kristos said as he eyed Sheppard.

"Five," said Lynn.

"Six," said Jonathan.

Lynn put a hand on his arm. "I really don't think we need that many. I'm only going because it'll make it easier on Kristos." She gestured to him. "And he's probably only going because of Naiya." She gestured to me.

Jonathan kissed her forehead and opened his mouth to say something.

She put a finger to his lips. "It's gonna be a packed car as it is, love. Between Shep and Kristos, I'll be plenty safe." She moved her hand along his jaw and kissed him. "I'll come back to you. I promise."

He searched her face a moment before sighing

and kissing her again. "Alright, Dreamer. But be careful. The Church wants you, too."

Matt nodded. "Here's to hoping they want Naiya more."

Ouch. The chime clanged a sour note along my muscles.

"You have the tact of a tetsubo to the face, Matt," Lynn said, wadding up her napkin and throwing it at him.

"Tact is for sugarcoating things," he said, batting it away and pointing at her. "You wanna be strong enough to take down vampire coteries and possibly dismantle Church dealings this side of the Atlantic? You get past the need to sugarcoat things."

"You'd fit right in with a church pack," Kristos said.

"Listen, Pack-killer—"

"That's enough," Sheppard said.

Something powerful shimmered through the air in the room, and the whole pack fell silent.

I narrowed my eyes at him and then arched a brow at Kristos. "'Pack-killer?'"

He sighed and slumped in his chair. "It was a mistake I made three hundred years ago."

My eyes went wide, and I snapped my attention to Matt. "You're that old?"

Kristos—at apparently nearly two thousand years old—barely looked forty to me, if that, and Matt looked decidedly younger, though I'd have only placed him in his early thirties at the most. Still, for whatever reason, I'd just assumed Kristos was the only one that was beyond-human-lifetime old.

Matt rolled his one good eye, though the milky one followed the motion too, and waved his hand dismissively. "I'm not even the oldest in this pack."

"Who is?"

"You really think anyone comes close to Kristos'

nearly two thousand years?" Matt's voice was incredulous as he crossed his arms and leaned back in his seat.

"Besides him."

Matt hooked a thumb toward Sheppard. "Mister Pushing-550 over here."

Sheppard snorted. "Still a handful of years to go till then."

"Close enough," Matt said.

"Either way," Sheppard said. "Here's to hoping they don't see it as a moving jackpot."

Kristos wiped at his face and looked at Lynn. "I'd tell you to stay, but I can't protect you if you do."

"Take my GLS," Daniel said. "It'll take a few fill-ups to get there and back, but at least it'll get you there comfortably."

Kaylah kissed his cheek.

"And it has the kind of power you'll need if you have to outrun goons," Jamie said.

I took another sip of my water before heading back to the bedroom I'd shared with Andy, pushing myself to act instead of feel sorry for myself.

Andy was leaving. He had to. So, I pushed a hand through my hair transferred a change of clothes from my duffle to my backpack, putting the laptop back in there, too, as I prepped for a reverse—and extended—version of the road trip that brought me here.

SIXTY-TWO

WE WERE on the road by two in the afternoon. The five of us were piled into Daniel's white Mercedes SUV with Sheppard driving, Kristos riding shotgun, Lynn in the backseat, and Andy and I on the third-row bench. The SUV had a navigation system that allowed us to find a route that avoided the metroplex —and, specifically, Midlothian—altogether. And since it got to be late at night on a Monday, it was a lot of empty highway between towns.

I watched the mile markers count down the distance, knowing that each mile gone was another mile closer to goodbye. I tried to rack my brain for any other possible solution, running over everything I already knew.

Andy couldn't stay here, because all it would take was capturing him, and I'd do whatever those assholes wanted to keep him safe. I couldn't go with him because that'd just get my family, Abigail, and anyone I'd come into contact with tortured for the information—tortured to find out where I'd gone.

Maybe there was another person who could do what Lynn could. Maybe someone stronger? If I got rid of the leopard, maybe then I could focus on just keeping Andy out of Mr. Loudspeaker's hands.

I leaned forward and tapped Lynn's shoulder. "There's not another *purgatum*, is there?"

Kristos turned around from where he sat in the front passenger seat. "There's not." He nodded toward Lynn. "She's the first in well over a thousand years."

"Well, isn't that special?" I said, sitting back with a huff.

Or maybe not.

"And you're *sure* you've never heard of other wereleopards? Or any other kind of were-something?"

If there was possibly even *one* other like me out there, maybe … well, maybe I wouldn't have to say goodbye. The chime clanged a hollow note.

Sheppard shook his head, as did Lynn.

Kristos turned to meet my gaze. "I wish like hell I had, Kitten. But it seems the best help you'll find is with a werewolf pack that takes in strays."

"How are wereleopards even a thing?" Lynn asked, turning to Kristos. "If the church created you, and then later created werewolves, is it possible wereleopards are something else they tried?"

Kristos shook his head. "No … well … perhaps. But if they did, it was well before werewolves, and they'd have all been culled by now."

"Maybe it skipped about eight thousand generations," I said, plopping my chin into my hand.

The corner of Kristos' mouth quirked up. "That seems unlikely. There's only been seventy-five or so since Jesus' time."

"I don't think she was being literal," Andy said.

I placed a hand on top of his and nodded. I was going to miss the everloving *hell* outta him.

We made a second or third stop for gas again some time later, and I stayed in the car this time, leaning against Andy, trying to memorize his scent. Honey. Dark chocolate. A hint of crisp fresh snow.

"I don't want to say goodbye to you," he whispered against my hair.

I couldn't say anything. I just nodded and turned to hold him as the tears poured down my face.

"It's worse that it has to drag out like this," he said. "I wish I had even a fraction of my power and my lab available to me. I could at least get the rift open right away."

"And rip it off like a band-aid?" I choked out.

He tilted his head at me as Lynn, Kristos, and Sheppard got back into the car.

I sniffled and wiped fiercely at my face. "A band-aid is a thing you put on cuts. An adhesive bandage. It usually pulls at the little hairs on your skin when you go to remove it, which often hurts worse on freshly healed skin. So the standard practice is just to pull it off quickly all at once so that it doesn't hurt as bad."

"Well then," Andy said, his tone sorrowful. "Yes. I wish I could make it like a band-aid for you … and for me."

He said the last part softer than the first, and I held him tighter to me, refusing to look out the window at the mile markers anymore. I didn't want to know. I didn't want to count down.

God only knew how long later, I dozed against him, and that song that was only familiar to me in my dreams floated to me, only this time it felt more mournful than it had before. I tried to reach for it, grasp it so that I could remember it when I woke.

Kristos' voice pulled me back to the waking world. "You see that, Shep?"

Lynn leaned forward. "What the hell is *that?*"

Andy's tattoos flared to pulsing iridescence, and my heart sank. The chime clanged a dull tone.

"A rift," I said.

I looked at the clock on the dash. It was nearly four in the morning.

Sheppard eyed the map on the navigation screen, tapping to zoom it out once before nodding. "We're close enough to Jess' pack that it's probably the one she's been monitoring."

Chad danced up over Andy's head and onto his shoulder before tinkling onto my hand, chittering happily. I pressed my fingertips to the sharp cool facets of the tiny creature, trying with all my might to etch him into my memory alongside Andy.

Sheppard had to take the next u-turn in the grass-median highway to get us back to it.

"What the hell are *those*?" Sheppard pulled the SUV off the road, past the rumble strip, and onto the grass of the shoulder.

"Whatever they are," Kristos said. "They don't belong here."

When we stopped, I could see more clearly the swirling purple-orange-green of the rift, but there was a whole pack of seven dark shapes out in front of it.

"Those aren't rift cats," I said, watching them stalk around in the brush. "I can track them alright."

"Penumbra dogs," Andy said. "They're partially on the elemental shadow plane—which is where they're actually from—so their bodies aren't all here."

"That's clear as mud," I said. "What do they want?"

He shrugged. "What any foraging wild animal wants, I guess."

"Hrmph," Kristos said. "How do you get rid of them?"

"You let me break their pattern so that they're only on this plane," Andy replied. "And then you … uh … take them out. They're generally malevolent creatures anyway, preying on things that fear them."

Break their pattern? What the hell did that mean?

"Sounds like you should get out of the car first, then," Lynn said.

Andy shrugged. "Sure."

Lynn opened the side door and he got out, calling his rapier to his tattooed hand with a flourish. He ran his other hand up his arm and flung little iridescent geometric shapes at the first of the shadowy creatures, which almost seemed like they were made of smoke. But when the shapes hit the first one, they coalesced into the creature's skin, and it seemed less shadowy than before.

The creature howled, a darkly melancholy sound that sent a chill down my spine, as it broke into a run toward Andy. The others followed suit, and Andy scrambled to fling shiny bits of geometry at all of them.

"I don't think it liked that, Andy!" I called.

"Yeah, I figured it probably wouldn't," Andy replied. "Look for the ones that seem more solid!"

Lynn and I clambered out the side door to help him.

Kristos pulled his shirt off as he came out of the SUV as well. He then stripped out of his sweatpants and groaned and grunted as he doubled over. Meaty cracks accompanied his guttural vocalizations. Whatever was happening to him sounded horrifically painful.

And then he was a bear. Or, at least, he was bear-shaped. He was larger than any bear I'd ever seen, and I'd been to a *lot* of zoos.

He turned to the first of the shadowy canines and tore its head from its body in a single fluid motion, using its skull to smash the one next to it.

Holy shit.

Though Andy was still shooting sprays of iridescent geometry at these things, they all redirected at the giant bear tearing their companions asunder.

The third one, he tore in half at the ribcage, and its dying yelps were almost heartbreaking. Sheppard smashed its skull in with a swift kick to stop the noise. Kristos tried to grab the next one, but his paw swiped right through it and it leapt for his throat.

"Andy!" I called, hoping he could do something before the thing killed Kristos.

"I'm on it!" He sprayed shapes at that one, and it coalesced into something more solid than it had been a moment before as Kristos bat it to the ground with a meaty crack of its spine. His paws crashed down on its skull as he landed.

I backed a step toward the SUV as my stomach twisted once.

I shook my head.

Oh, no.

Kristos had already torn open the jaws of the next one, making a total of four down.

I couldn't help here. The leopard didn't need to help here.

Another spray of geometry.

"That should be all of them," Andy called.

And I didn't want to be left naked on the side of the highway as I tried to get Andy home.

Sheppard intercepted the next one flying toward Kristos, using its own momentum to drive its head into the ground hard enough to snap its neck.

Besides, Kristos had this well in hand, and he was supposed to be the protector, right? I mean, with Sheppard's help, he had this, right?

Five down.

Andy's rapier flicked across the sixth as the last one leaped at Kristos. The bear tore out its throat as Andy slashed at number six once more.

And then there were none.

It was just the rift.

Okay, so maybe Andy's experience with these helped, too.

Andy flicked black ichor from the tip of his blade and then flourished it back into place inside his wrist as he turned to me.

There was a dark flash and then light poured from the swirling purple-orange-green rift, like it was daytime wherever it led. There was a town there, like something straight out of a medieval history book.

I jerked my chin toward it. "Is that close to your home?"

He looked over his shoulder and watched for a moment. "It's the city outside the Adamo stronghold." He looked back at me and grabbed my hands, tugging me closer to the rift. "Please, Naiya. Come with me."

The chime sounded within me, a deep thrumming sorrowful note as my vision blurred yet again. "I can't, Andy. I told you. They'll hurt everyone if I do. Please."

His mouth closed on mine then, and I tried to savor how good he tasted, how wonderful he smelled, how warm his hand was in mine.

"Besides," I choked out, breaking the kiss. "I don't belong there."

His hand went to my chin, lifting my face so he could look me in the eyes. I willed myself to remember the exact pattern of the stars in his eyes.

"You belong anywhere you want to," he said.

I looked over his shoulder longingly.

I couldn't go. Too many people would suffer. It would be the most selfish thing I could possibly do.

"We don't have time to argue, Andy." I fiercely wiped at the trail of tears on my cheek. "That rift won't stay open forever."

"Ny …" His mouth closed on mine again.

He wasn't going to go. Not if I didn't push him.

So I took a step toward him, and he gave ground.

Another step. More ground.

And another.

And another.

He pulled away then, his eyes searching my face. "What are you doing?"

"You have to go," I said, my voice breaking on the words. "This world isn't built for people like you, Andrezmes Kjelliho, but it is my home."

He opened his mouth to argue, a tear rolling down his cheek as the chime within me threatened to drown me in its sorrow.

"I will never, ever forget you," I whispered, brushing a thumb through the trail his tear made.

He leaned his forehead against mine, running his hands through my hair. "Nor I you, Naiya Kateri."

His mouth closed against mine once more, and among the honey and dark chocolate and crisp fresh snow was the sorrowful salty taste of tears—his or mine, I couldn't be sure. Likely both.

I pressed a hand to the center of his chest, feeling his heart pound against my palm as I tried to memorize the rhythm. I applied gentle pressure until he broke the kiss, his tear-filled eyes meeting mine.

"I love you, Naiya," he said, taking a step backward.

The rift was already shrinking.

I nodded. "I know."

He took another step.

"I love you too, Andy." That my voice even managed to give sound to the words was a miracle. I could hardly see through my sadness.

The next step, and he was on the other side. His hand brushed my cheek, his fingers wiping across the trail of tears as his other foot crossed through, and the rift began to shrink faster.

"And that's Lady Kateri, if you don't mind," I said with a half-hearted smile as his fingertips left my skin.

His expression and posture shifted then, his eyes more frantic than they'd been a moment ago. His mouth moved like he was saying something, but the rift closed before the sound could pass through, a fading wisp of inky black shadow the only indication that the rift was ever there.

And when that shadow dissipated, all of the strength keeping me on my feet went with it, and my knees crashed to the ground as sobs wracked my body.

Arms that were too thick and too strong and too big wrapped around me, the scent of worn leather edging out what remained of the honey and dark chocolate. I blindly pushed them away like a child mid-tantrum. I didn't want to lose the last little bit I had of him. I wasn't ready to say goodbye.

I suspected I never would have been ready to say goodbye.

I knelt in the grass by the highway for God only knew how long, crying out every ounce of energy and sorrow and anger and loss until I was empty. I numbly stared at the spot where the rift had been, aching for the words that would fill the hole it had left in me.

Sheppard and Lynn didn't even try to talk to me. There were no words that could have been said. Nothing that would have made any of this any easier.

Eventually, pre-dawn lit the horizon, bathing the world in a sleepy grey haze. The wind chimes sang a mournful tune along my muscles as a warm breeze blew my face dry.

And suddenly, I was terrified to move, terrified to face a world where the only person who I knew—beyond a shadow of a doubt—that I could trust was gone.

The mournful tone turned eerie and Kristos stepped over to me, placing a hand on my shoulder.

"We gotta move, Kitten. We're too exposed here." His voice was heartbreakingly gentle.

With unfocused eyes, I turned back toward the SUV, moving on autopilot as I got back in and moved to the third-row bench.

It was done.

Andy was gone.

SIXTY-THREE

Curled in the furthest seat back as I was, I hadn't realized until we were on our way that Lynn had taken over driving. Kristos was on the seat in front of me, turned sideways and studying me with honey-gold eyes. Sheppard sat in the front passenger seat and scrolled through his contacts as we pulled away.

I dragged myself to my knees to look through the rear window, watching the spot where the rift had been. The bodies of the dead penumbra dogs were gone. They must have dissipated with the rift as it closed. But that wasn't what I was focused on. A heavy hollow note thrummed through the wind chime tone.

"US-281, Bulverde, just north of the veterinary clinic, on the northbound side," Kristos murmured.

And if I was certain of one thing, it was that I would never forget that.

281. Bulverde. Northbound past the vet.

The exact location where the gaping wound inside me tore open.

Sheppard put his phone on speakerphone as he called whoever it was he'd found in his contacts.

A sleepy woman's voice answered. "Better be at my door, Alpha."

Sheppard chuckled. "How 'bout I do you better? Go back to sleep. We're all done here."

"You fucking kidding me?" She sounded instantly more alert. "You put out a call like that and then just clear up your business and be on your way without so much as a proper dinner between alphas?"

"I'm sorry," Sheppard said. "Truly, I am. But I wouldn't want to put your pack in danger by staying long enough for dinner. What I currently have in tow is being chased by an organization we have yet to identify for certain, but all signs point to the Church."

"Shit," she said. "And you brought that to my back door?"

Sheppard ran a hand through his hair. "Not exactly. We threw half of it through a rift, took out a pack of dog-like shadow animals that *definitely* aren't from around here, and are getting out of your hair before we bring down more on your pack."

"And I suppose I'm to thank you for the trouble?"

"Not at all," he said. "I owe you one. Truly. As soon as I lose my tail, I'll give you an opportunity to collect. And if it's a pressing need, I'll do all I can to help you while we get clear."

"I don't need your help, Alpha," she said. "But I'm hangin' on to that favor."

Kristos snorted and Sheppard arched an eyebrow at him over his shoulder.

"Fair enough," Sheppard said. "If anything sniffs around after us, and you need my help, lemme know."

"I got mine," she said. "No worries. Go brush up on your treaties."

The phone beeped as the call disconnected.

"She's a real peach," Kristos said.

"Jessica's not had an easy path to alpha," Sheppard said. "She's earned the right to her snark."

But it was like the whole conversation had

happened miles away from me. My mind was still on that spot.

281. Bulverde. Northbound past the vet.

The voices in the car fell silent, and the thrum of the wind chime turned dull and listless as we traveled on. We eventually turned onto a winding two-lane highway heading west.

We'd only been driving on that poorly maintained road for perhaps twenty minutes—or maybe it was twenty hours; what even was time?—when Lynn slowed down.

"Shit," she said.

Sheppard thumbed open his phone and started tapping out a message.

Ahead of us, completely blocking the highway, were four black SUVs with heavily tinted windows, parked in a diamond formation. A little white sportscar was parked in the middle, barely visible around the much larger black vehicles.

"They're not cops," said Lynn. "They'd have lights."

As we approached, Lynn slowed even more, and there was an arc of people standing just inside the two front-most SUVs. And one ballsy asshole standing on this side of the vehicles.

He was a lanky man, probably in his sixties, with a balding pate and a priest's collar. An angry note sang through the wind chime, and I furrowed my brow.

"Father Brooks," Kristos said.

Lynn glanced at him in the rearview. "The guy who wants you to keep tabs on me?"

Kristos nodded.

"What does he want?" Sheppard asked.

Lynn pulled the SUV to a stop but didn't cut the engine.

"And could he be any more cliché about it?" I

asked. His blockade looked like something straight out of an action movie.

Kristos opened the door and got out, his eyes on the old priest. "What's this about?"

"You didn't tell us the *purgatum* was taking a road trip, Brother Kristos," the priest replied, his voice chastising.

I stilled as ice coalesced along my spine, and the chime rang a shrill note. That was a voice I'd recognize anywhere.

Mr. Loudspeaker.

My heart started to pound like a wild thing caged and my palms grew slick as panic tried to choke me. Kristos leaned down to meet my eyes for a brief moment, a calm note replying to my shrill one in the resonance between us.

"That's because we're just making a quick round trip," he said, standing back up. "Barely planned to be gone any longer than forty-eight hours."

His calm note dulled the edge of my panic, though my heart still raced and pounded.

"Ah," Mr. Loudspeaker—or Father Brooks, was it?—said. "But you have something that belongs to me. Two things really."

White-hot rage defrosted the ice as a defiant tone rang through the chime. I clambered out the other side door, leaving it open as a sort of shield between us.

"He doesn't have *anything* of yours," I said. "People aren't property."

Kristos eyed me, something clanging against the tone singing through me. "Naiya—"

"We should speak in private, Ms. Kateri," Father Brooks said, turning his attention to me with a smug sort of satisfaction written across his features. "The matter between us does not concern the bear and his wolves."

I'd rather tear his face off. "I'm not going with you *anywhere* ever again."

"Perhaps you have forgotten what the consequences of noncompliance are."

He reached into his pocket and tossed an object in my direction. Kristos was around the SUV in a flash as it flew. He snatched it from the air, barely a foot away from me, and looked down at it for a moment before reaching behind him, offering it in an open palm to me.

"What game are you at, Father?" he asked.

My blood ran cold as I caught sight of the object in Kristos' hand.

It was the sun-faded Buddy Christ figure from the dashboard of Abigail's car. He was winking and pointing just like he did in that Kevin Smith movie, only this particular Buddy Christ's robes were colored like a kaleidoscope with clumsy marker lines from when Abigail's youngest—Adelina—decided he needed more color.

Had it been on her dash when she came to bring me my car? I couldn't recall. But I *did* recall how he'd pulled Abigail into a TSA interrogation room and nearly had her miss her flight just to leverage my compliance at the digital bench press after starving me for a week. So, what else had he done to her? Another note of fury, as well as one of fear, sang through the wind chimes ringing along my muscles.

It was answered by something from Kristos, I was sure of it, but I was too raw, too distraught, too *angry* to place it.

Lynn opened her door next to Kristos.

"Lynn," he said. "Don't."

She looked at him with steely resolve and stepped out of the SUV. She looked at me with concern in her eyes as the prayer bowl sounded. She reached a hand toward me. "Naiya—"

There was so much concern in her voice that it broke me. It wouldn't have taken much—I was so brittle anyway. But my hand closed around the Buddy Christ as my shoulders slumped. I brought the figure to my chest as a single tear hit the asphalt at my feet.

"There is no beating him," I whispered.

"What's that, dear?" Father Brooks called, cupping a hand to his ear. "Not all of us have supernatural hearing, you know."

I sucked in a breath and huffed it out, gathering myself. His snark fueled my anger, providing me the strength I needed to glare at him for a moment.

I nodded to Kristos and said, "I'll speak with him. Just wait here."

As I started toward Father Brooks, Lynn reached a hand for me. "But—"

I whirled on her, another clanging tone of anger coursing through me. "He has Abigail." I held up the Buddy Christ figure for her to see. "Your objections do *not* trump my family."

Kristos grabbed my hand, and my fury turned on him, but he didn't so much as flinch. "Just say the word, Kitten, and we fight."

I pulled my arm from his grip. "Maybe you can protect me, but you *can't* protect my family."

He pressed his lips into a line and nodded once, accepting my words—my fury—with resolute stoicism.

"How about we make sure this stays nice and friendly?" Sheppard gestured to our SUV. "You can chat in our vehicle."

Father Brooks gave him a rueful smile. "Mmm. I think not, though I will offer a somewhat similar alternative." He stepped over to one of the black SUVs, knocking on the window, which rolled down in response. "Ms. Kateri and I require the use of this vehicle for a private conversation." His tone was well-practiced authority.

"Yessir," said the driver.

The front doors to either side of that SUV opened in unison, and Grump and Blondie—yet again in matching black suits—exited the vehicle, their postures stiff and proper. They left the doors open. I tried not to let my reaction to them show, but I seriously doubted my poker face was up to such a task.

Father Brooks came around the front of the SUV, opening the driver's side passenger door and shutting the driver's door. He then turned to look at me, gesturing to the open door.

When I didn't move, he pressed his lips into a line and sighed, reopening the driver's door and turning off the SUV. There was a jingle of keys as he tossed them to Grump, who snatched them out of the air and tucked them into the inside pocket of his suit jacket.

"Just a conversation, Ms. Kateri." He shut the driver's door again. "I'll not try to abscond with you." He held his hands up to show that they were empty.

Not that I trusted him anyway. That asshole probably had extra sets of keys in his pockets, plus another set hidden in some compartment inside the car. But I was relatively certain that, at least on the surface, his words were true.

And he had my family.

So, against my better judgment, I nodded and stepped over to the SUV.

SIXTY-FOUR

He opened the passenger door on the other side and gestured toward the back seat. I waited for him to get in and to close the door before I sat down, though I hesitated to close my door and be in such a confined space with him.

He sighed. "Ms. Kateri. I intend for this conversation to be private. I do not intend any harm to you, nor to your companions. As I am sure you're aware, you can easily overpower me in this small space. Now, would you please be reasonable and shut the door?"

I narrowed my eyes at him and shut the door forcefully before placing the Buddy Christ on the console between the two seats. "I'm not going back to that facility."

He tsked at me. "I've learned nearly all I can of you from such a controlled environment. Besides, you understand freedom better now than you ever have, and I'm not keen to expend the resources necessary to break you enough to keep you under lock and key—nor am I so much a monster that I would wish to do such a thing."

"No," I spat. "Just monster enough to push me until I nearly drown from exhaustion."

He angled his head at me like a father patiently

walking a child through their mistake. "It did not kill you. Nor could it have. Do you truly think all the testing of your vitals was simply for show? You were told we were getting a baseline, and now we have it." He folded his hands in his lap. "I wonder. Did the *purgatum* try to pull the leopard from you?"

I blinked and tried to keep my expression passive.

"Ah, she did. Well. Fascinating that she was unsuccessful. No matter." He waved his hand dismissively. "From now on, you'll come in for a full physical four times a year. Evenly spaced, of course."

"Not a chance in hell."

"I think you labor under false assumptions, Ms. Kateri. Or perhaps you have forgotten where you stand? Let me make things crystal clear, shall I?" He opened the center console between us and pulled out the other objects he'd shown me at the facility: my father's watch, still ticking loudly, and my mother's music box. Closing the console, he arranged the objects with deliberate meticulousness.

White-hot fury roiled through me, chiming a dangerously ominous tone along my muscles. "These are not new threats."

He looked at the objects, then back at me. "I was unaware I needed aught but reminders to illustrate your precarious position. The status has not changed. You escaped. As you were always going to do. And do let me be clear." He steepled his hands. "Your family is in no mortal danger. They will not have their day ruined by a sniper's shot. Again, I am not so much a monster that I would do such a thing to innocent people. But you and I both know there are any number of ways each and every one of their lives could be harder. Recall, if you will, the example of your dear Abigail."

My hands clenched into white-knuckled fists as my jaw clenched.

"I'd hate for any of that to happen to your parents." He pressed a hand to his chest with a feigned gasp. "Why, they're overseas right now, aren't they? What sort of inconvenience might it be if their passports were found to be forged?"

He re-arranged the items deliberately on the center console.

Were my parents in a non-extradition country? Did that matter? Shit. I wasn't sure how bad it would be if international airport security decided my parents weren't who they said they were.

I glared at him, wishing it was enough to melt his skin from his body.

"You will remit yourself for testing four times each year to ensure the safety and security of your family and their current standard of living."

I removed the items from the center console, pulling them into my lap. "Twice a year, and you forget my family even exists. They are irrelevant to you."

He smiled, and I wanted to tear it from his face. "Not at all, Ms. Kateri. They are your *family*. They are just as important to my statistics as you are."

"Nice try, but I'm adopted. Or weren't you paying attention? There is no genetic link between them and me."

That asshole freaking tsked at me *again*. "You, of all people, should know that family is more than genetics. Lord knows the wolves certainly have that figured out. But it matters not. You are in no condition to argue or negotiate as you have nothing to offer beyond your compliance, which we have already established I can force if necessary." He pressed his fingertips to the center console, his tone turning more severe. "In point of fact, consider that you have *robbed me* of one of my test subjects, have you not? Or is Mr. Kjelliho simply hiding in the wolves' SUV?"

"He's beyond your reach."

"I see. Then you indeed managed to send him home through one of the rifts. A pity. You would have had leverage." He took a breath and folded his hands in his lap again. "Still, I am feeling generous. And the Lord rewards patience. You'll come to me three times a year, no fuss, and I'll forget Ms. Davis even exists."

He plucked the Buddy Christ from my lap and took my hand in his surprisingly strong grip. He placed the figure in the center of my upturned palm, closing my fingers around it. I wanted to break every bone in his body for even touching me. But he had a lot more people than I'd brought with me, and I doubted I'd get far if even a breath of harm came to this asshole.

"Ruminate on the opportunities you have deprived me of before you answer."

I narrowed my eyes as he patted my hand and then lit up with something remembered.

"Oh yes!" he said, pointing a finger in the air. "You left this behind when you made your departure."

He pulled a book from the pocket of his coat and placed it on the center console. I didn't need to look at it to know it was my copy of *The Last Unicorn*. I pulled it into my lap along with the other items as my throat closed up again.

I closed my eyes and took slow deep breaths as a motorcycle—or perhaps a distant helicopter—passed. He was right. I had nothing to offer that I couldn't be sure he didn't already know.

I didn't look up at him. He had turned me into a coward and a fool.

"Three times a year," I said. "Of my own choosing."

He waved a hand. "Fine. But they must be more than a full month—and a full moon—apart. Three times in the same week will be considered a single visit, so do not try to game the system. Perhaps in time, I can even help combat the nightmares that plague you."

"You can keep your damn meddling out of my nightmares," I said. "No sleep studies."

He pressed his lips into a line and cocked his head the other way. "Oh, there will most assuredly be sleep studies, my dear. Regrettably, your nightmares are too closely tied to your abilities to take that off the table entirely. But, if you'd prefer to keep your own counsel about said nightmares, I can work with that, so long as you stick to the arrangement."

I spoke through gritted teeth. "How do I know you'll keep up your end of the deal?"

Father Brooks smiled ruefully and reached across me to open the door. "How am I to be sure *you* will?"

The scents of a whole host of wild things wafted in with the breeze, and the deep wind chime clanged defiantly as he gestured out the door. That he didn't react to all the smells that I was certain hadn't been there before indicated to me that he likely was not, in fact, anything more than human.

Or maybe his poker face was just that good.

I gathered the items he'd brought and stepped out onto the asphalt. Backing toward the back bumper of the SUV, I made a wide circle around the open door. He stood and filled the space before I could focus on the movement behind the white SUV I'd arrived in.

"Neither of us trusts the other, Ms. Kateri," he said, folding his hands behind his back. "And for good reason. Still, I think you will find our arrangement quite agreeable in the long run. The Church is a powerful ally, and after all, you are the only wereleopard in the world. I'm afraid you'll never quite fit in anywhere, and—were I to hazard a guess—you just sent the only person you trusted whole-heartedly through a rift."

I heard most of what he said. Really. But my vision had locked on to the gorgeous redhead over his right shoulder. The one who stood shoulder-to-shoulder with Sheppard, Kristos, and Lynn but was a full head shorter than all of them. The one with no less than twenty wolves silently crowded around her. She was dressed in black and red motorcycle leathers, and her dyed cranberry maroon hair hung loose to the middle of her back. Her arms were crossed, but she winked at me with a smirk when I caught her eye.

"She'll never trust you," Kristos said.

Father Brooks didn't even look over his shoulder.

Dumbass.

My mouth pulled into a smirk as I rolled my eyes. "Why must *everyone* speak for me?" I met Father Brooks' grey gaze. "But he is right, Father. Man of the cloth or no, I could no sooner trust you than I could trust the wolves you sent to attack me in my cell." I looked over my shoulder and met the gaze of both Grump and Blondie in turn.

"A word of advice, if I may," he said. "The world is an exceedingly large place to be the only one of something. You should learn to pick your battles and recognize when you are outmatched. Perhaps you could take a cue from my friend, Brother Kristos. I have no doubt he can teach you such things."

Kristos' hand balled into a fist.

"She's not the only one-of-a-kind here," Lynn called, the Tibetan prayer bowl tone singing a harmony to the defiant clang of the wind chime.

Father Brooks *still* didn't look over his shoulder.

This was going to be good.

Kristos met my eyes. "And as long as she's with us, she's never truly alone."

The redhead cleared her throat, and the startled

surprise that lit Father Brooks' face was absolutely priceless.

Unfortunately, it was short-lived, and his mask of composure was back before he'd even finished turning around.

"Ah, Ms. LaRoux," he said. "I do apologize. I had hoped this matter would have been resolved quickly enough that it wouldn't come to inconvenience you."

"The Church would dare cause trouble for another pack's alpha in *my* territory without so much as a courtesy call to alert me of their presence?" Her voice was the same as the one that had been on speakerphone. This was Jessica, the apparent reigning Alpha in the area. I didn't know her, but the seething anger in her tone was unmistakable. "And in direct violation of treaties drawn up before your mother was even a glint in your grandfather's eye? It is *far* too early in the morning for such bullshit, Father. Your business is done here."

"You're right, of course," Father Brooks said, closing the distance to her. "However, Ms. Kateri has not satisfied all of the requirements to be party to and thus protected by such treaties."

I followed along, just behind his left shoulder.

Jessica pulled a folded piece of paper from the inside of her motorcycle jacket and offered it to him. "I think you'll find she has."

He stepped over and gingerly took it as the closest wolves to her heels pinned their ears back and bared their teeth at him. After unfolding it, he studied the paper for a moment.

"Ah," he said. "I see your signature on this document, but it must be affirmed by another alpha and witnessed by a non-ranking pack member."

Jessica held his gaze, her tone cool as a cucumber as she snatched the paper back. "Of course. How silly of me. Tobias, would you be a dear and help an alpha out?"

Tobias?

Sheppard clicked the pen that was already in his hand. "I'd be happy to." He turned to place the paper on the hood of the SUV and scrawled his signature on the line.

"Eric," Jessica said, looking over her shoulder at one of the wolves at her heels. "Need your John Hancock."

The dark grey wolf pulled his lips back and a snarl burbled in his throat.

"It wasn't a fuckin' question Eric," she said. "Now."

The wolf sighed and then contorted. There were meaty snaps of bones rearranging and I squinted my eyes closed as I winced and turned my face away until all the noise was done.

Except then there was a naked dude standing there, so I simply angled my body so his wasn't in my peripheral.

There was the sound of a pen moving across the paper on the hood of the SUV.

"Thank you," Jessica said, turning to hand Sheppard back the pen.

There were more guttural vocalizations and meaty snaps as Sheppard tucked the pen back into his pocket, and the grey wolf went back to his spot among the others.

"Well," Jessica said, holding out the paper. "Would you look at that? It appears Ms. Kateri falls under my jurisdiction."

What? My eyes went wide. Her gaze flicked to mine, and she winked again before turning her attention back to Father Brooks.

"It seems you're to leave her, her family, and those they employ in the keeping of their grounds and estate completely alone," she said. "Oh yes, and I do believe that if you check in with your head office, you'll find the same is true for one Grace Lynn Cartwright and one Kristos of Athens, both under Tobias Sheppard."

Sheppard turned to her, eyebrows raised.

Kristos' face was impassive, but the note singing along my muscles gave him away. Something very, *very* good for him had just happened.

Father Brooks held up a finger. "Now—"

"I'm sorry," Jessica said. "I wasn't aware this was a negotiation. Do you intend to break the treaties that were put in place specifically to keep infighting to a minimum so that we can keep our collective focus on the vampires?"

His gaze turned to steel. "Of course not."

"Then shoo!"

"Apologies, Alphas," he said. "I meant no disrespect."

"Of course you did," Jessica said. "And if I find you in my territory without warning again, justice will be swift and violent."

Father Brooks nodded, turning back toward the blockade. Grump and Blondie returned to the SUV as Father Brooks sat in the little white car parked in the center of the diamond formed by the four black SUVs.

A moment later, and they were off down the highway. Jess turned to the gathered wolves, gave a sharp whistle, and waved a hand in the air. The pack dispersed in virtually every direction.

"Jess," Sheppard said. "You didn't have to do that."

I turned to Sheppard. "What just happened?"

"I had to name you pack to save your family," Jessica said, handing me the paper Sheppard and Eric had just signed.

I took it. It looked like a contract, but I was going to need to sit and concentrate on it to know what it all meant.

"Naiya, Lynn," Sheppard said. "This is Jessica. Alpha of the San Antonio Basin pack. She's the Alpha of all the wolves you see there."

Jessica rolled a shoulder. "And a few you don't. Not everyone has their ringer on at six in the morning."

"So does this ... does this mean I don't have to go through with the tests I just agreed to?" I looked up from the paper and hooked a thumb back over my shoulder in the direction the blockade had been.

"Yeah, no," Jessica said, turning to me. She had to look up to me, but her presence was so much larger. "You don't owe the church shit. You're free."

Free.

"Th-thank you." My voice tried to crack. Probably from the exhaustion.

"A pleasure," she said, extending her hand to me.

I shook it emphatically.

"The paperwork's just a formality," she said, the corner of her mouth pulling into a smile. "And, of course, I'll have you transferred over to Sheppard's pack by the end of the week."

"I ... I'm—"

"Not pack." She nodded, waving a hand dismissively. "I know. Leopards don't really pack bond, so it doesn't surprise me that a wereleopard wouldn't be so quick to."

"But Lynn and Kristos didn't ..." Sheppard's voice was pleading.

She turned to him, reaching up to pat him on the shoulder. She was almost comically small compared to him.

"In for a penny, in for a pound," she said. "I had your signatures from your other pack members, so it wasn't hard to get my paperwork guy to splice them all together. Your *purgatum* is safe now. And the church will leave your bear alone too. No one's combed over those treaties in decades. I've been trying to get the word out about the paperwork, but no one's listening."

"What does the paperwork do?" Lynn asked.

I was thinking the same thing.

Sheppard nodded. "I'll tell you about it on the drive home. Jess, that—"

"It's incredibly kind of you," Kristos said. "Please. If there is ever anything you need."

"Oh don't you worry." She smiled at Kristos as she slapped Sheppard's ass. "This one owes me two already. Plus dinner."

Sheppard's eyes went wide, but he pressed his lips into a line and shook his head—though neither did anything to actually hide his smile.

"And you'll have a third from me," Kristos said.

"Look," she said, stepping over to the red sport motorcycle parked on the shoulder next to Daniel's SUV. "Just get the word out to the alphas. The Church is moving and shaking with these rifts activating and the vampires trying to make everything public. Any packs not tied to the Church need this paperwork to protect them."

"Because it's just one toe out of line," Sheppard said, "and we'll be fighting wars on two fronts."

"Exactly." She threw her leg over the sportbike and pulled her hair back with a tie from around her wrist.

"It's been great seeing you again, Jess," Sheppard said.

"Likewise," she said before pulling her helmet on.

"It was nice meeting you," I said.

"Stay safe, kitty cat." She flipped down the visor of her helmet as she turned the key and the bike's engine roared to life. She pulled off and down the road.

Sheppard turned to Lynn. "You good to drive the first leg so I can explain things?"

She nodded.

And with that, we piled back into the SUV and started down the road.

SIXTY-FIVE

WITH LYNN DRIVING, Sheppard rode shotgun, while Kristos took the middle row, leaving me the back bench seat I'd shared with Andy. Which was fine by me as I could still smell him if I concentrated. I put my parents' things and the Buddy Christ in my backpack so they would travel safely, along with my book.

Kristos watched me put the items away. "What are those?"

"My father's watch, my mother's music box, and the Buddy Christ from Abigail's car," I said. "Plus my copy of *The Last Unicorn*."

"I loved that movie," Lynn said. "But the book was so much better!"

I smiled gently, but my voice was morose. "It was." I didn't know if I could ever read it again without remembering every spot where Andy stopped me to tell me about Arcaniss or to ask me if something was real.

"We could stop by Dallas so you can drop those off if you'd like?" Sheppard said.

I shook my head. "I don't think I'm ready to face them yet."

Kristos furrowed his brow at me, his concern winding through the wind chime tone.

"All that work to keep them safe, and you don't want to see them?" Lynn's voice was incredulous.

I listlessly shook my head again. "They're not even in the country right n—wait. What day is it?"

"Monday," Kristos said.

"The twenty-second," Sheppard added.

I nodded. "Yeah, they probably aren't home yet."

"You should stay with us while we get the paperwork finalized anyway," Sheppard said. "But I won't keep you if you'd rather not."

"No, it's fine," I said. "There's just … a lot."

Kristos nodded and whispered, "You're free."

I met his gaze as a trill of joy shimmered into the note between us. But it was drowned out by the clang of the pit inside of me.

Sheppard turned in his seat to look at me as well.

Free. Fat lot of good it did me.

Andy was gone, and I'd just been claimed as pack by some Alpha I didn't even know. And I didn't have a *clue* what that meant. Hell, I was still hazy on the whole *consanguinea* and lost sister thing.

I pulled my knees to my chest, resting my feet on the edge of the seat as I put my chin down on my knee. I wanted to cry and scream and fall into a million pieces. But there was nothing. Just a pit.

"What does all of the paperwork *do*, Shep?" Lynn asked.

Sheppard nodded and pulled out his phone, swiping through screens. "Well, it should come as no surprise that the Catholic Church is largely just a bunch of people held together by a single faith in God, an agreed way to celebrate said belief, and a whole jungle of bureaucracy."

Kristos nodded. "The treaties Jessica referred to were the ones signed when we pushed the Anglican Church out?"

Sheppard nodded. "Those are the ones. The

Catholic Church absorbed and adopted them as well. It basically gave packs outside of Church jurisdiction a way to protect their power."

"But aren't they the Church's treaties?" she asked.

"No," Sheppard said. "They're the ones the free packs here signed to agree to stop killing the Church's alphas."

"So the people who hold all the power of those treaties are the packs that *aren't* part of the Church," she said.

"Exactly. Which is why there are so many provisions available to protect someone when they are named pack."

"So, why not do this *before* I sent Andy away?" I didn't have the energy to keep my voice level. There was pain and frustration dripping through every word, clanging into the deep wind chime tone. "Why did I have to say goodbye to someone I loved—probably forever—if this kind of thing existed?" My vision blurred, and wet warmth dribbled down my cheek as I squeezed my eyes closed, bracing against the abyss trying to swallow me.

"It couldn't have protected him," Lynn said. "Could it?"

"Andy is human," Kristos said with a nod, his voice gentle.

Sheppard bobbed his head side to side. "At least human enough to count for them. Even if you'd claimed him as your mate, the treaties couldn't protect him."

"The Church just hopes no one is paying attention to the corners they cut," Lynn said, sounding like a light bulb had just gone off in her brain.

"So, if you catch them," I said through my tears, "then you can beat them at their own game."

"Which is exactly what Jessica did," Sheppard said.

"So how is my family safe if they're human?" I asked, sniffling.

"The Church only cares about direct blood relation," Kristos said.

"But I'm adopted," I protested.

"But their names are on your birth certificate," Sheppard said quickly, "aren't they?"

I nodded, and my vision lost focus. "Bureaucracy."

Sheppard nodded. "As far as the Church is concerned, you're blood relatives."

Lynn met my eyes in the rearview mirror, her brow furrowed, and then refocused on the road. "But that doesn't apply to mates if they're human?"

Kristos snorted. "Only if you have babies."

"Oh," she said. "Blood relation."

"Correct," Sheppard said.

I looked up at him. "How does that protect Abigail?"

"She's considered part of the family's holdings because she is a direct employee of your parents," Sheppard explained. "Harm to her hurts your family financially, which would be considered undue pressure."

I considered that in silence for a moment, mulling it over with the conversation Jessica and Father Brooks had. "So … the Church is supposed to alert an alpha when they're moving people through their territory?"

"Any time more than two people are passing through," Sheppard confirmed, "yes."

"Most alphas alert their fellow alphas when they're moving their pack through as well, to avoid conflict," Kristos said.

"So." I looked at Kristos. "That guy, Father Brooks, is a friend of yours, huh?"

Kristos snorted. "Not even a little. He has me keeping tabs on Lynn for him. Though I apparently no longer need to do that."

I arched an eyebrow at him. "What dirt did he have on you to keep you doing that for him?"

Kristos pressed his lips into a line and looked at Sheppard. "He was going to have her pack killed if I didn't."

Sheppard took a deep breath, and though he looked calm on the surface, his heart had started to pound.

"Truth be told," Kristos said, "he still might if I don't do what he asked. Blood oaths likely trump treaties and paperwork."

Lynn's eyes snapped to his in the rearview mirror. "You're not free of them."

It wasn't a question.

He shook his head. "Likely not, at least not until Father Brooks passes."

"Blood oaths die with the one who made them," Sheppard said.

Kristos nodded. "So, the effort and kindness Jessica showed in including me in her arrangements ensures my freedom at that time. It is unlikely to be long."

"Until he dies," I said.

Kristos turned to me. "He is human and old and frail. I am nearly two thousand years old. It isn't like I'm going anywhere."

"We'll likely all outlive him," Lynn said.

Kristos turned back around in his seat and leaned back, folding his arms behind his head. "Exactly."

"Wait. Val had mentioned you guys were immortal."

"Nearly so," Sheppard said. "Close enough that it counts."

"Vampires truly are," Kristos said wryly.

"It looks like you are too, Kristos," Lynn said.

He shrugged. "Perhaps. I've never known a wolf who lived this long."

Sheppard snorted. "That's because apparently wolves haven't been around as long as you have."

"Okay," I said. "But am I?"

They all grew quiet for a moment. Either those three were just incredibly good at being still—unlike virtually every person I'd ever met—or werewolves were innately good at such things.

"I think you might be, Kitten," Kristos said softly. "At least as much as the werewolves are." He pulled his phone out of his pocket. "Let's take a picture now, and then another in ten years and see if you've aged."

Well ... that sounded as good of a method as any I could think of.

I nodded. "Sure."

I stilled while he snapped the photo and then thumbed at the screen on his phone.

"There," he said a moment later. "I've emailed it to myself and set it up with a reminder for ten years from now."

Lynn laughed. "It might be worth considering that you won't have that email ten years from now."

"I've had it for twenty years," Kristos said. "What's ten more?"

"A blip in your lifetime, sure," she said. "But electronics move faster than that."

Something from earlier connected in my brain.

"Wait," I said. "If Jessica transfers my protection to your pack, Sheppard, but that asshole decides to make a move and wipe out your pack because Kristos didn't keep up his end of the blood oath, then he'll have free rein to do whatever he wants with me and my family."

Sheppard blinked at me.

Kristos chuckled. "You're not wrong."

I furrowed my brow. "Then why are you laughing?"

"Because it means Sheppard's going to have to join his pack with Jessica's if he wants to keep the band together." His rich laughter took him then.

Sheppard was not amused. "I'll do no such thing."

Kristos laughed even harder. "Well, you'll have to figure something out, Alpha. I can't protect both the *purgatum* and this leopard *consanguinea* if they're in separate states."

"That sounds like a 'you' problem," Sheppard said. But his tone was wrong.

Kristos doubled over with laughter. "You don't even believe that, Shep! And in the meantime, you better tell that spitfire to keep Naiya under *her* treaty."

Sheppard wiped at his face. "I am going to owe her so many favors."

"Well, good," Kristos said. "Maybe if you work more with her, you won't keep runnin' back to the General who has to break rules to be on your side."

"I like General Buckheim," Lynn said.

"You're in the minority," Sheppard replied before turning to me. "He sets everyone on edge because he walks the line between us and the Church."

"Is he a werewolf?" I asked.

"He is," Sheppard said.

"And he's in the military?"

"He's the head of all of the US Army's werewolves," Sheppard explained. "Lynn has been helping him when the recruits he tries to turn go crazed."

"Crazed?"

"It's when a wolf gets stuck as a wolf and is violent and unpredictable," Lynn said.

"Like what Val was."

Lynn nodded. "Yes. Except her name was Hayley then."

Hayley. Like what Lynn had called her when she came to the door. "So even her name was a lie."

Sheppard shook his head. "No, she was given a new identity when Buckheim took her in. Whoever she was, she's Valerie now."

I nodded. Well, at least that wasn't a lie.

"But … if she was crazed …" I paused, putting pieces together and then whispered, "Am I like that?" I didn't feel like that now, but when I was in my leopard form, I definitely couldn't be sure I was … stable.

Kristos reached a hand back to me, laying it on the knee I still had pulled to my chest. "No, Kitten. You'd've attacked all of us when you panicked the other day if you were."

He was sure of it, and for a guy that's nearly two millennia old to be sure of something … well, it seemed silly to question it further. And though the pit threatening to swallow me did not close, it *did* feel like a weight lifted from my chest. Like it was just that much easier *not* to fall into the loss.

"So, what does it mean to be 'pack'?" I asked, swallowing down a lump and refusing to let the pit have me just yet. "I'm not really great at taking orders."

"That's good," Sheppard smiled. "I rarely give them."

"Clearly, Jessica does, though," I said.

He bobbed his head. "Yes. But she always puts pack first."

"Okay. Then what does pack mean?"

"It's a family," Lynn said. "People you can count on."

"We're there for each other no matter what," Sheppard explained. "Always in each others' corner. Always watching each others' backs."

"And you fight to keep it that way," Kristos said,

"by finding vampire nests and exterminating them, and by helping people not to fall prey to them anymore."

"We can work up to a hunt with you," Sheppard said. "But I'd like to start by seeing if we can't get you to change when you want to, instead of whenever your leopard breaks free."

Kristos met my gaze. "You said you killed a couple of vampires already?"

I nodded.

"Did you want to?"

"They made me. *He* made me," I said. "Father Brooks."

"But did you *want* to?" Sheppard asked.

I looked at him, trying to remember. "I did. They felt wrong—seemed wrong. Something inside me just said, 'kill it.'"

Kristos nodded. "So your instincts are similar to ours, at least. That bodes well."

"Okay. I have other questions, too."

"Shoot," Sheppard said. "We have time."

"*Consanguinea* means I am directly related to one of the brothers and sisters of Jesus, right?"

"Right," Kristos said.

I looked at Sheppard. "What's the chart you have?"

"It maps the bloodline," he explained. "It has every *consanguinea* on it."

"Including me and my father," Lynn said.

"But it doesn't have me?"

Sheppard shook his head.

I looked at Kristos. "Then how are you so sure I'm *consanguinea*?"

He speared me with a look that told me I should have already figured that out. A tone echoed through the dull wind chime.

"That," he said simply.

I nodded. "Okay … so then what's the whole lost sister thing?"

"Jesus of Nazareth had four brothers and two sisters," Sheppard said.

"Three," Kristos corrected. "Three sisters."

Sheppard nodded. "For purposes of explanation, fine. Four brothers. Three sisters. But the chart only maps four and two. Now, the church wasn't tracking *consanguinea* from the start, as I understand it."

"They weren't," Kristos confirmed.

"I'm not sure when they started then," he said. "But I know that whenever it was, they had to scramble backward to track where the line had been so they could better predict where it would be."

"The church knew from the start that there were four and three," Kristos said. "But when they could not trace the third sister's line, they simply pretended it had never been there. Except I was there when she disappeared, and I know how hard they were searching for her. It was not a matter of lost records or mistranslations. She simply vanished from the face of the Earth."

Sheppard looked at me. "And now you see why the church simply pretended she had never been there."

"Ha! Spoken as one who finally believes she existed!"

Sheppard speared Kristos with a look. "Don't patronize me. Of course I believe you. I just don't know how that makes Naiya possible. She's adopted, with sealed records."

I stilled, trying to remember if he'd been there when Ian and Daniel were asking me about my adoption status.

"You have a terrible poker face, Kitten," Kristos said, leaning toward me.

"Daniel is a lawyer," Sheppard said, "well-versed

in the bureaucracy of the courts. It wasn't much of a stretch for him to pull what strings he could to find out what there was to know about your birth parents. The problem is that the records are listed as sealed, but no one can find the records themselves."

I'm not sure I liked that. I pinched the bridge of my nose and sighed. "Could you at least please *tell* me when you do something like that?" I ran a hand through my hair. "I literally just escaped from a place that thrived off the information they had about me, but were unwilling to *tell* me." An odd note clanged in the wind chimes.

Lynn met my eyes in the rearview mirror. "Shep." Her voice was chiding. "That's not fair."

Sheppard nodded at her. "It's no less than we knew about you before bringing you in." He looked at me. "We had to know where you came from before I could sincerely offer our help. I'm sorry for not telling you sooner. I had not thought it to be an issue."

Well, at least he looked apologetic.

"Is there anything else you already know about me?"

Sheppard sighed with a nod and met my eyes. "Where you live, what your parents do, who Abigail is to your family, and full background checks on you, your parents, and Abigail."

My spine chilled and the tinkling chimes danced across my skin again.

Kristos made a grumbling sort of noise that definitely could have been a growl.

"Fucking hell, Shep!" Lynn exclaimed, lightly smacking his bicep.

"I know, it's a lot." He turned back to me and held my gaze. "But when you weren't a wolf and neither Kristos nor I knew where the leopards came from, I needed to be sure you weren't being played as a pawn. It was never you I didn't trust, Naiya."

I knew that was supposed to be a relief. I knew it was meant to be. But it wasn't.

"I'd like to see the files," I said. "What you know about me and my family."

He nodded once more. "Of course. You are free to all of it." He grabbed his phone from the center cupholder. "I'll forward you everything Daniel sent me."

I gave him my email address, but didn't bother to pull the laptop up to watch them come in. It was a far cry from what Father Brooks offered.

"So, if my records are sealed," I said, turning to Kristos. "Then whoever my birth parents are, they're part of this whole lost sister bloodline thing?"

"At least one of them is," Kristos said.

My head was starting to pound. "I think I've had a very long day."

Lynn nodded. "I think we all have, but you especially."

Kristos nodded and slumped into the seat, getting more comfortable. "Wake me when we stop for food."

"If we can," Sheppard said. "You aren't generally responsive when we try."

Kristos just waved a hand.

Sheppard looked past him to me. "You should try to get some sleep too, Naiya. It'll make the drive go faster."

I nodded and leaned onto my side, staring vaguely up at the sky through the rear window. A wisp of dark chocolate and honey touched my nose, and my eyes stung with tears as I inhaled as deeply as I could, trying to capture the scent forever.

281. Bulverde. Northbound past the vet.

The place where I said goodbye.

SIXTY-SIX

Time blurred as we continued on. I slept, I cried, and when I wasn't doing either, I stared at the sky through the back window, trying to make sense of everything that had happened. Eventually, Sheppard took over driving for Lynn, who reclined the passenger seat for a nap. We stopped a few times for gas, and once for fast food, but I don't remember eating.

We arrived back at Sheppard's modern glass house sometime after ten at night. The pack was out back playing woofball, the lingering scents of their grilled dinner wafting on the breeze.

I numbly watched them play, remembering how Andy had challenged me to join them.

Ian and Jamie tried to talk to me, egg me into playing, but I didn't have it in me. Kaylah made me a plate, tugging me over to a table to sit and eat it. I picked at my food as I watched the game. It was like they could play it for hours and never get bored.

A rumbling voice, more felt than heard, breathed into my ear. "You may be able to hide the worst of the pain from them, but you can't hide it from me."

Kristos took up the chair next to me. I hadn't even heard him come over.

A dark chord thrummed through me like a plucked bass string.

I blinked, my eyebrow arching, but I didn't say anything. I didn't have anything to say.

He watched me for a moment. "My patience is immense, Kitten. When you're ready to talk about it, I'm here."

I turned to him. "There's nothing to say. Andy's gone. What's done is done."

He held my gaze for a long, quiet moment before dropping his voice to barely more than a whisper. "You might be the only wereleopard on Earth, but you're not alone."

I nodded as my vision blurred. I wasn't sure I would ever have words to talk about the hole inside of me—the ragged, smoldering, crater that led to a deep dark abyss that threatened to swallow me if I toed too close—but it was nice to know that someone would listen if I ever could find the right words.

Sheppard turned to me then. "These guys are all antsy from everything and could use a run." There was something about the way he said 'run' that made me sure that woofball wasn't quite enough.

I shook my head, uncertain why he'd even mention such a thing to me. "So go?"

He nodded. "I'm gonna take them out to the reserve. If you had any control over your forms, I'd ask you to join. And you're, of course, welcome to come along anyway."

"Don't they close the parking lots?"

"Ha, this time of night?" Matt said. "We aren't driving."

"Oh," I said, finally catching his meaning. "You're going as wolves."

Sheppard nodded.

Ian turned to me. "We'll change here and head out from the backyard."

"Why don'tcha come 'long," Kaylah said. "Git some night air in ya."

I put my hands up. "Mmm, no thanks."

"You sure?" Lynn asked. "It's gonna be a pretty night."

"No," Chastity said. "It's going to rain."

Jonathan wrapped an arm around Lynn's waist, kissing the spot where her neck met her shoulder, and my heart panged its ache into the wind chime tone. "Perfect."

They all started to strip out of their clothes right there in the backyard, and my cheeks heated at the audacity of it.

"Oh yeah," Kristos said as I picked up my chair and turned it around to face the house. "None of them are shy about skin anymore."

Oh great. It was like joining a nudist camp.

And then there were all the awful noises of their bodies breaking and rearranging themselves before little barks and yips and short howls erupted behind me.

When I turned back, there were nine large wolves of all sorts of colors spread across the lawn. Almost as one, they took off at a run toward the back property line. I watched them run until I lost sight of them in the woods.

I took my plate inside, and Kristos went in, too. I contemplated going to the bedroom, but I wasn't ready to face that room without Andy. I'd only spent a night here—and I'd only been in his arms for a single night through—but he had been a constant presence in my life for nearly a month now. Every morning, when I woke, he was there. Every evening, when I slept, he was there. Every nightmare I'd had at that facility, he'd been there when I woke up.

Today was the 22nd of June. I'd arrived at the facility on the 28th of May.

Twenty-one days, four hours, and fifty-two minutes.

The memory of Andy's voice sent a pang through my heart like a hot poker.

I did the math. I'd spent a grand total of twenty-three days there. Add in his twenty-one, and he'd been there nearly a month and a half before he finally got free.

And now he was gone.

I took a slow, deep breath. It was shaky. It shuddered. But it didn't break.

Still, I definitely wasn't ready to lay in that giant bed without him.

So, I went back out to the back patio. It was a warm night. Sheppard didn't have a giant tree in his backyard, which would have been a nice escape—like I had in my favorite tree back home. But he did have a roof. And if the obstacle course at that damn facility had taught me anything, it was that I could jump much higher than I thought I could.

I looked for a low edge of the roof, surveying the lines where the asphalt-and-tar tiles met an edge that wasn't surrounded by rain gutters. The entire roof was one solid plane inclining gently toward the back of the house, so the gutters ran all along the backside of the house. But the side of the house was clear. I jumped for the overhang just before the corner, pulling myself up onto the nearly black asphalt shingle roof. I found a good spot and laid flat on my back, watching the clouds pass across the moonless sky, trying to let the night breeze fill the ache and blow it away as I counted and promptly forgot the number of sparkling stars. Except, the wind practically whistled through me. But it was better than crying myself to sleep in the last bed Andy and I had shared.

I chided myself for being so melodramatic as the promised rain blew in.

Maybe it wasn't even love anyway. Maybe it was just a crush.

Stupid. Of course it was love. Crushes didn't leave looming dark pits that made you feel like you'd been scooped out and left empty.

When the rain started, I reached my arms out to the sky and watched it fall, trying not to blink and failing with a little jolt nearly every time one landed right next to my eye.

"Aren't you going to come inside?" Kristos called from beneath me.

I shook my head, dropping my arms to my sides, and then remembered he couldn't see me.

"No," I called back.

He jumped for and pulled himself up onto the roof. "I'm not sure if lightning will kill you."

I didn't move or look at him. "You say that like it's possible it won't."

"You speak as if you have a death wish," he said. "Do you know I can't let you kill yourself? I very literally would have to do everything in my pow—"

"I'm not going to try to kill myself, Kristos, and I don't have a death wish." I lifted a hand, at the elbow, pointing to the sky. "Listen." I paused. "No thunder. So, probably no lightning."

"Hmm."

"You should give it a try," I said. "It's a humbling experience to watch the rain as it falls. Grounding in a … uniquely exhilarating way."

He laid down on the roof next to me, a little closer than I would have guessed, but not so close that I was uncomfortable with his presence. His scent was old leather with a hint of both salt and sweetness, and warmth radiated off him.

"In all my years," he said, folding his hands across his chest, "I don't think I've ever done this."

I arched an eyebrow, but didn't turn to him. "Can *you* survive a lightning strike?"

"I'm not sure … probably." There was a smile in his voice. "But, as you pointed out, no thunder."

He fell silent then, and we laid there on the roof, getting rained on until I started to doze lightly. As the rain lessened to a lazy drizzle, Kristos turned to me.

"If you stay here a while, like Sheppard suggested," he said, "I'll teach you lucid dreaming, so you can gain some control over those nightmares."

"Lucid dreaming." Hmm. I was pretty sure that was just some hokey cards and crystals mumbo jumbo. But the way he said it made it sound like it was real. And after everything Andy had said about Arcaniss … well … maybe it was worth reconsidering what I thought was mumbo jumbo these days.

"Maybe controlling your dreams," he said, "confronting what's terrifying in them, could help you gain control over your change."

"Mmm. I'm not so sure I want to try to stand down the angry leopard that stalks me and everyone I've ever given a shit about."

He sat up and looked at me, his expression surprised. "It's a *leopard* making you scream like that?"

I winced and sat up as well, turning my back to him to hide how my cheeks heated with embarrassment. I *hated* talking about what my night terrors were like. And yet … he was genuinely trying to help.

"It's always been the leopard," I said quietly.

He scooted a bit closer to me. "And you don't think maybe it's that she's a little angry that you keep ignoring her when she's just trying to protect you?"

I turned and glared at him. "I don't need your judgment, *Bear*. You don't know shit about what I've been through." I edged away from him.

"Maybe I don't," he said quietly. "But if you've

been to a place that tortured you for weeks and all you've got to show for it are some trust issues and nightmares of the thing you can turn into, then I think it's safe to say that *thing's* been trying to protect you the whole damn time."

That took the wind out of my sails. "Well, when you put it that way." I flopped back onto the roof. "That actually makes a whole lot of sense."

"Maybe keep the claws in next time, Kitten."

We passed the night on the roof of the house, watching what stars we could find between the clouds and the rain showers. The pack came back from their run at some point, and though Sheppard came to check on us, we were otherwise left alone. I wasn't sure why Kristos stayed, really. But I was glad he did. I didn't want to be alone.

SIXTY-SEVEN

THE NEXT DAY, after Kaylah's giant breakfast, Kristos got to work teaching me about lucid dreaming. He also insisted that meditation would be good, though every time I had ever tried to quiet my mind in the past, I simply fell asleep.

He started by explaining the concept of lucid dreaming and how it worked best when you were fully aware of your body when you're awake, so that you could tell when the sensations were being simulated by your brain during sleep. He lit a candle, had me feel the flame against my palm, and asked me to pinpoint where it was burning, pointing out that in a dream, it would not burn. He showed me how to do a simple reality check, in which I pointedly watched as I firmly and deliberately poked my left hand with the pointer finger of my right. He told me that in a dream, I would not feel the impact on the tip of my finger and my palm—that my finger would instead painlessly pass through my other hand. When I told him how unsettling the idea of seeing that was, he explained that it was much better than what would happen if I looked in a mirror in a dream. In your dreaming reflection, it's apparently typical to see a morphing, melting version of your face, because your brain doesn't actually know what you look like.

That was a terrifying thought.

Since I had yet to acquire a replacement cell phone, he set a reminder on his own phone to go off every thirty minutes, with the note 'reality check.' And so, every thirty minutes, at the sound of the reminder, I deliberately poked my hand with the other—watching the impact and focusing on the sensations of it in both the tip of my finger and my opposing palm.

The meditation, according to him, was to teach my mind to be comfortable in that liminal space between waking and dreaming. He had me concentrate on my breathing and the sensation of my muscles, how the latter supported the bones of my body. He had me sit on the roof in the glaringly bright midday sun and focus on the ringing in my ears caused by how tightly I was squeezing my eyes shut. He had me lay down like I was watching the rain and asked me to pinpoint every individual spot where a grain of gravel from the asphalt tile pressed against me. The tediousness of it was the whole point, it seemed.

The hardest part of the day, however, came when I had to ensure the room I was staying in was conducive to sleep. I had to return to the room in which I'd last been so wonderfully intimate and yet so deeply vulnerable with Andy. I could still smell him in the air, and it made my chest tight with the ache.

Worse, Kristos explained to me that the only time I was allowed to be awake in the bed was when I laid there, mimicking sleep. He told me that if I didn't—if I let myself just breathe in the scent of Andy on my pillow while I laid there and cried—I might not get to the point where I could lucid dream, and it would take that much longer before I could confront the leopard in my nightmares.

Not that I was terribly keen to rush that confrontation, even if I did recognize its necessity.

Additionally, I had to make sure to avoid any screens at all—whether they were TV or laptop or cell phone screens—for two hours before bed so that my body could produce the chemicals necessary to fall asleep faster and get a more restorative sleep. Kristos said he'd be happy to help with that by taking a late-night walk around the neighborhood with me, which seemed like a better option than sitting on the roof and meditating for two hours.

Most importantly, he told me that if I focused, if I did everything right, I could be lucid dreaming in just a few days. I apparently shouldn't try talking to the leopard the first few times I saw her. He suggested I instead try some easy things, like deciding I was at my parents' house instead of the facility, or that I could hover a few inches above the ground instead of fly.

As Sheppard had requested, I stayed with the pack. I sent my parents an email for when they returned home, indicating that I had picked up an unpaid internship in Colorado Springs that I was really excited for, and that I needed approval for a replacement phone on the family plan and a stipend. My father was skeptical at first, but Ian helped convince him that there was a great opportunity for me in the Springs to get exposure to the way businesses worked outside of Texas. They provided the approval when they were back stateside and asked for an address to send belongings to.

I shipped the watch, music box, and Buddy Christ back to them in an unmarked box. I didn't like lying to my parents, even if it was a lie of omission, but they would never have believed the truth of why I had them anyway, and an unmarked box at least left them with no knowledge that it was me who'd sent it.

During my meditation sessions over the subsequent days, I could sometimes almost *see* the gaping pit left behind from losing Andy. After the first couple notices, I reflected on its appearance to my subconscious eye and realized that the damage had only been exacerbated by the loss of the only other person who knew *exactly* what Father Brooks had put me through.

Val's betrayal was only able to cut me as deeply as it had because she made me feel like she was genuinely in my corner, genuinely against the things that had happened to me.

Although I was relatively certain the pack was getting tired of hearing my new phone buzz in my pocket every thirty minutes, Sheppard didn't push the issue of me trying to gain control of my change. None of them did. Instead, they simply spoke with a certainty that I would eventually gain such control.

I wasn't so sure, but I wanted to believe them.

I hadn't decided who in the pack I could really trust yet. I wanted to let myself trust all of them. It certainly felt like they were all relatively safe. But after three weeks at Father Brooks' circus of torture, and the betrayal from someone who had *so clearly* been my friend, trust wasn't exactly an easy thing I was willing to give away on a whim.

The matronly Kaylah certainly was in the running, as was their youngest wolf, Ian. I wanted desperately to like Lynn, who had said we were distant cousins, but it was hard to be around her and Jonathan without a stabbing ache poking at the raw edges of the emptiness.

And then there was Kristos: devastatingly handsome, built like a humvee, and the connection between us was simply undeniable. He always seemed to know what I was feeling, sometimes before I knew it myself. But he had an arrangement with Father Brooks, and though he'd made it clear there was no love lost between the two of them, I still couldn't be sure about him.

The late-night walks around the neighborhood with him helped me to trust him more. He reminded me to do my reality checks without so much as looking at his own phone or a watch. He, too, had recently lost someone he'd cared very deeply for, only his former lover had apparently been a vampire who tried to kill Lynn—a complication which almost literally had him choosing between his past and his future. It made me wonder if I'd perhaps sent my own future away, though I tried not to let myself focus too hard on that for fear of spiraling into an obsessive sort of depression.

Though Lynn and Jonathan had an apartment across town, they occasionally joined us on our walks, usually when they were at the house for dinner already. Lynn asked a lot of the same questions Val had as she tried to understand how similar I was to a werewolf. I asked a lot of questions about what it was like to be a *purgatum*. As it turned out, though this pack wasn't scared of her and her abilities, virtually every other werewolf she'd met was. Jonathan cracked jokes whenever the mood got too heavy, and though it was easy to laugh with him, I honestly liked it better when it was just Kristos and I.

When Lynn wasn't at Sheppard's house, I noticed the absence of the prayer bowl tone and asked Kristos about it. He was surprised that I was aware of Lynn's resonance with him, and explained that he hadn't had a lot of opportunity to be around more than one *consanguinea* at a time. Lynn and I tested whether we could feel each other by taking a trip to grab some fast food without Kristos—a test he decidedly didn't appreciate, as that left the two people he was trying to protect vulnerable, even if it was in full daylight—only to find that we could not. Kristos was the tie that bound us.

As day after day went by, I was able to be aware

of and even control scraps of my dreams—though, as expected, I'd wake up if I tried anything too outlandish.

Then the leopard began stalking me again, and every attempt I made to control the dream so I could confront the snarling creature in the edges of my consciousness was overridden by my need to run from it. When it caught me, as it inevitably did night after night, I woke covered in fur. Each and every time, Sheppard tried to use his power as alpha to push me back into my regular two-legged form, but it never worked. Kristos suspected it was because not only was I not technically his pack, I wasn't really pack at all.

Leopards don't really pack bond, Jessica had said.

The string of nightmares ended after a few nights, though it set my progress back more than I would have liked. It took another week before I shook my fear of it enough to control bits and pieces of my dreams once more.

After a few nights of that, it stalked me, just as it had before. Only when it caught me, and I woke up snarling and tearing at my bedsheets, Kristos was there. He grabbed my head, ignoring the scratches as my claws dug into his hands and forearms in my struggle to get free. His grip was firm and not at all painful. He held me until I calmed, only letting go once my breathing finally evened out. From there, he guided me through the meditation exercises he'd previously shown me, adapting them so I could learn awareness of this form as well. I took air deep into my lungs, rhythmically filling them like balloons as I forced my consciousness into every limb, every muscle of this form. When it finally released me, it was like the tumblers in a lock aligning just so, and I was able to return to two legs.

My elation at the experience sang triumph through the wind chime note that night, pushing the dullness of the aching pit away almost entirely for a fleeting moment.

Even so, the experience set my progress back when I realized the next morning that Kristos still had the scratches and bite marks from me from the night before. As it turned out, though he healed things as readily as I did—moreso really, to hear him tell it—wounds from a *consanguinea* did not heal at the typically speedy rate. Still faster than a normal human, but not werewolf or werebear fast.

That said, it was only a night or two before I was back to being able to control my own actions in my dreams once again.

SIXTY-EIGHT

AND THEN, finally, over a month after I'd started, I managed to *confront* the leopard in my dream.

It stalked me, as it always did, this time through the halls of Father Brooks' facility. As had been the case in previous dreams like this one, Father Brooks' voice garbled eerily from speakers overhead. But I pushed the fear down, swallowing around the trepidation as I tried to press my forefinger into my palm. There was no sensation of pressure as it appeared to make contact, and when my finger passed through my hand, I was certain this was a dream.

It was grounding and comforting and freeing all at once.

The fear at the thing snarling in the dark shrank to a controllable nervousness.

I made the scene brighter, bringing up the lights in the hallway so I could see the black creature covered in even blacker spots. It padded toward me as the light brightened, and I held my ground. But when it got too close, I took a single step backward.

At that, it stopped and plopped its butt on the ground. It studied me with eyes that were the same shade of green as my own.

"He was right, you know," the leopard said, her mouth moving out of sync with her words like a poorly dubbed movie. "I have only ever protected you. But we can be stronger together."

Her voice was like a smokier version of my own.

"Why are you so frightening?" I asked her.

"I wasn't always." She squinted her eyes closed for a moment and then spun, almost like a cartoon character, into a rather adorable little leopard cub.

A *familiar* adorable little leopard cub.

"The dreams from when I was little!"

She spun again, returning to her full-sized self. "You convinced yourself they were just dreams."

"But it's always been real."

She nodded and then studied me for a long moment, her head slowly angling to the side. "Why didn't you follow him?"

"What?"

"The boy." She shook a paw toward me. "The one with the crystal spider. He felt right."

I plopped onto the ground, my legs out in front of me. "I *know*. But he couldn't possibly be."

I swear I could feel the abyss open in the ground at my back, though I didn't dare look over my shoulder.

So she did, pulling her front paws from the ground to get the height to see over and behind me. "He left a very big hole."

I put my arms around my knees and laid my head down as tears trailed down my cheeks, dropping onto the tile floor with little plops. "I know. But he's from a different land. A whole different *world*."

"So what?" She angled her head the other way. "Leopards live everywhere—often away from the prying eyes of people who would notice." She straightened and puffed out her chest. "We should work together. Find him again."

. . .

That only made the tears worse, and I sobbed as I leaned forward, trying not to fall back into the gaping chasm.

A sound like a big motorcycle engine rumbling three streets over started and then grew closer. I looked up. She was much closer to me now, her head low as her nose reached for my face. The rumbling came from her chest.

I scrambled to the side, skirting around the edge of the pit to put more distance between me and her.

She did not pursue me, but instead cocked her head to the side again. The rumbling in her chest did not stop.

"Why are you angry at me?" I wailed, and though I was still crying, the tears now were also ones of fear.

"Angry?" She sat back down and cocked her head the other way.

I gestured vaguely at her. "You're snarling and growling!"

"Not growling." She straightened and shook her head. "It's a gentle noise. Meant to comfort."

I flopped onto the ground, arms out like a starfish. "Comfort."

She stood up and padded closer to me, bringing her face near enough to mine that her breath ruffled my hair, her whiskers brushing my face with gentle tickles.

But this was a dream, and—according to Kristos—my brain should not have been capable of mimicking such sensory details.

"Comfort," she said. The rumbling grew louder. "To help you not hurt. When you hurt, I hurt."

She hurt when I hurt. She was ... hurt.

Gentle comfort.

Purring! She was purring!

I'd learned as a kid that big cats don't purr, but

here she was, freaking purring like a giant house cat. Of *course* it would sound like a motorcycle engine!

I reached a hand up, but still, I could not bring myself to reach for her.

She did not hesitate. She leaned in and pushed her head against my hand.

I forced myself not to move away. Her fur was soft and shorter than I expected.

"Why do you chase me?" I asked quietly.

"Because you think you can run from me," she said. "But I am a part of you. Even if you try to run away, I am always there." She sat with a huff then, pulling her head away from my hand. "You should not run from predators—it entices chase."

"Like a game," I said.

"A game of chase." She showed me her teeth as she nodded. It wasn't a comfortable sight.

I sat up then. "Why do you sometimes attack my parents in my dreams? Or Abigail? Why did you hurt my father?"

She shook her head, and I got the impression she was sad. "Not all of your dreams are me. Some are your own fears. And he was attacking us."

"He wasn't! He was scared."

"You are often scared," she asserted like that was all there was that needed to be said.

She nuzzled against my chest with another of those rumbling purrs.

"We work together now," she said, keeping the top of her head pressed against my chest. "Okay?"

I pressed my lips into a line. "Mmm. Easier said than done, don't you think?"

She pushed me onto my back, and I squeaked out my surprise as she lay on my chest.

"Just call, and I will come," she said. "I am always here. But sometimes it is time for walking and talking and pretending, and sometimes it is time for teeth and claws and showing who we really are."

"Pretending?"

She lifted her head to look me in the eye. The garbled voice of Father Brooks overhead had stopped, but now I heard my own voice.

Not here. Not now. Not like this.

My mantra from the treadmill and from any number of the other things they had me do when I was held captive.

"We are not people," she said. "We are leopard."

I blew out a breath. "And people."

She put her head down. "Do people turn into leopards?"

She hadn't done his voice, but my mouth pulled into a smile all the same at the obvious mockery of Dr. Anderson from Saint Dymphna's.

"Well," I told her, "this people does."

"Then fine," she said. "We are leopard, and we are people. Like the ringing one is bear and people, or the boy is magic and people, and the rest of them are wolf and people."

Kristos. Andy. The pack.

I put a hand on her black-on-black spotted shoulder, ruffling the fur back and forth. "I can live with that."

She sat up and off me. "Want to try now?"

I blinked at her as I sat up again. "What?"

She waved one of her front paws. "Put your hand here."

I placed my hand on top of her paw. But my fingers sank into it instead. Fear tickled the hairs on the back of my neck.

Remembering my reality testing then, I took a deep breath. Of course my fingers sank through her paw. This was a dream.

The rumbling purr started in her chest again. "We are not dangerous unless we want to be."

I looked up at her. "Easier said than done, I think."

She nodded. "Then I will come to you. We are the same."

She moved to sit next to me, turning her head and deliberately positioning her body to match mine as closely as she could. I stilled to make it easier for her. She nodded when she was satisfied that she'd matched it and began to sidle toward me.

"Wait!" I put a hand out, palm facing her. "How do I *stop* being a leopard?"

She made a snorting noise through her nose. "We are always leopard."

"No, no." I shook my head. "I mean, how do I go back to walking and talking?"

"Oh." She nodded. "Just tell me so. We work best when we work together."

"So, why didn't that work before? When I was a lab rat at that facility?"

Her ears twitched away from me at my shout. "You needed me there, but would not let me out. When you were asleep, you let your guard down. So, I helped you then. I protect. Teeth and claws now?" She danced between her two front paws.

"Um." I took a deep breath and nodded. "Okay."

She readjusted her position, matching mine again before sidling into me, and then through me.

I came silently awake in the dark on four paws, my clothes shredded around me.

SIXTY-NINE

My heart pounded. My breathing was irregular. But I remembered the meditation exercises. First, I had to get off the bed. Because I was only allowed to lay in my bed if I was asleep or pretending to be. I dropped to the floor.

Okay. Meditation-as-a-leopard time.

Lungs first.

I stilled and inhaled deeply, pushing air down to the bottom of my lungs and filling them like balloons. In and inflate. I focused on how my lungs filled the space inside my ribs. Out and deflate. I focused on pushing every last little bit of air out. Again. In. Out. Inflate. Deflate.

Then the rest of me.

Breathing deeply, I pushed my awareness through my entire body. I had a tail. I had a *tip* of a tail. The tip flicked and swished gently side to side. I had a left rear paw. I had toes on that paw. I had *claws* at the end of those toes. I could extend and retract … well … kinda. I couldn't extend and retract each one individually. I *was* able to extend and retract just that paw's worth of claws. Same with the right rear paw. Same with the front left. And the front right. My neck had a good range of motion side-to-side and up-and-down. I rotated my head as well, trying to see how close to upside down I could get clockwise and counterclockwise before my shoulder tried to join the motion. I swiveled my ears around individually, paying attention to how doing so changed my hearing. I opened my jaw wide, trying not to let myself fill with fear at the teeth in my own mouth. I was leopard and I was people, and sometimes that meant teeth and claws and showing who we really are. I tested the mobility of my jaw and my tongue. I could easily lick my entire nose with my tongue. Interesting, if not a little gross. At least my tongue wasn't slobbery like a dog's.

Okay. Movement time.

I stalked around my room, paying close attention to the way the pads of my toes squished under my weight. The way my tail curled and gently bounced along behind me instead of dragging on the ground. The way my muscles worked together to make my body move.

My body.

This one was as much mine as the one shaped like a person. And it could have been the whole time if I had simply stopped fighting against it.

Time to show Kristos.

I padded toward the door, but remembered that to talk to him I'd have to be people, not leopard. And since I'd shredded my clothes—again—a blanket would be a better choice.

There was one on the chair next to my duffle bag. I pulled the creamy knit throw down, only to realize that I was going to have to awkwardly drag it through the house with me, including a trip up a flight of stairs.

Well, that would ruin the reveal, wouldn't it? So, I dropped it, leaving it on the floor next to my duffle, to be picked up later. I was sure there'd be a blanket or two on the sectional upstairs where Kristos slept. There usually was.

Thank God the doors in this house had the lever-type handles instead of knobs. I pawed my door open and headed down the hall on silent footsteps. The whole house was asleep. I hadn't thought to check what time it was.

Here's to hoping I even *could* wake Kristos.

I padded up the stairs, following his salty-sweet leather scent to the loft at the end of the hall. He might have been asleep, with his arm thrown over his face like it was, but Kristos didn't snore—at least, not that I'd heard—so it was hard to be sure. I gingerly nosed his hand and took a step back to sit down, a trill of a joyful noise dancing through the chimes.

I hadn't thought this through. He might have been the type to come awake fighting.

Instead, his arm dropped from his face as his honey gold eyes met mine. "It worked." There was quiet reverence in his voice as he sat up and then knelt on the floor between me and the couch.

Holding his gaze, I nodded.

An unfamiliar note sounded in the chimes. It was a deep thrumming, but it fluttered in my stomach like butterflies.

"You're beautiful, Kitten," he breathed.

He reached a hand for me, and I lightly pressed my cheek to it. He brushed his fingers along my jaw, and flattened his palm along my cheek, stroking down my neck to my shoulder.

The tip of my tail curled and uncurled rhythmically as he did.

"Sleek," he murmured. "And powerful."

Kitten.

A slow deep rumble, like a quieter version of the motorcycle engine sound from my dream, started in my chest.

The corner of his mouth pulled into a smile, and though he was obviously not as used to smiling as someone like him should be, it was beautiful on his face.

"It's clear even when you're on two legs, you know," he said. "You move with a smooth grace that belies what you are."

Grace? I was graceful?

His voice dropped to a whisper, and my ears flicked toward him. "How dare *anyone* think they could keep you locked away?"

I closed my eyes then, pushing the flutter of fear that came on the heels of the reminder of being held captive at Father Brooks' facility into the pit of loss that had opened when Andy stepped through the rift back to Arcaniss. No one was going to lock me away like that ever again. I had to make sure of that.

But if I hadn't been captured, I would have never met Andy.

Andrezmes Kjelliho.

Andy, who had been so wonderful and amazing.

Andy, who was gone.

A blue fleece throw blanket wrapped around my shoulders. I was people again, my knees hugged to my chest as tears leaked down my face.

"Oh, Kitten." Kristos wrapped strong thick arms around me as I melted into silent sobs that wracked my body. He rocked back and forth, stroking my hair as I cried.

It could have been an eternity, or only a few minutes. I couldn't be sure. But Kristos was still holding me when it passed.

"Sometimes I think this pit inside of me will swallow me whole," I whispered as I thunked my face into his shoulder. "How could I have been so stupid?"

He put his chin on my head. "You chose to keep

someone you care about safe. You'd rather suffer yourself than know someone you care about suffers."

I sniffled for a moment, rolling that around in my head. "That's why you made that blood oath with Brooks."

He nodded, his chin rubbing against the top of my head. "Better that the pack stays safe."

I sat in his arms for a long moment, listening to his heartbeat and breathing in the scent of him. With a sniffle, I resituated myself in his arms, laying my palm on the bare skin of his chest. He was so warm, and the heartbeat under my palm was slow and steady.

"Your heart's pounding, Kitten," he observed.

I sniffled and looked up at him. "Help … help me forget?

He raised an eyebrow. "Brooks? Or the kid you came with?"

I moved around in his lap again, letting the blanket fall away from my shoulders as I pressed against him. "Both?"

He pulled back, leaning against the couch, and studied my face as I chewed my bottom lip. "Are you sure that's what you want?"

I fiercely wiped the tears from my face with the hand that wasn't holding the throw blanket. My cheeks were already heated with the anticipation of the embarrassment of him likely telling me to stop whatever the hell I thought I was doing and go back to my room.

It didn't matter that he was decidedly beefier than I typically liked my men to be. It didn't matter that sleeping with him would undoubtedly complicate the hell out of things within the pack. In that moment, I'd had just about enough of being selfless.

"It's what I want tonight," I said.

He nodded as the corner of his mouth pulled into

a wry smile. "I thought as much." He wiped at the back of his neck. "Look, Kitten—"

My cheeks heated even more at his tone. "No, no. I get it." Don't sleep with the broken one. The chime clanged dully.

He hooked a finger under my chin, pulling my face up to look at him. "It won't close that pit." He poked at my chest.

My exposed chest.

I hurried to pull the blanket around me.

"I don't need it to," I said, my voice cracking. "I just don't want to feel like this all the time. I want to remember what it was like to not ache."

A tear blazed a new trail down my cheek. And another. And then the floodgates were open again, and Kristos pulled me tight to him.

I stiffened, but let him.

"I won't ever see him again," I whispered.

Kristos nodded, his chin brushing against my head. "At least he's safe."

"I just wish he was safe *here*. With me."

He kissed the top of my head. "I know, Kitten. I know."

I cried myself to sleep in his arms and did not dream. I couldn't be sure whether that was a blessing.

Kristos woke me with a gentle pat on my hip as the dawn light started to change the color of the sky.

"You're gonna want clothes, Kitten," he said softly.

Others were stirring in the house.

My cheeks heated.

He shook his head. "Pack doesn't care about skin. But, since you do …" He pulled the blue blanket over me. "Fur or blanket?"

Fur …?

Well. That would be a wonder to behold, wouldn't it?

I untangled my legs from his and sat up. Time to be leopard, then.

My perspective on the world shifted from one blink to the next.

He smiled. "That's a pretty spectacular trick."

I nodded once and snuck back to my room, nosing the door shut as quietly as I could.

As soon as the latch clicked on my own door, I decided it was time to be people again.

And I was.

I showed the pack what I looked like as a leopard later that day, and on Sunday night—the first night of the next full moon—I went with them to the reserve. I played stalk and chase with the pack, ran with them as they hunted rabbits back to their burrows, and piled with them when they rested in the moonlight.

Staying with the pack may not be my forever arrangement, but I wasn't really worried about that. The pack would be there whether I wanted it to be or not. But more importantly, I had options now. I could find a place of my own in this world without having to worry about Father Brooks and his team of assholes—and without having to worry about whether the creature inside me would take over and hurt the ones I loved.

There was no need to confront the leopard anymore in my dreams, and she did not stalk me through them. She and I were of a single mind now. We were one and the same.

My path was wide open in front of me, full of possibilities. And though there was still an abyss inside of me, I was ready to face whatever the world might throw my way.

I just wished Andy was there to face it with me.

EPILOGUE

Andrezmes

Kiyan looked at me over his mug of ale. His fifth mug of ale, actually. He was shorter than me by about three inches, with dark brown eyes that always knew both too much and not nearly enough about whatever was in front of him. He had close-cropped brown hair and there was a shadow of a brown fuzzy beard on his chin. He wore a white long-sleeved shirt and a black coat with heavy maroon embroidery. His matching hat with almost obnoxiously long feathers was hanging on a hook on the wall beside our table in the tavern.

It had taken me weeks to finally track down where he was. Even then, I'd had to wait another two for him to get back from his latest adventure, and it had taken however long it took him to drink five mugs of ale to tell him about where I'd been and how badly I needed to go back.

"So let me get this straight," he said, pinching the bridge of his nose. "You spent all this time in a place where there's no magic, but there are a whole *horde* of lycanthropes. And there, you found one of said lycanthropes that you liked the shape of, let her shove you back through a rift home, and only *now* you think maybe she was from here the whole time?"

I nodded. "I do. I thought it a lot while I was there, actually. Her pronunciation of my name should have been a clue, Kiyan. She picked it up like *that*." I snapped my fingers. "She did the same for everything else I taught her to say. But the rifts *translate* all of that. So, when she was on her side and said her name, I—on *this* side of the rift, heard the translated version of her name."

"You're doing that thing again."

"What thing?"

"That thing where you dance around whatever the lower planes it is that you're trying to say before you ever get to actually saying it." He flagged down one of the serving girls and pointed at his empty mug. She smiled and nodded.

"She thinks her family name is Kateri, but it's not. That's just how she says it because she was so young when she went there. But it's Klothyrian!"

The barmaid brought a new mug and picked up the old one, along with the coin he'd placed on the table.

"Thank you, love." He smiled at her with a wink and then turned his attention to me as he took a sip from the new mug—number six now. "Sorry, what?"

"She's not Naiya Kateri. She's Naiya Klothyrian."

He took another sip. "Klothyrian."

"As in Lyadah and Murohaat Klothyrian? Her parents were heroes."

He cocked his head to the side and took another sip. "Martyrs, you mean."

"Semantics!" I threw a hand in the air. "They died fighting Luca!"

The barmaid was back. "Need something?" She was looking at me.

Oh! I *had* flailed my arm like I needed her, hadn't I?

I looked at Kiyan and then back at her. "Can I get some bread and a bowl of the stew, please?"

She nodded. "A couple of rolls for him, I take it?"

"Please."

She nodded again and hurried off.

"From what I gathered, a year there is roughly two seasons here. She said she's twenty. And Luca was killed—what was it? Thirty seasons ago? Thirty-two?

"Thirty-four," Kiyan said. "Almost thirty-five now."

"Which means that Naiya must've been pushed across one of the rifts as a child. She couldn't have been more than a handful of seasons old."

"Okay."

The serving girl returned with a small basket of rolls and a steaming bowl of stew. I paid her and then she was off again to the next table.

"I have to get back to her, Kiyan. She needs to know. She *deserves* to know."

"So, you're going to tear holes in reality—open intentional rifts in reality—just to try to get back to her? That's not the same as plane-shifting, Andy." He put his mug down probably a little more forcefully than he meant before leaning over to me. "If the Adamos catch wind of you trying to pick up where Luca's spellcrafting left off—"

I waved my tattooed hand, leaving a trail of tiny angular shapes in green and purple. "I'll tell them myself. They should know she's alive. Who knows, if she's from here, maybe there are others there."

"All of Arcaniss is still recovering from Luca's destruction, Andrezmes." He tore off a piece of bread for himself. "No one's even *seen* a dragon since just after his defeat. You can't give people false hope that their loved ones aren't lost."

"So I won't. I'll just let Sir Drake and Lady Laila know that I found *her*, but that she's stuck on the other side of the rifts. They'll know what that means for the families who have lost people to Luca's rifts. They have to know that something akin to his arcana is going to be necessary to stop the rifts that are opening anyway."

Kiyan cocked his head, and his tone turned patronizing. "They're heroes, Andy. They don't have time for your theories"

"It's not a theory," I said. "I was *there*."

"And what proof do you have of that?" He arched an eyebrow at me, and my heart panged for Naiya.

I took a breath and ran a hand through my hair. "I have …" I ate some of my stew as I wracked my brain, trying to think of literally *anything* I had. Everything had all happened so quickly that I hadn't even managed to take a lock of her hair or anything. I'd have nothing at all to track her with when I got back there. Dammit.

"Andy …" Kiyan stared at me. Well … as good as one *could* stare with six mugs of ale in their system.

"I have … Chad as my witness." I put him on the table and he unfolded to dance up my arm to my shoulder.

"Chad?" Kiyan was incredulous. "The literal fragment of your psyche. You don't think maybe he's not a viable impartial third party? Since his existence literally depends on you?"

I dropped my head back. "Ugh, you're right."

"Besides," he said, "even if you *did* have proof—which you don't. And even if they *did* believe you—which they won't. Looking for her is a lost cause. Even if you could get a portal back to her world, you said yourself that it's huge. It's probably as big as ours." He took another bite of bread. "More likely you'll never find her again."

I shook my head. "No. Naiya is worth looking for."

"Because she's heir to the Klothyrii namesake? The namesake of martyrs in a world she knows nothing about?"

"No," I said, more adamantly this time. "She's worth looking for because I love her."

Kiyan's mug hit the table and his eyes sparkled with excitement as he leaned across the table to thump my bicep. "Well, now. It's about time! Why didn't you just say so in the first place? Let's go meddle with some rift magic!" He turned to the serving girl and waved his empty mug. "Another! And two for my friend here!" He slammed coins to the table.

He wasn't being sarcastic.

And my heart absolutely soared like a great eagle's at the thought of finally holding her in my arms once again.

It was only a matter of time.

ABOUT THE AUTHOR

Born and raised in Texas, Becca Lynn Mathis has been writing stories and daydreaming about other worlds since she was a little girl reading books in the branches of the tree in her front yard. As she grew, so did her love of stories, so much so that she often got in trouble at school for writing them, even if her other work was already done.

Today, she is a graduate of Lynn University in Boca Raton, FL with her B.S. in psychology. She is a dreamer of the highest order, involving herself in as much storytelling and geekery as she can manage, whether that's playing Dungeons & Dragons (or Pathfinder), prepping a musical performance for the next local renaissance or pirate faire, or simply getting lost for hours playing video games like Beat Saber or World of Warcraft. She lives in sunny South Florida with her amazingly supportive husband, their awesome blended family and two goofy dogs.

Be sure to visit her website and sign up for her newsletter to keep up to date about the rest of the Trials of the Blood series!

www.beccalynnmathis.com

CPSIA information can be obtained
at www.ICGtesting.com
Printed in the USA
BVHW091803240622
640596BV00012B/249